MELTDOWN

MELTDOWN

MAX MARLOW

NEW ENGLISH LIBRARY

British Library Cataloguing in Publication Data

Marlow, Max
    Meltdown.
    Rn: Christopher Nicole and Diana Nicole   I. Title
    823.914 [F]

    ISBN 0-450-53785-4

Published by New English Library,
a hardcover imprint of Hodder and Stoughton,
a division of Hodder and Stoughton Ltd,
Mill Road, Dunton Green, Sevenoaks, Kent TN13 2YE.
Editorial Office: 47 Bedford Square, London WC1B 3DP.

Photoset by E.P.L. BookSet, Norwood, London.

Printed in Great Britain by St Edmundsbury Press,
Bury St Edmunds, Suffolk.

This is a novel. The characters are invented, and are not intended to portray actual people, living or dead.

The events have not yet happened.

Contents

O dark, dark, dark, amid the blaze of noon,
Irrecoverably dark, total eclipse
Without all hope of day!

John Milton, *Samson Agonistes*

Prologue

With a creaking of windlasses the huge nets slowly rose to the surface. The trawler heeled as the great weight broke the water, swinging for a moment just clear of the swell, a teeming mass of struggling, slithering fish.

"That lot'll be it," Morrison said.

He had been leaning on the bridge wing, gazing down at the sea, waiting for the catch to emerge. Now he turned away to look aft and watch it being brought over the stern and emptied into the last of the refrigerated holds, and also to glance at the sky. But there was nothing to see in the sky, save blue. There was not a cloud in sight. The barometer was steady, and the sea, even in the very centre of the North Atlantic in April, had hardly a ripple on its surface. Only the ever-present swell, long and low, made the little ship move gently up and down.

Morrison had never known such a successful cruise. The weather had been fine throughout, and the catches had been superb. This last one was the best of the lot. Now his holds were jam-packed with fish, and in ten days' time he would be unloading, with a nice fat profit to show for it.

Which was not all that common, nowadays.

Morrison was inclined to take most of the credit himself; he had always been prepared to go farther afield than most in his hunt for fish, no matter how the owners had complained about fuel costs. Admittedly this field had been a stroke of luck. He had found it only two months ago, when he had been blown away from his normal ground some two hundred miles south of Iceland by one of the strongest north-easterly gales he had ever known.

The weather had carried him south-west for some six hundred miles and, when the storm abated, he looked in his echo sounder almost casually; his Loran placed him over the area known as the

Bight Fracture Zone, on the edge of the Mid-Atlantic Ridge, just about equidistant between Canada and Great Britain. And he saw fish. Masses and masses of fish. He couldn't believe his eyes.

The nets went down, and he returned home with the biggest catch he had ever taken. He swore his crew to secrecy, and they kept the secret; they knew when they were on to a good thing. He didn't know how long they would be able to keep that up, but just a couple more voyages would guarantee a profitable year. So they returned here again, and this time not only was the weather perfect, but the catch even bigger.

Morrison had no idea what was making the fish accumulate over this uneasy piece of ocean floor, where extreme depths lay side by side with surprising shallows – considered in hundreds of metres – but he wasn't going to worry about that: he was a fisherman, not a scientist, and the fish were there.

"Seven tons, skip," said Mate Finlay. "That is going to please the boss."

"He'll be over the moon," Morrison said.

"So . . . " Finlay straightened, gazing across the ocean, and grinned. "It's all happening. We could even take a whale home, if they weren't protected."

Morrison also stood straight, and gazed at the plume of water rising from the sea some four hundred yards from the port bow. Then he reached for his binoculars.

"Must be just under the surface," Finlay said. "See how the sea's bubbling?"

Morrison levelled the glasses.

"That's no whale," he said. "Goddam! It's an eruption." He leapt to the console, threw the engine levers forward and at the same time picked up the telephone. "Down there, Chief. Let's get the hell out of here. Full speed ahead!"

1

The Island

Geoffrey Dunning pulled his greatcoat tighter around his shoulders and pressed the street bell for the second time. When he left the taxi he had been almost warm, and merely threw the coat round his shoulders; now the north-easterly April wind, which was soughing up the Charles River and rattling windows in Binney Street, was biting around his ankles.

Still there was no reply; he decided she wasn't at home. At last he put the coat on, forced the brass buttons through their holes with awkward, gloved fingers, and turned away from the door, stepping down to the windswept street.

A man hurrying by gave him a quick glance, and went on his way into the gathering darkness. Seafaring men were not unusual in Boston, and in his blue coat and peaked cap Geoffrey Dunning could have been a local; it would have needed closer inspection to determine that his insignia was that of the British Merchant Marine rather than the American.

He paused with his hand on the area railings. "Damn," he muttered. "Damn, damn, damn." He had telephoned, but she hadn't answered. He assumed that was because she was always so busy; now he began to doubt if she was even in town. He wondered what to do next, and his face puckered uncertainly. It was a handsome face, long and lean like his body. Both were vigorous, mobile, positive. Geoffrey Dunning was only unhappy when uncertain.

As he stood at the bottom of the steps a voice came out of the speaker above him.

"That you, Ben? You're a little early, aren't you?"

Geoffrey spun round, nearly falling up the steps, calling, "It's Geoffrey."

There was a moment's silence. Then the voice said, "Geoffrey? Geoffrey Dunning?"

"The same."

The voice gave a little squeal. "Geoff! Oh, Geoff! Come on up."

There was a buzz as the street door was released. He noted that the apartment was on the third floor, ignored the elevator to take the stairs two at a time.

The door on the third floor was open and Anne Dunning was waiting for him in a dressing-gown, her hair wrapped in a towel.

"Geoff!" She hugged him close and kissed him fondly on both cheeks. "It's been so long!"

"Three years."

"Three years! But say . . . what're you doing in Boston?"

Brother and sister were very alike in height and colouring; the damp hair escaping from Anne's towel was as black as Geoffrey's, her mouth and jaw as wide and determined, eyes as mahogany and only careful plucking had lessened the density of her arched brows. The main difference between them was in their accents – Anne had lived in America for six years.

"Well, it's a short story," Geoffrey promised as he unbuttoned his coat. "*Skyhawk* touched something on her way up the St Lawrence . . . let me say right away I was not on watch at the time. Anyway, she wrecked a prop so she has to spend a week longer in Saginaw than usual, having her shaft straightened. So . . . I thought I'd nip across and see little sister."

"What a gorgeous surprise." She drew him into the apartment, and kicked the door shut with her foot.

Geoffrey looked around him, he had never been here before. The apartment bore all the visible signs of success: lavish carpeting and curtains, the latest in uncomfortable looking modern furniture, expensive contemporary paintings . . . it was a little daunting to think that Anne, three years his junior, was probably earning six figures, at least in dollars, which compared grotesquely with his salary as First Officer on board a rather small freighter.

Anne had always known what she wanted. She worked hard enough to gain a good university place, and the moment she graduated she got a job in the States in Public Relations . . . resulting in this splendid life-style. She had the looks, the brains, the drive for success, and was already an executive of the company.

He grinned as he hung his coat and hat in the smart lobby closet. He had always known what he wanted as well; to stand on the bridge of a ship as Master. He hadn't quite got there yet, but he would. Mum and Dad had been disappointed that neither of their older children had been the least interested in farming, and he and Anne had hated to hurt them . . . but the old folk were first to insist that they had to do their own thing.

"Come in here," Anne said, leading him into the bedroom. "Sorry for the delay in answering the door, I was washing my hair."

"For this fellow Ben."

"Correct. Say, where are you staying?"

"Well, I came straight here from the airport."

"So you're staying here, right. That settee in the lounge is a put-you-up."

"Well, if it's not inconvenient . . . what about this fellow Ben?"

"I'm cancelling him." She sat on the bed, punching numbers on the pink telephone. "Hi, lover. Say, tonight's off . . . sure, I know . . . I know it's late notice but something's come up . . . sure it's another man, my brother . . . oh, don't be a grouch. Listen, I'll call you, maybe Wednesday. 'Bye." She put the phone down somewhat brusquely. "Asshole," she commented.

Geoffrey winced. He had been standing in the middle of the room feeling rather embarrassed. Now he picked up a tie he saw lying across the chair. "You didn't have to. I mean . . . " he held out the tie. "If you and he have something going . . . "

Anne came towards him and took the tie away. "That's not Ben's. Yet. I just bought it for him as a sweetener after standing him up the last time." She put the tie in a drawer, glanced at the expression on her brother's face. "You didn't come all the way down here just to unravel my love life, I hope."

"I wouldn't dream of it."

"You're my favourite man, anyway." She kissed his cheek again. "Fix us a drink. Mine's bourbon and dry. No ice." She grinned. "I'm still English at heart. I just want to put the video on, then I'll get dressed. Where's that damn control?"

Geoffrey located the bar, predictably concealed in the bookcase. "Something you wanted to watch?"

"Yeah. They're doing a feature on this new island. Have you seen it?"

"Not yet. We were in the West Indies when it erupted. But I'm hoping to have a look at it in a couple of weeks. It's bang on our route from Halifax to Liverpool. You mean there's a programme about it tonight?"

"It started five minutes ago. But you don't want to watch TV. We've got so much to talk about. I'll tape it."

He handed her the glass. "We have all night to talk. I'd be really interested to see it."

"You're on." She had found her remote control, pressed the programme button and, curling herself on the settee, tugged the towel off her head and began rubbing her hair. "I can dress later, then we'll go out to dinner. Come and sit."

He sat beside her, stretched out his legs, cursing under his breath about modern seating that stopped halfway up your back leaving nothing to lean against.

"They've got that guy Mark Payton on. Heard of him?"

"No."

"He's a scientist. Comes from Boston. He says 'Bawston'. He's the guy who wrote that book trying to prove that our weather is affected by earthly phenomena, like when there's an earthquake somewhere it means more rain someplace else. Or is it less? I can't remember."

"I think I read a review of it. Not everyone agrees with him."

"I'm not surprised. I met him at a reception which we had organised. He's a complete asshole. Fancies himself."

Geoffrey winced again at the casual Americanism.

"But for all the critics I reckon he knows more about the subject than most." She pushed up the sound as the screen came into focus, looked at a bearded face. "That's not him."

"Then you did not actually see the island, Captain Morrison?" asked the voice-over.

"Naw, sir, ah did not." Morrison had a thick, Grimsby accent. "Soon as ah realised t'were an underwater eruption going on, ah got os owt o' there as fast as ah could."

"Were you overtaken by any tsunamis?"

"There was some big waves, sir. But ah reckon we were far enough away before she really blew. There weren't nothing we couldn't handle."

"Thank you, Captain Morrison." The presenter smiled at the camera. "That was Captain John Morrison, on Anglia Television, England. Now, I have with me here tonight Dr Mark Payton, who is one of the world's leading experts on volcanoes, earthquakes, and climatology. Hi, Mark, nice to have you with us."

"Nice to be here, Tom." Mark Payton was surprisingly young, probably in his middle thirties, Geoffrey reckoned. A large, athletic-looking body slouched in jeans and sweat-shirt, his feet were stretched towards the camera, the velcro-fastened sneakers looking hugely out of proportion . . . His face was square, eyes exceptionally dark blue and there was a deep cleft in his chin. All topped by an unruly mass of fair curls worn unfashionably long. Geriatric teenager, Geoffrey thought.

"I believe you were one of the first people on the island, Mark."

"*The* first."

"Okay. Now show us, just where is it?"

A huge map of the North Atlantic appeared behind Mark Payton's head. He got up, strolled round the settee he had been occupying, and picked up the waiting wand.

"There. Roughly forty-five degrees West, longitude, fifty-three degrees North, latitude. It's in an area known as the Bight Fracture Zone, but it's also part of what we call the Mid-Atlantic Ridge, which stretches from way down below the Equator right up to Iceland. You know, depths in the Atlantic proper are usually well over two thousand metres, more often four thousand, and in places a good deal deeper than that. But on the ridge they come up close to the thousand mark."

The figures clearly meant little to the presenter. "Tell us about the island."

"Sure." Payton resumed his seat. "Soon as we heard the news of an eruption over the Bight Fracture Zone, the Ballard Foundation despatched our ocean research vessel *Deep Sea Diver*. We got there five days after the initial eruption. By then there was quite a lot to be seen above water."

The screen was filled with a clip of the island, sinister in its slate-grey colouring, rising like a cone from the sea.

"You took these shots, right? Like how big is it?"

"Then it was maybe the size of a baseball pitch, cone-shaped. Like a large, hot rock just sticking up out of the sea, and smoking, just as you see it there. But it's growing every day."

The picture flicked back to the studio where Mark was still draped over the cream settee, his arms lying along the back, bent at the elbows and displaying a froth of sun-bleached hair above the wrists . . . and a massive diving watch. A potted palm had been carefully arranged behind his right shoulder.

"Okay." The presenter glanced down at his notes. "Say, Mark, this is a uniquely phenomenal event, isn't it?" as if he didn't know it.

"Well, phenomenal is the correct word, of course. But not unique."

"You mean there've been islands like this one . . . Misreal you've named it, haven't you . . . popping up before?"

"Sure. As recently as November 1963 there was an eruption just south of Iceland and an island appeared. Called Surtsey. Then a couple of smaller ones joined it. I'm told news of it kinda got lost in Kennedy's assassination. But it happened."

"Okay, now you say this island is growing every day. How big do you think it's going to get?"

"You won't get me making any guesses. It all depends on the intensity of the local seismic activity. There are also several unusual features about Misreal. It's come up over a fault, so that should mean it's polygenetic rather than monogenetic. But the magma is solid rather than viscous as one would expect in this area. Then it's a guyot, technically . . . " he turned directly to the camera. "That's a seamount, folks, a submarine mountain rising more than 3000 feet above the ocean floor, and with a flat top. It began life way, way down in the ocean. The normal course of events is for the pressure down there to act as a lid, so that the magma merely spills off to each side and forms lava beds on the ocean floor. But this one came straight up, and a good deal of that magma was scoriaceous, thrown high into the sky. There's a lot of pressure down there."

Anne laughed. "See what I mean? Why can't he talk English? Pompous ass!"

"The Yanks never use one short word when ten long ones will sound more impressive," Geoffrey commented.

Presenter: "You mean it's still erupting under there?"

"That's right. At this moment in time it appears that the viscosity of the magma is somewhat reduced, lessening the issue of pyroclastic material, but judging by the information collected, the activity in this area is not governed by the usual characteristic phenomena. If the volume of gas present creates sufficient pressure, it could reactivate at several times the previous explosive force, considerably increasing the spread of shredded magma. Right now Misreal is about a quarter of a mile in diameter, and rises two hundred feet above sea level. That's a lot of activity in three weeks."

"And you've actually landed on it?"

"We wanted to check out the temperatures and tabulate other data."

"Weren't you scared stiff?"

Mark Payton gave a calm smile. "I can't say it occurred to me at the time. We just wanted to get on with the job."

"Get on with the job," Anne sneered. "The jerk."

"So what was it like?"

"Pretty hot. And moving."

"The island was moving?"

"Shaking from time to time, yes."

"So what do you reckon is going to happen to it? Is it permanent?"

"It could be. But I think there's too much pressure for that. And much depends on the depth of the volcanic conduit. The most likely probability is that it may lie dormant for a while, then there'll be another eruption splitting the conduit into a wide chasm into which the mass may recede and disappear again. Or it may settle and just get eroded by the sea."

"Is that what happened to Surtsey?"

"No, Surtsey is still around."

18

"You mean this island really could be permanent?"

"Yes it could. Although my best bet would be that it isn't."

"You've called the island Misreal. Any scientific reason for that?"

Payton grinned; he had a most attractive smile. "Not one. When we landed, one of the guys said, heck, this is a miserable place. And another said, yeah, but it's real. Simple as that. Rolls nicely round the tongue . . . "

"You going back to . . . Misreal, Mark?"

"You bet your sweet life. We're just re-stocking the ship, then we'll be back out there."

"Okay. Now for the big one. Is this island dangerous?"

"Not so long as navigators remember it's there."

"What about the risk of an above-water eruption?"

"Well, like any eruption, if it's big enough it'll affect the weather. But dangerous . . . not unless you happen to be close to it when it goes."

"Thank you, Mark. Now . . . "

Anne switched off the set. "They mentioned an earlier one, in 1963. Just before I was born. Do you remember it?"

"For God's sake, I was only three."

Anne laughed. "Then maybe you don't. And you reckon you're actually going to see this on your way home?"

"You bet I am."

"Lucky jerk."

"Why don't you take some time off and come with us. There's a spare cabin this trip. Mum and Dad would love to see you."

Anne brooded into her drink. "I'd love to, Geoff. But I can't. Big conference." She stood up. "I'll fix my face and put some clothes on. Then we'll go eat. I know just the place."

Geoffrey kept his Ford Escort in a garage yard a short taxi-ride from the Liverpool docks. All direct routes, whether road or rail, led to London, almost at right angles to his destination near King's Lynn. Whichever form of transport, it was a damn nuisance but at least using the car eliminated hanging around cheerless railway stations as he crossed the country. He hated English motorways, but used them nevertheless; at least they gave one the feeling of getting there faster. The M6 was reasonably uncluttered and he was able to enjoy the warm May sun – relaxed driving before branching off east towards Peterborough.

He wished Anne could have come with him; Mum would have done her nut with excitement . . . he could just see her. Anne was a super girl but he was a bit worried about her. So gorgeous, vivacious and yet no steady bloke in the background. It wasn't brilliant to think of her sleeping around . . . well, not exactly that but one didn't doubt she did sleep with some of these types. Ben for instance; pity she'd cancelled her date, he'd like to have met the man, see what he was like.

He pulled left into the middle lane as a rusty pile of tin honked behind before shooting past at the rate of knots. "Fool!" he shouted after the dwindling green stern. Anne probably hadn't wanted them to meet; she knew he would be giving Ben the once over, vetting him. Doing his 'big brother' bit. He was the only member of the family who had ever dared lecture her. She was nearest to him in age and from the beginning the three-year gap had never mattered. They had always played together, got into scrapes together – shared secrets.

Strange, because Freddie was only thirteen months younger than Anne and one would have imagined they'd be closer; but Freddie was so different. He had never joined in their larks; he preferred to stay around the kitchen near Mum, and the cooking, playing with the cats and Jasper, the mongrel they'd had at that time. They tried to persuade him to compete in the famous pig race but Freddie went and locked himself in the outside loo and refused to budge. Geoffrey grinned to himself, remembering the trouble he and Anne got into when the darned pigs wouldn't stop and carried them through Tilney and St Lawrence crossroads. It was lucky Old Higgins' tractor had broken down blocking the road or they'd have probably been killed on the main road at St John's Highway. Dad didn't half lambast him for that – but Anne got off almost scotfree.

It was 2.30 before he finished his pub lunch and cleared Peterborough. He headed across North Level through Thorney.

A couple of curves and the road straightened, carrying him through the flatlands, vast fields as far as he could see in any direction, a patchwork of green and brown . . . oats and barley, beets . . . and there was a team of women picking green peas.

His smile widened. He was nearly home.

As soon as he swung off the Wisbech by-pass he saw the distant farm, white walls faintly pink-tinged by the sun, seemingly suspended in mid-air, separated from his horizon by long, thin strands of ground mist. This was the fen country, much of it at or even below sea-level, lying between the River Nene and the Middle Level Main Drain which joined the Great Ouse three miles south of King's Lynn. The Romans had been the first to drain this area. When their civilisation broke down, it reverted to marshland, and remained like that for hundreds of years. Now endless drainage systems dried the magnificent soil in convenient squares and rectangles for heavy crop production.

The farm took shape as he approached. In summer it would be impossible to see its outline, masked by weeping willows, but at this time of year the trailing thongs still carried catkins, the tiny pale leaves just daring to curl out of their buds. It was a lengthy drive from the five-bar gate to the yard, but before he drove in between barn and farmhouse he could hear Jason's happy bark. Climbing out, a little stiffly after his drive, Geoffrey braced himself as the Labrador's hefty body hurtled into his legs . . . closely followed by two shrieking children. The Rowlands were here, too.

"Geoff!" A short, stocky man with jeans stuffed down his wellies, a plaid shirt partly stuffed into his jeans and a flat, tweed cap making a feeble attempt to hold down an excessive amount of wiry brown hair, wandered out of the cowshed. "You made it at last. We were expecting you last week." His face crinkled into a lopsided grin.

Geoffrey threw a stick for Jason, and with his nephew and niece in each hand crossed the yard to greet his brother. "Freddie! You're really looking the part in that gear!" His hands were occupied and Freddie's were dirty so he gave his brother an affectionate dig in the ribs with his elbow. "I phoned Mum to say I was delayed. Didn't she tell you?"

"She may have, but I don't remember. My memory never was very good, was it?"

"Good enough to get you through college, which is more than I did." Little Jackie started to grizzle and tug away, so Geoffrey picked him up and asked four-year-old Jessica, "Where's Gran?"

"Shopping." She was still feeling shy of her big uncle.

"And Granpa?"

"Dad's gone down to clear a ditch near Fen's End," Freddie replied for her. "Jennifer's indoors, somewhere."

"And Charlie?"

"He'll be here for the weekend. Has to keep the wheels of finance oiled," he said slyly, referring to their brother-in-law's exalted position in a City banking corporation. He looked at his watch. "You had lunch?"

"Stopped at a pub for a Ploughman's. But I wouldn't mind a cup of tea. I'll go and put the kettle on. Come on, kids."

But Jenny had already taken a tray of tea into the sitting-room. She climbed out of a cretonne-covered armchair to put both arms round her elder brother's neck. "Geoff, dear. What happened to you? I came down last week to be here when you got home and the kids have been driving Mum and Dad potty ever since, waiting for you."

Geoffrey hugged her, lifting her off the floor. She would always be the baby of the family, a fact enhanced by her having remained smaller, daintier and fairer than her siblings.

"Had to spend an extra week in Saginaw for repairs. So I flew to Boston and visited Anne."

Brother and sister were still exchanging news when they heard Mum's car in the yard, shortly followed by Dad's Land Rover. Dog and children rushed out with a greeting worthy of at least a year's separation; and Freddie's voice joined in the kitchen mêlée.

"I'd better go and make a fresh pot." Jennifer picked up the depleted teapot. "Won't be long."

"I'll go and get my stuff in from the car before it starts raining." Geoffrey was smiling. It felt so good to be home with the family, here at Dunning Farm. He looked out of the sitting-room windows at the lovely garden his parents had created – lawns, borders, hedges and a pretty, octagonal summerhouse in the far corner under the largest willow. It was neater, now, than in his childhood; Dad and Mum had been too busy in those days, trying to build up the farm and raise four kids, to spend time on such luxuries. Now they could afford luxuries aplenty – holidays abroad every year, a decent car each, trips to London theatres . . . they were even talking about putting in a swimming pool.

And was this what he wanted – eventually? Yes, eventually, but not now. He had to see the world first, achieve his ambitions . . . but it would be nice to have a place like this of his own, one day, in which to raise a family.

Mary Dunning loved having her family around her more than anything else in the world. Since the children had grown up and left home she had filled her life with all the things she had itched to do for years but lacked the time and money. For the past five years she had worked on her garden, restocked with canvasses and oil-paints and joined an art class in King's Lynn – and the local church choir. On occasional trips around the countryside with John she bought pieces of antique china to add to the collection started by her grandmother at the turn of the century, and these now had pride of place in the sitting-room; all the dining chairs were re-upholstered with the tapestries she had worked while sitting at the bedsides of elderly patients in her role of local hospital visitor . . . all very conventional, comfortable and gratifying. But nothing compared to the satisfaction she felt now, sitting at the foot of the family dinner-table opposite John, with her grown-up children around them and the grandchildren safely tucked in bed upstairs.

She had worried when Jennifer determined to get married so

young, barely nineteen. Charles was of a very different background, town people, banking people. That sort of marriage didn't
always work out. But Jennifer and Charles had made it work, had
been gloriously happy from the start. At first, Charles had visited
the farm in navy pinstripe and tie, removing his jacket as a gesture
towards melding with the new in-laws. Jennifer had sorted that one
out. He would doubtless be arriving on Friday night in jeans and a
pullover, probably hoping Freddie would allow him a turn driving
a tractor. Of course their life-style was very different from the rest
of the family. Charles drove a big Mercedes and they maintained a
villa in Spain for their summer holidays, while in their Greenwich
home they seemed to have dinner parties every week . . . but it was
reassuring to feel that one of her daughters had married both
happily and prosperously.

She spooned roasted parsnips on to Geoffrey's plate.

"Never see these anywhere except at this table. Can't think why,
they're the most delicious veg there is." His mouth was watering as
he spoke.

"I like them mashed with butter, too," Freddie said, helping
himself to leeks.

"You like anything that's put in front of you," his mother
laughed.

"And a lot that isn't, as well," Jennifer teased. "In fact I notice
there's an awful lot of tummy hanging over the top of your
trousers."

"Rubbish! It's just the way I'm sitting," Freddie grumbled, feign-
ing offence when everybody laughed.

"Stop it!" Mary ordered. Freddie's always had a hefty appetite."
She felt extra protective of her younger son. He was a gentle
creature, soft, loving, willing and cuddly, wholly lacking the determined drive of Geoffrey and Anne . . . even of Jennifer. Yet he had
done so well at Horticultural College; it was lovely having him
living at home with them . . . but for how much longer? He seemed
very keen on Dr Bolting's receptionist, an attractive girl but would
she have the stamina to be a farmer's wife? And if they did make a
go of it, would they live here or want a place of their own? The
thought of sharing a kitchen didn't appeal all that much, but it was
preferable to losing Freddie.

"What time did you finish milking?" John asked.

"'Bout five or soon after." Freddie reached for another piece of
Yorkshire pudding.

"Getting later. Bigger yield?"

"Yes. There's good grass down there past the road."

"Won't last long."

23

"Now we're down to only the five of them it will see them out for another week."

"Changing the subject, Geoffrey, did I hear you mention that you'd passed that new volcanic island on your way back?" his father asked.

Geoffrey's description of the island lasted until the end of the meal, with only a pause demanded by Mary and Jennifer as they cleared the plates into the kitchen and fetched the Queen's Pudding for dessert.

Question time was over coffee in the sitting-room. Everyone was very interested though Mary wanted to know more about his visit to Anne.

"Tell us, what's her flat like?"

"A bit like a movie set, all in grey and pink with huge contemporary pictures I couldn't make head nor tail of on every wall," he told them.

"That sounds like Anne," Jennifer giggled. "And what about a boyfriend? Anyone in particular?"

"I would say definitely not."

"Tck, tck. About time she settled to a bit of comfortable domesticity," his father growled.

"I reckon she's extremely comfortable the way she is." Geoffrey found it hard to keep his face straight as he said it. It was not easy to imagine his business-orientated sister swapping all that immaculate luxury and personal freedom for a team of screaming kids and the three-meals-a-day-seven-days-a-week syndrome. Yet he wondered, as his eyes drifted around the sitting-room ... surely, having been raised in this close family atmosphere, she must sometimes feel awfully lonely? Certainly he'd hate to end his days a bachelor, but then he was only thirty; he wouldn't have to settle down for years yet. He changed the topic. "How's business, Freddie?"

Freddie glanced at his father before replying. "Very well, I'd say."

"He's being modest," John chipped in. "The farm has never done better. Mind you, I still think it's been mainly luck that some of his crazy, computerised ideas have paid off."

"You mean he actually uses that infernal machine he's installed in the office?"

"Maybe if you installed something like it on your bridge you wouldn't hit things in the St Lawrence," Freddie remarked casually over the top of the *Telegraph*.

"I might tell you I was asleep at the time ... "

"Really! Worse and worse!"

"No, you blockhead . . . "

The howl of laughter from his parents and sister put paid to Geoffrey's excuses. But he knew they weren't necessary. His family would believe the best of him, as he would of them. That was what families were all about. Funny. Sometimes, when he first arrived home after a two-months round trip, he wondered why the hell he'd chosen a career at sea . . . Home was so wonderful. Yet he knew that before the end of one week he'd be restless to get away again. Much as he adored Dunning Farm, he adored the sea more.

Throughout the summer the island of Misreal continued to grow. And to the surprise of the experts, the volcanic activity was continuous, but in low key: small eruptions sent lava flows out of the cone but very seldom hurled any of the magma high into the air, nor were the earth tremors sufficiently strong to be dangerous.

The island was a continuous source of news and interest. In June an American entrepreneur chartered a small steamer and advertised a 'Voyage to the Newest Place on Earth', with lectures by Dr Mark Payton, organised by Anne Dunning's PR Agency. Every berth was taken within forty-eight hours.

On the spur of the moment, Anne decided to go along herself, rather than send one of their reps. This way she could see the volcano for free. She had to share a two-berth cabin, but it was only for just over a week.

Everyone was on deck as the cone-shaped island emerged from the horizon early on the fourth morning after leaving New York; there were oohs and aahs and a steady clicking of cameras. The Ballard Foundation's research vessel lay a mile off, as it had done since Misreal had first appeared, and after an exchange of signals a launch came across and Mark Payton boarded the ship.

He looked very much as he had done in the TV studio, save that he had added a windcheater. He grinned at the eager passengers, then climbed up on to the bridge and addressed them through the ship's tannoy system.

"That island *is* the newest place on earth, folks," he announced. "And in just a little while you're going to be standing on it. But first, I'm going to tell you a little about it.

"What we have here is a guyot, or seamount, that is, a volcano which is the result of an undersea eruption. But what causes a volcano in the first place? Well, the centre of the earth is filled with a molten mass called magma, and this stuff spends its time trying to get out. In prehistory the whole earth was a mass of volcanic activity, but over the centuries the various cracks and fissures in the surface closed up, and now volcanoes, like earthquakes, normally only take place in certain well-known and defined areas: nearly half of the world's volcanic activity is, for example, concentrated along the western coastlines of the Pacific Ocean. There is some volcanic activity, maybe thirteen per cent of the whole, in the Atlantic, but there's never been any in this particular spot. So this guy, this guyot" – he laughed at his own joke – "is a bit of a maverick. On the other hand, he's come up from a piece of the ocean floor named the Bight Fracture Zone, just where the ocean floor rises up into the Mid-Atlantic Ridge, and it's possible some kind of vent has been forming there for some time.

"But Misreal is a tricky one for other reasons. As I said, a guyot is a seamount with a flat top, but you'll see the shape is like a cone with the top sliced off, or just what we'd expect with a volcano on land. Inside the cone there's a crater." He grinned. "I haven't actually looked inside, because it's still active, but I know it's there because I've flown over it. It's one great red glow down there. But it's come up more than two thousand feet, and that's unusual. Something pretty big must have been pushing it and still is pushing it. Let me say that there's nothing to be scared of at this minute. Right now the pulses are slow and easy, and we're monitoring them all the time. Every day they're getting weaker. You'll find it's pretty hot on the island; wear stout shoes. And just pretend that you're taking a walk back through time. Because that's what you'll be doing. Okay, folks, let's step ashore."

The steamer's boats had already been swung out, and now with a great deal of excitement the sightseers, most of them were in early middle age, clambered down the accommodation ladder. It took some time. Anne hung back. She was wearing white trousers and a blue blazer and had her hair tied up in a scarf. She only hoped her thick-soled sneakers would provide sufficient protection.

She was in the last boat to go ashore. The engine was slipped into neutral as they approached the black-pebbled beach, and sailors were waiting to help the ladies over the bow to prevent their feet getting wet. Seabirds, which amazingly had already started to nest on the island, rose into the air with alarmed screeches.

Anne gazed up at the cone, now rising some four hundred feet above her head; little puffs of smoke emerged continuously. In her university days she and some friends had bicycled down through France and Italy, and crossed to Sicily. From there they had made the excursion north of Messina to the Lipari Islands, and visited Stromboli, where the volcano is active, and is reputed to erupt every six minutes without fail. Each eruption is nothing more than a puff of smoke and a faint rumbling.

Misreal reminded her strongly of Stromboli.

As they strolled round the lower slopes of the cone, she suddenly found herself next to Mark Payton, who was chatting in turn with the various groups and answering questions.

When he turned and smiled directly at her she said a polite "Hi," wondering if he'd remember her.

"Well, hi," he replied with interest. But he was greeting an attractive young woman; he clearly had no recollection of ever having met her. On the other hand, she thought he might remember her after this meeting, as his gaze drifted up and down.

"I've been comparing Misreal with Stromboli," she said conversationally.

"Good point."

"The Italians say that as long as Stromboli keeps up its mini-eruptions every six minutes it'll never really blow its top. Do you think that applies here?"

"Absolutely. If Misreal were to stop smoking, you guys wouldn't be standing here."

"Meaning you would?"

"Probably. Goes with the job." His tone was so pretentious in its casualness it irritated.

But she had to remain polite. They were going to be thrown together a lot during this trip. "And do you enjoy the job when it entails trailing dumb sightseers over a scientifically exciting area?" she asked, a slight edge of cynicism in her voice.

Mark stopped and looked at her, and for a moment she wondered if she'd gone over the top. Then his face spread into a huge grin. "No! I most positively do not!" His laugh echoed across the black beach.

"What's so funny?"

"I guess I sussed you out all wrong."

"How come?"

"Must have been your snazzy gear and that stiff, English accent. And then bringing this bunch along, I guess I had you down for another of the rubberneck gang."

She wasn't sure how to react. "I imagined you'd be happy to have all these people along, interested in your subject."

Again he laughed. "Sure, I would be . . . if they were. But this lot! Have you heard their questions and comments?" He bent and picked up a lump of lava. "Gee, look Professor," he pitched a squeaky falsetto, "this rock looks like a horse's face. See, here are the eyes and the ears . . . " he pointed a finger at the indentations . . .

It was Anne's turn to laugh; he looked so ridiculous.

"You'd think this stuff was kids' modelling clay!" He threw the lava out into the sea. "I'm sorry," he suddenly looked tired and chastened, "I really thought I was coming along to lecture to folk seriously interested in one of the greatest natural phenomena of our time."

They walked in silence, following the group of chattering tourists.

Anne stared up at the lip of the crater. "If it did blow, would it be a big one?"

"If this island ever really blows," Mark Payton told her, "coming up all of two thousand feet or more from beneath the ocean bed, it's gonna be the biggest bang this world has ever heard."

2

The Eruption

British Ocean Transporters was a shipping company specialising in the trade of light metals. One of the smallest of their fleet of carriers, SS *Skyhawk*, followed an unchanging schedule. In Jamaica she loaded raw bauxite; the ore was taken north and up the St Lawrence River to the town of Saginaw, where it was converted into aluminium. *Skyhawk* then loaded treated aluminium – from bauxite cargoes carried on earlier voyages made by herself or her sister ships – across the North Atlantic to Liverpool. In England the aluminium was made into household goods, and the third leg of *Skyhawk's* triangle was carrying such goods, dishwashers, washing machines and the like, out to the West Indies.

Each round voyage took two months, and the odd incident like touching a rock in the St Lawrence apart, was as predictable as if one were driving a car over a familiar road. There were storms from time to time, but nothing the ship and her experienced crew could not handle. As *Skyhawk* was now quite an elderly lady, there was the occasional bit of engine trouble but, again, never anything Chief Evans couldn't fix, and there were no serious breakdowns.

Skyhawk was eight thousand tons, a conventional vessel with all her accommodation and machinery aft; the three holds occupied the midships and forward sections of the ship. She was a happy ship. Captain Fogarty was a veteran now, and due to retire the following year; he left much of the day-to-day running of the ship to his First Officer, whom he knew to be a good man.

Geoffrey in turn had the utmost confidence in Second Officer Lloyd Turnbull, and their junior, Harry Trent, was a promising lad.

The purser was George Abercrombie, and the doctor Ian Bennett; for *Skyhawk* also carried passengers. In addition to the officers' quarters, there were six double cabins on the deck below.

These were small, and by no means luxurious; one on each side had an en suite bathroom, the other two on each side shared. However passages on *Skyhawk* were comparatively cheap, and the owners had intelligently guessed that there were still a large number of people in the world who wished to travel by sea without great expense, and without the forced jollity and gourmet meals of a cruise liner. The food on *Skyhawk* was simple but very good, the passengers eating with the officers in the small dining-saloon in an atmosphere of one happy family.

Few people came for the round trip. Most on the outward leg were businessmen travelling to the West Indies and using the ten-day voyage from Liverpool to Kingston as a holiday. West Indians travelling up to Canada made up the largest part of the northern leg, and on the home leg more often than not there were students crossing from the New World to the old, vacationing and enjoying themselves.

This meant a constant change of faces, which suited Geoffrey. He was gregarious but mistrusted close relationships, especially with the opposite sex. He would not forget Sally in a hurry, even if she had apparently managed to forget him overnight. He thought the most humiliating thing that could happen to a man about to be married must be to have his bride-to-be call it off when actually before the altar; the next worst was to have an envelope turn up at your house on the morning of the ceremony containing your ring and a note with a single word, *Sorry!* He had telephoned, but she had already left the country. As one of his West Indian friends might have said, it left him feeling like a pennyworth of ice in a hot sun. It emerged later that Sally had done this before, twice; but her apparent inability to face decisions had not really helped. He still wondered if there was something about him that was unacceptable to a girl.

That had been six years ago – six years of telling himself that she wouldn't have made a good partner and it was better it had happened before the wedding than after; six years of wondering if it had somehow been his fault for failing to give her the necessary confidence – which didn't alter the fact he had loved her and that it still hurt. Nowadays his female friendships were in very light-hearted vein, the first suggestion of serious involvement bringing a brusque, not to say off-hand reaction. Which fitted admirably with his work. A good-looking, personable young First Officer was virtually expected to conduct a mild flirtation with any unattached females who happened to be on board; it was an amusing duty, fun, but not one to be enjoyed by a man committed, and with a conscience. It was important to keep these relationships light – no heavy stuff and certainly no visiting the passenger cabins, not that it would be practical on a ship as small and intimate as *Skyhawk*, with her crew of twenty-four knowing each other so well.

Passengers for England boarded in Halifax, *Skyhawk's* last port of call before crossing the Atlantic. Here, at the beginning of September, Geoffrey stood on the bridge wing and watched them filing up the gangway. They consisted of a middle-aged couple with two children – boys – occupying A2 and A3; two male students who would be in B3; a single man who would be in B2 – the other berth was vacant – and a prosperous-looking fairly young and clearly upward-moving married couple who were obviously adventuring, in A1; a rather grim-faced elderly maiden lady who would be in B1; and a young woman who would be sharing that cabin.

Geoffrey straightened his cap, and glanced at the list in his hand. The latter's name was Elizabeth Bowman, and mounting the open gangway she appeared decidedly attractive – short, but with a good figure, auburn hair blowing in the breeze, and a delightful smile. It promised to be a pleasant week.

Geoffrey's duties kept him on the bridge until the ship was clear of the port, and he remained on watch until eight o'clock, when he was relieved by Turnbull and went down to dinner.

There were three tables of six in the saloon. The Captain presided at one, with the doctor and four guests; Chief Evans presided at the second, with the Purser and four more guests; and First Officer Dunning presided at the third, when available, while Second Officer Turnbull took charge in his absence, as one of the two watch-keeping officers was always on the bridge; the second place was occupied by young Trent, thus being groomed early in the art of small talk. As with the others, there were normally four passengers at Geoffrey's table as well, but as they were one passenger short on this voyage he had only three, and was disappointed to discover that his guests consisted of the two students and the single man. The family was with the Chief, and the Captain, predictably, had the Yuppie marrieds and the two single ladies. Maybe the situation would be varied as the voyage went on.

There was a small cocktail party before the meal, to effect introductions all round.

"I do hope we are going to see Misreal, Captain," the Yuppie wife enthused. Geoffrey had shuddered at the sight of her miniskirted dress with voluminous sleeves and weird hair-do cut short as a man's on one side, revealing a row of studs and hoops pierced into her ear, and drooping over eye and ear on the other.

"Oh, we shall, Mrs Crawford. We pass quite close to it." The old man was so inured to this routine he could handle passengers' questions almost without conscious thought.

"We've seen it twice now," Trent said brightly. He had admired the blue-stockinged knees.

"Must be old hat," Yuppie Crawford remarked. He was equipped with baggy trousers and a large, spotted bowtie.

"Is it as dramatic in real life as in the TV pictures?" Elizabeth Bowman asked.

Geoffrey's black eyebrows shot up in alarm as the Australian accent – which he should have anticipated after a look at her passport in the Purser's Office before dinner – floated across from the other table. Great Scot! Was it possible to dance attendance on a voice like that for seven whole days? Of course, providing she kept her mouth shut it might not be too difficult. The passport had also told him that she was aged twenty-seven, single, and that she had a scar on her left thigh. The various stamps indicated that she had entered the United States at San Francisco eight months before, and had moved across the border to Vancouver four months later. So she was not only attractive but probably adventurously interesting or, looking on the black side, running away from an emotional hiatus. And she dressed well. Her outfit was a multi-coloured blouse, cut Cossack style, with a matching ankle-length skirt and wedge-heeled shoes, a sane choice for negotiating companionways. And now she was on a British ship travelling from Canada to England. Geoffrey decided that despite the ghastly drawl this was definitely worth working on.

"Every bit as dramatic, Miss Bowman," the Captain replied.

"And is it still growing?" asked the grim-faced lady.

"Seems to be. But you'll see it all for yourself, in three days' time."

The meal over, Elizabeth Bowman fetched a heavy windcheater from her cabin and went out on to the small promenade deck behind the passenger accommodation, where there was some shelter from the wind. This deck was sufficiently high above the engine-room for the noise to seem very far away, a mere background rumble, and astern the bubbling white wake stretched forever.

Geoffrey, having monitored Elizabeth's movements, allowed about two minutes before wandering outside himself. The two students were also there, smoking and chatting, but they were not speaking to Elizabeth, who was leaning on the rail, looking at the night.

He leaned beside her. "That's the Plough."

"Yes," she agreed.

"You don't see it in Australia."

"True. But I've been away awhile."

"Exploring or escaping? Or am I being nosey?"

She smiled. "I'd say you're being nosey, Mr . . . " she glanced at his insignia. "I'm terribly sorry, but I'm hopeless on titles and names."

"Aren't we all when a bunch of them are thrown at us all at once. The name's Dunning. Geoff Dunning."

"Then you're First Officer?"

"Correct. And you're Elizabeth Bowman."

"Well, you remembered my name."

"That's part of my job."

"Yep. Reckon there's more to running a ship than standing on the bridge. And in answer to your question, you could say I was escaping, Mr Dunning."

"Oh, Geoff, please. We have seven days ahead of us."

She gave him another glance. "Then you'd better call me Liz."

"Okay, Liz. Now, First Officers are also father confessors to their passengers. What's your problem? Unhappy love life?"

"Oh, no. I'm just looking . . . for something I just don't seem to find in Oz. So . . . "

"Something? What kind of something?"

She shrugged. "Just tell me and I'll be halfway there. Mebbe I just had ants in my pants. Bored with the local scenario."

It sounded a bit deep and involved so he changed course. "Did you enjoy your dinner?"

"It was great. I hadn't expected the chow to be so good on a freighter."

"Oh, the food is guaranteed. I was thinking of the company."

"Well . . . I don't really know them, yet. My cabin mate, well . . . "

"Looks a bit of a dragon." He made a grimace.

"Dunno if she's good mates material, but I'll have a go at sorting her out."

"A pity, but we can't do anything about it, I'm afraid. Voyages like this are very much pot luck. But . . . would you like a change of scenery, meal times?"

Liz Bowman turned round to rest her back on the rail and look at him. "Are you this direct with all the passengers?"

"Only the ones I like," he grinned.

"And I suppose you don't have a wife and four kids waiting for you in Liverpool."

"No way!" He laughed.

"Ah," she said. "Find 'em, feel 'em . . . "

"Oh, no!" he denied hastily, before she could go on. "It, well . . ."

"Goes with the job," she remarked, and he realised he was making about as good an impression on her as Mark Payton had on Anne.

There was little point in pretending otherwise. "True. And very enjoyable with the prospect of interesting company for the journey."

She studied him in silence, her face not unsympathetic.

"So, if I got the Purser to make a discreet change in the seating arrangements night after next . . . "

She raised an eyebrow. "Not tomorrow?"

"I won't be at dinner tomorrow. I'll be on watch. Lloyd Turnbull will have my table and I'm not handing you over to him," he said in mock seriousness. She smothered a smile. "We stand watch and watch," he explained. "The day is divided into six four-hour watches. Lloyd is on now. He'll hand over to me at midnight for the Middle Watch. I'll be on duty until four, then he'll take over for the Morning Watch. I'll replace him for the Forenoon Watch until twelve, then he'll take over for the Afternoon Watch, at four."

"Hold on," Liz said. "That means you'll be on watch from four until eight again tomorrow, and free for dinner."

Geoffrey shook his head. "To make sure the watches alternate, the period between four and eight in the afternoon is split in two. They're called the Dog Watches. So I'll be on from four to six, the First Dog, and Lloyd from six to eight, the Last Dog. Then I take over for the Night Watch at eight."

She looked totally confused. "Why are they called Dog Watches?"

"I have no idea. And neither has anyone else."

"I see. And when do you sleep, while all of this is going on?"

"Well, tonight I'll sleep from four until quarter to eight tomorrow morning, and if I need to, I can have a siesta tomorrow afternoon."

"But normally you'd be in bed now, making sure you're awake at midnight."

"Normally."

She smiled. "I think you should get your sleep. I'm going to bed now anyway. But . . . " she paused, grinning. "Don't forget to switch my table, night after next."

The weather at two o'clock the following afternoon could have been described as bracing, Liz Bowman decided as she reeled gently along the main deck.

She didn't know if passengers were allowed down here, but no one had objected as she descended the ladder from the very limited promenade deck . . . and it was certainly a good place to get noticed from the bridge.

The wind tangled her hair into a bird's nest and she licked salt from her lips, hugging her windcheater close over her chest. She was waiting, hoping that this Geoff person would appear soon; his was the only character on the ship who appealed to her. She wished now she had chosen to fly the Atlantic, instead of crossing on this old tub; a fruitless waste of a week. Fruitless? What fruit was she hoping to pick? Of course she hadn't been completely honest last night with Geoff. True she was escaping, but mainly from Bob and Company. She'd had Bob up to the eyeballs. They had lived together for two years, during which she'd done the secretarial work for his plant hire business, cooked his meals, washed his stubbies, mended and cleaned for him . . . for the magnificent reward of the occasional smile and a regular screw. Away from his 'mates' he was a nice enough bloke, but together they all seemed hell-bent on their macho image, drinking themselves stupid night after night. What the others were like in the mornings with their wives and/or girl friends she had no idea, but Bob had been bloody. She could do nothing right . . . and if she dared raise a voice in self-defence he was not above lashing out with a fist at any part of her anatomy within reach. Sure, he was always sorry afterwards, even tearful when she announced, as she did at least once a month, that she'd had enough and wanted to chuck it in. But when she had finally walked out, left Tweed Heads and pitched into the anonymity of Sydney, he had traced her, come knocking on her door, pleading, weeping, begging. He waylaid her in the street, even tried to manhandle her into his car. So she had left a perfectly good job after only three months and headed for Melbourne . . .

The foam-streaked water coasted away from the hull and over the swell; she was remembering Bob's face and the better times they'd shared. Perhaps it wasn't possible to have it all good in a relationship with a bloke. Maybe she was being naive to expect the traditional fairy-story happiness. Her search for it in Melbourne had been a disaster. First Chuck, then Andy, had made her feel human, normal and trusting before heading her straight into the Bob syndrome again. For months she had believed there was something wrong with her attitude, until girls she palled up with at work started talking about their own mates . . . and they all sounded as bad as each other. It was on the bus going to work one morning that it occurred to her that perhaps men outside Australia were not all male chauvinist pigs. And at twenty-six it was time to go and investigate before it was too late.

Of course, this Geoff bloke was a non-starter; she knew all about shipboard romances, and he was showing all the classic signs of tail-chasing. But who knew where an introduction in England might lead? It was worth getting to know him a bit better if only for that reason.

And here he was.

The First Officer was heading for the forward hold, making a round of checks as he came off duty, before putting his head down for a couple of hours. His decision to check the hatch covers was made when Liz emerged on to the deck beneath him. Now he pretended he hadn't noticed her before. "Oh! Hi! Breezy out here today." He paused. "Does the movement upset your stomach at all?"

"Reckon I was born with a cast-iron gut. Nothing, but nothing separates me from my chow." She beamed a welcoming smile. "Your stint through now?"

"For a couple of hours."

"But you're gonna take a siesta, check?"

"When I've done my rounds. Would you like to join me?"

"Why not?" She fell in beside him and together they examined the fastenings over the holds. He made more of an issue of it than he normally would as Liz was obviously pleased to be taking part, and he debated whether to forgo his nap and stay with her. But this was only day two and it could set an exhausting precedent.

Fifteen minutes later Liz said, "Now you've run out of checks . . . and reasons to stay out of your hammock. Don't think I'm being personal but I reckon you need your beauty sleep. Go on," she added as he started to mouth a protest, "go siesta, sailor, and I'll see you tomorrow."

"You're very understanding. Thanks." He appreciated her gesture almost enough to change his mind and stay. But he didn't. He smiled into her green eyes and murmured, "Till tomorrow, then."

She watched him go and decided he improved on knowing.

Next day he realised he was looking forward with genuine pleasure to seeing Liz at dinner. The Australian accent wasn't really so bad, in fact he was beginning to like it, and there was a laid-back directness about her which was very open and refreshing.

She was wearing the same colourful outfit as the first night, when she came through from her cabin. Geoffrey excused himself from a boring monologue about stockmarkets round the world, delivered by the male Yuppie, and went forward to greet her.

She had the elderly virgin in tow. "Geoff, meet my cabin mate, Rose. She's Canadian."

"Hello, Miss er . . . " he held out his hand.

She took it and shook it. "Rose," she affirmed. "No way we use stuffy surnames all through the trip. Anyway I hate being called Miss Taggart. I've retired from teaching. Had scruffy brats yelling *Miss Taggart* at me all my life." She repeated her name in squeaky mimicry.

Geoffrey realised that behind the thick glasses her eyelids were faintly blue and she'd put on some lipstick; her stout body was enveloped in a pale blue, full-skirted dress, and she wore pearl necklet and earrings. Her grey hair framed a severe face which became transformed when she smiled. As she did now. "Thank you, Rose," he said. "I'm Geoffrey, your First Officer."

"I thought Liz said your name was Geoff?" She was still holding his hand.

"Oh, er, yes. Yes, please call me Geoff." Nice that she was so relaxed, but was she going to stick with them for ever?

Apparently not. "You two can entertain each other, I guess. I'm going to nail the Captain for a while." Rose released his hand and for a moment he thought she winked at him . . . then decided it was his imagination.

"I was wrong; she's quite a gal," he remarked to Liz.

"You wanna be a fly on our cabin wall. She's a wow. The day she retired she rubbed the magic lamp and took off. You should see her in her fancy bra and panties!"

Geoffrey smothered a laugh. "With what in mind?"

Liz snorted into her drink and splashed it down her front.

"Sorry about that." He was trying to straighten his face. They were still laughing as they took their places at table.

Liz appreciated having her chair held as she sat down. She liked the way he hadn't made any snide remark about preferring to see her in undies. He didn't seem to be trying the fast and loose game. And she did like those mobile black eyebrows.

Unfortunately the Crawfords were also at their table tonight. "I was telling the Captain how lucky Melissa and I feel to get berths on your boat," Henry brayed. "Just in time, I should say. Old tubs like this are surely being phased out, now."

"That so! Why?" Liz demanded, a dangerous light flashing under her long lashes.

The steward placed plates of colourful hors d'oeuvres before each diner: sardines, boiled eggs topped with caviar and little heaps of Russian salad nestling on beds of lettuce and tomato.

"Obsolete, dear gel. Obsolete. In fact as I told him, she must have been running at a lorse for years." The spotted bowtie of the first night had been exchanged for one with yellow stripes. Geoffrey thought that anyone who'd be seen dead in gear like that had to be a clown. The man surely spoke like one.

"Reckon the Keptun musta bin real happy to hev you tell him, cobber. He obviously hesn't realised ut, hes he?" Liz's face was deadpan as she delivered a heavily exaggerated accent.

Geoff kept his eyes glued on his plate. If he glanced at either Liz or Trent he was lost.

Unfortunately humour was not Henry's strong point. It never occurred to him that his observations might be received with less than the seriousness with which they were spoken. And it was also unfortunate that the sight of the colourful hors d'oeuvres, together with the delicate scent of sardines, should dampen his spirit of adventure and upset his equilibrium. Suddenly he was looking quite grey round the gills.

Melissa Crawford's eyes narrowed. She couldn't believe that any-one could treat the English language so badly, and wondered if it was that, or the increasing roll of the boat, that was affecting Henry's colour. "Are you all right, darling?"

The ship slid into an extra deep trough at that moment, and glasses, cutlery and the colourful hors d'oeuvres slipped daintily towards Melissa's lap, held at the last minute by the fiddles. "Aayy!" she shrieked.

Henry tried to swallow the excess saliva swilling in his mouth. "Oh hell. I don't think . . . er, I wonder if you will excuse me a moment . . . " he staggered to his feet.

"I'll come with you, darling." Melissa's skintight yellow catsuit, which matched the striped bowtie, wiggled after him past the tables. She wasn't looking too good, either.

Harry Trent held back his explosion till the saloon door closed. "Miss Bowman, you were magnificent!" Tears of laughter blinded him.

Geoffrey glanced hastily towards the other tables; his charges were creating a near riot . . . but no one seemed to notice, though the Captain and the family man were still watching the spot where the middle section of catsuit had disappeared.

"Did I say something wrong?" Liz asked. Her eyes were wide with startled innocence and Geoffrey noted they had little brown flecks in the green.

"No. Nothing. Nothing at all," Geoffrey assured her with an absolutely straight face. As First Officer he was trying to maintain the dignity of the ship's dining saloon. But he couldn't keep it up; the corners of his mouth twitched . . . and then the three of them were in stitches.

The incident had developed a certain camaraderie between the

three remaining diners at Geoffrey's table, and he found it difficult, afterwards, to shake off the friendly Trent without offending
him. Liz excused herself, whispering to Geoff that she would fetch
a coat and return in five minutes. He retired to his cabin, leaving
Trent to wander off to join the other diners over coffee in the main
saloon.

"That was crafty of you," he remarked when she joined him in
the gangway. "Do I gather you want some fresh air before turning
in?" He took the coat and held it out for her.

"Harry's cute, but very young." Liz slid her arms into the sleeves.
"And yes, I do intend to take a turn around the deck. Were you
thinking of checking the holds again?"

One black eyebrow twitched as he peered down into the dancing
eyes. "Why not?" She was very tiny; he could fit her under his
armpit. But he resisted the temptation and stood aside to allow her
to go first. Be careful, he told himself. This little Aussie is heating
your cool.

Wind and sea made walking difficult. Liz lurched, and bounced
off an air vent. Geoff caught her and held her arm as they swayed
together forward along the deck. Away from the aft superstructure
the wind tore at their clothes and carried away their shouted
remarks, killing conversation. Liz's small mouth was stretched to
the limit in pleasure as she raised her chin to the salt spray, hair
dragged back from her face and streaming behind, exposing her
gold stud earrings. Geoffrey had a violent urge to kiss her, but
didn't. He just stood watching the long, closed lashes sweeping her
cheeks, wanting to protect her from any sudden powerful gust.

She knew he was there. Knew he was looking, and wondered
what he was thinking. He was being a true Pom, a real gentleman,
making no move whatever to touch her. Pity. She was in the mood
to be touched, right now. But only touched, and maybe kissed. No
heavy stuff. What the Aussie boys would call prick-teasing. Would a
Pommie call it that, too?

She was almost thrown off her feet as the elderly freighter
screwed down into another trough. Geoffrey grabbed her and
guided her aft to shelter. Here the wind twisted under the bridge
wing and companionway, whipping Liz's hair across her face and
into her eyes. Trying to help brush it away with one hand while
holding her steady with an arm behind her shoulders, Geoffrey
was aware she was, effectively, in his arms, and when her face tilted
up, his mouth accidentally closed over hers.

He felt her arms slide up round his neck.

Geoffrey took over the watch at four the next morning. The

darkness was just beginning to fade.

"There she blows," Turnbull commented.

Geoffrey looked into the gloom. The glow on the horizon was like a light, winking at them. He glanced into the radar.

"Thirty miles off," Turnbull said.

"The small blip beside it?"

"I'd say that ocean research vessel is still keeping an eye on things."

"Must be costing a fortune," Geoffrey remarked.

"Steering East by North one half," Turnbull said.

"Got it."

"Have fun."

The Second Officer left the bridge and Geoffrey checked the compass setting. The ship was on autopilot, but a coxswain stood by to monitor the course.

The wind had dropped, and although there was the occasional whitecap the sea was no more than moderate. Geoffrey went out on to the wing to gaze at the glow for a moment, then stepped inside the radio office. Harper was asleep, however, so he returned on to the bridge, sat in the chair, and remembered last night. He could still taste Liz's lips, feel her body against his. For a moment there he had been carried right away. And so had she, he suspected. He could almost have imagined himself falling in love . . . before sanity had returned. But they had kissed again. And there were another four nights to Liverpool.

Slowly it began to grow light as *Skyhawk* steamed east at a steady fifteen knots, and the island rose out of the ocean like a beacon. But even in daylight its tip glowed red, which was more activity than Geoffrey remembered from the last time.

He went back to the radio office, where Harper was showering. "You spoken with those research people?"

"Not yet. You want me to?"

"Might be an idea."

But even as he said it the radio came to life, calling the vessel approaching Misreal.

Harper grabbed his mike and sat down, wrapped in a towel. "SS *Skyhawk*," he answered.

"*Skyhawk*. We would recommend you stand a little farther off the island," the voice said. "There is more seismic activity than usual."

Geoffrey took the mike himself. "You mean there's a risk of an explosion?"

"We reckon there is. The mini-eruptions ceased two days ago, and since then pressure has been building."

"Roger," Geoffrey said. "Keep in touch with them," he told

Harper, and returned to the bridge to telephone Fogarty. The Captain's cabin was actually only a few feet away on the same deck, but he was better roused by phone. Geoffrey explained the situation, and a few minutes later Fogarty was on the bridge.

"Distance off?"

"Eight miles."

"Well, you'd better alter course East by South for a couple of hours."

"East by South," Geoffrey told the coxswain, who adjusted the pilot; *Skyhawk* promptly came round to starboard. "That'll disappoint the passengers."

They were now starting to appear on deck, having set their alarms, armed with cameras, and oohing and aahing as they gazed at the island.

It was Liz who, glancing aft at the wake, noticed the alteration in course.

"Say!" she called up. "You guys chicken?"

"Definitely," Geoffrey said from the wing above her.

By the time Turnbull relieved Geoffrey at eight, Misreal was dropping astern, although as she was still only thirty miles off she remained visible, and still glowing.

Geoffrey went down to join the passengers for breakfast, which was always a buffet, with everyone sitting as they chose. Liz was waiting for him, and they sat together with their plates of egg and bacon.

"What did you think of it?" he asked.

"Impressive, what we saw of it. But why did you turn away?"

"Seems it's rumbling a bit. Did you get any shots?"

"Shouldn't think so, with my old . . . " she paused, her mouth half open, as there came a distant noise.

Geoffrey was on his feet in an instant, running for the promenade deck, and staring aft, at the huge pillar of light and smoke and black matter which was rising out of the horizon.

"Holy shit!" shouted one of the students. "It's blown its top!"

Cameras clicked, although at this distance all that would be recorded was the cloud and the flashes of light. Henry Crawford's video camera was whirring. Geoffrey was reminded of an atomic explosion, as the black mass spread across the sky in mushroom form – but an atomic explosion that was still going off, as the darts of red and black continued to spark at the base.

"Goddamit!" Liz said. "What a shame we're not closer."

"I think we're close enough," Geoffrey said, wondering what the aftermath was going to be, seawise. Thirty miles was a good distance, but . . .

"First Officer to the bridge," said the tannoy.

"I have to go."

"Say, let me know what's going on," she asked.

"Will do." He went up the ladders, and straight to the radio room, where both Fogarty and Turnbull were with Harper.

" . . . fore and aft," the voice was saying. "Abandoning ship. As quick as you can, old man."

"Geoff," Fogarty said. "Seems the bang was bigger than the research people expected, and they've been bombarded with burning rocks. Now they're on fire and they can't douse it."

"Hell!" Geoffrey commented.

"We're the only vessel in the vicinity, so . . . "

Geoffrey nodded.

"You want to take her?" Turnbull asked.

"No. You keep control, I have things to do."

"Do I tell them we're coming?" Harper asked.

"Just as fast as we can," Fogarty said.

"We're on our way," Harper said into the mike, and looked at Geoffrey.

"Ninety minutes," Geoffrey told him. "Tell the Chief to push the speed right up, Lloyd."

"Geoff," Fogarty said. "The passengers . . . "

"I'll tell them," Geoffrey promised. But he had more important things to do first. He got on the telephone, summoned both the boatswain and the carpenter. By then Trent was on the bridge as well. "I want all hoses rigged," Geoffrey told them. "And the moment we enter range of whatever is coming out of that spout I want them played, all the time. Especially I want the hatch covers soaking, and the launches." He grinned. "Can't be too careful. Chips, I want deadeyes over every bit of glass, and all bulkhead doors secured."

"What about the paying public?" the carpenter asked.

"All cabins and the saloons as well. I'm going to speak with them now. You fellows get to it."

He slid down the ladder, went aft. By now the passengers had discovered that the ship's course had been reversed, and they were clustered in the saloon, staring through the huge plate-glass forward windows at the pyrotechnics in front of them; the two young boys were jumping up and down with excitement.

"We going back for a closer look?" asked one of the students as Geoffrey entered.

"Not exactly. That research vessel is in trouble, and we're going to take off the crew."

"In trouble?" Melissa Crawford's voice was shrill. "Then we'll be in trouble if we go back."

"We've been asked for assistance, and we must give it," Geoffrey told her. "They were taken unawares, but we'll be taking every precaution."

There was a babble of conversation, and people crowded round.

"Ladies and gentlemen, please!" Geoffrey shouted. "There is absolutely no danger to *Skyhawk*. I assure you of that. But there may well be bits of flying rock and other matter. I must therefore ask that no one goes out on deck again until we are out of range of such missiles. Your ports and the windows are all about to be covered with steel shutters. We will keep you informed about what is happening. But I repeat, no one is to venture on deck until permission is given. Thank you."

The babble started up again and he went to the door.

Liz stood beside him. "You serious? About there being no danger?"

"You just believe it," he told her.

"Geoff . . . can't I come up? I mean, trapped down here with this lot . . . "

"Sorry," he said. "I can't discriminate. Please understand."

She looked as if she would have said more, then nodded. "I understand. You take care, huh?" The green eyes were staring at him intently.

Skyhawk was now making her maximum speed of eighteen knots. Smoke streamed astern from her funnel, and she was throwing white water to both sides as she hurried to the west.

And with every minute the sight from the bridge windows became more horrifyingly dramatic. They could see the entire cone exploding in huge arcs of red, while the black cloud was spreading ever higher; and now the noise was reaching them, a tremendous groaning rumble, as if the whole earth was tearing itself to pieces.

Which, Geoffrey supposed, was exactly what it was doing.

Half an hour later they could see the red tracer-like streams as the exploding cone hurled molten rocks far into the sea, and they could see, too, the blazing research vessel, the fires now definitely out of control.

"How many millions of pounds' worth of equipment do you reckon are going up there?" Turnbull asked. "How the hell did it happen? I thought those people were experts."

"That is one big explosion," Geoffrey suggested. He watched the hoses being run out along the decks, and listened to the various bangs as the carpenter's crew covered every vulnerable port . . . but

43

was aware of a tightness of his stomach muscles.

There was a lot happening out there, and now the sea was churning and steaming, as sizzling pieces of rock were hurled into it. One landed on the foredeck, and there was a spurt of flame, which Trent and his crew, wearing yellow safety helmets, quickly extinguished. But there would be more.

"I hope you have all your gear ready," Captain Fogarty remarked to Doc Bennett.

"I think I'm going to need it," the doctor agreed.

Something bounced off the bridge roof with a tremendous clang.

"Check up there," Geoffrey told one of the waiting seamen.

The man opened the door, and they were assailed by an immense heat.

"How far off?" Fogarty asked.

Geoffrey checked the radar. "Fifteen miles."

"Damn, if we have to go much closer . . . where the hell are those people?"

"Three miles, two points to starboard," Geoffrey said, having deciphered the two small blips from the amazing amount of material which was cluttering the screen.

"Alter course two points to starboard," Fogarty said.

Geoffrey left the bridge and slid down the ladder to the lower deck where Trent and the boatswain were waiting.

"It's like being in the middle of a bloody firework display," the boatswain commented. His men were now playing the hoses along the decks, which were being constantly bombarded with pumice and magma, all glowing red.

"We'll be out of here in half an hour," Geoffrey told him. "Drop your accommodation ladder; we've people coming alongside."

He levelled his binoculars; the boats were now well in sight. They had been hit once or twice, and men were frantically pouring water over the smouldering fibreglass; some of the men were obviously injured.

"Stand by, Doc," Geoffrey called up.

Seen from this distance, the island was like a huge torch rising out of the sea, glowing and throbbing, hurling its guts far and wide, and dominated by the great black mushroom-cloud which was rising ever higher. Now, although it was a clear mid-morning, the sun was obscured by the black layer, and *Skyhawk* seemed to be steaming into some replica of hell.

Yet amazingly the sea seemed if anything to have gone down even more, and there was no wind; it was as if all the energy in this part of the universe was being sucked in and then thrown out of the volcano.

"I guess, next time we come by, there won't be anything to show the guests," Trent said almost sadly.

The boats were coming closer, their men waving at the freighter. The accommodation ladder was down, held just above the surface of the waves, and Fogarty signalled engines to neutral. *Skyhawk* continued to plough through the sea for another half a mile, until they were within a hundred yards of the boats, and then came slowly to rest, rolling gently, while the accommodation ladder was fixed in position.

Now only eight miles from the volcano, the engine noise much reduced, the morning was awe-inspiring. The roaring, belching and groaning was continuous; so was the expulsion of matter – the surface of the sea was constantly peppered with flaming fragments, and occasionally quite large rocks came hurtling through the air . . . one struck the side of the ship with a clang like an unexploded shell, and left a large dent in the steel. The sky was now completely obliterated by the ash-cloud, which was rising and spreading with every minute. Between *Skyhawk* and the island the research vessel continued to blaze, its flames dull compared with the pyrotechnic backdrop.

The men in the boats were suffering severely from the bombardment of molten rock; one or two had collapsed. These had to be helped up the ladder; Fogarty had adjusted his course so that the ship was between them and the volcano, thus supplying some shelter. Geoffrey and Trent were in the gangway to help the injured men on board, and Lucas the steward and several sailors were waiting to guide or lift them into the sickbay where Dr Bennett waited, ready masked and scrubbed.

Last on board was Mark Payton.

"What happened?" Geoffrey asked Captain Ritchie, who was physically uninjured, but looked mentally shattered.

"Sheer fucking freak," the Captain growled. "We knew there was a bang coming, and we were ready to move off to a safe distance. But the first one was bigger than anyone expected. I rang for full speed, but before we got moving this flaming ball of rock . . . must've been all of eight feet across . . . came aboard as if fired from a gun. Did about as much damage as a SAM missile, too, smashed through the after bulkhead into the laboratory and sent the whole thing up in flames. Before you could move a muscle it was out of control . . . " he shook his head. "My fucking ship. Just like we were in a fucking war."

The accommodation ladder was taken up.

Fogarty leaned over the bridge wing, also wearing a yellow helmet. "I'm abandoning your boats, Captain," he called. "We've got to get out of here."

"Sure," Captain Ritchie agreed.

The engine telegraph trilled, and *Skyhawk* began to move.

"Seems to have quietened down, though," Trent remarked, staring aft at the blazing cone.

"Don't you believe it," Mark Payton said. "That monster hasn't even started yet."

3

The Tsunami

"First Officer Geoffrey Dunning." Geoffrey held out his hand.

"Mark Payton." Payton squeezed the proffered fingers.

"I saw you on TV when Misreal first appeared," Geoffrey confessed.

"Yeah?" Payton continued to stare at the island. His normal insouciance had quite vanished, yet he didn't look scared, only somewhat irritated. "That goddam thing took me by surprise," he said.

"When you say it hasn't really blown yet, what do you mean?"

Payton shrugged. "There is one hell of a lot of energy still down there. I don't like this sudden quiescence after the first explosion. Your boy there remarked it has simmered down. I would say it's simmering up, gathering its strength for another one."

Geoffrey grinned. "You'll be telling us you'd like to hang around to see it. Sorry, but we have a schedule to keep."

"This is no place to be when she does blow," Payton said. "But where are you bound, anyway?"

"Liverpool."

Payton gave him a sharp look. "Liverpool, England?"

"'Fraid so."

"And just when do you get there?"

"Four days."

"Holy shit!" Payton commented. "What kind of a tub is this, anyway?"

"Coffee, gentlemen?" Lucas asked. "I'm serving in the saloon lounge.

Geoffrey took a quick look around. *Skyhawk* was steaming east as rapidly as possible, beneath the huge black cloud. She was still being bombarded, but most of the fragments were by now small, and there was no immediate danger. Behind them the research vessel continued to blaze, and he reckoned she would soon sink. He glanced at Captain Ritchie, who stood beside him, also gazing at the burning vessel. There was nothing to say. Geoffrey had never been in the position of watching his ship destroyed, but he knew there were no words which could adequately convey sympathy. Equally, there were no words to compensate for the loss of gear and equipment these men had just suffered.

It was only just after eleven in the morning; he was not due back on watch until noon.

"Any of you fellows care to put our passengers in the picture?" he suggested.

"Sure," Payton said, and led them into the saloon, where there was a hush as he was introduced, and then a spate of anxious questions.

Payton soon had them quiet.

"Our instruments told us she was building," he said. "That's why we suggested you give her a wide berth. But the explosion was far more violent than we expected. My fault," he confessed. "I'm supposed to be the expert."

"She's a maverick," Captain Ritchie said. "Nobody could've known what was going to happen."

"Can't we go out on deck and have a last look at her?" Liz Bowman asked.

Geoffrey looked at Payton, who gave another shrug. "I think it's probably safe enough at the moment. But I'd leave those steel shutters in place, if I were you."

The passengers ventured on to the promenade deck, gazing astern at the island, followed by Mark and Geoffrey.

"How far off are we?" Liz inquired. To Geoffrey's irritation she was looking at Payton, rather than himself.

"Twenty, twenty-five miles."

"And that stuff is still coming down," Crawford said in awed tones as he gazed at the peppered sea.

"Look at that cloud!" shrilled his wife. "It's black!"

It was ten to twelve. Geoffrey went up on to the bridge, checked the radar; the island was just over thirty miles off, the gigantic glow barely visible to the naked eye.

"And so we say goodbye to sunny Misreal," Turnbull said. "I'm off to have a shower before lunch. See you."

Geoffrey nodded, sat in the navigation chair, brooding at the bridge windows; the centre steel shutter had been raised here to enable the coxswain to see forward. But Geoffrey was thinking about Liz, standing beside the big-headed Payton. The scientist was

48

clearly going to monopolise all the passengers for the rest of the voyage. Damnation! Or maybe fate was doing him a favour. He had been getting rather too fond of that girl.

Lucas brought up his plate of sandwiches, and the coxswain was relieved. Geoffrey chewed thoughtfully.

It was a quarter past one, when the ship shuddered from the stem to stern ... followed a few minutes later by the biggest explosion he had ever heard.

Geoffrey leapt out of his seat at the shudder, the plate crashing to the deck. His first impression was that there had been an explosion in the engine-room, but the growl from beneath his feet was smooth and unchanging. He ran on to the wing, and looked aft. Misreal itself had sunk below the horizon half an hour before, but now the entire western sky seemed to be a blazing mass, etched against the black ash-cloud ... as the ship vibrated to a massive, rolling, long-drawn-out explosion.

Fogarty and Turnbull abandoned lunch to join him on the bridge, followed a moment later by Payton and Ritchie.

"Jesus Christ!" Turnbull whispered. "It looks like the end of the world."

"What do you think has happened, Doctor?" Fogarty asked.

"I reckon she's split from top to bottom," Payton said. "How far off are we?"

Geoffrey looked in the radar – but of course the blip had disappeared. Although there were a lot of smaller blips on the forty-five mile marker. "Just on forty-five miles."

Payton appeared to make a hasty calculation.

"What are you worrying about?" Turnbull asked.

"Tsunami. That explosion is pushing one up right now, I would say."

"Yes, but surely we're all right at this distance."

"I agree that a tsunami doesn't mean much danger to a ship on the open sea, but that's wave height we're talking about. It's still going to be travelling at something like fifty miles an hour and we're way too close for comfort, I'd say." He ran the fingers of both hands through his tangled hair. "It's what happens when it reaches land that spells out real trouble. That tsunami is going to hit England hard enough to cause damage, and we happen to be in between. It'll go the other way too, for Newfoundland and then down the US coast."

Trent had joined them on the bridge. "Oo-oh shit!" His choice of expletives was limited but they rolled off his tongue with considerable feeling.

"Then what do you recommend?" Fogarty asked.

"Well, Captain, I think you should prepare your ship for a bit of a bump. But the most important thing is to get on your radio and warn both the States and Europe what's coming their way." He stretched his lips in a thin humourless grin. "And pray."

In the saloon, while waiting for lunch, Carter Marne and his wife Carol had been playing a Star Wars version of 'Snakes and Ladders' with their sons, watched by the two students; the morose and bearded Eli Baumer was immersed in a book as usual; Henry Crawford fiddled with his Zenith portable computer, Melissa beside him turning the pages of this month's *Architectural Digest*, while Rose and Liz talked quietly in a corner. But everyone had risen together at the sound of the explosion, hurrying on to the promenade deck to gasp in a combination of wonder and terror at the kaleidoscope of sinister colours filling the western sky.

They turned anxiously as Mark joined them. It had been agreed on the bridge that, as he was the man with the most answers to their probable questions, he should again go down and explain the situation to them.

Rose guessed he had been delegated for a job. She watched him duck under the lintel as he emerged, and thrust his hands into his pockets, before he started talking. Not only was this young man physically large but she gauged he had considerable mental stature, too. Not a stature he had assumed . . . for that one required an over-developed sense of self-awareness. No, Mark Payton was a man obsessed with his life's work and keen to explain it to the world, if necessary. Like so many men who were expert in their particular fields, he credited his fellow human beings with a great deal more knowledge and understanding of his subject than was justified.

Perhaps because of the presence of the youngsters, on this occasion he did simplify his terminology. He explained slowly and clearly what had happened behind them, and about the tsunami which would be rising from the source of the explosion and the need to get as far away from it as possible before it reached them, stressing all the time that for a well-found ship the wave, which would not rise very high while out in the middle of the ocean, posed no real threat.

They were not entirely reassured. He was interrupted by Melissa's complaint to Henry that she hadn't liked this idea of his, to cross the Atlantic in some old freighter, in the first place.

Everyone else glared her to silence so that Mark could continue. And when he had finished, one or two people asked questions. But, for the sake of the children, no one actually voiced the big query in all their minds – what were the chances of disaster? Could this voyage turn into a *Poseidon* situation? One didn't want to alarm the boys, though judging by the white faces of the parents, the older Marnes were already shattered. It was all very well for herself, Rose thought, she'd had nearly her three score years and ten, and though she hoped for another ten or fifteen years of this new-found fun and freedom, if the writing was on the wall, well it wouldn't be so bad.

But how tragic for all these people, the children especially, and their parents so terrified for them. And those two young students just breaking free from academic regimen and slog. She had already had a basinful of the boring Crawfords, with their flat which was *wonderful for dinner parties* in Sloane Square, wherever that was, and their *darling* weekend cottage which was such *fun* to dash off to in the Porsche, whatever that was, no doubt taking their Organiser Diaries with them, without which, they had assured the dinner-table last night, life would be *utterly impossible*. Rose had little time for poseurs, or life's impostors as she called them, but on the other hand she didn't wish them ill . . . or dead. And as for this little Australian girl, setting off across the world to seek a new life, what a tragedy if she didn't find her goal. Rose knew she had already become quite fond of Liz, probably, she thought ruefully, because she was one of the few people in life prepared to give the time of day to a short-sighted old schoolmarm.

"Okay, folks, that's it for now," Mark stood up. "Captain Fogarty and the crew are working like crazy to secure every darn thing on this ship. I guess your portholes will stay shuttered, making it kind of gloomy in the cabins, but the Captain says old *Skyhawk* has ridden out hurricanes before now, so she should cope with a tsunami like she was surf-riding." He had accepted responsibility for them, calming them as much as he could, speaking with a cheerfulness Rose guessed he far from felt.

"Seems a fair enough bloke," Liz commented as Mark left the saloon.

"Got a brain, too," Rose added.

"Sure. But he didn't wrap the whole thing up in a load of crap . . . beg pardon, technical jargon, like I reckon he might have done." Liz was quiet for a moment, then said, "Nice looking bloke, too. Movie material."

None of the officers had any inclination to leave the bridge. They kept watching the radar screen, or scanning the stern horizon with their binoculars.

"When do you reckon it'll catch us up?" Turnbull asked.

Payton had returned to the bridge. "We were forty-five miles off when Misreal blew just after one, and we're making eighteen knots . . . it'll catch us up about a quarter to three."

"Just time to finish the passengers' lunch," Fogarty commented. "Mr Trent, nip down and tell Lucas to start serving now. And you'd better open up the lockers and distribute lifejackets to all passengers and crew." He turned as the door opened. "All well down there, Chief?"

Evans had also come up to the bridge. He looked hot and bothered, as well he might. "At the moment," he said. "But just how long do you want this full speed kept up? Those engines weren't built yesterday. And after that spot of bother up the St Lawrence back in the spring . . . "

"Another couple of hours. Can you do it?"

"I suppose we'll have to. I'd better get back down there."

Harper came in from the radio office. "I've contacted both Halifax and Liverpool," he said. "And they've promised to circulate the news and warn all shipping in the area. They'd already had reports of the eruption from aircraft. Seems one jumbo was directly over the volcano, at 35,000 feet, when she blew, and all but copped it. Now all trans-Atlantic flights are being cancelled where they can't be re-routed. Liverpool wants to know if we require assistance."

"We don't know that yet," Fogarty said. "You keep in touch."

"There," Geoffrey said, gazing at the radar.

They crowded round, and saw a line of white across the western edge of the screen, moving forward at a very obvious speed.

"God Almighty!" Fogarty said. "It takes up the whole screen."

"A tsunami can be more than a hundred miles long," Payton said. "And this was always going to be a big one." He gave another of his thin smiles. "There's still time for a quick lunch."

"You'd better go down and sit with the passengers, Lloyd," Fogarty said. "I'll stay here. Geoffrey . . . "

Geoffrey nodded. "I'll just check everything's secure."

He slid down the forward ladders, and found Payton beside him.

"What did your engineer mean about engine trouble earlier this year?"

"We touched a rock. Had to have a new prop and shaft."

"And he's not sure about them?"

"He's a little pessimistic." Geoffrey glanced at him. "Ever been in a tsunami at sea?"

"No. You?"

52

"No. I reckon they don't happen every day. But the books say there's no problem in deep water."

"That's the theory. You reckon she can handle it?"

"Well, let's put it this way: I've been in some pretty nasty weather in *Skyhawk*, and I'm still around." Geoffrey grinned. "Any good?"

"Most reassuring," Payton said drily.

They had reached the bow, and Geoffrey was checking the chain hatches were securely in place and bolted down, while the chain itself had been winched as tight as possible to prevent any chance of the anchors breaking loose.

"All correct?" Payton asked.

"As correct as we're going to be," Geoffrey agreed. He looked aft, at the superstructure, white against the blackness behind, the Red Duster proudly streaming in the breeze, and then up at the obliterated sky. "That thing is still growing," he suggested.

"Because Misreal is still exploding. This could go on for days."

"And at the end of it?"

"Your guess is as good as mine," Payton said. "Should be some pretty sunsets for the next year or so. That's what happened after Krakatoa. There's our friend."

He pointed, and Geoffrey gazed at the line of white across the bottom of the black horizon, as if someone had drawn with a chalk across a blackboard; it stretched out of sight north and south.

"That's travelling quicker than we thought. We'd better get ready to face it," Geoffrey said, and they hurried back to the bridge.

"Twenty miles," Fogarty said. "Say just under half an hour. Mr Turnbull, tell the passengers to abandon lunch and sit tight. Lucas should clear the tables right away. And I want everyone in their lifejackets." He picked up the telephone. "Ready down there, Dave?"

"Ready," Evans said.

"We're going to have to do this on engine controls," Fogarty warned him. "Stand by. Helm hard to port, coxswain."

"Hard to port it is, sir."

"Hey, what're you guys at?" Payton was amazed. "You going back to it?"

"We have to take a wave like that on our strongest point," Fogarty told him. "That's the bow. That way we stand the least chance of sustaining any real damage. Take it on the stern, and were it to lift us up so that the rudders broke the surface, we could lose control."

Payton scratched his head. "I guess you know your job."

"Will you take her, Geoffrey," Fogarty said, as *Skyhawk* came

53

round in a semi-circle, now steering due west. The Captain had to remain in overall command, and not tie himself to the helm.

Geoffrey nodded. He left the coxswain on the helm, grasped the engine telegraph. His business was to get through the wave in as short a time as possible, because the real danger to any ship in bad weather came from weight of water on deck; this would not only cause physical damage but again raise the possibility of loss of control.

"Do you wish to go below, Dr Payton?" Fogarty asked.

Mark shook his head. "I'd kind of like to stay up here."

"Very good, but hold on. Drop the steel shutter, Mr Trent."

The shutter was rolled down. Now all Geoffrey had to work with was a Clearview Screen, a circular hole in the shutter filled with an electrically operated sheet of glass; when water was thrown against the glass, the speed with which it was revolved kept it clear, and because of its small size it was less vulnerable than the bridge windows.

There was also the radar of course, and Trent had taken his position in front of this.

"Five miles," he said.

"Five minutes," Payton muttered.

"How are the passengers?" Geoffrey asked over his shoulder, as Turnbull came up from below.

"Nobody ate much," the Second Officer replied. "But they're behaving pretty well."

"I think you had better get back down and stay with them," the Captain said.

Turnbull hesitated, then obeyed.

"Will everyone please hold on," Fogarty said.

Geoffrey stared through the screen at the approaching wave. It was moving at tremendous speed, and this was the greatest danger; with *Skyhawk* travelling at eighteen knots they would meet at a combined speed of over seventy knots, and although the tsunami actually wasn't very high – not more than eight feet at this stage he reckoned, the size a good surfer would appreciate, a height which would not normally bother an 8,000-ton ship in the least – it was going to be some impact. On the other hand, all of his training warned him that the quicker he broke through the wave and, literally, threw the water aside, the safer the ship would be.

"Stand by," Trent said.

Geoffrey rang for slightly reduced speed as the freighter came up to the surge, then as the bows plunged into the foaming white, he called for full ahead.

The response was instantaneous. *Skyhawk* plunged at the wave, and white water shot in every direction, cascading high into the sky and coming down on the foredeck and the bridge windows with a tremendous crash. For a moment even the Clearview Screen was obscured. The ship itself shuddered from stem to stern; even having clutched the grab rail with both hands Trent was thrown across the bridge and Geoffrey had to grasp the telegraph with all his strength to avoid following him, while there were various unhappy noises from below. Then the ship was through, rattling and shaking, plunging and trembling.

In a real storm, the true danger was going too far through wave number one, and burying the bows into the next, possibly losing control. But here it was easy. They entered a confused sea, but nothing *Skyhawk* couldn't handle.

Geoffrey pulled back the telegraph.

"Hard starboard," he said.

The coxswain spun the helm, and *Skyhawk* came about, following the tsunami to the east, in a turbulent but not dangerous sea.

Lloyd Turnbull had rejoined the passengers, as instructed by Captain Fogarty. He wanted to remain on the bridge, be where the action was, not cowering down here with a bunch of women. But he made the best of it and had done a good job of clearing the saloon of everything that wasn't actually screwed to the sole or bulkheads: at least if the ship rolled they wouldn't have furniture hurled on top of them.

The passengers were sitting along the bench settees fixed to the bulkheads, all rather uncomfortably, being unable to lean back properly in their cumbersome lifejackets. The younger of the two Marne boys was sobbing, tears staining the front of his mother's lifejacket.

"Relax, young buddie," Lloyd told him. "You've seen film of guys going out to sea through surf on one of those big beaches . . . "

"Bondi," Liz cut in.

"That's the one – Bondi Beach. Well now, that's the way it's going to be. We're going to breast this wave and we'll just coast down the other side, like we were getting ready to surf-ride," he said, praying there might be some truth in what he was saying. "There's no danger at all."

"Then why are we wearing lifejackets?" asked the older boy.

Trust the little nerd to come up with that. "Er . . . "

"So we'll bounce if we fall on the floor," Liz helped him out again.

Brilliant. The little Aussie girl was a peach. Lloyd flashed her a smile. Christ! He swallowed hard as the ship swung violently, she's going over! He had been crouched on his haunches in front of the children and was immediately tipped on to the saloon carpet, to slither gently and purposefully towards the open doorway, coming to rest clutching the door frame.

But the ship remained comfortably upright. Liz gave a shout of laughter. "Do you always travel round the ship on your bottom when the going gets rough?" she called to him.

His reply was lost in the shrieks and giggles from the boys. And everyone else laughed, some obviously forced, as they started to get up. Henry Crawford stood stretching, colour flooding back into his face. "That wasn't so bad . . . "

"Siddown!" Lloyd yelled, realising that they had not yet met the wave. "Hold on!" There was a bone-rattling crash, followed by shrieks of fear, and the ship tilted at an increasingly crazy angle. Oh God! She's standing right up on her arse! He lost his grip on the door frame and rolled into the corner against the stern bulkhead . . . where he was joined by a miscellaneous number of arms, legs and lifejackets. Lloyd's ear was pinned to the carpet, through which he could hear the engines tearing their hearts out. Dave Evans was gunning them with everything they had . . . And then they seemed to cut . . . He held his breath, forgetting the shouts and wails around him. Was it deliberate? Had they already crested or had the elderly engines caved in? Though it was only a few moments, it seemed like a lifetime before he realised that the pressure of bodies against him had eased. The ship had levelled . . . Oo-oh shit!

With renewed shouts and yells the heap of bodies disintegrated . . . to reform against the forward bulkhead. This time Lloyd was on top of Liz immediately under him. He was to remember that moment for the rest of his life . . . the way his arms had slid round her, quite automatically, to hold her as close as their combined lifejackets allowed, his face buried in her hair. Later, he supposed it had been the picture in his mind of *Skyhawk* hurtling downwards, hell-bent for the ocean floor, that had prompted him.

"Okay, folks, it's all over." The Captain's voice boomed out of the tannoy. "You can relax and take off your lifejackets. Crew remove shutters. Lucas will you serve coffees or whatever else our guests require, compliments of the Captain?"

Lloyd didn't really want to let go. He gazed down into the face of the girl in his arms, scarlet to the roots of his hair, still clutching her lifejacket close to his. "You were dead right!" he exclaimed.

"What about?" she laughed helplessly, unable to move.

"The purpose of the lifejackets!"

"Halleluyah!" Mark Payton's body filled the doorway. "Are you folks okay?" He jumped forward to help untangle the heap and pull people to their feet.

No one was hurt; Rose was braying with laughter and soon had the others joining in. Liz knew it was hysterical relief.

"Is the big wave gone?" the younger Marne boy asked, eyes wide and anxious.

"Yes. It's way past us," Mark told him.

"Did you see it?" his brother demanded eagerly.

Mark nodded. "Sure. And I'm telling you, it was a biggee."

"What was it like?"

"How can you be sure it won't come back?"

Liz was amused to see the huge man fold himself on to the bench seat, lift the younger boy on to his knee and commence a very simple version of a lecture he must have given many times before.

When Geoffrey finally left the bridge he dropped in to the saloon. Order had been restored. The furniture was back in place, coffee, biscuits and brandy were being served . . . and the passengers, minus lifejackets, were clustered round Mark, listening in hushed silence.

He turned and headed for his cabin. He wondered if the wise guy was telling them what was likely to happen when that wave hit the land – in either direction.

The Rowlands' house in Greenwich was nearly two hundred years old. Nestling in a quiet, narrow road on the outskirts of the ancient village in the shadow of the Observatory, behind a tiny front garden spilling over with golden rod, Michaelmas daisies and late climbing roses which had gone berserk, the small frontage concealed the extent to which the house had been developed at the rear.

Jennifer, at the top of a step ladder balanced precariously on the flagstone path, was holding on to the tangle of old man's beard which obscured the sitting-room window, trying to cut through the vigorous growth with a pair of rather blunt secateurs. In skimpy jeans which failed to meet her teeshirt by at least six inches, she wanted to finish the job before her friend Angela brought Jessica home from playschool, and before Jackie woke up from his midday nap. Most important, she was determined to watch the TV coverage of the tsunami, which was due around lunchtime. All the world was waiting for the big wave thrown up by the explosion of Misreal to hit, and the west coast of Ireland was first in the line of fire.

Yesterday had been a flat panic, as soon as the newsreader had mentioned, casually, that one of the vessels nearest to the volcanic eruption had been SS *Skyhawk*, and had told of the dramatic rescue of the crew of the research vessel. Jennifer and her mother had been back and forth on the phone, trying to get more information, but it seemed that the ship had survived virtually undamaged.

They had then tried to contact Anne in Boston, but the trans-Atlantic lines were jammed solid. Instead, Jennifer and Charles had cancelled a dinner engagement and spent the evening in front of the television, listening to the accounts of air passengers who had looked down on the eruption, many of whom had received a considerable buffeting from the huge force so suddenly released. Most were equally bemused by the searing black cloud in which they had been enveloped, and more than one aircraft had had a narrow escape, falling several thousand feet until the jet intakes were blown clear of crippling ash blockage.

A pile of detached greenery cascaded on to the path and with a sigh of relief Jennifer clambered down and began to stuff it into a huge, orange plastic sack.

"Mummy, Mummy, Mummy!" Jessica shouted from the gate.

"Hello, darling. Back already!" She stood up, face red and wet with perspiration. "Hello, Angela. You managed to avoid the traffic jams today."

"Yes. Weren't we lucky." Angela, cool in a primrose linen trouser suit, unhitched the garden gate to allow the child through.

"Got time to pop in for a drink?" Jennifer asked her.

"Don't think so, thanks awfully. I'm parked on a yellow line; Jeremy has wet his pants in the car and I'm dashing to get home in time to see the tsunami hit the Irish coast while I dish up the lunch." She looked at her gold Cartier. "In ten minutes."

"Crumbs! Is that the time? My turn to collect Jeremy tomorrow at 8.35. 'Bye-ee!"

"Super! 'Bye."

Coping with Jessica, the steps and the garden refuse didn't leave Jennifer any time to clean herself up before the programme started, so she wiped her hands on the seat of her trousers and switched on. Brilliant sunshine, reflecting through the kitchen windows from the white walls of the back courtyard, washed out the picture, so she had to draw the curtains . . . swearing as dirty fingermarks appeared on the pale material.

The rocky Irish coastline, bathed in sunshine, made a beautiful setting for the attractive girl presenter. "Behind me, in a few minutes' time, you should see the huge wave fill the horizon . . . "

"Mummy, I'm hungry," Jessica complained.

"Of course you are, darling. Your lunch won't be a minute. I'll have to fetch Jackie. He's just woken up." With a last look at the screen she flew off up the stairs at a gallop. Jackie needed to be potted, and when she got back to the kitchen, the veges had nearly boiled dry. She was trying to get their lunch on the table before . . .

A quick glance at the screen . . . and everything stopped. She stood with her mouth open watching. It was awesome! The camera angle, with the girl in the foreground, gave horrifying perspective to the massive, white-capped wall of water.

"We are 350 feet up, here, at the top of cliffs that fall sheer to the sea, but I have to tell you that it is very scary." Indeed the girl looked extremely nervous.

A man appeared. "Don't worry, Jane. The helicopter is standing by and will take us all up before the tsunami hits. No water should reach here – if all the estimates of its size are correct. But we won't be taking any chances."

"Come on, Mummy!"

Bang, bang, bang went Jackie's spoon on the tray of his high chair.

The two children were settled and her own plate on the table in front of her . . . when the phone buzzed. "Oh, shit!" She looked at it, looked at the screen, wondered whether just to leave it . . . and couldn't. "Yes!" she snapped.

"It's me, darling." Charles's voice.

"Yes!"

"I wondered if you had the television on?"

"Yes."

The reporters and camera crew were in the helicopter now and the unbelievable monstrous wave was only yards away from the cliff . . .

"Are you all right?"

"Ye-e-es!" Yes, yes, yes. I'm watching!"

"So am I. Isn't it fantastic?"

"Yes. See you later, darling." The receiver crashed back on to the base at the same moment the wave hurtled into the cliff-face.

Shockwaves from the impact rocked the helicopter, and the white mass which had wiped out the entire picture turned to blue and green as the camera swung to the sky and then to grassland. The pilot steadied the craft and a man's voice said, "That, viewers, is a sight I never wish to see again." Slowly the water sucked back down the cliff, leaving white waterfalls gushing in its wake. The whole picture had paled as the lens attempted to penetrate the haze of spray which curled hundreds of feet up, hung in the air and then fell like rain over land and sea. And through it, it was possible to see the backwash sweep out into the ocean, draining the beach, sucking away boulders which had lain undisturbed for centuries.

A newsreader appeared at a desk. "Normal programmes for the

remainder of the afternoon will be suspended, so that we can bring you up-to-date reports from other parts of the British Isles and from the eastern seaboard of the United States, where the tsunami is expected to hit this evening."

"No, Jackie! You may not throw your shepherd's pie on the floor. Now eat up." Jessica's plate was clean . . . but Jennifer had hardly eaten anything. Her appetite had disappeared.

Repeatedly, during the afternoon, various 'experts' assured viewers that apart from the possibility of extra high tides in the early hours of tomorrow morning, which the Thames Barrier at Silvertown should handle, there was nothing left to worry about. Jennifer found it hard to believe that a wave of that destructive force, and an eruption powerful enough to create it, could vanish . . . leaving no aftermath.

Geoffrey was at sea somewhere in that. And what about Boston, and Anne?

When Charles opened the front door that evening, Jennifer flung herself into his arms. She was still shaking with horror.

Together they looked at the sky, and at the huge black cloud, very high up, which obliterated the setting sun.

Pink candles flickered in their pale pink china candlesticks, clustered on the pearl grey tablecloth beside a single pink rose floating in a small crystal bowl. The plates were alternately plain pink or plain grey and the stems of the wineglasses were pink, too. The napkins were a pink and grey floral design of the same material as the floor-length undercloth.

Anne Dunning looked at the finished table and sighed. She had loved the idea of pink and grey, at first. She'd worked hard to put this apartment together, carrying out the theme she had fallen for in *Homes and Gardens* . . . but now it bored her. Oh, it was smart enough, true. But it lacked character. Illogically her mind drifted back to the cretonne covers and massed family photos in her mother's sitting-room back in Norfolk. How plebby she had thought home was in those days. Old-fashioned. Now it was her own apartment which was old-fashioned. Cluttered Victoriana was in. "To hell with it!" she exclaimed out loud. "You can't win."

The door phone buzzed. "Yes?"

"Ben."

"Come on up." She pressed the door release. Waiting for him she flicked the remote on the TV and switched to mute . . . she didn't want to miss the news.

"Hi, Annie girl!" Ben shut the door behind him, "Wow! Does

that look good! His eyes swept admiringly over the table. "I'm honoured."

"And very patient and good-humoured." She had to stand on tiptoe to kiss his cheek: he was one of those long, loose-limbed guys who don't look like they have any joints, just rubber bands. He reminded her of Pooh, the Teddy bear she'd left behind at West Walton. No one could describe Ben as dynamic; he had soft, sleepy, sexy eyes almost hidden under luxuriously long, dark lashes, and sensuous lips. He moved slowly and thought slowly . . . and drifted slowly from job to job. For the past two months he had been attempting to sell cars but not with any success to her knowledge. He was nice, a real nice guy, a comfortable creature to have around, to cuddle up on the settee with to watch TV . . . and to go to bed with. But if you were looking for stimulating company, someone to hit the town with . . . forget it!

Ben picked up the TV control. "Do I kill this?"

"No way. I want to see the news."

"Why?"

"I want to hear about the tsunami."

"Come again?"

"The tsunami, for heaven's sake. This big wave that's heading for us. Apparently the ship my brother is on has just ridden it out in the Atlantic. Hey, pour yourself a drink and come and sit down."

He came over and placed the glass on the coffee table, draped himself over the settee like a leopardskin, with his arm around her shoulders and his hand dangling loosely over her left breast . . . the fingers making almost imperceptible circling movements on her silk blouse. "M-mm," he purred.

"Not before dinner, honey," Anne warned.

"When's dinner?" he asked, nuzzling her hair.

"After the news. Here we go." She re-pressed the mute and sound filled the room.

"Reports from Sable Island establish that the tsunami thrown up by the eruption of the volcano Misreal yesterday afternoon carries a height of a hundred feet, and is travelling at fifty miles an hour; it was not, as hoped, either slowed or reduced by the Grand Banks. Damage in Newfoundland and along the Labrador coast has been extensive, and Sable Island itself is being pounded. From Europe there are reports of even more widespread damage.

"It is estimated that the wave will reach the American mainland around midnight tonight. The evacuation of the islands and Cape Cod is just about complete, but we wish to repeat our earlier warnings: under no circumstances attempt to go out to see this wave. Stay away from waterfronts. This is a highly dangerous wave . . . "

"Nothing about *Skyhawk*," Anne muttered and switched off the set. "But they must be okay; they rode it yesterday. And guess who's on board? Mark Payton."

"Who?"

"The vulcanologist, goofball. Seems his ship caught fire. I know him." Well, she supposed she did, even if he probably wouldn't remember her again. She wondered how Mark Payton and Geoff would get on, trapped in a small ship in the middle of an exploding ocean.

"Great stuff," Ben said, without much interest.

"You think that wave is going to get into Boston harbour, Ben?"

"I'd say the islands should break it up. But seems like a lot of activity down on the waterfront. Half those people not wanting to be evacuated, the other half panicking to get out."

"Let's eat," Anne said. "And pray it doesn't get this far."

"Am I invited to stay?" Ben asked as they cleared the table.

"I rather feel like company tonight." She swung away from the sink to give him an affectionate peck as he passed, plates in hand. "But it won't bother you if we have the newsreel on in the bedroom around midnight, when the wave is due to hit, will it?"

"I guess it's too much to ask I get possession of your mind as well as your body." He gave a deep sigh.

Anne knew it wasn't for real. "Hey! Come on! It's not 10.30 yet! Surely you can work up an interest in an hour and a half!"

"Are you telling me I get to have both if I promise to come off before your programme starts?"

"Ben, I love you!" She wound her hands, still in their rubber gloves, round his neck.

"But not enough to marry me!" he complained. "Or even live with me. All you want is my body."

"You're damn right. And now." She tore off the rubber gloves, threw them on the draining-board and grabbed his hand. "Let's get to it."

He was fantastic as ever and, as ever, eager for an almost immediate repeat. Her brain swam with contentment. Almost . . . almost, at moments like this, she could agree to marry him. But not quite. She always forced herself to think ahead to the morning, to his total lack of 'get-up-and-go'. Twice she had had him stay for a whole weekend, and both times she had ended up so bored she couldn't wait to get rid of him. God knew, she enjoyed sex, couldn't live without it . . . but there were other things in life. At least there were in hers – but apparently not in his.

She looked at the time display on the video at the foot of the bed. 11.30. She groped for the control and pressed. "Let's just see if anything is happening . . . "

Ben's long arms pushed her back on the pillows. "Mmmm." He buried his face in her breasts.

"Oh, come on. Look at the crowd out there!" She forced herself up again, staring at the screen. "I thought people were told not to go down."

"Okay, sweetheart. Howsabout you have your wave programme and I have your body?"

"No. I want to concentrate."

"On sex or TV?"

"Shush. TV."

"Oh, shit. Well I might as well fetch a beer. Want one?"

Anne's eyes were riveted on the reporter on a dockside of the Naval Annex in Boston harbour. " . . . attempting to secure all craft. Whether they stand a chance is something else. Latest reports estimate the height of this giant threat at eighty to ninety feet . . . and look around me, folks. Does that mean trouble?" A camera panned the area, great superstructures looming out of the dimly lit night. "In daylight over the other side there, you'd see the mast of USS *Constitution* opposite the Museum Wharf. What chance has she? What chance for any of the buildings standing around me? Or Logan Airport between us and the wave?" He gave the viewers a dramatic pause before dropping his voice. "We can only pray that the historic buildings across the Charles River Basin, in central Boston, may be spared."

"I don't believe it," Ben commented, standing naked beside the bed, beer can in hand.

"Nerd!" Anne pressed mute. She had been six years in the US of A and still found it hard to stomach the media's obsession for drama. "How come old *Skyhawk* could survive this darn thing out in mid-Atlantic, and Boston can't?" she demanded. "We'll go take a look in the morning."

In the morning it was impossible to go anywhere.

4

The Shadow

"Oh, Geoffrey! It's so good to see you!" Mary Dunning hugged her eldest son again. He had of course put in a ship-to-shore telephone call to reassure his parents that he was all right, but she still needed to see for herself.

"Have you heard from Anne?" were his first words.

"Yes. She called yesterday. Seems the lines were down before then. She's all right; her flat was well away from the sea. But Boston is in a mess."

"The entire Atlantic seaboard is in a mess."

"And it's still happening," John Dunning said. "That fellow Payton says this is the biggest continuous volcanic explosion in history. Apparently it threw a series of shockwaves which went past ten on the Richter scale. He says the whole underwater map of the North Atlantic may have to be redrawn."

"I gather you saw the interview," Geoffrey remarked.

"As he came off your ship, yes. Quite a scoop, picking up an international figure like that."

"I suppose you could say that," Geoffrey agreed with a shrug.

Payton had proved every bit as much of a pain as he had feared, from the point of view of a First Officer trying to run a ship and flirt with a pretty girl at the same time. The vulcanologist had monopolised the ship's radio to hold discussions with colleagues back in the States, and press conferences with, it seemed, every newspaper or TV station in the world. When not on the air he had spent his time snowing the passengers. Mostly he talked about weather and volcanoes and earthquakes; one would have imagined everyone would have been bored after a while – but right then those were the things they wanted to hear about.

They had all gazed at him with stark admiration, and scurried about with desperate enthusiasm to find changes of clothing for him, and the crew members from the research vessel, to wear. As Mark was a very large man it had been difficult to fit him out, and that had caused much amusement – and even more admiration. When on their last night out Geoffrey had invited Liz Bowman for a stroll on the foredeck as he checked the hatch covers, she had politely declined: Mark was going to tell them about Krakatoa in 1883.

The hardest thing of all to bear was that it was obvious Mark Payton was not a poseur, nor was he consciously arrogant. He did know everything there was to know about his subjects, and he did like talking about them. It never seemed to occur to him that there were people who might not want to listen. Neither did it occur to him that in the circumstances in which they had met, a pretty girl like Liz Bowman would be easily swayed.

But now at last he was gone. So was she, of course, down to her aunt in London. But Geoffrey had an idea about that; she had at least given him her address and telephone number.

He paused to fondle an excited Jason, then followed his mother into the farmhouse kitchen where she filled the kettle.

They were joined by Freddie, and a young woman.

"Doreen Wright," Freddie explained. "You remember Doreen?"

"Of course I do," Geoffrey lied. "Let me see . . . "

Doreen Wright was short and plump, with an attractively up-turned nose. "Your last medical, Mr Dunning. I'm Dr Lister's receptionist."

"Of course," Geoffrey said. He gave his brother a hasty glance in an attempt to establish the relationship, if there was one, but Freddie ignored him.

On the other hand, Mary was saying, "Be a dear and put out the plates, Doreen." Which suggested the young woman was a regular visitor.

"What I don't understand," Freddie said, after they had exchanged one or two inanities, and he had explained to Doreen that his brother had just returned from an exciting North Atlantic passage – something she clearly knew already – "is how these tsunamis could be so huge and do so much damage, and yet it seems *Skyhawk* steamed through it without trouble. That doesn't happen in the movies. There was that one with Fred MacMurray in the East Indies, and what about the *Poseidon* story?"

"Well, I hate to say it, but these things are too often souped up. A tsunami really is only dangerous in shallow water; then it builds up very rapidly. We had nothing higher than eight feet. Mind you, it was travelling pretty fast. And we did sustain some damage. Mostly to crockery, but the owners have put the ship into dry dock for a thorough overhaul just in case any hull plates were strained."

"Oh, splendid! That means you'll be home for longer than usual," his mother cried enthusiastically.

"Well . . . yes. But I rather thought I'd nip down to London for a day or two, if that's all right with you." He wasn't going to mention anything about a girl; that would get her all excited. She was forever nattering on about her three eldest 'settling down', as she put it. "Now tell me, have you had any damage up river here?"

"Not a thing," his father said. "I believe the last couple of tides were higher than usual, but that's all."

Geoffrey wondered if he really knew what he was at. Undoubtedly Liz Bowman was an attractive girl, once one got accustomed to her accent and her occasionally earthy vocabulary. But he had flirted with a good many attractive female passengers in his time without ever wishing to see them again once the voyage was over.

Could it be that for the first time he had had competition? But Mark Payton had not really seemed to appreciate that Liz was around; she had just been another rapt face in the audience.

Could it be that they had faced danger together? Though the fact was, there had been no real danger. He had survived more than one severe storm at sea, including a hurricane, without feeling any special affinity for any of the passengers.

Maybe it was visiting Anne earlier in the year, seeing her somewhat convoluted but utterly relaxed life-style. Maybe he wanted to find a woman like that, and maybe Liz Bowman was the one. She had certainly seemed relaxed.

He was only sure of one thing, that he wanted to see her again, and that he wanted to kiss her, hold her, listen to her funny accent, and . . . Further than that he couldn't allow himself to think.

"Nice girl, that Doreen," Geoffrey remarked next morning as he put his suitcase in the back of his car. "Serious?"

"When do you think this weather is going to clear?" Freddie riposted. "It's been overcast now for four days."

"That's not overcast, that's the ash cloud from the volcano," Geoffrey told him. "Didn't you watch the news last night?"

"I never watch the news if I can help it," Freddie confessed.

"Well, that cloud covers the whole North Atlantic and is still spreading, at a height of about 35,000 feet and rising. That's why there's been this enormous mix-up over trans-Atlantic flights ever since those planes on the first day took ash into their intakes and all but came down."

"Nasty. So when does it clear? There's been no sun since it

appeared. I'll tell you, the milk yield will be down if it goes on much longer. I'm damn glad we don't run a big herd, like Phil Hendon up at Newfield."

"All depends on the jet stream," Geoffrey told him. "And that's too far south at the moment and apparently very weak. We could have it for a day or two yet. But it's still rising, apparently. It could break up at any time."

"Cheer me up," Freddie remarked, and stepped back from the car. "Give my love to whoever it is," he shouted.

"And you take care of young Doreen," Geoffrey retorted. But his younger brother was a discerning fellow.

Geoffrey could appreciate how the cows were feeling. The weather was definitely oppressive, as if some huge dark blanket had been pulled right across the earth, or at least the Northern hemisphere. There was no wind, and there was no fog; it was warm enough to drive with open windows. And yet there was no sun, either, and no glimpse of the sky.

When that stuff starts to fall, Geoffrey thought, there is going to be one hell of a mess.

The volcano was of course still the main media concern. Following the initial report from *Skyhawk* six days before, plane after plane had flown over to look at Misreal, keeping well below the ash layer and carrying reporters and cameras; new research vessels had clustered round the spot where the island had been; it had now entirely disappeared although there continued to be underwater rumblings and no one had discounted the chance of another eruption. But for the time being, Misreal seemed to have done its thing – and written itself into the history books.

Experts were putting the cost of the tsunamis at multi-billions of pounds. The great waves had roared ashore from Greenland to Cape Hatteras, from Iceland to the Norwegian coast, and if the British Isles had acted as a breakwater for Europe – and Ireland had done the same for much of England – big waves and high seas had been thrown up as far south as Biscay and along the north-western Spanish coastline. Fishing boats, yachts and other small craft on both sides of the Atlantic had been hurled ashore from their moorings, piers had been ripped apart, and in exposed ports and resort towns the water had poured into the seafront areas smashing houses. Boston had taken one of the hardest blows, with its waterfront a mass of shattered wreckage, and even quite large ships stranded. Cape Cod had all but disappeared. The miracle was that so few people had been killed, fewer than five hundred on both sides of the Atlantic.

Geoffrey could understand Freddie thinking that it was odd that if one had to be near the sea at all, the safest place, in a tsunami, was the middle of the ocean.

But now, nearing London, not even the ash cloud could dampen his spirits any longer. In a few hours' time he might be with Liz Bowman.

He had telephoned from the farm and booked himself in at a modest hotel on the Cromwell Road. The moment he got to his room he called the number Liz had given him.

And was delighted when she answered the phone herself.

"Hello there," he said. "Geoff Dunning. Remember me?"

"Geoff!" She sounded quite pleased to hear from him. "Don't tell me, I forgot something on the boat."

Geoffrey winced, as he nearly always did when he first heard her voice – quite apart from describing *Skyhawk* as a boat.

"Nothing like that," he said. "I'm in town."

"Which town?"

"I'm here in London," he said patiently.

"Oh, are you? Hi, that's great. Maybe we'll see each other some time."

"That's why I'm calling. How about dinner?"

"When?"

"Well, tonight."

"Oh, heck! I can't. I have a date."

"Already? When did you get to London?"

She laughed. "Same day we docked. Day before yesterday. Except that it was night before yesterday by the time the train pulled in. So I'm a fast worker. But not that fast. I'm eating out with Dr Payton."

"Oh," Geoffrey said. "I thought he'd be back in the States by now."

"He decided to stay over a couple of days. Seems as soon as we landed he was grabbed for lectures and for various chat shows. He's doing one tonight, in fact, after dinner. So he asked me to go along."

"You are appearing on a chat show?"

"Don't be a wally," she giggled. "I'll be in the audience."

"Well then, what about tomorrow?"

"Tomorrow," she said thoughtfully. "Look, Mr Dunning . . . "

"Oh, Geoff, for heaven's sake. We were shipmates, remember?"

"Okay, Geoff . . . listen, call me tomorrow, will you?"

"I may just do that," Geoffrey said.

*　　　*　　　*

What the wretched girl had really meant was, if Mark Payton asks me out again tomorrow I'm going to accept. Geoffrey nearly checked out and drove straight back to Norfolk. Then he reflected that Payton was only going to be around for a couple of days more.

He went to a movie, got thoroughly bored, had dinner at the hotel. He was in bed by 10.30, and then remembered the chat show. Well, why not? He could pretend he was sitting in the audience beside Liz. He might even see her!

The programme had just started.

" . . . Norton Edwards, of the British Meteorological Society . . . " pan to a rather precise-looking man with a pencil moustache, wearing a very well-cut suit, "and Dr Mark Payton of the Ballard Foundation in Massachusetts, the vulcanologist and environmentalist."

Mark was dressed as carelessly as ever, tieless and wearing a windcheater — Geoffrey wondered just where he'd taken Liz for dinner — but the clothes were obviously brand new. He also looked as relaxed as ever, which was more than could be said for Norton Edwards, who clearly had not taken to the American.

"Now Dr Payton," said the presenter. "From the very first appearance of Misreal, you said that it could be a very big eruption. How does it feel to be proved right?"

"It feels like hell," Mark said.

"Come again?"

"This is a bigger explosion than I ever anticipated," Mark told him. "It is the biggest explosion in the recorded history of the world."

Edwards cleared his throat somewhat noisily.

"And you were actually in it," the presenter agreed. "Your ship was sunk and you were very fortunate that a British freighter was standing by to pick you up . . . " just in case any viewer had been buried alive for the past week and didn't know what was happening. "But what I hope we'll discuss tonight are the possible effects of the eruption on the environment. Now, we have had the tsunamis, and there has been an enormous amount of damage and considerable loss of life. Since the island has disappeared, need we anticipate any more of these tidal waves?"

"Not unless there is a further increase in activity below the surface."

"Do you expect this?"

"Not at this time."

"Well, then, that leaves us with this ash cloud." The screen became filled with the latest satellite picture of the North Atlantic, and it really was startling; nothing of the Eastern United States or

Western Europe could be seen at all, just a huge black pall. "That thing stretches from Chicago to Berlin. What effect will that have when it begins to fall?"

"If it falls," Mark said.

"Of course it must fall," Edwards put in. "And it is going to be pretty unpleasant, I can tell you that."

The presenter grinned from face to face, having got the beginning of the confrontation he was seeking. "Why do you say it may not fall, Dr Payton? Surely what goes up must come down?"

"Not if it goes up far enough," Mark pointed out. "That stuff is already very high, over 40,000 feet at the last check."

"That's not high enough to break the force of gravity," Edwards remarked.

"It's where we know there is already a considerable amount of dust and other detritus floating rather than returning to earth," Mark said.

"And you think the ash cloud may mingle with that . . . and stay up there?" The presenter looked genuinely concerned.

"That could happen. I think it is happening."

Edwards was showing signs of being about to erupt himself.

"And how long do you think it will stay there?" the host asked.

Mark shrugged. "That depends on high altitude winds. Right now there doesn't seem to be a lot of them."

"Dr Edwards?"

"I am bound to say that that is pure speculation, and has no basis in meteorological history."

"Misreal has had no equivalent in volcanic history," Mark pointed out quietly. "Equally, our understanding of that dust layer is fairly recent."

"Now, what will be the likely effects of that ash cloud?" the host asked. "Upon weather here on earth? Will it make it warmer, or colder this winter?"

"Well, of course, ash and dust can work in one of two ways," Mark answered. "Either it can repel the sun's rays, which will mean a cooling down of the planet; a heavy normal water-cloud layer will do that for instance, or it can admit the sun's rays, but not let them escape again. So far, the dust and carbon dioxide mixture up there appears to be having the latter effect. The vital question is, will the ash cloud mingle with the dust and increase that effect, or will it reverse it? I suspect it will increase it, because it isn't composed of water vapour – it's dust itself. Now, when we talk of the sun's rays warming the Earth we are actually speaking of radiation. The strength of the solar beam striking the surface of the Earth, at right angles, is presently just under two gram calories per minute. This is what we call the solar constant. Obviously it is less as the Earth curves away from the right-angle plane; exactly where this is depends upon the Earth's position *vis-à-vis* the sun. Now, as you probably know, not all of this radiation is absorbed; a good proportion of it is re-radiated into space. We have a nice balance here, which creates the conditions on Earth necessary for the support of animal and human, and even more important, plant life. For instance, grass and crops absorb around seventy-five per cent of all this sunlight, and throw back the rest. Forests absorb well over half, depending on the colour of the leaves. Deserts also retain some sixty per cent. The mavericks are the seas and the ice caps. The sea absorbs nearly all of its heat when the sun is overhead, but throws back something like eighty per cent when the sun is near the horizon. While the ice caps only retain about ten per cent at any time. Now, recently there has been some evidence that the amount of reflected heat has been diminishing, due to that amount of dust and carbon dioxide in the upper atmosphere. That is, the Earth has been tending to grow a little warmer, as more heat is retained at the surface. If the ash cloud reinforces that, well . . . the results could be interesting."

"You're really talking about an acceleration of the greenhouse effect," the presenter suggested.

"Yes."

"What sort of an acceleration?"

Mark gave another of his shrugs. "If the cloud were to stay up there any length of time it could be quite dramatic."

"Can you be more specific than that?"

"If temperatures were to rise, say, by ten degrees it would make a very considerable difference to agriculture. It could also involve widespread melting of the polar ice cap, with a rise in the sea level, which will of course have an important effect on our way of life." He grinned. "And where we live. The possibilities are endless."

"What do you think about that, Dr Edwards?"

"The greenhouse effect is a total exaggeration of what is really a perfectly normal meteorological pattern," Edwards declared. "People don't seem to realise this, and I suspect that a lot of so-called experts are sadly deficient in history. Several million years ago, the world was a much warmer place than it is today; England, for example, was far warmer than it is even on the Equator today. Then there came the Ice Ages, what we call the Pleistocene. There were seven major glacial periods, stretching from about one-point-five million years ago down to quite recent times. However, each Ice Age was separated from the next by an inter-glacial period, when temperatures rose sharply.

71

"We happen to be in an inter-glacial period now, and have been for the past twenty thousand years. The average inter-glacial was a good deal longer than twenty thousand years, therefore we are possibly not yet halfway through our present one. The point is that the warming up of the Earth during an inter-glacial is historically a perfectly natural process, which, in this instance, has been going on for, as I have said, twenty thousand years. It is not a constant process. We know, for example, that the European climate in the tenth to fifteenth centuries AD was much warmer than it is today. Then in the sixteenth century a mini-ice-age set in, which lasted for some four hundred years. You've read of the sort of thing, fairs on the frozen Thames in the seventeenth century, three-day cricket matches on the ice during the winter of 1878–9. This gave our immediate ancestors the idea that the world was cooling down. But this was a hiccup. Since the turn of this century the climate has been steadily warming up again. And now everyone is saying it is because of man-made substances pumped into the atmosphere. I'm not saying dust and carbon dioxide are good for us. What I am saying is that the effect they are having is nothing compared to the purely natural, and historical, warming pattern. And incidentally, most experts are of the opinion that volcanic dust acts as a reflector rather than as an absorber of heat. That is, the weather should grow colder, not warmer, while this layer is up there."

"Dr Payton?"

Mark gave one of his disarming smiles. "Every word Dr Edwards has said is absolutely true. But he is talking in historical terms. I am speaking of the next year or so. As for the ash layer, no one knows for sure. It is a fact, for instance, that the world started to recover from the so-called mini-ice-age in the 1880s, that is, *after* the eruption of Krakatoa, which is the last eruption comparable in size with Misreal, and it is equally a fact that temperatures have reached new record highs throughout the 1980s, following the eruption of Mount St Helen's. It is my opinion that if that ash cloud does mingle with the dust and carbon dioxide that we know is up there, and acts as a non-reflection shield for the Earth, then it is going to have the most profound ecological consequences." He turned his smile away from the camera to the studio audience. "That is going to affect you and me, folks."

The cameraman obligingly panned over the faces in the chairs nearest the stage, and Geoffrey spotted Liz Bowman in the very front row, wearing an emerald green dress and looking far more attractive than ever he remembered her on board the ship. She was gazing at Mark with rapt attention.

"Bugger that," he muttered, and reached for the control.

As he did so, the host asked, "So what would be your weather forecast for the coming winter, Dr Payton? In a sentence."

Mark grinned at him. "It's going to be mild. And then some."

Geoffrey and Liz had agreed to meet on the Westminster Embankment by the steps down to the riverboats, and Geoffrey wished they hadn't. It was drizzling, she wasn't there and he was already soaking wet because he didn't have an umbrella . . . he was also increasingly dirty, for the rain certainly had an element of ash in it and left black splodges everywhere. But no doubt that was to the good, if it meant the cloud was breaking up.

She was four and a half minutes late, according to his watch. The customers thinned out at one of the ticket kiosks so he bagged a spot under the awning, which kept the wet off his head and shoulders.

Others had had the same idea and one of them jostled him out into the rain again. He turned to protest and a voice said, "Oh, hi!" Liz was standing smiling up at him from his dry spot. "I've been looking for you! Didn't know you with all that gear on." She was hatless, her hair plastered flat to her head and clinging round her cheeks, down which there were dirty streaks.

"You're going to catch your death of cold," he admonished, resisting the violent urge to wrap her in his arms.

"You joke. The weather may be wet but it's not cold."

Geoffrey wondered how he could ever have disliked the Australian accent. The way she pronounced her vowels was delicious. "Possibly, but it's not brilliant for a boat trip down to Greenwich."

"Why not?" Her expression drooped. "I was all set for it."

"Really? Well, I suppose it will be okay inside." He also thought they might drop in on Jennifer to dry out, if necessary.

He bought polystyrene mugs of coffee on board and they settled down to listen to the commentary on the tannoy for tourists. Liz was excited, bubbled and bounced, dashing from one side of the boat to the other to peer through windows steaming on the inside, streaming on the outside, soaking her sleeve in an attempt to clear her view. It was like having a new puppy.

Immediately they landed Liz fell in love with the *Cutty Sark* and wanted to explore her. Geoffrey had never been over the famous old clipper himself and was as interested as she was, though slightly less boisterously. They had to see how the bales of tea were stowed, where and how the crew had lived and operated, and, far below, admire the ancient and colourful ship's figureheads.

"Didn't you say you had a sister living in Greenwich?" Liz asked as they left the ship an hour later.

"Fancy you remembering that!" He hadn't mentioned it today. "Shall we go and cadge a drink off her before lunch?"

"Sure. I'd love to meet her."

The still prolific old man's beard dripped down their necks as they waited at Jennifer's front door, so they huddled close under the lintel and almost fell into the hallway when Jennifer flung open the door.

"Geoffrey!" Jennifer squealed, throwing herself into his arms. "Ugh! You're filthy!"

"Blame the weather." He hugged her then held her away. "This is Liz, a friend of mine."

"Hi!" Liz held out her hand. "And no prizes for guessing where I'm from."

Jennifer shook the hand and examined the face. "Hi!" she responded. "Might it be Koala land?"

"You got it in one," Liz grinned.

Geoffrey was beaming. The two girls had obviously taken to each other immediately.

"Take off your wet things and I'll throw them in the tumbledryer while we have a drink. Would you like to borrow a hairdryer, Liz?"

"Ta. That'd be great."

"Nice girl," Jennifer commented while the hairdryer hummed in the bathroom. "But boy, what an accent!"

"Do you think Charlie would have a fit?"

"I pride myself I've knocked all those rough edges off him. Hadn't you noticed?"

"He's become very much more relaxed, I must say. One might almost describe him as laid back nowadays."

When Liz rejoined them, hair dry and wavy again, she said, "Jenny, I go for this house, it must be yonks old."

"Built about 1770, I believe," the English girl told her.

"Gee! Before my pommie ancestors were sent out to do time!" The idea of criminal antecedents didn't seem to bother her.

"Like to see the rest of it?" Jenny offered.

"Love it."

"Don't be too long," Geoff warned. "We have to go off and find lunch as soon as our things are dry."

"You are more than welcome to stay. Irish stew and screaming kids on the menu."

Liz was obviously keen to accept, but Geoffrey wanted her to himself – a point that Jennifer already realised.

"Thought we'd try The Captain's Pennant," Geoffrey said – quickly. "It's just down the hill. But thanks very much for the offer."

"I'd love to see your kids, too, before we go. Is that possible?" Liz begged.

"Of course, if you're feeling brave enough. Jessica will be home any minute and I can hear Jackie talking to himself upstairs in his cot. We'll fetch him as we do the grand tour."

While they were gone, Geoffrey flicked through *The Times*. It was all pretty depressing, still endlessly concentrating on the aftermath of the eruption, and the cloud.

Jessica arrived home just as the others came downstairs with Jackie, the two little ones hurling themselves on to their uncle. The Australian girl loved children and they loved her. She lay on the carpet and helped Jackie load his dumper truck, and crawled into a corner to join a doll's house tea party with Jessica. Dragging her away for lunch proved a problem and by the time they walked down the street after protracted good-byes and followed by Jackie's screams of frustration, it was far later than Geoffrey had intended.

The restaurant was popular, old, quaint and nautical, the walls festooned with antique bits of rigging. They were lucky to get a table in the window, just vacated by early diners, where they settled themselves with the menu and aperitifs.

"You'd better decide for me," Liz said, "I'm spoiled for choice." So Geoff settled for salmon mousse and traditional steak and kidney pie.

They sat in silence until Liz looked up to see him staring at her. "I've missed you," he said.

"And I've missed you, too. You're the nicest Pom I ever met." Her voice was bright and chirpy but he couldn't gauge how much she meant it.

"Is that a compliment?"

"It was meant to be. But come to think of it, I reckon I haven't met that many. And there wasn't all that much choice on old *Skyhawk*, was there? That nerd with a pebble in his mouth, Crawford . . . "

" . . . would make any alternative an improvement?"

"Hell, he was enough to make any Oz turn for home!"

"But what about Mark? You liked him."

She stared back at him, head cocked on one side. "He's no Pom. He's a Yank."

"So that gives him a head start, anyway?"

"Hey, Geoff Dunning, I do believe you're jealous!" Her nose wrinkled as her face spread in a wide grin.

Geoff made a move. "You're damn right I am!"

"You've no reason to be." For a moment his spirits lifted but then she went on, "You and I only kissed a couple of times on board

75

ship. And I guess that's standard routine for you sailors."

"True. And that's the way it was, at first. But," he hesitated, "you are the first passenger I've ever dated after a voyage."

She raised one eyebrow. "You're kidding?"

"No. Honestly. So you see I don't want any damn Yankees queering my pitch." He spoke with a smile, but she could see he was serious.

"Sorry, Geoff, but I have to tell you that I'm lunching with Mark tomorrow." She was confused, blushing.

"Then you're free tonight?"

"No-o. I have to spend some time with my aunt. She's got us theatre tickets for this evening."

The waitress brought their first course, staying to pour the wine, and the subject was changed to food.

"That was tremendous," Liz said after the steak and kidney. "Really fantastic. I'd love to know how they did it." She waved away the dessert menu. "Couldn't face another thing. Ta. But if there's coffee I'll go for it."

"Same for me," Geoff nodded to the waitress.

"Say, look. There's nothing so special about this date with Mark. Why don't you join us tomorrow?" Liz reach out to touch his hand.

It was Geoffrey's turn to raise an eyebrow. "You can't be serious? He'd be livid! I know I would be if I'd dated you first."

"I don't know the bloke that well, but from what I've seen of him so far I'd say there's a good chance he won't even notice you're there."

"Cheer me up!"

She giggled. "I mean, half the time he doesn't seem to know what the hell's going on round him, any road. No, come on. He'll probably enjoy having someone a bit more intelligent to talk to."

"Are you sure it's intelligent conversation he's looking for?" Geoff queried.

"He hasn't tried to kiss me yet, if that's what's bothering you."

Much to Geoffrey's surprise Mark greeted him like a long-lost friend when they arrived together at Liz's aunt's house in Hammersmith. The three walked together to an Indian restaurant in King Street, recommended by the aunt, commenting on the way that at that moment it wasn't actually drizzling. But it was still heavily overcast.

"You'd think that with all this black rain, the cloud would be starting to break up," Geoffrey remarked.

"What's falling is peanuts. That cloud is several miles thick," Mark replied, without looking up. "I don't like it. Bad vibes."

"Do you think it's drying up a bit?" Liz asked.

"No chance. Whether it's raining right now or not, that cloud is up there waiting to make a nuisance of itself."

"Let's hope it does it at night, then. I want to do some sightseeing while I'm here," she retorted.

The restaurant was decorated in blue and white, divided by white-pillared arches and banks of tropical plants. All the tables were round with blue cloths and napkins and each had a vase of fresh flowers. The ambience was artistic and appealing; the menu and service good and the food delicious.

Mark was always polite but his mind was not consistently in gear with the conversation and Geoffrey realised the man was actually worried; which he found disturbing, as well as beyond his immediate understanding. He was one of the world's workers, who had his points of view, and did his share of voting, but was perfectly willing to accept that his ideas on what was wrong with the country were unlikely ever to be considered, just as he had been forced throughout his life, and particularly at sea, to accept the weather as it came and make the best of it. But here was a bloke who actually had a say in what the weather was going to do, and therefore had very positive ideas on how to cope with it.

The more they talked the more he mellowed towards the American. Not only was Mark's supposed pomposity simply him being absolutely natural; but, for him, speaking in layman's terms would actually have required 'talking down'. If the man came across as a 'know-all', it was because he did know it all. To pretend otherwise would require him to pose as ignorant as the man-in-the-street. Why the hell should he?

Geoffrey finished the meal considerably more concerned about the current environmental situation, and impressed by Mark's observations. Liz was less so. When the vulcanologist hurried away to a lecture after they left the restaurant, Geoffrey said, "That man is brilliant! What a brain!"

But Liz shrugged, commenting, "He knows his subject, but so does anyone who devotes so much time to a limited field of study. How would he make out helming a ship into a tsunami, I ask myself?"

Geoffrey smiled; he had no inclination to argue.

The three ate together again twice, in the next few days, and much as Geoffrey wanted Liz to himself he took to the American more and more. When Mark admitted to being a Bostonian, Geoffrey immediately brought up Anne's name.

"Your sister!" Mark exclaimed. "That gorgeous dark-haired courier on the cruise ship to Misreal? Well, I'll be darned! Super girl. I'd like to call her when I get back and tell her you and I met. Er . . . May I ask for her address and phone number?"

Whatever Anne's original assessment of this man, she had to be wrong, Geoffrey decided. "Here, look her up, sometime." He handed over the address. "And meanwhile, why don't you two come with me to visit my family in Norfolk? Find out what rural England is all about."

"I'm overdue back in New York because of these lectures," Mark replied. "But I'd really like to take a raincheck on that. May I?"

"You'd be welcome anytime, but of course I'd prefer to be there with you. Keep in touch and we'll try to arrange it."

"I surely will, but how?"

"I wrote Anne's address on the back of my own card. It has the ship's radio call sign on it."

"I'd like to come," Liz chipped in.

"You would! When?" Geoffrey's voice rose an octave.

"I thought I might try to get a temporary job in London. I've made a few enquiries. But if I'm going out of town it had better be before I start work, so the answer to your question is, how soon suits?"

The rain did not stop for more than an occasional hour, usually at night. Mary Dunning thanked heaven for her tumble dryer; it was impossible even to dry things on a line in the utility, let alone hang them out. Anything not kept in a centrally heated room felt damp and she was obliged to keep even the empty bedrooms heated, otherwise they soon smelled musty. Yet the weather was so unusually warm for the time of year; the house was unpleasantly hot with the heating on, yet without it the damp crept in immediately.

Mary had been part of a farming community all her life, but she never remembered having to cope with so much mud for so long. Freddie was trying so hard to keep the yard hosed down and reasonably clean, but cars, tractors, cows and people replaced the muck almost hourly. And what could you expect, with the fields and driveways soggy, a veritable sea of mud in some places? You couldn't set foot outside the door without wellies on. She finished mopping the utility and kitchen floors for the second time that day, standing on the footscraper outside the back door to empty the muddy water down the drain, hurriedly put away the mop and bucket, and then returned to check that the sitting-room was reasonably tidy before dashing upstairs to change. The bedside clock told her that she had just under ten minutes before Geoffrey and the girlfriend were due.

She paused in front of her vanity mirror. There wasn't time to cleanse off the morning make-up and draw in her face again, though the Lord knew it needed it. Quick dabs of lipstick, powder and perfume would have to do. She glanced at the clock again, and threw her tracksuit – how did one ever exist without them in the old days? – into the bottom of the wardrobe and grabbed the tweed button-through from its hanger.

She wasn't at all sure what sort of impression she hoped to make with Liz. Weren't all Australians supposed to be terribly laid back? Thank heavens Jennifer had had the sense to ring up and tell her about the girl; of course one was quite used to the accent now, with the various Australian plays and soaps on television, in fact recently she'd become quite hooked on one.

Jason, who had followed her upstairs, suddenly woofed excitedly and dashed through the door. They'd arrived.

The first thing Liz said was, "Oh, no! Will you just look at all the mud we're tramping in on the clean floor!"

Geoffrey kissed his mother . . . so Liz did, too, and John and Mary were impressed with her natural friendliness.

"Did you have a good trip up?" Mary asked.

"What we could see through the rain and the steamed-up windows was really interesting, but I could wish I'd picked a better time to visit England." Liz allowed Geoffrey to take her mackintosh and shook drops of rain out of her hair.

"Would you like to go straight up to your room and freshen up, or have some tea first?"

"I'm dying for a cuppa tea."

"Good. Kettle's on. Come through to the sitting-room." Mary led the way, Jason following 'carrying' the visitor's hand to make sure she came too.

"What a lovely picture of Jessica and Jackie!" Liz disentangled herself from her new admirer and crossed to pick up the silver-framed photograph on the bureau. "Don't you just love them?" Still holding it in her hand, she swung slowly round taking in every detail of the room. "What a fabulous collection of figurines. You know, Mrs Dunning, it is so obvious Jennifer's your daughter. She's inherited your style. Don't you think so, Geoff?"

"I've never thought about it . . . " he began.

"Nor had I," his father said. "But you know, Liz, you are absolutely right. What you didn't add was whether you like their taste."

"Dad! It's a bit mean to put her on the spot like that. She hasn't been in the house two minutes."

Liz carefully replaced the photo, came to sit beside Geoffrey on the settee and patted his knee. "Don't panic! Fortunately I can truthfully say I love it. Really comfortable and relaxed. Kinda soothing. But pretty, too. Jenny was kind enough to show me over their place; I'm looking forward to seeing more of this one."

"You can see all you want, indoors. Outside is going to be difficult, though," John commented. "Pity the garden is almost obscured, it is normally lovely from these windows. Maybe it will clear up before you go."

But it didn't. Geoffrey took Liz out in his car to show her a bit more of the countryside, but if they kept the windows up and the rain out, the car steamed up immediately, the de-misters clearing two halfmoons on the windscreen, but only constant mopping with a dirty old duster let them see to left and right. They explored the older parts of King's Lynn under umbrellas and dried off over a pub lunch.

"I'm so disappointed you're seeing it all in these conditions," Geoffrey moaned later when they were alone in the sitting-room.

"Maybe you'll ask me back another time when the sun is shining."

"Of course, if you're still over here when this damn cloud finally lifts. You haven't told me yet how long you're staying."

She ambled over to the window. "I don't know, myself. I think I'd like to stay on a while and see something of the rest of the country . . . and Scotland and Wales. And that means getting a job to bring in the lolly."

Geoffrey went and stood beside her. "What about us? I want to see a lot more of you."

Liz turned into his arms. "Yep. I reckon you're getting to be a habit with me."

"Is that all?"

"I don't know."

"You mean you can't decide yet whether . . . we might be falling for each other?"

She stood back, shrugging. "Maybe I'm scared of the subject. You see, back in Oz . . . "

"I never imagined I was the first bloke in your life. Naturally I'm interested to know all about you – past, present and future. But you don't have to explain anything if you don't want to."

She smiled up at him, green eyes shining under long, thick lashes. "You are one real nice bloke. My trouble is I've thought that of two or three other blokes and it turned out I was wrong. Conditioned reflex. Don't get to like a bloke too much then you don't get hurt. I'm sorry, Geoff."

He pulled her back into his arms and held her face against his chest. She was so tiny. So tough in some ways, yet underneath she was fragile. He'd been aware of that the first time he'd got really worked up kissing her goodnight in her aunt's Hammersmith sitting-room. His hand had begun to roam over her sweater, feeling the delicious shape of her breast cupped in his fingers; and without making an issue of it, she had gently manoeuvred herself out of his grasp. He had known she wasn't playing the prissy virgin; her kisses indicated she was becoming as worked up as himself. Whereas the average modern girl would have had a hand in his pants days ago, and either stretched him on the sitting-room floor or hauled him up to her bed, Liz proved to be anything but average. Suddenly she was nervous, backing off like a frightened filly. God alone knew how much he wanted to sleep with her; too much to risk upsetting her by forcing their relationship too quickly. This was to be no one-night-stand. "Darling Liz. Don't worry. Don't apologise. Dammit, we've only known each other for a couple of weeks. Jut so long as you stay over here and don't go running off to the other side of the globe, we've got all the time in the world. I've got to return to *Skyhawk* in two days' time, of course. It'll be hell being away from you but we'll see each other when I get back. Right?"

She hugged him round the waist, listening to his heartbeat with her ear on his chest. "I'm being a crazy, illogical female, I know, but I just don't want you to go!"

He kissed the top of her head. "I'll soon be home."

"When?"

"Two months."

"That's nearly as long as forever! You'll miss Christmas, won't you?"

"Yes, 'fraid so, and New Year's Eve. We normally try to be home for one or the other, but those two weeks in drydock have messed up our schedule. We'll celebrate the New Year together as soon as I get back!"

This was the first time ever he'd regretted having to go back to sea!

Liz had totally reversed her aunt's opinion of young people from down under, so much so that she was invited to stay in the house in Hammersmith indefinitely. She got herself a clerical job in a hardware shop in King Street and, from the shatteringly low salary they offered, she paid her keep, wondering how local girls managed to handle rents or mortgages as well.

She found London, despite the weather, a fabulous city, full of life and interest, ancient and modern. She palled up with a girl at work and went to a couple of parties with her; she visited the Tate and the Royal Academy; stood outside the gates of Buckingham Palace to gawp at the royals and watch the changing of the guard

... And all the time she felt she was only half enjoying it because Geoffrey wasn't with her.

Jenny rang up and invited her to spend a weekend down in Greenwich, which was great. She told Jenny she wished she could babysit occasionally, but Hammersmith and Greenwich couldn't have been much further apart and it simply wasn't practical. She had bargained without Jennifer's quick reactions.

"Oh, that's no problem! You'd come for the weekend, anyway, and Charles will take you home on Sunday evening."

So Auntie Liz was soon established as a favourite visitor with Jackie and Jessica, and when they went up to Norfolk to visit the farm, she was invited with them.

If only the weather would improve, she thought. As November drifted into December, the ash-cloud remained suspended in the upper atmosphere. The heat was continuously oppressive, as though a thunderstorm was imminent; tempers were short and there was an epidemic of coughs and colds. Pale and listless, people appeared to be waiting ... for something to happen.

5

The Long Warm Winter

"Course south-south-west, speed fifteen knots," Lloyd Turnbull said as he handed over the watch. "Wind one knot, barometric pressure nine-nine-two. Visibility poor."

Geoffrey looked in the log. But he knew what he was going to see there. Three days out from Liverpool, bound for Jamaica, and not one of the figures given him by Lloyd had varied since they had dropped the pilot.

The only variant had been the rain, sometimes heavy, most of the time fairly continuous, although at present it had stopped.

That would give the watch a chance to do something about the deck; it was covered in black ash. But not apparently enough of it had come down. It was twelve noon, and above their heads the sky remained black. There might not have been a sun up there at all.

He peered into the radar screen. The ocean was empty within forty-five miles of them. Not for the first time on this voyage, he felt a sense of the uncanny, as if *Skyhawk* and her complement were the only living creatures on a dead planet.

The prevailing depression was affecting the passengers, too; most of them had their sealegs by now, but no one was the least cheerful. That suited Geoffrey. He was not in a very convivial mood himself, and although there were two single girls on board, pretty and vivacious, on their way home to Jamaica, he had no intention of flirting with anyone.

He just wanted to think about Liz.

Had anything definite developed there, or not? He couldn't be sure. Of course it would have been unthinkable to pry, but he would dearly have loved to be able to learn something of her experiences with men in Australia. She hadn't wanted to talk about it.

Maybe he should have come on strong and pushed her into bed. If Mum and Dad, with their instinctively old-fashioned outlook, clearly had never even considered he might wish to share a bedroom with his new girl friend, he did not imagine anyone would have minded had he wandered down the corridor at night. Hell, he had been tempted.

But the thought of a girl like Liz saying no couldn't be considered. He didn't want a one-night stand. He wanted Liz.

This was the first time he had ever actually admitted it to himself. He was in love.

"Ever sailed south of the Equator?" Captain Fogarty asked, leaning moodily on the bridge rail and staring at the mist.

"Not yet," Geoffrey admitted. "It's something I've always wanted to do."

"But you know about the Doldrums?"

"I've read about them."

"They stretch a good way either side of the Equator," Fogarty said. "Slack low pressure, hardly any wind, heavy rainstorms, and thunderstorms, too. This is just as if the Doldrums had moved up into the North Atlantic." He grinned. "At least in the Doldrums you see the sun. And it's damned hot."

They saw the sun three days later, after they had passed the Tropic of Cancer.

It was like looking at the edge of the world, because long before the skies opened they could see the edge of the cloud, where it would clear; Geoffrey was reminded of the few occasions *Skyhawk* had been sent down to Guyana on the South American mainland rather than Jamaica to load bauxite. When the ship was still ten miles off the land – and as the coastal strip is very low-lying it was not yet visible to the naked eye – one could see a definite demarcation line, where the blue of the ocean turned to the brown of the silt-filled water brought down by the great Guyanese rivers, the Essequibo and the Demerara, the Berbice and the Courentyne. Now he was looking at the same thing, in reverse. Everyone was on deck to watch the magic yellow beam approaching. Then it was a gala day. Taped music was played, and they danced, Geoffrey doing a tremendous reggae with the two Jamaican girls before everyone, even Lucas the steward, joined in a conga line which snaked up and down the decks and into the engine-room, to the annoyance of Chief Evans.

"How the folks at home would love this," Turnbull said, standing on the bridge wing with his face turned up to the glow, while below them the promenade deck had suddenly become a mass of sun-seeking naked limbs and torsos.

"Yeah," Geoffrey said sombrely, and looked aft, at the huge black pall which was slowly dropping astern.

Now the barometer began to move, and soon they had a breeze. In place of an almost smooth dull grey swell, white water sparkled against blue.

Life took on a whole new meaning, and by the time the ship had docked in Kingston, Geoffrey had struck up a friendship with the older of the two Jamaicans. It was difficult not to. Angelina had a mind of her own and left him in no doubt of her ultimate objective. She was a charming, pretty girl who had followed her elder brother to England some years before, but had finally decided she didn't like it.

"The place, or the men?" Geoffrey asked, as she leaned against him seductively on the promenade deck, late on their last night at sea.

"The men ain' bad," she said. "Some of them. The place ain' bad. But the weather . . . man, we don' have weather like that in Jamaica. And this las' month . . . you ever known anything like that?"

"No," he said.

"I can' hardly wait to get home," she said. "How often you come to Jamaica?"

"Every second month."

"Wowie! How lucky can a man get." She turned so that her breasts rubbed his arm. "You mus' come to see me."

He looked down at her; at the huge dark eyes and soft, pouting lips, at the stiff bra-less points pushing out against her white blouse. Asking for it. Just waiting to be invited into his cabin. Well, that might be difficult, but it would be simple to follow up the invitation after they docked. And why not? Liz had turned him on like crazy but never followed through. Only left him feeling randy as hell. And they'd made no commitment before they parted. Well, not exactly.

The Jamaican girl's thigh was pressed against his own, stepping up the pressure. Every second month, he thought. That would have been very nice if only it had happened on the voyage before last.

He kissed her nose. "You don't want to have a sailor as a boy-friend."

She gave a delightful little laugh, and kissed him on the mouth. "Man, they is the bes'. They don' get in the way." Her arms wound round his back and he allowed the delicious sensation to wash over him.

Captain Fogarty was a stickler for Company rules, and it was a Company rule that members of the crew, and that included the officers, did not use the ship's radio for calls to their loved ones, except in case of emergency.

The moment he got ashore in Kingston, therefore, Geoffrey telephoned Liz's number, having worked out that, as it was four in the afternoon in Jamaica, it should be nine at night in London.

He was suffering from a conscience, because on that last night necking with Angelina, there had been a certain amount of hand play as well; Angelina had gorgeous big breasts. Now he was distinctly put out, to think that he had only once ever attempted to touch Liz's breasts – and had stopped immediately she moved away. Was he being a complete fool, trying not to offend her?

After the third attempt to get through, he heard the ringing tone in London. "Why, Geoffrey," Aunt Madge answered, "how nice to hear you. Have you had a good voyage?"

"Splendid, thanks. Hope you're both well." And before she had a chance to tell him if they were, he added, "May I speak to Liz, please?" He decided not to ruin her evening by telling her how much the call was costing him.

"I'm afraid Liz is out."

"Out?"

"I think she's gone to a show."

"Oh." She would hardly have gone to a show by herself, he thought. And here he was, feeling guilty. "Well, could you tell her I called, and . . . I'll call again, same time tomorrow?"

"I'll do that, Geoffrey."

He went to dinner with Angelina and her parents, who lived in Port Royal, and spent the entire evening wrestling with the decision whether or not to bed the girl afterwards, as she obviously expected, and as he would have done three months ago. Across the table she was looking at him, waiting. There was no way he could ever imagine himself in love with a girl like Angelina, but she would provide something he was wanting right now. On the other hand he could picture Liz, her dancing eyes laughing up into his own, telling him in her adorable accent how much she was going to miss him. Was she still missing him? Was she, in fact, sitting beside a girlfriend at the theatre, wishing he was there with her? Or was she dating someone else and having the time of her life?

Angelina looked hurt and angry as she waved him good-bye from her front door, when Geoffrey left immediately after the meal. He had never realised that being in love could make such a balls-up of a man's life.

"Geoff!" Liz cried. "How lovely to hear your voice. I'm sorry I was out last night. But . . . "

"You went to a show. Who's the new beau?"

She laughed. "I don't have a beau . . . in England. I went with your sister and her husband."

"Oh!" He felt an utter heel. "Was it good?"

"I enjoyed it more being with them. They're great fun. Charlie never stops ragging me about my accent, mimicking me. So I put a bloody big pebble in my mouth and mimic him back."

God, what a little enchantress, to have won over the stiff-necked Charles! Her voice bounced over the Atlantic so perfectly that he was convinced he could feel her lively personality vibrating, responding to the remote contact with himself, reflecting the electric charge she produced in him . . . He desperately wanted to reach out and hug her.

"So, sailor boy, did you have a good trip?" she was asking.

"Boring. I kept remembering the last one."

"Well, I guess it's a good thing there aren't volcanoes dotted about all over the place."

"I was thinking of the company. Liz, I do miss you."

"Me too. London's not the same without you."

"Will you marry me?" Christ! What was he saying?

"Wha-at?"

He hesitated to repeat it, then decided she must have heard anyway. "I asked you to marry me."

"Geoff! What a proposal!"

Maybe in Australia they didn't do that sort of thing. "All right. Will you live with me?"

"You don't get back for six weeks." She sounded breathless. "You'll have changed your mind by then. But . . . if you haven't . . . we can talk about it."

There was a weird sensation somewhere in the middle of his gut. "Promise?" he shouted. Bloody fool! Thirty years old and you're acting like a ruddy schoolkid.

He telephoned Angelina and cancelled their date for that night, remaining on board in the privacy of his cabin, writing a soppy love letter. He didn't go ashore again until the loading of the bauxite was completed.

Jamaican television had brought them up to date on the ash cloud and world opinion. It now seemed fairly obvious that it was going to pose a long-term problem, although no two experts agreed on the precise form the problem was going to take. The jet stream had done one of its meanders north during October, but had blown at lower altitudes than normal, and had apparently had no effect on the cloud at all. Certainly it was raining more heavily than usual for December throughout the northern hemisphere, and much of the rain contained an element of ash, enough to make everything dirty, but this too was apparently in no way diminishing the volume of the cloud, while temperatures remained unseasonably high.

"So it looks like being a Black Christmas," said one jocular newsreader. "But who's worrying? If this weather keeps up it's sure going to be a warm one."

The passengers who boarded in Kingston were all very excited at the thought of what they were going to see, and rather like the voyage out in reverse, they crowded the deck as *Skyhawk* took the Florida Passage. The Bahamas and South Florida were basking in their usual warm sunshine, although Geoffrey gathered from weather forecasts that there had been more rain than usual down here as well, for the time of year, but they had not yet got abeam of Cape Hatteras when they saw the black cloud looming in front of them.

"Ooh, isn't it scary?" cried one of the women passengers.

"Don't worry about it, Mrs Louden," Captain Fogarty said. "It can't harm you."

Geoffrey wished he could be quite sure about that.

But he was going home to Liz.

"Here we have the latest pictures from the Space Shuttle," announced the newsreader. "Once again you'll see that the ash cloud isn't moving. I'm going to call in Bob Lowe from the weather desk to tell us what's happening worldwide, relating to this phenomenon."

Anne Dunning curled up on the bed with her supper. When she came in from work feeling as shattered as she was today, alone and with no date impending, she occasionally indulged in a really lazy evening watching TV from bed; Ben, who'd contrived to talk himself into a rather more upmarket job, was out of town on some sales convention. She felt a little jealous, as she knew – from organising them – what conventions were all about. A lot of chat, and pretty girls; a lot of liquor, and pretty girls; and a lot of bed, with pretty girls. She wasn't jealous of Ben, as such, only of the mores that dictated such a scenario. Anne had been on conventions herself, had wound up in bed more than once, and as a convention-attender as opposed to a convention-entertainer; but neither she nor any of her women friends had ever been able to let themselves go in the way men did. Quite apart from the consideration of AIDS, there was something essentially cheap about sleeping with any guy who threw his arm round your shoulders in a bar . . . apparently a purely feminine hang-up. Not a problem Ben suffered from.

There was no chance of any other callers, which was a great relief, so she had shed her sticky clothes, showered, and raided the fridge. The eats were not wonderful: one slice of left-over ham, somewhat curled up at the edges, a slightly shrivelled tomato, a banana and a bag of potato crisps.

She took a sip of wine, and listened to Bob Lowe.

" . . . as high as seventy-five degrees Fahrenheit, which for Moscow in December is unique. Stockholm also reports exceptionally high temperatures, while right here in the midwestern United States we're having a kind of Indian summer – except that there is no sun. Rainfall throughout is above the average, and seems likely to continue that way. Right now that isn't a severe problem; the summer harvests are all in. But some rivers are already rising, and state governments are keeping a careful watch on their dams and levees."

"And still no sign of a break in that cloud?" prompted the anchorman.

"Not a crack. As you can see from these latest satellite shots, it is solid. Unless something decisive happens in the next couple of weeks, this could be the warmest winter in recorded history. There is, of course, an additional problem: pollution. The lack of barometric movement, and the consequent absence of anything like normal wind strengths and shifts, means that all the effluent from our factories is rising straight into the sky . . . and staying there. There is already evidence that the incidence of acid rain is both increasing and spreading. Again, there is a danger of the skies over the northern hemisphere turning into a kind of aerial version of the Mediterranean Sea, simply because the absence of tides has meant there has been no adequate force to sweep all the effluent away."

"Thank you, Bob. We now have our political correspondent, Michael Robinson, waiting on the steps of the Capitol. Mike, what's the weather like down there?"

"Warm, muggy, and overcast. How's it with you?"

"Same, but with a lot of rain. What did the President have to say?"

"Well, as you know, Dick, this is the first press conference at which the President has allowed questions on the weather. He was in good, relaxed style, but there can be no doubt that here in Washington there is considerable concern about the effects this extraordinary weather may have during the next few months. The President said he was particularly worried by the number of beef herds suffering from footrot because of the unceasing damp; milk yield is down as much as thirty per cent in some areas, and some poultry stocks have been decimated by a mysterious viral epidemic. The horticultural industry in several states has fared even worse, with winter crops rotting in the fields, and it is feared that if the cloud is not dispersed soon, lack of sufficient light will inhibit bud initiation in a wide variety of early crops. And added to all this is the strong possibility of severe flooding in the midwest if the rain doesn't let up and there is no drop in temperature. And, as Bob has just told you, there is the pollution problem to be taken into consideration, as well."

"Did the President offer any suggestions to remedy, or at least ease these problems?"

"Well, he wouldn't be drawn. He said that the Administration is keeping a careful watch on the situation, and that funds would be made available to stricken farmers. But that was all. However, from private talks I have had with one or two senators, it would appear that certain other options are being considered."

"Options to manipulate the weather?"

"That's right."

"But say, haven't they been tried before, to cause rain, or break up hurricanes, without too much success?"

"That's right," Robinson said again. "But maybe they didn't try hard enough. One suggestion that is being touted down here is to loose off a couple of hydrogen bombs in the atmosphere to disperse the ash cloud."

Dick, the anchorman, was clearly as taken aback as Anne herself and, she suspected, several million viewers.

"Is that a serious suggestion?" Dick asked at last.

"In some quarters it is."

"But what about things like fallout."

"Well, Dick, it seems to be a matter of balancing one possible ecological disaster against another. There are those who feel that if that cloud isn't dispersed within the next couple of months we could be headed for a major catastrophe. A catastrophe even greater than what would result from a couple of atmospheric atomic explosions."

"Does the President feel like that?"

"As I said earlier, he wouldn't be drawn on what measures the Government has in mind. He kept saying these are early days, and the cloud could start to break up at any moment. But he's obviously keeping his options open."

"Well, thank you, Michael Robinson. Now for the rest of the news. Here in Boston the great clean-up after the tsunami is continuing, but the Mayor warns that it will be weeks, maybe months, before the waterfront is back to normal. And . . . "

Anne switched off, and stretched; she was living with the Boston clean-up, she didn't have to watch it on TV. Hydrogen bombs in the atmosphere! Sounded crazy. But man has to eat, and if food stocks were threatened . . .

The bedside clock said seven twenty-seven. She re-tied the girdle of her robe and padded barefoot into the kitchen to pour herself another glass of wine before returning to her book . . . and the door phone buzzed.

"Who?"

"Mark Payton. Remember me? We were on that tourist cruise round Misreal together."

Of course she remembered him, but what the hell was he doing here? She looked down at the scruffy towelling robe, not ideal for entertaining visitors. "You'd better come on up. I'll have to go get some clothes on so I'll leave the door on the latch. Just walk in."

"If it's a bad time . . . "

"Forget it. It'll be nice seeing you again." Was that just a polite lie? she wondered as she replaced the receiver and ran back to the bedroom. No. She'd finished up that cruise thinking he wasn't such a bad type, after all. But he might have called by phone first, before actually buzzing the door.

She had pulled a white sweatshirt over her head and zipped up white denim jeans when she heard him shut the front door and walk into the lounge. "Go into the kitchen and help yourself to a glass of wine from the fridge," she called through the open door. "Pour one for me, too."

"Will do." He had a very deep voice.

Might as well give him the treatment, she decided, applying two rapid splodges of eyeshadow and another of lipstick. There was no time to do anything much with her hair so she brushed it loose over her shoulders, pegged big gilt studs into her ears and fastened a white leather belt with an elaborate multi-coloured buckle loosely over her hips.

Mark was engrossed in a *National Geographic* when she walked in.

"Hi. Sorry to keep you waiting." She held out her hand as he jumped to his feet. To her amazement he was wearing a button through shirt with a jacket and tie.

91

"I do apologise for dropping in on you like this," he said. "I promise you, I did try calling you earlier but there was only an answerphone and I hate the damned things." He shook her hand, holding on to it until he finished speaking.

"I never get in till between six-thirty and seven. No problem." They sat in armchairs facing each other, sipping wine. "So what brings you to Boston?"

"Believe it or not I live here, though I don't get to see it much these days."

"And I'm intrigued to know how you came by my address?"

"Your brother Geoff was kind enough . . . "

"Geoffrey! Of course, he fished you out of the ocean."

"Well, that's one way of putting it."

"And then gave you my address?"

He told her about dating Liz and Geoffrey taking her over.

"Terrific! So big brother has himself a girlfriend! Tell me, what's she like?"

"Cute little Australian girl, but with an accent that needs a meat-chopper."

"Honestly? Well, that takes the biscuit. My stuffy, ever-so-English brother dating a thick Australian accent?"

"You'd better believe it. It looks like a hard case with them both. But," he leaned forward, his huge face split in a wide smile, "I didn't come here to talk about your brother. I hoped maybe you'd come out for some dinner with me."

She made an attempt to cover her astonishment. Mark Payton! Coming to Boston to ask her out to dinner! It was almost laughable after all the gruesome things she'd said about him to Geoffrey. Well, presumably Geoffrey must have thought him a reasonable character or he wouldn't have handed over her address . . . or would he, just for a lark? No, big bruv would not do such a thing to her. Anyway, she had already changed her opinion of Mark, and now here he was . . . So, did she accept the invite? Why not? He would certainly be more stimulating company at table than Ben, though undoubtedly not in bed! "That is a super idea, especially as I'm ravenous." She thanked heaven she hadn't had time to demolish the garbage from the fridge which was sitting on her bedside table. "Where had you in mind?"

He shrugged, and she noticed he'd had his hair cut: it no longer reached his shoulders. "I don't know much about Boston restaurants; I don't get up here all that often. We could try the Ritz Carlton. I guess that's always a safe bet."

Either he was getting a helluva high salary for a lecturer or he expected her to go Dutch. "That sounds a bit upmarket and stodgy, and I'd have to go change into a dress. There's a funny little pseudo-Italian place just round the corner from here, run by a large, redfaced Irishman known as Paddy. It's quite good and they serve some nice, genuine Italian wine. Howsabout that?"

"Mean I won't have to wear a tie?" He looked hopeful.

"Come to think of it, you'll look odd if you do," she said obligingly.

Mark immediately tugged the tie off, throwing it on to the coffee table where Anne could see the price tag still attached to the narrow end.

When their drinks were finished, Anne threw a fun fur round her shoulders and grabbed a huge red and yellow brolly saying, "I imagine we'll need this."

Mark nodded sadly at the brief reminder.

Paddy welcomed Anne as an old friend. "Yuv not bin near us fer weeks," he admonished. "Ah wus begunnin' ter t'ink t'e beg wave a' got ye."

"It wouldn't have dared, Paddy, not knowing what you'd have done to it if it tried." Anne allowed him to pump her arm up and down before adding, "This is a friend of mine, Mark."

The Irishman's eyes squinted up into Mark's face. "Ah'll swear ah've sin ye before. Doan' tayll me. Ut'll com' ta me in a munnut." He led them through tables of earlier diners, to an alcove where a mural depicted a window overlooking the artist's idea of an Italian scene. The painting had become rather grubby with age, but the essential donkey was still struggling up a narrow street carrying panniers of grapes, which appeared to have been garnered from the sea.

"Ut's t'e Frascati ye'll be wantun'," Paddy informed them and quickly returned with a bottle which he uncorked at the table. "Ye can see t'e menu if ye loike," he said as he poured, "or tayke me wurd t'at t'e best t'ing is spaghetti wit' a moshrum sauce ta stort, an' t'en a noyce piece of tender toybut."

Mark gave Anne a bewildered glance.

"That sounds lovely, Paddy. Spaghetti and turbot okay with you?" she quizzed at Mark for his agreement, and he nodded.

"Your Paddy is almost as hard to understand as Australian Liz," Mark said, watching the Irishman disappear behind a bead curtain. "How the hell do you follow him?"

"With difficulty. Maybe being born in Norfolk, England helps, though I can't imagine why."

"You look very like your brother," he said suddenly. "I noticed it the minute he said who you were."

They talked of family origins, Anne aware all the time that Mark

93

was strangely shy and awkward; he had never struck her that way before. This was the super-confident lecturer who could address an audience of hundreds, millions maybe on TV, looking like he was in his own home talking to his granny; but at the moment he didn't appear to know how to string two sentences together. She tried getting him on to his own subject by telling him about the news report she'd seen earlier.

And then wished she hadn't for it only released a spate of technicalities she found hard to assimilate. He continued in full flood till Paddy reappeared with their spaghetti.

"Ahh! Ut duddn' tayke me tew lorng ta work ut owt," the plates were dumped heavily onto the chequered cloth. "Yor t'e volcayno expayrt. Ut's on t'e telly ah've sin ye. Royght?"

Mark smiled acknowledgement, but they were spared Paddy's impending opinion on the situation by a summons from another table.

"Do I gather you go for this crazy hydrogen bomb idea?" Anne asked.

"It could be the only answer."

"But . . . "

"There are worse things than hydrogen bombs, oddly enough," he said.

There was enforced silence while they wound spaghetti unsuccessfully round their forks and sucked the swinging ends up into their mouths.

Mushroom sauce spattered down Mark's jacket lapels and Anne jumped up with a laugh to help him clean it off.

"Never could handle this beastly stuff," he muttered.

"Don't you like it?"

"Love it. But it seems to hate me."

Anne decided to get his mind off spaghetti . . . and off hydrogen bombs as well; he just couldn't be serious. "How long will you be in Boston?" she asked.

"Well, I'm home for Christmas with my folks. That apart, as long as it takes, I guess."

"Come again?"

"To get to know you better."

"Me!"

"Sure. I kinda took to you right there on Misreal."

She realised her mouth was hanging open. "I'd no idea."

"I never was any good trying to say the right thing to a girl." He gave a feeble laugh.

So that was why he was being so shy! She didn't know what to say, knew she was blushing. Watching him make one final, miserable attempt to manoeuvre spaghetti, she felt a surge of sympathy for him; so expert in his one field, so helpless at the ordinary things that come naturally to others. He looked like a grossly overgrown schoolboy. "Sounds like you're progressing, to me," she told him, then wondered what she was at. Did she want him to progress with her? She looked at him objectively for the first time, despite recognising his awareness of her analysis.

A man with a dual personality, for a start. He had made no noticeable attempt to engage her interest when they had been on Misreal; had talked on his subject at length, increasingly irritated by the paying public's ignorance of and indifference to the scientific aspects of the phenomenon they were visiting. For all the world he had come across as having a one-track mind. Yet he had not only asked Geoffrey for her address, he had taken time off from lectures in New York and meetings in Washington, to come calling on her in Boston . . . or had she been an afterthought – he was actually here to visit his parents?

But instead of turning up in his usual uniform of jeans and sweatshirt, he had obviously equipped himself with a brand new shirt, jacket and tie. Especially to impress her! This man whom she had supposed to be objectionably arrogant! He was surely coming over as the nice-boy-from-next-door, but no way could he be described as a sexual timebomb.

He was watching her face intently, a nervous smile twitching the corners of his mouth.

The turbot arrived to replace the more or less empty spaghetti plates, the silence broken by Paddy's chatter.

The fish was beautifully cooked, served in a simple white wine sauce with freshly prepared vegetables. "Nothing beats fresh, cold water fish," she commented.

"This place is good. Interesting."

"Paddy once explained to me that when he first came here he wanted to clean down the walls and freshen the decor," Anne told him. "But the regular clients who got to hear of it objected so strongly he thought he would lose custom. Whether it's true or just an excuse for laziness I don't know."

"One has to feel sorry for the poor bloody donkey, carrying a load twice his size up a four-in-one gradient."

It was filler talk, to avoid the alternative silence.

As they neared the end of their main course, she knew she had to make a rapid decision. Taking a deep breath she asked, "Do you want a dessert or would you like to come back to my place for coffee?"

*   *   *

95

They sat together on the settee with their coffee and brandies.

"Did you say you are staying in Boston for Christmas?" Anne asked.

He answered with another question. "What about you?"

"Yes. I usually go to friends for Christmas Day lunch, over in Duxbury."

"Are you busy on Boxing Day evening?"

"No."

"My old folk are giving a party in the evening: very mixed ages. Would you care to come?"

Meet the family, huh? She accepted more out of curiosity than any other reason. He wasn't giving her any other reasons! He just sat there, repeatedly turning to look at her, smiling, but positively keeping his hands to himself. Could it be that he just wanted her for a friend? He showed no signs of wanting her for anything else. Which would have made a pleasant change, but for the fact that she suddenly had an urgent desire to kiss him.

He looked at his watch and stood up. "Better get moving. Thanks for a superb evening. And for coffee. And sorry for just turning up like that out of nowhere."

Anne followed him to the door. "I am so happy you did." And she meant it.

When he shook her hand she put the other round his neck, pulling him down to peck both cheeks. His free arm circled her and he found her mouth. It was a brief, awkward, toothy kiss with their handshake trapped between them, but he made no attempt to do the thing properly. "May I call you tomorrow?" he asked, backing against the door.

"Sure. But early, before eight-thirty, or after seven in the evening."

She ran to the window to watch him down the street.

Anne laughed at the sight of the plate of leftovers by her bed. Salvaging the banana she threw the remainder in the trashcan, removed her make-up and went to bed smiling.

The thought of Ben with all those pretty girls at the convention didn't even cross her mind.

Freddie was in the yard to meet the Rowlands as the big, mud-spattered Mercedes edged up as near as possible to the backdoor. He approached Charles's window as it wound down. "I'll carry the children in," he said solemnly without offering any other greeting, "but not you. I presume you're wearing boots."

"We've all got our green wellies on," Jennifer leaned across from the passenger side. "Still it would be better to carry the smalls, thanks."

"And can you get me over your shoulder, too?" Liz called from the back where she was wedged between Jessica and Jackie.

"I may well get over-excited and drop you," Freddie warned.

The business of carting kids, suitcases and a plastic washbasket full of brightly wrapped Christmas parcels into the utility, and trying to separate them from the mud before proceeding into the house, took a full ten minutes, and twice as long to convey everything upstairs to the appropriate bedrooms.

Hot buttered scones, iced fancies and a big tray of tea was waiting in the sitting-room, with Mary presiding and John emerging from the *Telegraph*.

Jennifer was unusually quiet as she bent to kiss her father. "Daddy, it's awful out there. I had no idea how bad things had become."

"I thought Jennifer was keeping me up to date with the situation, sir," Charles added as he shook John's hand, "but I have to say I feel rather concerned about getting back to town next week."

"Which way did you come? The main road isn't too bad, as yet. They've had a JCB mechanical digger out there deepening the ditches at the trouble spots."

While the flooding by the near-continuous rain was being discussed, Jessica was telling her grandmother about the school nativity play. "I was an angel, Granma, with a halo and gold wings and . . . "

" . . . an' I was a sheeper!"

Mary looked up from the teapot at the cherub face wreathed in soft, blond curls. "What's a sheeper, darling?"

"A man who looks after sheep, of course!" Jackie couldn't believe his grandmother could be so dense.

"I took time off work to go to the play with Jenny," Liz added. "It was marvellous. And guess who were the best kids on the stage?"

"We were!" the children chorused, hurling themselves into her arms. Jason demanded the right to a share in the fun and tried to climb up into her lap.

"Down, Jason, you idiot," Freddie ordered. "Dammit, you're bigger than she is!"

Doreen Wright joined them for Christmas lunch, and everybody made an effort to maintain traditional Christmas cheer, but it was not easy. Water and pollution were foremost in everyone's thoughts. Jennifer struggled to produce other topics when they gathered for drinks before dinner, after the children were in bed, but she was anxious about the farm, wanting to know what emergency plans Freddie and her parents were making.

"At the rate the watertable is rising, I would say we are just about okay here for another four to six weeks," Freddie said. "But we will have to move the cows into the barn permanently. Well, there's nothing for them to graze on outside anyway. In fact, fodder is going to be the big problem. Even the hay in the barn is mouldering, let alone the ricks standing out there in a foot of water."

"But what about next year's crop? Do you think the Government will grant assistance here?" Charles automatically thought of the main financial aspect.

John tapped his pipe out on the cork hump in his ashtray. "One hardly dares think that far ahead. There was always a flooding problem here in the Fens, but with our ditches and canals we've probably been better off than many other areas. Where that leaves us in regard to Government funding I don't know. Still, the fact is that the continuous rain, with no sun at all to dry off any moisture, is bound to leave even the soil that isn't flooded impossible to plough or sow."

"That's right," Freddie nodded. "We've already had to get a bulldozer in twice when the tractor got bogged down. About all it's good for out there at the moment is rice." It was an attempt at humour.

"I imagine it's warm enough," Charles grinned.

"Probably. But then the minute the cloud disperses, if it ever does and I'm beginning to wonder about that, we'd get bloody ice and snow and lose the lot."

Jennifer felt for her brother. He was speaking jovially, but it was forced. He had worked so hard to prove to their father that the contemporary methods he'd learned at Horticultural College were worthwhile, not just a load of theories and hot air dreamed up by impractical intellectuals. He'd been winning, too, when this damned weather started. "This can't go on much longer," she said. "It's already broken all records for duration."

Mary and Liz murmured their agreement, Charles smiled brightly, saying he hoped she was right. John continued to look very glum but Freddie, calm, solid, dependable Freddie, said he was darned if he was going to let it wreck his Christmas and how soon could they get out the rummy cards. He needed an alternative method of making money.

Skyhawk stayed an extra couple of days in Saginaw over the holiday, but it was too unreal to be enjoyed. Instead of having to follow ice-breakers up and down the St Lawrence they hardly needed a pilot, the river was so high.

"First time in my life we haven't had snow by Christmas," added Tom Lewin, the Port Superintendent. "This is downright depressing."

Geoffrey agreed with him, when he thought that he could be enjoying himself at the farm, with all the family there, save for Anne. His parents had asked Liz to join them for the holiday, knowing her aunt was taking her annual Christmas cruise with friends.

He very nearly repeated his trip of the spring by flying down to Boston. But he reflected that at Christmas Anne would most certainly be shacked up with Ben, and wouldn't be very pleased to have big brother make a third.

In any event, time was short, as the day following Boxing Day *Skyhawk* again put to sea.

Because of the unusual time of sailing – due to that fortnight lost in September when the ship was in drydock – there were only four passengers prepared to spend New Year's Eve at sea, or to take on a winter crossing of the North Atlantic, when stormy weather could almost be guaranteed. Except that this time was different.

"The Met people say the barometric readings haven't altered more than four millibars, up or down, since the end of September," Lloyd Turnbull remarked. "That has to be unique."

It rained most of the time, a slow, steady, dark downpour, which limited visibility to less than a mile. This was no problem to navigation, as the radar screen provided a perfect picture of the sea for forty-five miles in every direction, but for the passengers it meant they stood no chance of seeing anything of Misreal.

"There's nothing to see," Geoffrey explained. "It's gone." He grinned at them and jerked his thumb at the sky. "It's all up there, now."

Yet as they approached the position of the volcano, he was aware of a certain tension. The scientific watch on the area had been abandoned some weeks ago, he knew; the seabed seemed entirely quiescent. But as it was night when he reckoned they were within twenty miles of the collapsed volcano, he kept remembering four months before, peering through the bridge windscreen, half expecting to see that eerie glow coming out of the darkness.

"There's something happening," remarked Seaman Walsh, who was on watch with him, and peering into the radar screen. His voice trembled slightly.

Geoffrey took his turn before the screen, and felt a distinct shiver go up and down his spine. Fifteen minutes before, when last he had looked, the screen had been empty. Now there were several blips, none of them as large as the island had been, but some of them the size of a ship, and clustered fairly close together.

"What are they, sir?" Walsh asked.

Geoffrey studied the screen. Ghosts of an old volcano, he thought. But that was nonsense.

The distance to the nearest blip was twelve miles, therefore the objects were low, and of irregular shape, which was why they hadn't been picked up by the radar at greater range. And they were moving, from north to south, very slowly, but right across the path of the ship, while as he watched, they seemed to multiply; it was almost as if they were approaching a huge fishing fleet.

Geoffrey reached for the engine telegraph, rang down for 'Slow Ahead'. Almost immediately the rhythmic throb of the engines died, and the freighter began to lose way. Then he reached for the telephone, but before he could pick it up, it buzzed; like any good captain, Fogarty was instantly alerted by changes in either the weather or the handling of his ship, no matter how deeply he might be asleep.

"What's the problem?"

"Considerable radar activity ahead of us, sir," Geoffrey said. "Distance ten miles."

Three minutes later the Captain was on the bridge, still buttoning his jacket, and staring into the screen.

"Icebergs," he said without hesitation.

Geoffrey frowned at him. "In this latitude, sir? At the end of December?"

Icebergs seldom became a problem this far south much before February or March, when the enormous ice islands that fringed the icepacks became too top-heavy and broke off. Besides, he had seen icebergs on the radar before, and they were always much larger than these blips.

Fogarty straightened. "Alter course two points to starboard," he said. "We'll see if we can go round them."

"Two points to starboard, cox," Geoffrey said. "They look a little small for icebergs, sir," he suggested.

"Growlers," Fogarty said.

A growler was the name given to pieces of an iceberg which had calved: from which smaller bergs had broken away.

"Then where's mother bear?" Geoffrey asked.

"That's what I'd like to know," the Captain agreed.

Skyhawk having altered course, the blips were now on the port bow. Geoffrey picked up his binoculars and went out on to the wing, where it was distinctly chilly, despite the above-average temperatures, and stared into the darkness, but could see nothing.

"Damnation," Fogarty growled.

Geoffrey hurried back inside, stood at his Captain's shoulder, and watched several more blips, these smaller than before, and both dead ahead and to starboard.

"Reduce speed to Dead Slow and wake Harper," Fogarty said. "Tell him to broadcast a general warning that there is considerable ice in this vicinity."

"Yes, sir." Geoffrey worked the telegraph, then woke up the sleepy radio operator, before returning to the bridge.

"They stretch for miles to either side, but they all seem pretty small; we're going to have to go through them," Fogarty said. "I want visual lookouts, forward, with night binoculars and walkie-talkies. Some of those bastards may be so low on the water they won't show on the box."

Geoffrey used the telephone to summon the rest of the watch, who were below sitting in front of a video. Reluctantly two of them pulled on their greatcoats and gloves, and made their way along the deck.

"Get Turnbull and Trent up," Fogarty said.

Geoffrey called the other officers. "What about the passengers?" he asked.

Fogarty considered for a moment. "Let them sleep," he said. "At this speed we're not going to hit anything too hard." He grinned. "If we hit anything at all."

"You really taking her through, sir?" Geoffrey asked.

"Yes," Fogarty answered tersely.

"Then I'll go forward as well, if that's all right with you."

"Good idea," Fogarty said.

Geoffrey buttoned his coat tightly, selected a pair of infra-red glasses and a pocket radio, and went along the deck behind the sailors.

"What're we looking for, Mr Dunning?" one of them asked.

"Growlers. We're approaching a nest of them."

Fogarty had now resumed his original course, as there seemed no way round the ice; he was relying on being able to manoeuvre his ship through the mini-bergs. With her speed reduced to hardly more than steerage way, *Skyhawk* was coasting almost silently through the gentle waves, only the slightest swish coming from the bows; what noise the engines were making was inaudible this far forward.

Geoffrey stared into the darkness, once again aware of the peculiar crawling sensation between his shoulder-blades. This particular stretch of ocean was taking on the characteristics of a new Bermuda Triangle, at least to him.

"There's one of the blighters," Gladwin said.

"And another," said Pearce.

"Two growlers close to port," Geoffrey said into his radio.

"We have them," Fogarty replied. "Watch the sea."

Geoffrey peered down at the dark water, but could not help looking up again as the icebergs came closer. They might only be growlers, but they were still massive ice rocks – several of them were nearly the size of *Skyhawk*.

There was a sudden alteration of course, and he saw another of the monsters sliding by to starboard. Fogarty was handling his ship with consummate skill.

Then the sea was open.

"We're through," Fogarty said on the radio, his voice redolent of relief. "All right, Mr Dunning, you can . . . "

"Dead ahead!" Gladwin's voice was hoarse with excitement.

Geoffrey looked, and gulped. It might have been a whale, just breaking the surface, not a quarter of a mile away, and directly ahead.

"Submerged growler four hundred yards ahead," Geoffrey snapped.

"Keep watching it," Fogarty said.

Travelling so slowly, *Skyhawk* answered the helm slowly as well. Geoffrey watched in agonised silence as the bows moved away from the huge dark mass; the problem was, he could not tell how far under water the ice shelf stretched.

"We're clear," Fogarty remarked over the radio. "Well done, Mr . . . "

Before he could finish the sentence, there was a scraping noise from beneath the surface, and the ship trembled.

"Get down there, Geoffrey," Fogarty snapped.

Skyhawk was still turning away. Geoffrey ran aft, and above the main hatchway met Allen the carpenter who had already rolled back part of the cover and opened a slat, and carried overalls for both of them, as well as rubber boots. They pulled these on and went down the ladders one after the other, switching on the huge lamps as they did so. To either side the aluminium sheets which were the main cargo were piled and secured, but an inspection corridor had been left between each pile.

The two men made for the starboard bulkhead. *Skyhawk* had a double bottom, used in part for fuel storage. One or two of these tanks were empty, but it was not usual practice to open any of them while at sea. This had to be done, however. Allen unscrewed the manhole-type cover and they crawled into the reeking interior, hardly able to breathe because of the stench of the heavy oil.

The carpenter had also brought along powerful flashlights, and these were played along the rivets of the external hull.

"There," Allen said, and pointed to where a dribble of water was trickling down the steel plates; the plates themselves had been pushed in, but there was no obvious break.

"You reckon it'll hold?" Geoffrey asked.

Allen was examining the dent, looking for actual cracking of the metal.

"She's fine," he said at last. "A couple of those rivets are strained. But I wouldn't call it serious."

"What about when we increase speed?"

"She'll hold, Mr Dunning. I'll get some of the lads and shore it up anyway. If that dent actually cracks, well, we'll have to flood the portside tank to even her up."

Geoffrey nodded, went up to the bridge. There were lights on in the passenger saloon and he gathered that everyone had been alerted.

"Well?" Fogarty asked, with massive calmness, aware that he might be about to be told his ship was sinking.

"There is a dent and some strained rivets in number three storage, starboard," Geoffrey told him. "Nothing the pumps can't cope with. Chips is shoring it up now, but he reckons it'll hold anyway."

"Then you can tell the passengers to go back to bed," Fogarty told an anxious Turnbull, and rang down for Full Speed Ahead. "As I intend to do." He grinned at Geoffrey. "Looks like another lucky spot of leave for some people while they knock that one out," he said. "But British Ocean Transporters won't find this latest interference with their schedule so lucky." Which thought wiped the grin off his face.

Geoffrey went out on to the bridge and looked astern, at the dwindling humps of ice. He listened to the excited chatter coming up from the promenade deck, as the four passengers discussed what had happened; they were wearing heavy coats over their pyjamas and nightdresses, and were clearly far too excited to consider going back to bed.

Lucas was serving hot coffee laced with brandy.

At this rate, Geoffrey thought, the next time we cross the Atlantic without running into some kind of trouble, everyone, passengers and crew, is going to be very disappointed.

6

A Question of Heat

Mark Payton peered down from the window of the aircraft. He knew he was looking at the Nares Strait, the stretch of water which separates Greenland from Ellesmere Island, northernmost of the Canadian Arctic territories, but he could see nothing. The Arctic night was at its deepest, and although in the middle of a January morning it was usually a kind of dwindling twilight, now, with the sky obliterated by the ash layer, visibility was nil.

Yet the people at Thule Air Force Base in Greenland, some three hundred miles behind them to the south, did not seem too disturbed.

"At least we haven't had any blizzards yet this year," Colonel Kelly had remarked. "That has got to be good."

Temperatures at Thule had been above freezing, for the first time on record in January. Three hundred miles further north, and at a height of five thousand feet, there were only traces of ice on the wings.

"It's the damndest thing I ever saw," said Dave Obrenski. Dave was in his fifties, and was the Administration's expert on weather. Having read and approved Mark's book, he had invited the vulcanologist to accompany him on a fact-finding tour of the Arctic, and Mark had jumped at the idea.

Well, almost.

He still found it difficult to assimilate the events of Christmas and the New Year. The fact was that his life had been too bound up in his work for the past fifteen years, first of all in learning his subject, and then in practising his profession. All work equates a dull boy, as he well knew. He had always accepted his social dullness – it hadn't seemed to matter when there were volcanoes to be investigated, and weather patterns to be studied in order to sustain his theory that what happened under the earth affected what happened above it. There was nothing dull about that.

But girls had always passed him by, literally, however they might hang on his every word as part of a selected studio audience.

And then, Eureka!

Maybe he hadn't tried hard enough before. He hadn't made much effort with Liz Bowman, partly because he doubted her intellectual ability, but also because she was the chatty type of female who constantly intruded on one's thoughts. Anne Dunning was different however. When he had taken her address from Geoff, it was with the intention of investigating further a character who on the slightest acquaintance, on that awful trip to Misreal, had revealed a trained, businesslike mind; a mind too sophisticated, too independent to be overawed by a lecture full of scientific data. On Misreal she had discussed the volcano and its implications intelligently and with obvious interest, but then, suddenly switching roles, had politely but most definitely played big sister to her charges, shepherding them like a lot of children on a Sunday School treat. He had wondered what so forceful and worldly a woman might be like in her private life.

Now he knew. Anne Dunning was no poseur. From the moment he had walked into her apartment, rigged out like a tailor's dummy and wondering if this would turn out to be one of the more stupid missions of his life, he knew she had to be exceptional. He admired anyone who could organise both their business and domestic lives efficiently, and having already experienced her at work on the cruise, one glance round her comfortably relaxed yet immaculate apartment confirmed that she was one of those people. It was the way she could switch her mind from one department of her life to another, like selecting a file on a computer, which really struck him. He had always prided himself on being totally organised in his work, but his domestic arrangements could only be described as chaotic, for which he exonerated himself on the excuse of being too busy. He'd had a girl friend, two years ago, who'd tried to reform him. She'd fussed and cleaned and left him lists . . . which he always mislaid. She repeatedly telephoned him when he was abroad, wanting to know if he was thinking about her, which he wasn't, and resenting his preoccupation when he was working on projects. 'Togetherness' was a big word with her.

He could imagine Liz being a girl like that . . . but never Anne. The moment they had parted, that first evening, she had programmed her next day, so that when he called her in the morning she was ready with an invitation for him to take supper with her in the apartment that night. And having spent most of the day in New York with a client, she had produced a perfect meal, accompanied by two bottles of wine which he had named the night before as his favourite – the Lord knew where she had found them – and, most magic of all, she hadn't spent more than five minutes in the kitchen the whole time he was there. It was all done so casually, easily.

Only four days later, equally casually and easily, she had slid into bed with him.

He could try telling himself that she was merely an extreme representative of modern urban womanhood, vigorous, self-confident, capable . . . and amoral. Her sexual knowledge had been frightening to a man who could count experience on the fingers of one hand, but wildly exhilarating as well. She was a girl to be received – one simply could not dream of using the word 'taken' with regard to Anne Dunning – when she was in the mood to give, and savoured, and then . . . forgotten? He could not contemplate that; for the first time ever, leaving Boston had been a wrench.

This expedition was important. It would play a big part in formulating Government policy towards this unique, and rather frightening, weather situation, and it totally absorbed his mind . . . But when he put his head on the pillow each night he was already dreaming of getting back to Boston.

And now what? Should he aim at a permanent relationship, despite knowing about her life-style to date, the fact she would need the fingers of maybe a dozen hands to tot up *her* track record? Was he thinking of marrying her, just to know that she'd always be there waiting when he returned from a tour project or conference? He suspected that Anne would laugh at that, and say, 'Why, you darned male chauvinist pig, you.' Or might she say, 'Great! We will need to plan our respective work schedules to coincide'?

Lights appeared out of the gloom, and fifteen minutes later the piston-engined amphibian – it was fitted with both wheels and skis – touched down on the strip outside the township of Alert, at the northernmost end of Ellesmere Island.

"You know this is the first time I've ever landed here, on wheels, in January?" Hudson the pilot remarked. "Never been possible before."

While the scientific team disembarked and began unloading its gear, Mark looked around him. Alert was a small place, a close-packed cluster of little houses huddled together against the nine-month-long Arctic winter, which was now at its peak. There were traces of a recent snowfall, and one or two of the puddles in the roads were covered with a thin layer of ice, rather as one might expect to find in Boston at the first onset of cold weather. But this was January, on latitude 84° North.

Sergeant Martinsen of the Royal Canadian Northwest Mounted

Police was waiting for them.

"Some weather," the Sergeant commented. "Looking for something special?" It wasn't every day he met a planeload of VIPs up here.

"Just looking," Obrenski told him.

The instruments were set up, holes bored into the ground for the thermometers, heat-measuring gauges pointed in the right directions, while groups of curious Eskimos stood around and watched.

Obrenski and Mark lunched with the Sergeant and his large, jolly wife.

"Warmest weather we've ever had up here, this time of year," Jenny Martinsen told them. "Could be August. Excepting there's no sun."

"What's your average January temperature?" Obrenski asked, as if he didn't know.

"Minus thirty degrees Fahrenheit," the Sergeant said. "Fifty-two degrees of frost. Man, this village just about disappears under snow and ice. But look at it now."

For the next two days they checked their instrument readings. Their lowest temperature recording was plus twenty-nine degrees Fahrenheit – three degrees of frost – and that was taken at two o'clock in the morning, while their figures for radiation were startling.

"We have to check out the Pole itself," Obrenski decided.

They flew the further four hundred-odd miles to the Pole, and after some searching found a place where they could set down on skis.

Mark gazed at the endless stretch of snow and ice, disappearing in every direction into the gloom. He had never been in latitudes this high before, and found it awesome. But it wasn't cold enough! Obrenski had insisted they all wear their thermal suits and snow goggles; there was not an inch of skin exposed to the Arctic air. Yet he felt as if he could strip off and not suffer the least injury.

Obrenski had his people check the depths of the ice cover between them and the water; the geographical North Pole is actually situated in the centre of the Arctic Ocean – unlike the South Pole, which is in the centre of a continent – where the water is covered with ice. In the summer this ice can be as thin as ten feet thick and breaks up in places to expose water; in the winter it is as solid as dry land, and can be as thick as fifty feet. When the steel poles found water at seventeen feet, Obrenski said, "Let's get the hell out."

*   *   *

It was a year for firsts, Mark reckoned; he had never been in the Oval Office before, either.

Amazingly, the President seemed to have read his book, or at least been briefed on its contents, but there was little time for niceties.

"Here we have it, Mr President," Obrenski said, spreading an Arctic chart between them. "Temperatures inside the Arctic Circle are some fifty degrees higher than normal for the time of year. This means that the ice layer over the sea, for instance, is very thin, almost down to summer readings. We flew over places where there was actually water showing . . . within something like a hundred miles of the Pole. Our radiation readings have been startling. You know that every square metre of the earth's surface receives approximately three hundred and eighty-five watts of radiation per annum – and land surfaces re-radiate more than half of that. Any change in that give-and-take process is likely to have severe effects on our ecology, and on us. Over the oceans, and particularly at the Poles, the reflection of sunlight is much more than that as a rule; at the North Pole not more than ten per cent is usually retained – this is what keeps the ice cap there. Now, sir, the amount coming in has been reduced by this ash cloud, and is averaging about three hundred and fifty per annum, as far as we can make out . . . "

"Shouldn't that have caused a freeze-up?" the President cut in.

"Sure, if the normal amount went back out. But as far as we can make out, the re-radiation has dropped an overall average of some twenty per cent. That means that every square metre of earth in the northern hemisphere is retaining maybe as much as seventy watts of radiation more than normal, and has been doing so since last September. But I repeat, it is the Pole which is the most significant factor; there radiation is actually being retained on a level which, so far as I know, hasn't been achieved since the beginning of the Ice Age."

"So what are you telling me, Dave?"

"Mr President, this is January, and we have May temperatures in the Arctic Circle. May temperatures down here as well. If that ash cloud doesn't move, it's only going to get warmer from here on. Come June, when temperatures around the Pole average normally between 32 and 50 Fahrenheit, they could reach as high as the seventies and eighties."

"At the North Pole?"

"It's a possibility."

The President stroked his chin. "What are we talking about in terms of effect?"

Obrenski shrugged. "Should the ice cap begin to melt? We are talking about releasing a volume of water maybe as large as the whole United States, cubed. There could be a water level rise of fifty, a hundred feet."

The President looked at Mark. "You agree with that figure, Doctor?"

Mark didn't, actually; he thought Obrenski was going a bit over the top. But he wasn't going to risk arguing, and possibly losing out on Administrative action. "Near enough. It's got to be one hell of a rise, sir," he confirmed.

"In June," said the Chief of Staff, sitting on the President's right. "That's five months away, gentlemen. Are you seriously suggesting this cloud won't dissipate for five months?"

Obrenski looked at Mark.

"We'd expected it to start breaking up well before now," Mark said. "It hasn't shown any signs of doing so."

"What happened after Krakatoa?" inquired the Press Secretary.

"The cloud began to dissipate after a couple of months, although enough ash remained in the atmosphere to affect weather for over a year."

"I don't remember reading of a sea-level rise of any consequence," the Press Secretary said. "Apart from the tsunamis, of course."

"Krakatoa was in the tropics, Mr Desmond, not very far off the Equator: there was nothing to melt. Here we have a cloud sitting over the polar ice cap. What is more, the Misreal explosion was several hundred per cent more violent than that of Krakatoa. I would say that ash cloud up there shows every indication of being around in June."

"When you would predict significant flooding along our eastern seaboard," the President said.

"And in Western Europe, sir."

"To add to what's happening in the midwest as a result of all this rain. So what do we do about it?"

It was Mark's turn to look at Obrenski; they had discussed this on the flight down from Thule.

"Dr Payton feels that the ash cloud simply has to be dissipated, and as quickly as possible," Obrenski said.

"Christ," remarked the Chief of Staff. "We're not back to hydrogen bombs in space again?"

"Failing any other suggestion, yes," Mark said. "After proper consultation with European heads of government, of course."

"Oh, they'll just love that," the Press Secretary said. "Have you any idea what you're suggesting, Dr Payton? Can you imagine the fallout?" His face reddened with sudden anger. "The damage? And I'm not talking in a purely ecological or human sense, either. There happens to be an election next year. You want this party to be thrown out of office for the next fifty years?"

Mark kept his temper. "With respect, sir . . . " he addressed the President, "I would suggest this crisis transcends party politics. I think if you put the issue squarely to the people of this country, you would obtain a consensus to support your action. But I would also suggest that even if you didn't obtain such a consensus, you should begin talks with other governments and try to persuade them of the imminent danger in which we all stand." He looked from one tense face to the next before adding, "Otherwise you, we, the whole world, is going to be faced with an ecological and human disaster which is going to make the fallout effects of a couple of hydrogen bombs seem like a snowstorm."

"Nuts," the Press Secretary said. "We don't even know if letting a device off up there will shift the cloud. But we sure as hell know what'll happen down here after."

Mark glared at him, and the President intervened.

"Thank you, Doctor, thank you, Dave, for giving us this briefing. You may be sure we shall study it, and the overall situation, most carefully." He stood up and held out his hand.

"I told you they wouldn't go for it," Obrenski said as he and Mark walked down the corridor. "Hydrogen bombs are too emotive a subject."

"You don't reckon letting a fair proportion of the earth's population drown is emotive?"

Obrenski extended his arms in a gigantic shrug. "It won't ever come to that. We'll get 'em all moved."

"And then watch them starve to death as all the crops fail, or die of pollution."

"Hell, that cloud'll shift, sometime."

"Maybe. Lord knows I'm not advocating we fire the bombs off immediately. All I hope is to see these guys who press the necessary buttons get their act together. I want them prepared to take action whenever, and if ever, it becomes vital to do so. Hell! These fucking politicians give me the shits, pussyfooting around worrying about the next election when the chances are that half their bloody voters'll be swimming to kingdom come before then!"

Dave Obrenski had thought he'd gotten to know this big, laid-back scientist pretty well over the past couple of months, reckoned he was way too cool ever to lose his rag. How bloody wrong can you get? he asked himself. He allowed Mark a couple of minutes to calm down before casually asking, "Where are you off to now?"

"Boston," Mark told him. "I'm looking for sanity."

Actually he was looking for a lot more than that, with sympathy topping the list. He was mad at himself for snarling at Dave the way he had, leaving the White House. It wasn't Dave's fault that the hierarchy hemming in the President, inhibiting his thinking, was so totally self-motivated. Or at least Party motivated. Dammit, he hadn't asked them to fire off the bombs tomorrow, not at any specific date. All they had to do was prepare the ground, politically and in the practical sense, so when and if it became vital for the sake of thousands of lives and the whole future of the environment to press the Red Button, the populations of the countries of the northern hemisphere would be ready to take evasive action against possible nuclear fallout. A delay of months in which to prepare could be fatal.

So what had happened? They'd talked down to him like he was an over-eager, ignorant school kid. The one with the smooth, round face and gold-rimmed glasses, Jimmy Desmond, had actually sneered at the waste of the President's time listening to him. Made you wonder why you worked so hard at a subject so far beyond the comprehension of the country's leaders, only for them to dismiss your findings as puerile.

He stood on the steps of the apartment block waiting for Anne to answer the buzzer, asking himself if her reaction would prove any better.

He needn't have worried.

"Stupid bastards!" she commented, winding her arms round his neck, lifting her face for his kiss, her earlier reservations about his proposed plan for saving the situation quite dissipated by his knowledge and certainty. She was wearing some slippery, satin type housegown that made her body feel fantastic as his hands slid over and down her back. Her silky black hair was loose on her shoulders, the way he loved it. "First things first?" she asked.

"Unquestionably!" he agreed as they headed directly into the bedroom.

"I didn't want to put a damper on your impending visit to the White House, when we spoke on the phone," Anne remarked later over a beer, "but I guessed the way it would be. Admin, at whatever level, is invariably the same. Any form of public office automatically ties a blindfold on a guy. Women are not quite so bad usually, though maybe I shouldn't say that."

"Honey, I have to tell you it's so good to get back to sanity." He lifted his glass. "Three cheers for intelligent womanhood."

"You trying to get me back to bed?"

"Don't want to disappoint you but the smells from the kitchen have pushed thoughts of your body way back into second place!"

"Thank God for that. I'm starving."

It took Anne precisely three minutes to serve the roast chicken and all the trimmings. Mark wondered how the hell she did it, and was grateful when she didn't ask him to carve but set about it expertly herself.

"So what were you doing while I was away?" he asked.

"Conference in Chicago. Meeting of the moguls of the car industry."

"How were you involved?"

"Organising the operation, the hall, the decor, the seating, the hotel accommodation, the transport . . . "

"Are you trying to convince me you haven't missed me?"

"You'd better believe it!" she laughed. "I don't have time to breathe on one of these functions, let alone daydream about my favourite man."

"Favourite?" His forkful of chicken remained poised in mid-air.

She stopped eating to look him squarely in the eye. "That's what I said."

He stared back and put down his fork. "I decided I was in love with you the first time I came calling."

She smiled. "Funny, two people getting the same feeling at the same moment, like that." She piled more meat on his plate. "Here, let's finish eating before it gets cold."

It rained virtually all the way from Liverpool to West Walton, near his home. Geoffrey looked at vast areas of normally fallow land which had turned into swamp, and every few miles there were notices warning of detours because this or that road was impassable; according to the radio, several streams had broken their banks, and the rivers were becoming dangerous.

But even this sombre news had not prepared him for the condition of the farm. He drove through a puddle so deep, and right across the road, it almost brought him to a halt just before the gates, and the entire drive was more than an inch deep in water.

The house itself, together with the barn, was on a slight rise, and was clear of standing water, although the ground was soggy when he stepped out.

Freddie came out to greet him, clad in heavy coat and rubbers.

"What a mess," Geoffrey commented.

"Bloody awful. If this keeps up there's going to be no spring sowing." He looked at his older brother. "*Can* it keep up?"

"It never has before."

"Oh, yes it has. I've been looking it up. There was apparently a year like this in 1316. It had rained pretty solidly for the two years previously, and that year there was a complete agricultural break-down, with no harvests of either wheat or fodder. One in ten of the population died of malnutrition or disease."

"Nice. What caused it?"

"God knows. The history books don't say. But it must have been something pretty horrendous. Just a generation later they had the Black Death."

"And we're all still here," Geoffrey pointed out. "Now let's be serious. Any real flooding?"

"Well, nothing dangerous. The drains can cope, except at high tide. Then the water stands for a bit."

"What happens if these doom and gloom merchants are right and the ice melts sufficiently to force the sea level to rise? Then the flood water won't be able to run off, at least here in East Anglia."

"I thought you said we were all still here?" Freddie asked.

"Any Government action?"

"Not a damn thing. There are the occasional questions in Parliament, and the usual reply that the situation is being monitored. Then someone pops up and says, this Government cannot legislate for Acts of God! Loud cheers from the Government benches, boos and hisses opposite."

Geoffrey grinned and led his brother into the house; Freddie at least hadn't lost his sense of humour.

But Dunning Farm had lost its sense of fun, and the news on the television was all bad. Geoffrey had in fact noticed that the air seemed thick the moment he had stepped ashore, but apparently pollution-related illnesses were now reaching epidemic proportions, with the very old and the very young chiefly affected by the thickening atmosphere. Mother and Dad were clearly very worried, and so was Freddie, beneath the 'we'll-ride-it' veneer. Geoffrey was glad to get away again; besides, he had things to do in London.

He was waiting in Aunt Madge's sitting-room when Liz arrived home from work. She was pretty, attractive as ever, but he saw immediately that there was a dullness, a grey cloud of gloom, over her. The vigour with which she would normally have flung herself into his arms was missing. She stood against him, hugging him, but her flesh lacked the solid vitality under his palms to which he'd grown accustomed.

Still they kissed, long and anxiously, aching for reassurance not only of each other's continuing love and loyalty, but that life, their existence, was not threatened; that the vast cloud of depression hanging over them was not real, only a passing nightmare which would vanish at any moment and allow them to return to normality.

Geoffrey had come home determined to ignore the cloud and its effects; determined that their lives must proceed as ordained, in anticipation that tomorrow, or in one of the other tomorrows, they would gaze up together into clear, azure skies, confident of their future.

"I'm here for your answer," he told Liz. "Will you marry me?"

Ever since his phone call from Jamaica, Liz had turned the idea over in her mind. There was no doubt at all that she loved him; wanted to say yes. But were they the only people involved? Hers was a loose-knit but united family. Mum had gone out to work as long as she could remember and she, being the oldest girl, had played domestic understudy after school until Mum got home. Wayne, her senior by one year, Luke, two years junior and baby sister Sue, had sought her and fought her, like a mother. And as each came fifteen they went their own ways: Wayne to Perth as geologist to a mining company, Luke, the accountant, to Melbourne and Sue to nurse in a hospital in Adelaide.

Dad and Mum continued to work all daylight hours solely to finance their devotion to music. They had both developed fine, if amateur, voices and took part in big choral works. Latterly, Dad had taken a course in choral conducting, and Mum, who had always played the piano, learned guitar and clarinet. So how would they feel if their elder daughter decided to settle on the other side of the world? She didn't want to distress them, but she had never been as close to them as Geoff was to his parents. They had their music: full, happy lives . . .

The more important question was how she herself would feel about staying here. Here under this God-awful cloud. There was no doubt in her mind that Geoffrey was the man she had been looking for when she left Australia, but would the love, the need she felt for him now, survive the dreariness of living in England? It wasn't just the weather, either. So many of the people were dreary. Maybe if she had got to know them before the Misreal eruption she would have found them quite different. As it was, people on the trains and buses, serving in shops and restaurants, all seemed so morose, aggressive . . .

But dammit she wouldn't be marrying them. She would be Geoffrey's wife; and wasn't that what she wanted above all things? She stood back to look up at him: at the long, finely chiselled face, dark brown eyes overhung with heavy black brows; the wide firm mouth which could be so gentle. There was really no doubt about the answer.

"Yes, Geoff darling. I want to marry you more than anything else in the world."

7

April Showers

John raised his glass. "Congratulations, Geoffrey and Liz! We wish you every happiness and all the luck in the world."

"Geoffrey and Liz! Liz and Geoffrey!" Everyone sitting around the Dunnings' dining-table chorused to raised glasses.

"And a special welcome to Madge," Mary added. "We've heard so much about you from Liz and it's lovely to meet you at long last."

"I am so happy to be here," Liz's aunt responded. "Despite the rain and flooding, your home surpasses all the glowing reports I've heard from Liz."

Charles and Jennifer had come up earlier, Liz and Aunt Madge arriving by a later train as soon as Liz could get away from her work. Geoffrey had driven down from Liverpool, arriving only half an hour before Mary put dinner on the table.

"It's really very obliging of you two to give us something to celebrate," Freddie told them in mock seriousness. "There has been a marked lack of material for jubilation lately. Have you decided where to have the wedding?"

"Yes. Geoff gave me the dates he anticipated being on leave this year and told me to call my folks in Brisbane," Liz explained. "They were all excited, but they agreed the sensible thing would be to have the wedding over here. My brothers and sister are scattered all over Oz. So Mum and Dad are going to combine the wedding with a tour of the Old Country."

"That's wonderful," Mary beamed. "They must stay here with us."

"Why, is the ceremony to be held in Norfolk?" Freddie asked.

"Where else?" Liz demanded. "Geoff and I went to your dinky little antique church near here last time he was home. We have an appointment with the vicar tomorrow to discuss arrangements."

"Have you decided on a date, yet?" Charles asked.

"April twentieth. Happens to be Liz's birthday," Geoffrey told him.

"How splendid to get married on one's birthday!" Jennifer trilled.

John and Mary winked at each other down the length of the table. It was good to see smiling faces round them again, hear laughter in the house and anticipate such a joyful event. Life had been far too depressing in recent months.

"Have you decided where you are going to live?" Madge wanted to know.

"We plan to go house-hunting in this area tomorrow, when we've finished with the vicar," Geoffrey said. "There's not much point in settling for London. It's that much further from Liverpool, for a start, and unless we found something near you, Liz would be pretty lonely when I'm away. And anyway, London is so darned expensive."

"You can say that again," Charles said with feeling, to nobody in particular.

"That will mean giving up your job, Liz," Madge pointed out.

"I might try to get something in King's Lynn or nearby."

"Can you swim? You can always come and work here on the farm," Freddie offered.

"That's a thought," Liz responded, trying not to laugh. "Tell you what, howsabout we go into business together breeding frogs with nice fat legs?"

"You're on! You catch 'em, I'll market 'em!"

Everyone joined in with idiotic suggestions, laughing like mad. John opened another bottle of wine and even Madge got a bit tipsy.

Roy Chubb, the vicar, was young, wiry, red-haired and enthusiastic, hammering all the details on to his computer as they talked. He insisted on Christian names all round for all generations, and Liz was thrilled when she realised that theirs would be a relaxed, happy ceremony.

Roy wanted to hear all about the Bowmans. "I went out to Oz before starting my training," he told them. "Thought it would be a good idea to get as far away as possible from my home environment before making the final decision. My father is in the ministry, you see, and I was afraid of entering the calling simply because Dad was in it."

"Where did you go? What did you do out there?" Liz wanted to know.

"Bondi. Surfing."

"No! You're joking!"

"Straight up! Why did you think I'm kidding?"

"The thought of a parson on Bondi! What did the blokes think of the back-to-front-collar?" The accent automatically thickened.

Geoffrey looked from one to the other in alarm, but Roy was grinning, enjoying himself.

"They thought it was great. Kinda hedged their bets in the biggees!"

"You're having me on! You never wore it on the beach!"

"I couldn't. I hadn't made the decision yet, remember? Now," he turned back to the screen on his desk, "you tell me your folks are into music. Do you think they might like to do something for us during the service? My wife, Babs, usually plays the organ, with a bit of help from our two-year-old; but it would be super if your parents could sing or play for us in the interval instead of the old idea of making a long ceremony of signing the register."

"I'll ring and ask them," said Liz.

"Mike! Mike, where are you?" Doll Bowman stood in the shade of the porch outside the lounge window.

"Here." Mike peered round the backrest of the sunlounger, groping on the paving for his can of beer. The movement twisted his tanned body, revealing a fair-sized paunch in an otherwise strongly muscled torso. He wore only sunglasses, with a pair of shorts hooked over the back of the lounger in case someone rang the front door bell. He looked at his wife appreciatively as she strode naked towards him, long bronzed legs swinging easily from her hips. Her belly was flat, breasts high and firm; there were only a couple of grey wisps in her short, brown hair. Nobody'd believe she was fifty.

"That was Liz on the blower."

"Again? Jees! This Geoff bloke must be made of money!" he tilted his head to allow the cool beer to slide down his throat, replaced the can in the shade under him and rolled back, face up to the evening sun. "What did she want?"

"The parson wants us to sing at the wedding."

Mike sat up, reached for the beer again and twisted round to stare at Doll, to see if she was serious.

She nodded. "On the level."

"Sing what?"

"They said they'd leave the choice to us."

"Um-mm." He rolled back onto the lounger. "So! Young Liz is really putting her act together. You know, we haven't celebrated the engagement, yet. Let's have a party, huh?"

"Right. I'd better let the other kids know now. Maybe one of them can get home for it."

Mike's forehead wrinkled. "Out of whose pocket?"

"Yours, you big berk! Who else?" She got up. "I'm going in to get pen and paper. We'll make a list."

"Of what to sell to pay for this wedding?"

"Don't need to write a list for that. We'll flog off your wine cellar." A brightly coloured cushion sailed through the air and landed on Doll's behind. "No," she giggled, grabbing it and hurling it back, "I want to make a list of folks for the party . . . oops!" The cushion flew past Mike into the pool.

"No wonder neither of your sons are any good at cricket. You couldn't hit the side of a house from six feet." He got up and reached for the pool scoop.

The party materialised very quickly, only three days later. Sue couldn't get up from Adelaide, and it was too far for Wayne to fly across from Perth, but Luke arrived home half an hour before the first guests arrived, in time to act as barman while Mike worked on the barbecue.

It was a typically relaxed pool party. The men arrived in shorts over bathing trunks, the girls in bikinis and wrap-arounds. Nearly everyone knew each other, and stood about in groups, chatting, stretched out in loungers, or took to the floating armchairs in the pool, their iced drinks wedged in the glass holders cut in the polystyrene armrests.

"When do we eat?" Bob Starky asked. "Mike's making my mouth water."

"Soon as the sun's down and the pool lights go on," Doll told him. "You'll have to wear a clothes peg on your nose for the next ten minutes. Would another G and T help?"

Doll had laid out salads and quiches on the kitchen table, where their friends could help themselves. The noise level rose as the sun subsided behind the trees, and Mike yelled above the din, "Okay. Come and get it."

Luke carried round a tray loaded with plastic glasses of wine, and Bob's wife, Meg, helped Doll pass baskets of hot garlic bread to everyone. Some people perched on the edge of the pool, feet dangling in the water, plates balanced on their knees, others were at one of the tables or on loungers; one group sat cross-legged on the grass.

Bob, short, round and bald and Mike's best mate, stood glass in hand, banging on the table beside him with his fork. "Okay, folks, let's have some hush."

"Why don't you stand up, mate, so's we can see you?' someone barracked.

119

Bob jumped nimbly on to a chair. "Is that better for the elderly and short-sighted?" Shouts of laughter. "Here's where we say 'cheers to Liz and . . . what's his name . . . Geoff'." He held his glass high.

"Liz and Geoff."

"Congratulations."

"God bless 'em."

"What I can't understand is why they're getting married over there," Bob continued, "when the weather is so God-damned rotten . . . "

"Next thing you know all the Pommies will be over here getting their sun tans," someone called.

"But I've heard on the grapevine . . . " Bob refused to be interrupted, "that Mike and Doll have been asked to sing at the wedding . . . "

He was interrupted by a chorus of shouts and cheers.

" . . . and I think it only fair to Liz that we should vet the rendering tonight."

More cheers.

"So what's it to be, Doll?"

"We haven't decided yet . . . " she began.

"'Sweet Nellie Dean!'" a voice yelled from the lawn.

"'The Ball of Kerrymuir'," was suggested from the pool followed by shrieks of laughter.

Bob held up his hand. "No, seriously, folks." He looked across at Mike. "Have you really not decided yet?" And when Mike shook his head he said to Doll, "Well, have you thought of doing the love entreaty from *Samson and Delilah*? Everyone laughed again.

"Try 'The Nun's Prayer'."

"Or 'The Good Ship Venus'."

Suggestions flew thick and fast, getting more and more crazy.

"You could do the twenty-third psalm to *Crimond* together," Bob murmured to Mike.

"Yeah. Maybe. Great for weddings but tonight it would be one helluva party pooper. I'll get the guitar out and we'll have a sing-along, everyone joining in. Huh?"

Doll crawled into bed beside Mike at three the next morning. "Wow! That was some party. Pity Liz wasn't here. She'd have been tickled pink."

"I videoed some of it and sound recorded the rest. Played back a bit while you were mucking about in the kitchen, just now. It's hilarious."

"Good on you, honey. We'll take it with us when we go." She was asleep in ten seconds, dreaming about the outfit for the bride's mother.

"That's it." Geoffrey slowed the car at the top of the lane and they both stared down the gentle incline at a pretty cottage nestled between willows behind a privet hedge . . . and at the lake in which it stood.

"Oh no! Are you sure?" Liz studied the specifications collected from the estate agent in King's Lynn. There was no doubt, from the front photograph, that this was indeed the prospective home they were looking for. "But how do we get at it?"

Geoffrey switched off the motor. "I'm not sure that we can."

"It must be possible. Aren't there people living there?"

"No. I think this is the one they said had only been used for weekends for the past couple of years. Where's the brolly? I'll take a quick look round and see if there's another approach."

Liz sat hunched in her seat and waited. This was the third attractive possibility they had found, all half-submerged in floods, and her spirits were beginning to submerge with them. She watched Geoffrey clamber over a gate halfway down the lane, and wade back to the car shaking his head. Above his head thunder rumbled almost constantly although there was little lightning; this was almost encouraging, as it was the first sign of real weather they'd had since October.

"Just as well I listened to Mother and wore my wellies," he said. "No good, I'm afraid. And even if we could reach it, I wouldn't like to bet that the water hasn't caused serious damage; more than mere painting and decorating. And as for these damned mos-quitoes . . . " He swiped at the back of his neck.

"I've been bitten on my hands and face, look." She showed him the red blotches on her cheek and forehead, and on her hand.

He took the hand and held it up to kiss the palm. "I'm so sorry about all this, my darling. We're not having much success are we?"

Her fingers stroked his cheek. "That was the last of the houses. I reckon it just wasn't meant to be." She screwed the papers into a ball and dropped them by her feet. "Come on, let's get home and dry out. I feel like a bath sponge."

John was in his chair in the sitting-room staring into space, empty pipe clenched in his teeth, the *Telegraph* lying unopened on his lap. He looked up when they came in. "Find anything?"

"Nothing that wouldn't require selling the car and buying a boat," Geoffrey replied, dropping on to the settee.

John sighed. "Mum's bringing the tea in."

"I'll go give her a hand." Liz disappeared and came back with a

121

plate of scones and a fresh jam sponge.

Mary sailed in with the loaded teatray. "Here we are. Let's tuck in while everything's hot. See Freddie?"

"He was in the yard when we came back. Said he'd be in in ten minutes," Geoffrey said.

"I'm here," his brother spoke from the doorway. "Mum, got anything for bites? The mosquitoes are having a field day out here."

"In the cabinet in our bathroom. Yes, we'll have to screen the windows soon, I was chewed up in the night."

Freddie reappeared two minutes later, his face white with cream. "How did you get on with your house-hunting?"

"Hopeless."

Mary looked up from the teapot and raised an eyebrow at John. Who cleared his throat. "Look here, you two. We've been talking, Mum, Freddie and I."

Having handed round plates, napkins and scones, Liz sat beside Geoffrey, both leaning forward and wondering what was coming.

"We thought you might like to consider the Granny wing."

"I thought it had been turned into a junk store," Geoffrey frowned.

"It has, in a manner of speaking. But there's nothing to stop it being turned back again. The bathroom is okay, I think, though the kitchen has been used during the past couple of years for making animal feed and special medications. It's in a bit of a mess, but why don't you take a good look at it? At least it's above the watertable." John opened his tobacco pouch and busied himself with his pipe.

"That could be a fantastic idea. But what about all the stuff that's in there?" Geoffrey was beginning to feel better. It *could* be a wonderful idea. He remembered the way it was when Gran was alive, filled with her heavy, carved furniture and the exquisite china figurines that Mum now had. He used to love creeping out into the yard when he was supposed to be doing homework, around the side to her front door which he could never recall being shut. Gran was a doer, always making something, cakes or cushion covers, mosaic pots or painting watercolours, and never averse to accepting help. Pretty negative help, he imagined on reflection. But her home had been a warm, interesting place.

"We've ten times more barn space than we use, now that we've cut down the herd," Freddie told him. "Stick it all in there."

"What about you?"

"Me?"

"Well, Doreen . . . "

Freddie gave a sheepish grin. "I think you can forget that. When the time comes, we'll find someplace else. Or by then you will have."

Liz was starting to bounce up and down on the edge of the settee. "I've never been inside it."

"I'll show you when we've finished tea," Geoffrey promised.

"But I want to see it now!"

"No! Eat up!" he teased.

Geoffrey need not have worried about Liz's reaction; she was enchanted from the moment the door swung open on its squeaky hinges. The kitchen was in a mess, as Mary had warned, but the living-room, long and low-ceilinged with an old stone fireplace and raised hearth, made her gasp, speechless with excitement despite the dust and cobwebs. She prowled around the stacks of boxes and bags of meal, edged behind a discarded fridge to get into the bedroom. "I don't believe it!" she exclaimed. "Geoff, will you come and take a look at this old bedstead – it's got real brass knobs on!"

"Have you seen Gran's old dresser? And the carved dining-table?" he called back.

Later, when the family reassembled in the sitting-room before dinner, Mary asked, "Well? What did you think?"

"Fantastic!" Liz enthused. "But . . . it seems such an imposition."

"Rubbish!" Freddie retorted. "It was my idea. I need you around to catch all those frogs."

"From a purely selfish viewpoint, I have to say I think it would be lovely to have you here," Mary remarked, "especially while Geoffrey's away. It does get lonely when the men are out on the farm."

John blew a cloud of smoke at the ceiling. "And it's a good way of getting the place cleaned up and decorated for free."

"Families are wonderful." Liz gave a mock sigh. "They make you feel wanted, needed."

"We'll have to talk it over from the business angle . . . " Geoffrey began.

"If you wish," his father said. "But as far as we are concerned, until, ah, it gets too small for you, you are welcome to it. The fact of tidying it up and seeing to the maintenance will more than make up for any form of rent."

"What about Gran's furniture?"

"I'd meant to sell it when she died. We had all we needed in here. But your mother flatly refused to part with it."

"I couldn't bear the thought of it going out of the family," Mary said. "All this," she waved a hand over the contents of the sitting-room, "came from John's people, but I grew up with most of the stuff in there. It's such a shame to think of it covered in dust and

123

going mouldy. I know it's old-fashioned and heavy, but do you think you could live with it, Liz?"

"Live with it? I think it's fantastic. All of it, especially the bed."

The gloom that had developed over the past few days' unsuccessful house-hunting vanished and the remainder of Geoffrey's leave was spent working furiously to prepare the wing for decorating.

"Your folks are just wonderful," Liz said.

"Aren't yours?" Geoffrey asked.

"Sure they are. But somehow . . . I'm easier coming to live with yours than if you were coming to live with mine. Oz is a kind of, well . . . individual place. You either fit in, or you don't."

"Meaning, I wouldn't."

She grinned. "You're the ultimate Pom. But maybe that's why I love you."

They were alone in the sitting-room, still side by side on the settee. The fact of their engagement and imminent marriage, and even more the fact of his imminent departure on another West Indian voyage, had not been lost on the family, who had at last departed to bed.

Geoffrey wrapped his arms round her, felt her face tilt back to receive his kisses. Theirs was going to be a fabulous marriage. They were so right for each other: such a perfect balance. It amazed him how similar their tastes, attitudes and opinions were. Only in temperament did they differ: she so open, trusting and friendly with friend and stranger alike, drawing him out of his English reserve. They liked each other, had enormous fun together, and this, Geoffrey had no doubt at all, was the ultimate basis for a happy and successful marriage. He had been assailed by doubts, from time to time. It was all very well having a girl to dream about when you were away at sea for weeks at a time, but it didn't automatically follow that you'd see eye to eye about every subject, and they had come from two such completely different backgrounds. But during the past couple of weeks all his doubts, and hers, had been swept aside: which had to do with Mum and Dad's attitude towards her and the offer of the Wing. Maybe for the first time Liz felt truly relaxed, not merely politely welcomed, but enveloped in this so family-minded family.

From his point of view, the fact that she would not have to mope around a house or a flat on her own while he was away was an enormous relief, and he could tell it was for her too. It was slowly beginning to penetrate his rather self-centred masculine personality that Liz was a terribly lonely, terribly vulnerable person, for all her apparent laid-back Aussie frame of mind . . . or maybe because of it.

Of course mutual sexual attraction had been there at the start of their relationship, yet that relationship had remained amazingly asexual. There could be no doubt after their passionate necking sessions that they did turn each other on, yet they had never slept together. He had admired the fact she had not tried to jump into bed with him when they first met, and somehow since then there hadn't been time, or the ambience hadn't been quite right . . . but she was clinging to him now, responding to his caresses, her tongue circling his . . . wanting more of him as he was wanting her. Urgently.

Suddenly she drew back, held him away from her, studying his face. "Say, how much more does a girl have to do round here to get laid?" she asked, her expression deadpan.

"Didn't know you were psychic, as well as gorgeous." He jumped to his feet. "Nothing, is the answer to your question. Follow me, my darling. I don't intend waiting another minute." He grabbed her hand.

"But . . . " She raised her eyes to the floor above.

"Forget them."

"They might hear . . . "

"So what?"

Nevertheless they tiptoed up the stairs and Geoffrey started towards his room. Liz tugged at his hand, shaking her head, so he followed instead to her room.

"If anyone's going to be caught wandering the landing in the middle of the night it's got to be you," Liz said firmly, as her door closed. Then she started to undress.

He had never even seen her in a bathing suit. He stood motionless as each garment slid to the floor revealing more and more pale golden flesh.

"I've been away from home so long my tan has faded," she said, moving towards him and starting to roll his jumper up.

Geoffrey lifted his arms. "I only tan briefly when we're in the Caribbean." He bent to kiss her mouth, while both pairs of hands were busy with his remaining clothes.

Then with her arms round his neck and her legs wound round his waist, he carried her to the bed.

8

Ultima Thule

The buildings of Thule Air Force Base loomed out of the gloom, invisible at four hundred yards.

"You reckon this is fog, or water-level cloud?" asked Colonel Kelly.

"It's water vapour, anyway," Mark agreed.

They stood on the tarmac and looked into darkness. In March the long winter midnight was coming to an end, but there was little apparent change here in Thule . . . and they were nearly a thousand miles south of the Pole.

The clouds had accumulated slowly. For six months there had been almost no variation in barometric pressure and therefore no wind. The entire northern hemisphere was gripped in an Equatorial vice with temperatures dropping only slowly, down to February. Now they were rising again. Mark was wearing an open-necked shirt beneath his windcheater, and he was only wearing the windcheater because it was liable to start raining again at any moment.

Satellite photography being useless as the ash layer still covered the lower atmosphere, Mark had followed the normal aerial photographs of the clouds accumulating over the Pole, forming a layer within the ash layer . . . and his worries had grown. The water vapour was being sucked up by the sheer warmth of the air, not by the sun. The result was that it was not rising high enough to condense and fall as heavy rain, but remained within a few hundred feet of the surface, leaving everything wet and damp in the drizzle.

And it was spreading south.

He had returned to Washington and spoken with Dave Obrenski, hoping to obtain another interview with the President. But the President was preoccupied with the latest Middle East

126

crisis, and besides, his advisers had told him the ash layer was beginning to thin.

"It is, you know," Dave had said.

"Sure it's beginning to thin," Mark had agreed. "Like a million-gallon water reservoir with a pin-hole for a leak. Anyway, I'm not sure the damage hasn't been done. I think we should take another look up north. You seen all these reports?"

"Okay," Dave had said. "So we have some obvious water-level increases. In Holland they're talking about an average of two feet above normal and there's had to be some evacuation. It's about the same in certain areas of Canada. So that means there has been some melting of the ice cap. We can live with two feet, Mark. We have to."

"Dave, the ice cap hasn't started to melt, yet. So what happens when it gets up to a hundred feet? That's the figure you were quoting just six weeks ago."

"I was OTT. And you knew it at the time. Once that ash layer really breaks up, we'll have a return to normal. You wait and see. Anyway, we're monitoring the situation very carefully out of Thule. Believe me."

"So let me see the latest reports from up there."

"Can't be done, old buddy. Not even for you. That's classified information."

Mark reckoned Dave had been nobbled. The problem had no precedent, and no short answer, therefore the attitude was, pretend it isn't there and it'll go away. But obviously the news coming out of Thule hadn't been good.

Thus he'd persuaded the Ballard Foundation to finance another trip north, as the Government wouldn't co-operate. But now Kelly was proving equally unco-operative.

"All aircraft are grounded north of Thule," he explained. "It's just too goddam dangerous. You were lucky to get in here."

"So you have no idea what's happening at the Pole?"

"We're getting radio reports from places like Alert all the time. So it's an exceptionally mild winter. They happen."

"Do you really believe that, Colonel?"

Kelly slapped a handful of mosquitoes on his arm. "Could be summer," he growled. His shoulders hunched, as he thrust his hands into his pockets. "Look, Doctor, I'm a serviceman. I obey my orders and leave strategy to the big brass."

"And the big brass are doing the three-monkey-trick. Let me go up there, Colonel."

Kelly gazed at him, lips twisting as he tried to make up his mind.

127

Then he shrugged. "I reckon they're playing it wrong, too. If you can find someone to fly you . . . "

Mark went back to Hudson. "Sure," the pilot agreed. "I've been kind of hankering to have another look myself. I don't know I'll be able to put her down, though."

He climbed until they broke through the mist layer. Then, at about 5,000 feet, they were in relatively clear visibility, although it was still a twilight world, and high above their heads the black pall continued to obliterate the sky.

"One thing's for sure, the incidence of skin cancer should drop this year," Hudson said with an attempt at humour.

Mark saw the mountains of Greenland peeping above the mist layer, the huge ice sheets which marked glaciers that had existed for tens of thousands of years, and gasped. Most of the ice was still there, but there was bare rock showing through in places, and he was looking at peaks several thousand feet high. What might be happening at lower altitudes, beneath the fog, was frightening to suppose.

The mountains fell behind, and Hudson checked his charts. "We're over the Lincoln Sea," he said. "Want to take a look?"

"If you're game."

Hudson grinned. "I don't reckon there's anything down there to hit save ice, and that's all at one level. Here we go."

The aircraft sank, and the mist came up to meet them. A moment later they were totally enveloped. Mark watched the altimeter as they went down, down, very slowly. At a hundred feet Hudson levelled off. Now the mist was patchy, and every so often they could see the ice beneath them . . . but these were floes. Several of them were enormous, the size of small islands, yet in between there were lines of blue water.

In March?

"You want to try to find a place to land?" Hudson asked.

"I don't think that will be necessary."

"Well, that's the best news since Christmas. What d'you reckon, Doc?"

"I reckon things are one hell of a lot worse than we thought. Once that ice breaks up a little more, it is going to start to drift, and then it is going to melt. You know something, Dick? We're watching the start of the break-up of the Polar ice cap."

"Shit!" Hudson pulled back the yoke and they soared up through the mist. "You want to try for the Pole itself?"

"Just get me back to Thule," Mark told him.

*   *   *

"The chief would like a word, Mark," anchorman O'Ryan said.
"Well, I had to show him the script. He's very sensitive about public
responsibility and that kind of thing."

"That's why I came to you," Mark agreed.

"Yeah," O'Ryan said doubtfully. "Well, fifteenth floor."

Mark looked out of the window of the outside elevator as he rode
up the Universal Broadcasting Company building. Springtime in
New York. The mist hadn't reached here yet, and the city was fully
visible, and dirtier than he had ever seen it; no one was really
attempting to clean it up any more. People might have saved a
fortune in heating bills this winter but the absence of sun and snow,
the intermittent dirty drizzle, had left everyone feeling vaguely
frustrated. Tempers were short.

"Hi, Doctor. Mr Kinnear's waiting for you," said the attractive
middle-aged secretary. "Go right in."

"Mark!" Tom Kinnear was a large, bluff man who smoked cigars,
wore expensive suits, and never spoke a full sentence unless he had
to. Well, as President of the Universal Broadcasting Company he
could afford to be terse. "Good to see you." He shook hands
vigorously. "Sit. Smoke?"

"Don't."

"Wise." Kinnear sat down himself, tapped his desk. "This script.
Controversial."

"That's the idea."

"Controversy must be responsible. Responsibility. That's the
name of the game."

"That's what I'm trying to achieve, Tom, instil some kind of
responsibility into Washington."

"They have information."

"So do I. And I'm damn sure mine agrees with theirs, only
they're keeping theirs under wraps."

"Shoot."

Mark leaned forward. "Tom, I've been up there. I've flown over
the Lincoln Sea, north of Thule. Three days ago. This time of year
that should be one solid sheet of ice, thick enough to march an
army across. Right now it's a mass of floes. Just lumps of floating
ice."

"So?"

"Tom, that ice has broken up to a summer state, but in March.
Normally the ice starts breaking up in July and August. Then it
begins to melt. But it can't have much effect on world sea levels
because within another month temperatures drop below freezing,
and it all starts to come together again. This year, there are no
temperatures below freezing up there. That ice is melting *now*, and

129

temperatures are going to continue to rise and ice is going to melt even faster. The pace can only increase. But up till now we've been talking about sea ice. Like I said, it melts during the summer and freezes up again during the winter. The earth can cope with that; it's been doing it for over twenty thousand years. But what really holds the Arctic together is the huge area of permafrost, on the land. In some places it extends just a couple of feet below the surface. In others it's 300 feet thick. It stays that way even in summer, when temperatures rise maybe twenty degrees above freezing. It stays that way because in the winter temperatures get more than double that *below* freezing. But right now, and as far as I can make out all winter, temperatures have been hovering just around the freezing mark. Okay, that's kept the permafrost together and that's kept the Arctic together. But if this trend continues, and temperatures continue about twenty degrees above normal, come July you're going to be having tropical conditions up there, and that means the permafrost is going to melt." He paused to let what he had said sink in. Then he went on, "For Christ's sake, Tom, the whole Arctic area right now is like one gigantic freezer with the door left open into a centrally heated room. There are billions and billions of gallons of water tied up there, and it's all going to be released."

"Government knows this?"

"Of course they do. But they can't make up their minds what to do about it."

"What happens when that water is released?"

"Floods. On a scale no one's seen since Noah's Ark."

"Fact?"

"Oh, I can't be dogmatic about it. But yes, fact."

"Can't be proved, eh?"

"The temperatures can certainly be proved. They're right here in the thermometers. It doesn't require genius to work out what has to happen if you subject ice to 70° Fahrenheit."

"I mean, you can't prove what's going to happen, how high the water will rise, what areas are going to be affected."

"No, I can't prove that. There's no way of telling how long the ash cloud will remain. But logically, it has to happen. And there are other aspects of the situation. From Labrador to the Pole there is thick mist, a couple of thousand feet thick, lying on the surface of the earth. Believe it or not, that's heat exchange. That mist is going to spread, Tom. It is already spreading. Try thinking what that's going to do to the communications network, either flying or driving, for that matter. Then think of this. The ash cloud is going to move eventually. When that happens, there's going to be a sudden return to normal. High winds, proper temperatures . . . and all that water. Figure that."

"So?"

Mark sighed. "We're facing catastrophe, Tom. They have to act. Now. So it's going to be grim. But every day we put it off, the end-result is going to be worse. We have to put it to the nation."

Kinnear tapped the script again. "Hydrogen bombs in the atmosphere? Suicidal."

"Necessary. It's the only way."

"Can't be done. I'm killing the programme, Mark."

Mark stared at him in disbelief. "You can't do that."

"My decision. Sorry. I agree, we have catastrophe on our doorstep. But you don't solve one catastrophe by creating another. Final."

Mark hesitated. Then he got up and left the office.

Anne Dunning hurried along the pavement with a bag of groceries under her arm. It was already dark and of course drizzling, but like most people she was getting used to the irritation of it. Plastic mac manufacturers were having a bonanza, marketing a vast range of fashion styles, and Anne was wearing a shiny white one, with a matching medicated face-mask to help her combat the really unpleasantly thick – and apparently germ-laden – atmosphere, her hair securely tucked up under a matching, wide-brimmed hat. But as with all macs, hers quickly became hot and sweaty inside – which meant she would need a bath when she got in.

It would have to wait, though, till after the programme. Mark had called her in some excitement to say that he had secured an interview on UBC television at prime time this evening, in which he was going to blow the lid off the weather situation and demand that Washington take immediate action.

It at least promised to be amusing.

"Hi, honey!" A familiar voice broke into her thoughts from the top of her front steps.

She peered at the hunched figure in a dripping raincoat. Oh Lord! "Hi, Ben," she mumbled through her mask.

"Tried calling, but it's always the Ansaphone." He wasn't wearing a mask, and his voice was hoarse.

She'd taken up leaving it on even when home. "Yeah. I've been kind of busy. I have been meaning to call you."

"You reckon we should stand here in the rain?"

"It's not convenient to ask you up right now, Ben. Can we make a date to talk, sometime?"

"You giving me the brush-off, sweetheart?"

Anne sighed. She had hoped to avoid a scene like this.

"I thought we had something going," Ben persisted.

"We did, Ben. We did. But . . . "

"Something better has come along, right?"

"Oh, Ben . . . look, now's not the time, huh? Like I said, let's make a date . . . "

"If it's only to say good-bye, it's not worth it. Waste of time." He stood over her, hair plastered to his head and little rivers running down the sides of his face. "Say it, Anne, baby. Say what you have to say here, right now, or ask me up."

She hadn't wanted to be this abrupt about it. Ben had been a dear – she would always remain so fond of him – but what was to be gained by asking him up to talk, other than a prolonged argument? Better to get it over, rapidly.

"Ben, dear, I have to tell you that a very important guy has come into my life . . . "

"Yeah? Since when?" His voice was harsh.

"Christmas."

"Christmas! Shitting assholes, Anne! Why the hell haven't you told me before?"

"Because you've been away on your conferences, knocking off dollybirds." She was trying not to lose her rag, but hell, he had no right to take that tone . . .

"Well, we never made any . . . I mean, so there's another guy around. So what? Does that make a difference? There have been others before."

"Yes. This time there is a difference. Mark and I are in love."

They gazed at each other. "Now there's a word I never thought to hear from those pretty lips," he said at last. "So be happy, honey." He brushed past her down the steps and walked off into the darkness.

Anne ran to the elevator wanting to cry.

Upstairs, she went straight through to dump the groceries in the kitchen, and poured herself a drink before turning on the TV, standing in front of it to unfasten her mac and tug the hat off her hair.

" . . . the interview with Dr Mark Payton, which was to be shown at this time, has been postponed indefinitely owing to circumstances beyond our control. Here instead is an edited version of last week's game between the Rams and the . . . "

Anne switched off the set and swore.

Evening flights to Boston had been cancelled due to adverse weather conditions, so Mark went up by Amtrak. He had called

Anne to say he'd be in very late and would eat on the train, so when the vendor came through the carriage with his trolley, he bought sandwiches and a Coke, placing them on the tray in front of him. He reclined his seat, put his feet on the footbar and tried to relax with the *Evening Post* . . . but it was too unwieldy and got in the way of his sandwiches, so he discarded it and reached for *Time*. 'Black New York', ran the lead, with various articles on how to clean up the city; and some idiot had done a double spread on the need for new reservoirs in the midwest. He drained his can of Coke, leaned his head back, eyes closed . . . but instead of counting sheep he was counting icefloes.

Anne was waiting for him with a pot of hot chocolate, love and sympathy. She made no comment about the dark circles round his eyes, or the fact that his programme hadn't been shown. She sat quietly, waiting till he finished his chocolate, then shoved a bath towel in his hand and pointed him at the shower.

Hair still damp, he flicked off the light and crawled into bed beside her, reaching out to pull her naked body against his own, feeling the softness of her breasts under his cheek.

Gently she smoothed the hair away from his forehead, aching for his misery and worry. Two minutes later he was asleep.

She had not told him about Ben. Nor that she had decided to fly over to England next week to visit her family and meet Geoffrey's Liz.

9

The Ash Cloud

San Francisco was on the very edge of the shadow cast by the ash cloud, but the passengers on the jumbo had seen it looming in the distance, their attention drawn to it by the pilot, all the way up from Hawaii.

"It's enormous," Doll Bowman whispered, holding Mike's hand. "Did you ever see anything like it when you were flying?" Mike had been a commercial pilot. "No, and let's hope we never see anything like it down under," Mike replied.

Meg leaned forward from the seat behind. "Must be ghastly living further east, right under it."

Bob stared gloomily through the scratched perspex, and shuddered.

All four were vaguely hungover, because the last few days before leaving Australia had been one round of parties. The Bowman kids had all been mad they couldn't accompany their parents to Liz's wedding, but it just wasn't a financial proposition. No one had supposed that Liz, clearly fleeing a succession of unhappy love affairs in Oz, would want to get married within a year of leaving home. Of course Doll was delighted, but it was all being done in such a rush . . . it was seeing the cloud made her wonder if maybe her daughter *was* in a rush. That cloud made her think of the end of the world.

Mike had other things on his mind. So much had been going on over the past week that Doll had watched almost no TV or opened a newspaper. Neither had he, but he did know that there had been two jetliner crashes in the States over the previous ten days. In each case the cause had not been determined, at least officially, as yet. 'Full scale investigations' were being launched.

As a pilot Mike knew there could be a hundred and one reasons for a big jet to come down. There was the usual talk about the possibility of a bomb on board, or structural failure . . . but the fact remained that two supposedly safe modern aircraft had just fallen from the sky, killing all on board.

Equally he knew that plane travel was still the safest form of transport in the world, and judging by the statistics, the fact that there *had* been two recent crashes made them all the safer – another one wasn't due for at least six months. But he hoped Doll didn't find out about them. She was a nervous traveller at the best of times.

It drizzled all the time they were in San Francisco, no encouragement to sight-seeing. Besides, their stopover was only half a day and one night. The two women had managed to drag Mike and Bob to a big shopping mall the previous afternoon, where Doll had found a fabulous turquoise and white dress and jacket which she liked even better than the wedding outfit she'd already bought.

"I hope I can find a hat to go with it in London," she said to Meg as they sat waiting for their flight in the airport lounge. "Liz says you can't go to a wedding in England without one."

"That'll be quite something."

"It'll be the first hat I've had in years."

"Hope Lizzie won't mind me parading the old blue. My Ma wore it to every christening, wedding and funeral she ever attended, and lent it to her sister, too."

"Liz'll love it. She adores antiques." The two of them giggled into their coffee cups.

"Can't figure why the Yanks call this beer," Mike said morosely, as he drank something called 'Lite'. "Say, you reckon they have Foster's in England?"

"Don't be a wally," Doll hooted. "Foster's just about owns England."

Their flight was called an hour and a half late. Once they were all seated, the stewardesses did their routine. "Ladies and gentlemen," the purser said, once they had been taken through the safety drills, "we apologise for the delay on this flight. Due to the exceptional weather we are experiencing, all flights are taking approximately an hour longer than usual. This is because there is a great deal of electrical activity in certain areas, and to ensure the flights are comfortable the captains wish to avoid extreme turbulence wherever possible. With this in mind, may we ask you to keep your seatbelts fastened at all times except when actually moving up and down the aisles – and that you use the aisles only when necessary. Thank you, and have a nice flight."

135

"You know something," Bob said, leaning forward over the back of Mike's seat. "That girl sounded scared."

"So am I." Doll shuddered.

Mike turned his head in concern. "Now, come on, Doll. What's there to be scared of? It's probably the first time that kid's ever used the radio."

"Well, I'm scared," Doll snapped. "Mike . . . can't we get off and catch a train or something?"

"You know we can't, Doll. We'd have to change all of our bookings . . . And it's too late. We're moving." He pressed the call button over his head, and when the stewardess came, asked, "How soon can we get a drink?"

"Just as soon as we're airborne, sir," she replied, and returned to her seat.

The take-off was smooth enough, and there wasn't very much heavy cloud over the city, but it was awe-inspiring to be climbing towards the blackness.

"Wasn't there a play or something called *A Long Day's Journey into Night*?" Doll asked. With a G and T in her hand, she was feeling better.

"We don't actually go up into that thing?" Mike asked the stewardess.

"Oh, no, sir. That's over 40,000 feet. We cruise at 35,000 feet."

"Don't seem a lot different to me," Bob muttered. "What happens if it comes down?"

The stewardess giggled. "Everyone's been praying for it to come down for months, sir."

"Wouldn't be much fun if we were underneath when it did," Mike pointed out.

And indeed, when the aircraft levelled off at its cruising altitude, the cloud seemed almost close enough to touch, while below them was another thick layer of cloud. "I feel like the filler in a sandwich," he remarked.

Yet the flight was quite smooth. The Captain came aft, smiling, to chat reassuringly with the passengers, and lunch was served. Fortunately the meal had been cleared when the warning buzzed and red alert lights came on. The stewardesses came round to make sure every belt was fastened. "There's a widespread area of turbulence ahead," they explained. "We should be through it real soon."

Meanwhile the in-flight movie was put on, something about a girl and her horse, kid's stuff in Mike's opinion. He'd had several beers and some wine with his lunch, so he drew his blind and closed his eyes. Doll watched the movie, more to occupy her mind than a desire to see some chick singing in the saddle.

Poor old girl, Mike sighed, she really was in a flap, and that was totally unlike his Dolly. Of course it was alarming, being able to see damn all in the middle of the afternoon, just looking up at that huge blackness. But he reckoned that if planes were allowed to fly it had to be safe.

Yet what had caused those other crashes?

He was disturbed by a violent shaking of the aircraft, a louder noise than usual, and sat up.

Doll clutched his arm. "Hell, Mike! What was that?" She was white as a sheet.

There was a considerable rustle throughout the cabin.

"Please remain seated, ladies and gentlemen," the stewardess said over the intercom. "We are in the middle of an electrical storm. We'll be through it in a few minutes."

The child star was weeping on the screen . . . her horse was sick.

Then there was another boom, and this time the screen went blank, while the whole aircraft seemed to sizzle. The engines changed their note, and the plane began to descend.

Mike looked up at the intercom, but there were only clicks and gurgles coming from that. Then he pulled back the shade to look out of the window, and gasped in horror. The afternoon had been very nearly dark anyway, but now it was 3 o'clock, and the black was sticking to the glass.

The cloud *was* coming down! Or some of it.

Hastily he closed the blind again so Doll wouldn't see, but others had, and there was a chorus of shouts and even screams from around them.

The stewardesses had got the intercom working. "Please don't be alarmed. The pilot is merely taking evasive action. Please . . . " She gave a startled exclamation as the plane gave another violent bump and lurch, and the engine noise altered for the second time – but this time was now quieter.

"Oh, shit," Mike muttered.

"What's happening?" Doll moaned. "Oh, what's happening?"

They'd lost an engine, Mike knew, but he didn't say so. "Dunno," he tried to sound casual. He pulled back the shade to look out again. But he could see nothing in the prevailing blackness. At three o'clock in the afternoon!

People were shouting, despite the stewardess's attempts to reassure them.

A few moments later another engine went.

"Ladies and gentlemen . . . this is your Captain speaking," his voice was amazingly calm. "I am afraid we have sucked ash into our intakes, and have lost *three* engines. This means we cannot maintain altitude. We are therefore descending on our remaining engine. I wish you to know that the aircraft is still under control, and there is every probability that we will be able to blow the jets clear as we drop away from the ash cloud. However, should this not be possible, we will be obliged to make an emergency landing on the nearest convenient airfield. The cabin crew are fully trained to help you and I would ask everyone to obey their instructions implicitly."

There was a moment of stunned silence after the Captain finished speaking, then a babble of sound broke out, punctuated, as before, by shouts and screams. But the hostesses were already moving about the cabin, speaking to each row of seats in turn.

" . . . all spectacles, and jewellery and shoes, specially high heels. I'm sorry, madam, but if we do come down you won't be able to take even your bag with you. False teeth . . . "

"Shit," Mike growled. He'd always hated anyone to know he had false teeth.

"Must do it, Mike," Doll told him, suddenly much calmer.

Mike passed his hand over his mouth and whipped out the teeth, transferred them to his jacket pocket. But the damned girl had seen him do it.

"Thank you, sir," she said. "Now remember, if the Captain does have to make an unscheduled landing, you bend forward and clasp your arms as shown in the emergency leaflet."

"What happens after that?" Doll wanted to know.

"Once we're down, all the emergency exits will be opened, and we'll have everyone out of the craft in ninety seconds," the girl assured her, and gave a bright if obviously forced smile. "We do it all the time in training."

As she spoke, the last engine failed, and the aircraft dropped like a stone.

The late night horror film ended, as usual, with the hero and the girl scared but reunited. Liz yawned and groped around for the control panel to switch off. It wasn't under the newspapers and magazines . . . "Aunt Madge. Hey, wake up, it's time to go to bed!"

Madge's knitting fell on to the floor as she sat up with a jolt. "Eh? Oh dear, I must have nodded off."

"You always do when we watch late. Have you seen the control?"

" . . . to bring you news just coming in of another air disaster, this time just south of Salt Lake City." The programme had switched to a newsroom.

"Ah, here it is. I can't think how it got into my knitting bag. Which button is it?" Madge peered shortsightedly at the hieroglyphics.

"They say things always work in threes," Liz commented.

"What?"

"Another plane down. That's the third in the past ten days."

They both watched the screen.

"We understand that this was Translink flight 303 out of San Francisco . . . "

"Oh God! No, it can't be!" Liz scrambled to her feet. "Where's Mum's letter?"

Madge understood immediately. "You put it on the mantelpiece, there, behind the clock."

Liz snatched it and flicked the pages. "Here . . . oh!" She sank back on to the settee, colour draining from her face.

Madge took the letter and read the details of the flight, twice, then stood taking deep breaths. "I'll put the kettle on."

" . . . has come down in a desert area north-west of the town of Lynndyl. It is reported to have two hundred and seventy-three passengers on board and a crew of ten. Rescue services have reached the scene but there are no reports yet of any possible survivors."

Mum! Dad!

" . . . programmes will continue, and we will bring you news flashes as more information comes in. Meanwhile, if you are concerned about friends or relatives on this flight, here is a number to call for information." Figures appeared on the screen. Then it went blank.

Liz came out of her trance. "Oh, hell! I didn't get it."

"I did." Madge put her notepad on the mantelpiece. "Kettle's nearly boiling."

Liz wasn't weeping. She didn't know if it was because her brain had gone numb or whether the thought of Dad and Mum's plane going down was just too impossible to believe. The idea of them being dead was ludicrous; they were far too alive, bouncy, full of fun. Mum was only fifty, and Dad fifty-two – they had years and years of living ahead . . . Maybe they'd missed the plane – Mum was never on time for anything. She got up and looked at the telephone number Aunt Madge had taken down.

"No good calling yet, Liz," Madge said over the mugs of tea. "Here, take this but don't scald yourself." She wondered if she should go upstairs and get her Bible, and pray. But either they were alive or dead, prayer couldn't make much difference now. Could prayer help Liz, though? She could hardly remember Mike and Doll. Doll was her sister's daughter, which made her Liz's great-aunt, actually. Doll and Mike were still only courting when she had married her Pommie RAF sweetheart and come back to England with him. Norman had taken her back to Oz on a visit five years ago, just one year before he died, but she had no desire to go back and live there. Her friends were here in London. She looked at her great-niece, sitting transfixed, wide eyes on the muted screen, unseeing, unblinking. She had come to love this lively, humorous, sweet-natured kid, and the hurt which was just beginning to penetrate the girl's mind was already hurting Madge herself. Almost as though this was the daughter she had longed for and never had.

The word *Newsflash* came up on the TV and she re-pressed the mute button.

" . . . no live coverage yet, but rescuers report wreckage scattered over a wide area. They tell us there can be virtually no hope of any survivors. The pilot, who was in continual radio contact, had reported successive engine failures, due, he believed, to the intake of volcanic dust at a height of 35,000 feet. Having received permission to make an emergency landing at Salt Lake City, he was beginning a gradual descent . . . "

"35,000 feet," Liz whispered. No one could possibly survive a fall from that height.

" . . . list of passengers will not be released until next of kin have been informed."

They sipped their tea in silence.

Madge and Liz both spilt tea in their laps as the old-fashioned phone bell jangled.

Madge got up to take it. "Yes? Oh, Sue. Yes. Yes, that's what we think. Yes, would you like to speak to her?"

Liz took the receiver "Sue? Was that the flight they told you? Yes, it's the one I was going to meet tomorrow morning . . . this morning I guess. That's the number I have on Mum's letter." She listened. "Do you think there's a chance they missed it? Oh, she called you this morning." A tear formed in the corner of her eye and began its way down the side of her face. "He called you from Perth? No, I haven't heard from him. Maybe he doesn't know about it yet. What about Bob and Meg's family?"

When Liz put the phone down Madge had to support her to the settee. There was no longer any doubt in their minds; no hope.

Mike and Doll were dead.

"Mummy? Jennifer here. I'm round at Liz's place."

Mary turned down the gas under the breakfast she was cooking.

None of the family had slept after hearing the news, but the men had had to go out for their morning chores as usual. "How is she?"

"Absolutely devastated."

"Is she going back to be with her family?"

"No. Not right now, anyway. They've talked it over and decided against. There is nothing for her to do there but grieve, you know."

"Quite. Well, what does she want to do? Is the wedding going ahead?"

"No. She wants to delay it for the time being. She needs time to get over it, I think. No point in walking up the aisle with tears streaming down one's face. Anyway, she's planning to fly across to the States to identify the bodies and arrange for the funerals."

Mary sighed. "Poor little lass. Give her a big hug from us both and tell her we're thinking of her all the time. Oh, and tell her, do, that we totally agree that the wedding must be postponed, but she is very welcome to come here and stay with us for as long as she likes. When she gets back from the States."

"I'll tell her. But I think she intends returning to work. She says she doesn't want to let them down as she'd promised to work on to the end of the month. I think she means to ask if she can keep the job."

"Bless her. What a dear kid she is. Thank goodness Madge is with her; such a level-headed person."

"They're both coming to stay with us for the weekend. The children's chatter will create a diversion, hopefully."

"Good idea, Jennifer darling. Come and see us soon."

"Yes, Mummy. We might bring them down next weekend. I'll see how they feel about it. Bye bye. Give Daddy and Freddie my love."

"And kisses from us to Jessica and Jackie. Bye bye."

Mary put down the phone and looked at her husband, who had just come in, having attempted to clean his boots outside the kitchen door. "Did you hear?"

He nodded. "Tell me . . . has anyone thought to tell Geoff? He was due to leave Halifax yesterday afternoon local time. He won't exactly have been watching TV."

"Reports indicate that the whole North Atlantic is a sea of ice," the pilot told Fogarty and his officers as *Skyhawk* steamed out of Halifax harbour. "Seems like the entire Arctic Ocean is moving south. Most of it is pretty thin at the moment, and is melting, but of course there are some growlers and even proper icebergs. You guys want to keep your eyes open."

The Captain nodded. "We've been routed further south than usual. And we're to operate at reduced speed." He grinned. "But

we have a problem. My first officer is getting married in a fortnight, so we can't afford to be late."

"Better late than never," the pilot pointed out, as he descended
to his launch. "But congratulations, buddy."

Geoffrey had just taken over the middle watch from Turnbull, and
was surprised to discover the old man still up – it was a measure of
his concern. Well, he was pretty concerned himself, although not
about the ice they were likely to meet. He was thinking more of the
implications. Melting of the ice in the Arctic Ocean had to mean a
rise in sea level. That didn't matter in the middle of the ocean, but
it surely would in coastal areas; he wondered what was happening
to East Anglia . . . and to Dunning Farm.

The whole world was turning increasingly topsy-turvy. As
Skyhawk proceeded into the night there were vivid flashes of lightning all about them . . . but these were sheet lightning, merely
caused by excessive heat. While the surface of the sea was covered
in a cloying mist; thank God for radar. Admittedly it was April, but
the atmosphere was like a really muggy summer's night.

"I'm off to bed," Fogarty said. "Call me if you see anything big."

"Will do." Geoffrey sat in the navigator's chair from where he
could watch both the Loran read-out and the radar screen. Walsh,
the coxswain, monitored the auto-pilot and the other instruments.
Below them the engines hummed reassuringly, and as there was no
wind there was no other sound.

Geoffrey looked at the chronometer, and grinned. Every second
that ticked away was taking him home, and to Liz. With all the
joyous future that lay ahead.

They had only slept together the once. But how he was looking
forward to repeating that, while knowing a pang of conscience that
he should be thinking of sex when this was a matter of love. He did
love her; sex was merely a by-product, an expression, of that love.

He thought of the wedding, the church and the flowers, the
morning suit for which he had already been measured, as had
Freddie. Freddie, in a morning suit!

"Ice." Walsh interrupted his reverie.

Geoffrey was on his feet and looking into the radar. It actually
looked like clutter, there was so much of it. But even after he'd
fiddled with the controls it was still there.

He rang down to reduce speed to Half Ahead, and the phone
buzzed.

"All right?" Fogarty asked.

"Looks pretty thin," Geoffrey told him. "I'm maintaining
course."

"Send men up front if you feel the need," Fogarty said.

Geoffrey decided to do that, just in case; it was so warm there was little chance of discomfort, much less frostbite. Now they were into the ice, and various clangs and scrapings came up from below, but so far as he could hear there was nothing dangerous; the plates damaged on the previous voyage had been replaced and strengthened.

Slowly *Skyhawk* moved ahead, while Walsh now watched the radar and Geoffrey peered out through the bridge screens . . . if the whole voyage was going to be like this, it was going to be a slow business. Still, not even a half-speed crossing of the Atlantic could make him late for the wedding . . . although it might be a near-run thing.

He looked at his watch. A quarter to four. Turnbull would be up any moment to relieve him, and brother, was he going to sleep! Presumably it was peering out into the night all the time, but he had never been so sleepy.

He half-turned his head as someone entered the bridge, but it was Harper. "Don't tell me, someone's broadcasting an ice warning," he suggested.

"There's a message for you, Geoff." Harper's voice was dull.

Now Geoffrey did turn, frowning. "For me? In the middle of the night?"

"From home," Harper said. "Here, you'd better read it."

Geoffrey took the sheet of paper covered in the print-out from Harper's receiver, and slowly sank into his chair.

Brrrr. Brrrr. Brrrr.

"For God's sake." Anne Dunning opened one eye, and draped an arm out of bed, seeking the telephone. There was a clatter as it fell off its rest and bounced on the carpet. "Oh, shit!"

Mark helpfully switched on the light, blinked at the glow. Like her, he had a head; as it had been her last night before departing for England and her brother's wedding, they had tied one on, dinner, dancing, and then a long evening's love-making. Now . . . it was five o'clock in the morning! And some idiot was telephoning?

"What?" Anne was saying. "What? You can't be serious. Oh, my God! But . . . how's she taking it? Shit! Oh, I'm sorry, Mummy. But . . . does Geoffrey know? Yeah. Yeah. Yeah, six o'clock this evening. Oh, don't worry, I'll find my own way. Should be with you for lunch tomorrow, anyway. Okay. I love you too."

Slowly she replaced the receiver.

"What's happened?"

She turned to look at him. "Mr and Mrs Bowman. Liz's parents.

They've gone down in a plane crash."

"Oh, no. Another?" Mark sat up, frowning. "That's the third in ten days."

"Mummy didn't have any details . . . save that the wedding's off." Anne found the remote control and switched on the television. She had to try several channels to find an early morning newscast.

" . . . there can be no doubt that ash sucked into the air intake caused this crash, as it seems to have caused the two previous recent crashes of high-altitude aircraft, despite official reluctance to confirm this. This is raising speculation that the ash-cloud may be breaking up and coming down to earth. The FAA has just announced that all big jets have been grounded until further notice."

"What the hell? I'm flying to England this evening," Anne shouted.

Mark was already in the bathroom. "Looks like you may have to cancel," he said, through a mouthful of toothpaste.

"Oh . . . " she couldn't think of an appropriate swearword. "And just where do you think you're going? It's only five-thirty in the morning."

"I'm catching the first available plane, or train, or bus, to Washington. If that thing is coming down . . . wowie!"

10

Crisis

"There is no real break-up of the cloud, so far as we can ascertain," Dave Obrenski was saying. "There has been intense electrical activity over the Rockies during the past few weeks, some at a very high altitude, and this has caused some of the ash to descend, which resulted in those crashes. Perhaps the Federal Aviation Authority should have acted sooner, but it is one mighty great decision to axe all high-level flying over this country or the Atlantic. Our decision is causing quite a furore amongst European and foreign airlines, which haven't yet encountered our problem. Our civilisation lives on air travel, Mark. Speed of communication is everything. Now the airlines are saying that if they have to fly at lower altitudes it will mean a whopping increase in fuel bills and therefore in seat prices, not to mention a hell of a drain on fuel supplies, and they're demanding compensation. So what do we do? Tell them to go out of business?"

"We're talking about survival, Dave," Mark pointed out.

"Yeah, so you say."

"You had any information on the situation in the North Atlantic, recently?"

"Sure, it's full of ice. But nothing heavy. We're monitoring the position hour by hour, and we have icebreakers out there ready to cut through anything big. Shipping is being slowed up, sure. Hell, the whole world is being slowed up."

"And no doubt you're also monitoring the flooding," Mark said.

"Of course we are. There's a lot of it in coastal areas. Of course it's no worse than it is in any normal year during storms. This time it's just lasting a little longer."

"And at least after a storm everything has a chance to dry out."

"True. Which it can't do right now. Even the water from the tsunami hasn't dried out completely. And as for the damage . . . I

145

don't know if Cape Cod is ever going to recover. It's sure going to be a different shape." He shoved his spectacles up his forehead and sighed. "We are having some problems down in the Carolinas, too, but we're still only talking about three feet."

"Because it's still just cool enough to keep the ice cap from really starting to melt, yes. But the temperature is climbing every day. What we have in the Atlantic is just peanuts compared with what we're going to have."

"Maybe. But we have to worry about what is serious right now. Flooding! You want to take a look at the midwest. And the boss is on the verge of declaring the south a disaster area because of the height of the Mississippi. We've been evacuating people by the thousand. And that's on top of the East Coast. Christ, when is that cloud going to move?"

"It isn't, Dave. Not without a shove. Look, you have got to get me another appointment with the President."

Obrenski scratched his ear. "You think he's going to listen?"

"He has to," Mark told him.

Liverpool was full of talk about the flooding. Everywhere the sea was a couple of feet higher than usual, and in many coastal areas people were permanently sandbagged against each rise of tide.

"At least it makes navigation easier," Lloyd Turnbull commented.

People were also discussing the ban on high-altitude flying, which was just beginning to be noticeable. Opinion seemed to vary from the well-what-will-they-think-of-next to the loudly voiced opinions of the airlines, businessmen and travel agents. On the other hand, there was apparently a queue for rebooking North American or Scandinavian holidays in the Mediterranean or even further south, where there were no problems, as yet . . . apart from exceptionally heavy rainfall, but this was expected to ease off in the summer.

Geoffrey went ashore and telephoned Aunt Madge's. Liz wasn't in so he left a message with Madge to say he was on his way. Then he called West Walton.

"It's pretty grim down here," Freddie told him. "But right now it's nothing but standing rainwater. The drains are still working at low tide, and no salt is coming up the river. Yet. But the North Sea levels are maintaining a good couple of feet above average. If it gets any higher . . . "

"What's the Government doing?"

"Oh, there's talk about building dykes like they have in Holland. Apparently the Dutch are coping pretty well at the moment, although they have their problems too. But of course the big one is money. The Government seems to be trying to get a consensus on cutting back spending on social security to fund a massive coastal protection scheme, and the Opposition isn't having any. So when are you coming down? If you stick to the main roads you should be all right."

"I'm going to London, first," Geoffrey said.

"Of course. Liz will be expecting you. Give her our love."

Love. She'd need a lot of that in the next few months. Perhaps he should apply for extra leave . . .

Geoffrey stuck to the motorway and found the going fairly easy, although it was disturbing to see the masses of water lying in every low-lying area he passed. He also had a shock the first time he stopped for petrol. He had a long-standing personal custom of never letting his tank get less than half full, which was just as well, because the pumps were manned, and the forecourt attendant would only allow him five gallons.

"We're behind with deliveries," she explained. "There's been trouble with tanker crews demanding more pay for unsatisfactory working conditions." She looked down at the black smudges left on her white overalls by the last shower of rain. "Unsatisfactory, and they're complaining. Shit!"

After that Geoffrey topped up at every other station, with the result that it was dusk before he drove into London. Here again the traffic was very heavy, but he had been warned by his radio as he approached the city; apparently the continuous wet and the flooding had caused the cancellation of many mainline trains.

He went straight to Aunt Madge's house, guessing she would offer him a bed. Luckily he found a parking space in the same road, but was dripping by the time he pressed the bell, and immediately the door was flung open by Liz.

She looked smaller than he had pictured her, and though she had obviously made a great effort to compose herself to greet him, it was necessary for her to bite hard on her lower lip. Gently he pushed her backwards into the hallway, closing the door behind him before taking her in his arms. He felt her shuddering sobs, pressed her head against his chest and let it all flood out.

She took a tissue out of her skirt pocket and blew her nose. "I should be in the States," she muttered. "But they are not sure if they've found all the bodies yet. Now they tell me I can't get there, anyway, except by boat. Oh, Geoff . . . "

As the tears streamed down her face again he half-carried her into the sitting-room and sat her on the settee, kissing her eyes and forehead, nose and mouth.

"Oh, Geoff," she sobbed. Then sniffed, and seemed to pull herself together. "Fix yourself a drink."

He poured Scotch. "For you?"

She didn't reply so he poured her one as well and sat beside her. "So when and where do we get married?"

"Oh, Geoff . . . how can we?"

He frowned. "What do you mean? You don't want to call it off altogether . . . ?"

She shook her head. "No. But don't you think we ought to postpone it for a while?"

"What sort of while? Days? Weeks? Months?"

She shrugged. "Months, I guess."

"Why?"

"Well . . . "

"Liz, I can't say anything helpful about your parents. I feel like hell about them. But we can't alter history. Do you still love me?"

She raised those deep green eyes to look at him, and he had his answer.

"I understand you don't want a big wedding," he said. "But I think we should get married, just as quickly as possible."

"How can we?" she asked again. "I mean, they've only been dead a week."

"And I only have a fortnight before going back to sea. And nobody on earth knows what's going to happen next. Don't you think, knowing that we love each other, your folks would want us to be married?"

She nestled in his arms again.

"I'll organise it," he said. "Just say 'yes'."

Geoffrey bought the special licence next morning, while Liz worked the last day of her notice at the hardware shop. The first date he could obtain at the Register Office was three days hence, but that at least gave Liz time to buy herself an outfit, Geoffrey time to buy her a ring, and both of their time to telephone everyone who mattered. Dunning Farm was delighted, and Jennifer got very excited.

"We'll do the reception," she said.

Aunt Madge was relieved; Liz's mood of depression had been bothering her and though she did argue that *she* should be doing the reception, she was only too happy to hand over the responsibility so that she could concentrate on helping Liz. They telephoned Australia, and Liz's brothers and sister also agreed. There did not seem any hope now of their parents' or Meg's and Bob's bodies ever being positively identified, and because of the ban on flying – while the question of altitudes was being worked out – there was no prospect of any member of the family reaching the United States for the mass burial of the crash victims. So life might as well go on as best it could.

John, Mary, Freddie and Doreen came down in the morning, and Geoffrey, Jennifer and Charles met them for a drink before going to the Register Office. The children were left with a friend and would return home for the reception.

Liz was sufficiently old-fashioned to insist upon not seeing Geoffrey, on the day, until the ceremony at twelve, so he spent his wedding eve at the Rowlands'. The local Borough Council had given the old courthouse building a facelift the previous year, brightening the Registrar's Office considerably, and Jennifer had worked wonders that morning with floral arrangements, so that the whole ambience was infinitely better than either Geoffrey or Liz had anticipated. Jennifer had gone shopping with Liz for the bridal outfit and convinced her, with the help of the saleswoman, that her parents would be horrified if they knew she was considering anything the slightest bit funereal.

"You owe it to them, to Geoffrey, and to yourself to make this as happy and cheerful an event as possible," Jennifer lectured. "You will get over the grief in a year or so, and you don't want to be stuck with miserable photos to show your children and grandchildren."

The happy couple from the previous ceremony posed on the stairs as it was too wet to stand outside, while John, Mary, Charles, Jennifer and Doreen filed up past them to the waiting-room, followed by Geoffrey, his uniform just back from the drycleaners smartly pressed and smelling of chemicals, and Freddie, who was one of the witnesses.

Mary had abandoned the hat she had trimmed so lavishly, in favour of a simple navy and white straw which complemented the little navy suit, trimmed in white. Jennifer, furthering her theory about not looking sombre, wore the outfit she had originally bought for the wedding, pink and white chiffon which clouded round her as she walked. Charles had suggested he carry a black tie in one pocket and grey in the other, to change as might be deemed necessary. Jennifer had whipped out a Golf Club tie and told him to wear that and shut up.

The six of them had moved into the office at the Registrar's invitation, before Liz and Madge finally arrived at five past twelve. The bride had not found it easy to leave her beautiful wedding dress hanging on the wardrobe door, a lovely, dreadful reminder of how much happier the day should have been, and Madge had had to gentle her through repeated bouts of tears during the morning. Geoffrey was relieved to see her smiling and dry-eyed as she walked towards him to the strains of Mendelssohn's Wedding March played on the Registrar's tapedeck, as well as a great surge of affection at the effort she had made with her appearance. The dress of palest green had a scalloped neckline and flared from her tiny waist to a scalloped calf-length hem. Shoes, gloves and picture hat were a perfect match and she was wearing his gift of diamond pendant and earrings, and carried a spray of orchids. Auburn curls framed her pale face and though she was obviously wearing make-up, her deep green eyes predominated, huge, against the almost translucent skin. She looked so tiny, so vulnerable. It was hard to believe this was the same bubbly, bouncing, confident girl he had met . . . just before Misreal exploded.

Madge, Liz's only relative in England, was the second witness, adding her name below Freddie's in the register.

The ceremony itself lasted only a few minutes, but the Registrar was kindness itself and particularly so to Liz.

Charles had organised a fleet of three taxis, and these conveyed them to the nearest dock, where a river launch waited to carry them down to Greenwich exactly as Liz and Geoffrey had done on their first date.

"What a wonderful surprise!" Liz cried, and thought it was even more splendid when she discovered that Charles had ice-cold bottles of champagne waiting to be served.

"Oh, Charles," Mary said. "You have done us proud."

"Must have cost a bomb," Freddie remarked.

"Yes, you must let me know what I owe you," Geoffrey muttered.

"Regard it as a wedding present, old man," Charles told him.

Miraculously it wasn't raining, and it was so warm that they were all able to stand in the stern and wave at the passing boats and people on the shore.

"Oh, Geoff," Liz said, holding his arm. "I feel almost happy. Is that very wrong of me?"

"It's what your mum and dad would have wanted," he consoled her. "And that makes me happy too."

By the time they reached Greenwich they were all slightly tipsy, and walked from the dock to the Rowlands' house, where the children were waiting with Jennifer's friend, in a state of high excitement. The sitting-room was filled with flowers and a modest but beautiful wedding cake stood on a round table in the centre of the carpet. Charles produced more champagne while Jennifer hurried into the kitchen and in a few minutes appeared with serving dishes of finger buffet, a large proportion of which was hot.

"You did all this at three days' notice?" Liz cried.

"Not too difficult in a modern kitchen. But I'm not in Anne's class. She'd have done it in one."

"What a shame Anne couldn't be here," Mary said. "You've never met her, have you, Liz?"

Liz shook her head. "I guess we all have a lot of meeting to do."

"I know, we could telephone her," Freddie said. "Let's do it."

Jennifer looked at her watch. "She'll be at work, probably, but we can try." She lifted the handset to dot out the number from memory, and waited. "Hello, sister dear! We were just saying 'wish you were here'. Geoffrey and Liz were married a couple of hours ago and we are all back here in Greenwich for a little family reception. What are you doing?"

Liz and Geoffrey were both called to receive Anne's congratulations, with Mary queuing up to speak to her older daughter.

Geoffrey joined Charles standing by the window looking out at the rain, which had started again.

"How're things in the money world?" Geoffrey asked.

"Pretty awful, most ways. I mean, business is still going, from our point of view. We're still handling the same number of clients who need their money looked after. But one hell of a lot of people are having to liquidate sizeable portions of their portfolio because of the fall in the stockmarket. Frankly, we're telling most of them to convert into gilts, because there doesn't seem any end in sight." He chuckled. "If enough do it, I suppose I'll be out of a job."

"Um," Geoffrey said. He had never earned sufficient money to know much about portfolios.

"You planning on a honeymoon?" Charles asked.

"No time. We'll have a night here in London, then it's out to the farm to try to put the Granny Wing together before I go back to sea. We'll have a honeymoon in the summer; I'm due for a month off then." He grinned. "If we can find anywhere the sun is shining."

"Why don't you nip down to Spain, old man? Have our villa in Javea. You've never been there, have you?"

"No, I haven't."

"I think you'd enjoy it. No view of the sea, I'm afraid. It's not actually on the coast, but on a mountain called Montgo some five kilometres back. About three hundred feet up. Lovely views of the valley, and not too hot in the summer."

"Well . . . " Geoffrey said hesitantly.

"You really are welcome to use it," Charles said. "Jennifer and I and the kids are going down there at the beginning of June." He grinned. "It'll be the last time we'll be able to beat the summer visitors, as next year Jessica will be at school. But we'll be back by the middle of the month, and it'll be all yours in July and August. When are you due home from your next voyage?"

"Well, June."

"Ah ... but that's no problem. As I said, we'll be back by the middle of the month. You can have the last fortnight. It's actually the best time to go."

"That sounds great. I'll have a word with Liz and let you know. But thanks, anyway. You're sure it isn't raining in Spain as well?"

"As a matter of fact, I believe it is. But they're used to it down there. Anyway, it'll have stopped by the summer. It always does."

After they had demolished most of the buffet, and Jackie had made himself sick on endless chipolata sausages, John proposed a toast to the bride and groom. They had agreed to avoid speeches; there was little anyone could say without touching on the tragedy which was in all their minds. Together, Geoffrey and Liz cut the cake, and then it was Jessica's turn to gorge herself – on icing.

A taxi arrived for the newly-weds. There were hugs and kisses all round. Freddie said, "See you tomorrow," and Charlie added, "Don't forget about Spain."

"What about Spain?" Liz asked as Geoffrey slid on to the seat beside her, and became quite animated as he explained.

"Could be a good place for a late honeymoon," Geoffrey suggested.

Geoffrey had booked them into the Derwent Hotel, reasoning it would be better to luxuriate in splendour for one night, rather than something cheaper for a longer stay. Their room was spacious with a vast double bed, a lounge area complete with settee, armchairs and crystal chandelier, a huge marble bathroom and excellent room service from which they had ordered optimistically. But the coq au vin just served by the floor waiter didn't look as though it would fare much better than the half-eaten prawn cocktails he had removed.

The forced gaiety of the reception had proved exhausting, particularly for Liz, and seeing the strain in her face as she tried to keep up some form of conversation, Geoffrey wanted to say "Stop! You don't have to weary yourself anymore, just for my sake." But he didn't, reasoning that it was better in the long run for her to keep going. This was not going to be the honeymoon night he had been dreaming about throughout the last voyage.

They both pushed their dinner plates away at the same moment, and the coincidence made them laugh.

Liz grimaced at the amount of food still untouched. "What a waste." She sighed. "Poor darling, I'm so sorry it has happened this way."

"Just as long as you don't regret going ahead with the wedding . . . "

"Certainly not. It was the best possible decision. The thought of spending another night alone in my little room at Aunt Madge's, fighting to sleep, trying to escape mental pictures of the crash, was horrendous. Dearest Geoffrey . . . " she left her chair to come and stand behind him, hug his head against her chest, pressing kisses through his hair.

Inevitably the waiter knocked at that moment and she rushed back to her seat.

"Dessert?" the Italian asked as he removed the dishes.

"Only coffee for me. Decaffeinated," Liz said.

"Same for me," Geoffrey agreed. They both needed a good night's sleep. He didn't anticipate much else.

"It's only 9.30," he remarked when the table had been wheeled away with the coffeepot. "Do you want to watch some television?"

"I'd prefer a bath." Liz yawned and ran her fingers through her hair. "How about you?"

"You go ahead and give me a shout when you're finished."

"What, won't you tub with me, you stuffy Pom?"

He turned to stare at her. "Seriously?"

"Start as you mean to go on, I say." She moved away towards the bathroom door, hands reaching over to wrestle with the top of the zipper on the back of her dress.

Geoffrey jumped out of his chair. The evening was beginning to brighten.

The hotel supplied little bottles of shampoo and bath foam. Liz emptied the latter under the tap while Geoffrey attacked his beard for the second time that day, and when he turned round she had almost disappeared under the meringue topping that climbed out of the bath and up the tiles.

Geoffrey dropped his towel on the floor and climbed in, gasped as his back touched the hot taps. His toes slid up the outside of her thighs leaving him feeling extremely vulnerable. "Careful with those feet of yours," he warned.

"Why? What of?" she asked innocently, reaching with her toes to tickle the vulnerable area and completely disappearing under the foam. She surfaced, spluttering. "Ugh! You'd think in a smart bathroom like this they'd install decent double baths."

"London hotels are built for respectable citizens. They do not cater for Australian morals," her husband explained. And had his head smothered in a blanket of foam.

The tussle that followed ended with them in each other's arms, kissing and caressing under the foam.

They dried each other on huge bath sheets, turned the hairdryer on each other's heads, laughed; forgot about the tragedy, the cloud . . . everything.

"Where's this scar?" he asked.

"How'd you know about that?"

"I saw it on your passport, on board *Skyhawk*."

"You bastard. Do you look at all the women's passports?"

"When they're worth looking at, yes."

She stuck out her tongue at him, then bent over to show him the discoloured area tucked in beneath her right buttock.

"Looks like a bite."

"Right first time."

"You must've known some funny fellows in Australia. And he must've had a big mouth."

"He was a she."

"Now you tell me."

"A sow."

"A what?"

"She went oink, oink, just before coming at me, if that helps. I was twelve, she was just a mother, and I was too close."

"Lady," Geoffrey said. "You have *lived*. Do you show everyone that?"

"Only when they're worth the look," she answered wickedly.

When they reached the bed they were roused, wanting. Liz pulled him over her, needing his immense body to envelop her, crush her. She loved him, passionately, wanted to lose herself in his love, take him into herself.

He tried to be gentle, afraid to hurt her, afraid to seem too eager when she must be feeling so fragile . . . but she lifted to him, surged against him, leaving him in no doubt that she needed this passionate consummation of their marriage to erase the agony of the past few days.

But Liz knew it was more than even that. When, after falling into a deep, healing sleep they had made love again in the small hours, she knew the fears, uncertainties and miseries resulting from all the failed relationships she had had with other men in the past few years were also erased. This total awareness and understanding of each other's needs, this fervent mental and physical loving, was truly different from anything she had ever known before.

Geoffrey felt her deep sigh of contentment, and smiled into the darkness.

In the morning the rain was quite heavy, hitting the windowpanes, reducing the meagre light edging round the curtains. Geoffrey awoke from a dream in which he and Liz were both on the bridge of *Skyhawk* clinging to each other as the ship plunged through a storm, and then realised that she was actually in his arms. His wife! He felt an immense sense of elation, and an even greater sense of responsibility.

She opened one eye. "Hi!"

He kissed her. "Breakfast?"

"That sounds great."

He switched on the bedside light, but nothing happened. "Damned bulb is blown," he complained. "I'll get them to change it when they bring up the meal." He dialled Room Service.

"I'm sorry, sir, but a cooked breakfast is not possible at this moment, sir," Room Service told him.

"Why not?"

"There is no electricity, sir. We can make coffee, and heat croissants in our gas oven, but our main facilities are inoperable."

"Oh, hell. Well, coffee and croissants it will have to be." He thumped the receiver back in place.

"Don't tell me, there's a power failure," Liz said. "There have been several of those this last month. Seems that fuel supplies aren't getting through to the power stations, because so many people are out on strike. Complaining about the working conditions. And then there are problems with conduits getting wet because of all the rain. Brrr. Nobody seems able to cope."

"Let's get back out to the farm," he decided. "Just as soon as we can. Find some sanity."

Being married, Geoffrey decided, was wonderful, and Liz seemed to think so, too. To be able to enjoy sex in a leisurely fashion in the morning after breakfast, to stand naked thigh to naked thigh while they cleaned their teeth, and then share a shower together, to watch Liz dress, inspired a feeling of intimate togetherness he had never suspected possible, made him wonder why he had waited so long . . . except that had he married earlier he would not have found Liz.

"Sorry about the brief honeymoon," he said as they got into the car. "I did phone Captain Fogarty about extending my leave but the company is desperately busy at the moment as the sea is the only method of crossing the Atlantic. He would have said yes if I'd insisted, but he is obviously under such extra pressure I hadn't the heart. Anyway, there will be a better chance of some sun later in the year."

"Yes," she said, "we sure could use some."

It continued to rain all the way out to Norfolk. The journey took several times longer than usual, because once they left the main roads there were endless detours around flooded areas, while the car radio kept up a constant stream of travel information: breakdowns here, subsidences there, warnings about boiling all water because of contamination from overflowing reservoirs, interspersed with economic news, of wholesale lay-offs in many businesses both because of strikes by workers unable to cope with flooded shopfloors or because of a catastrophic drop in demand for consumer goods, and sad news of whole flocks of sheep and herds of cattle caught by floodwaters and drowned. The stock market, as Charles had forecast, was down to its lowest level for several years, and the volume of trading sluggish.

"I had no idea things had deteriorated so badly over the past couple of months," Geoffrey said.

"Your country is grinding to a halt," Liz agreed. "But it's even worse in Scandinavia and Russia. Apparently they can't handle the exceptional weather."

"I wish I could take you to sea with me," he said. "It's all still relatively civilised there. We make our own power, and we're used to the weather."

Geoffrey was even more distressed when he saw Dunning Farm. They arrived following a large covered lorry, which splashed through the yard and came to a halt in front of the barn. This was sandbagged, but Freddie and John were waiting to move the bags and greet the truckers, who promptly began unloading sacks of artificial fodder.

"This is the only way we can feed the animals," Freddie explained. "It's a Government service for areas where the hay has all rotted. But I haven't kissed the bride since yesterday." He enveloped Liz in a bearhug, and John was waiting to do the same, while Mary beamed from the shelter of the doorway.

"You know something . . . I feel I've come home," Liz said, trying not to give way to an emotional outburst.

Mary hugged her. "That's good to hear. You and Geoffrey will have five lovely days together installing yourselves in The Wing. The heating is on gas, which is holding up quite well, but it is still a bit smelly."

"Do you want me to carry you over the threshold?" Geoffrey asked.

"Later," Liz smiled. "Your Ma and I are going to have a cup of tea first, in her kitchen, I think."

So he left the women together, while he surveyed the farmland with his father and Freddie. It was entirely under water which was several inches deep, saving only for the knoll where the buildings were situated. As the Government lorry disappeared in the distance, he turned to his father. "How much did that lot cost?" he asked.

"Not a penny. It's a Government handout," John told him.

"Then things aren't quite so bad as I thought."

John glanced at him. "Because we can keep half a dozen cows alive free of charge? That's it, Geoff. Our winter crops have all been lost, and we should've been sowing these last six weeks. There is going to be nothing this year. Absolutely . . . bloody nothing."

Geoffrey gave a low whistle. "Surely the Government will help there too?"

"They're talking about it. And the Farmers' Union is lobbying like hell. But then, so is everybody else. There just isn't enough money available to cope with a disaster like this. And there's no end in sight. That's the horrifying part."

"Okay, Doctor," the President said. "Looks like you were right and we were wrong. That cloud doesn't appear to be going anywhere."

Today he was flanked by the Chiefs of Staff.

"So tell us your prognostication."

"Well, sir," Mark said, "I think we are already too late for this year. In another few weeks it's going to be summer, and there is no way we are going to arrest the melting process now. But I believe it can be ameliorated, and we have to think of next winter. This summer we are going to have flooding on a gigantic scale, and we will have virtually to re-finance our entire farming community. But by restoring the status quo we can make sure that the ice cap reforms and the water is taken off next winter, then at least we're back to square one. If we do not accomplish that, then we have to face the fact that life on this planet may not ever be the same again."

The President glanced at his advisers.

"And your solution is to disperse the cloud by the use of atomic explosions," said General Mitchell.

"I cannot think of any other way it is going to be done, sir."

The General turned to the Colonel at his side. "Colonel Hawes?"

"Based on the latest estimates of the amount of ash still up there," the Colonel said, "I would say we are talking of several twenty-megaton warheads. These can be delivered by ground-based missiles, timed to explode at the appropriate altitude. However, without an international consensus, we would be breaking international law, not only because we would be in breach of the general Atmospheric Test Ban Treaty but because several of the bombs would necessarily have to be detonated over the territory of other nations."

General Mitchell turned to the man on his left. "Major Worthington?"

The Major cleared his throat. "We would be dealing here with an indeterminate problem as regards fallout. Okay, so the devices would be detonated at a height of 40,000 plus feet, and one device would probably have an effect of not more than ten plus Rems here on earth . . . "

"One moment, Major," the President said. "Define Rem."

"A Rem, sir, is a measurement of radiation, from any cause; it is equivalent to one Rad of X-rays."

The President smiled. "Then perhaps you had better define Rad as well, Major."

"A Rad, sir, is the basic unit of radiation dose: it equals one hundred ergs of energy transferred to one gram of tissue. I should stress that this is a very small unit. For example, one pound of tissue receiving one Rad is absorbing energy equivalent to a three-hundredth part of the necessary energy to lift the pound one foot."

"Ah," the President said, looking somewhat baffled. "What is the lethal dose for man?"

"That is the variable factor, sir. The atomic bomb dropped at Hiroshima produced as many as 5,000 Rems in certain areas; in that case death was virtually instantaneous. Some people received between 400 and 800 Rems, and death there was pretty certain, although some took longer than others. Most of those who received in the range of 150 Rems plus survived, although often with significant hair loss and internal damage, and of course, genetic damage as well. We generally reckon that 150 Rems is about as high as man can take and live. I'm talking about a single dose, of course. Under that, well, in most people a dose of less than 100 Rems is not even noticeable, at least in the short term. But there have been cases where 30 Rems have caused severe illness."

"You're speaking about immediate effects, Major," Mitchell said. "But isn't it true that a single Rem is actually lethal in the long run?"

"Well, sir, you could say everything, or anything, is lethal in the long run. Depending upon a person's general state of health, every

Rem received shortens life by between two and fifteen days. But then an overdose of sun can inflict a Rem. It is a generally accepted principle that man's whole body can take ten Rems every thirteen weeks, without suffering discernible ill-effects, and a dose of say twenty-five Rems once in a lifetime, again without observable ill-effect."

"So you reckon that if a fallout of ten Rems reached the earth there would be no serious risk to health," the President said.

"Correct, sir. However, we're talking about using several devices, in which case the Rem incidence could be conspicuously greater."

"The bombs would be as widely spaced as we could make them," Hawes said.

"That may not necessarily have the effect of limiting fallout, Colonel. Much will depend on the wind strength and direction immediately after the explosion."

"There isn't any wind," Mitchell pointed out.

"At the moment," Mark put in. "That's because the cloud is maintaining an almost even pressure pattern across the northern hemisphere. Once the cloud breaks up, or even starts to break up, there's going to be a lot of wind. In fact, this is something we have to discuss."

"Say, I thought this was your baby, Doctor?" Mitchell demanded.

"It is. I just want to make sure there are no misapprehensions."

"How's about we just fire one device?" Hawes suggested. "That might just get the whole thing going."

"And if it doesn't we have to start all over again," the Press Secretary remarked. "You guys keep talking about fallout. Any of you calculated the political fallout when this idea becomes known? They're gonna be lining up from the White House to New York to protest."

The President stroked his chin. "All right, gentlemen. Now I want one-word answers where possible. Certainly one sentence. Doctor: what are the odds on this cloud breaking up under its own volition before next winter?"

"Long, sir. It's been there six months already."

"Right. You reckon that anything we do this minute will have no effect on what's happening now?"

"I believe we can check it, sir. Right now there is no real evidence that the permafrost has started to melt. If we can restore temperatures now, before the weather gets too much warmer, then we can keep flooding limits to the present heights, with which we can just cope. If we do nothing, odds are the temperatures in August may be equatorial. In which case the flooding problem is going to be massive."

"But the vital thing is to get that water back where it belongs, in the Arctic Circle, by next winter?"

Mark hesitated. Then he said, "Ultimately, that has got to be our objective, sir, yes."

"So we just let all air travel and a hell of a lot of other things, go hang, is that it?" the Press Secretary inquired. "That ain't gonna pull in too many voters either."

"We'll have to get the situation across to them," the President said. "That's your baby, Jimmy. General Mitchell, I wish you and your staff to prepare a detailed study of the amount of energy we are going to need to disperse that cloud, and the estimated amount of fallout that is going to result. I want that report as soon as possible. Dave, I want you to put together a staff of top scientists, and the moment we get that report, they, and you, head off to every capital which can possibly be involved, and sell the story. I hope you will be associated with this, Dr Payton."

"Of course, sir."

"Joe, I want you to get hold of all the leading manufacturers of protective clothing, and assemble them here in the White House for a chat. Jimmy, ditto with a selection of the more influential Congressional leaders, and then the media. You'll say nothing about our decision, just that the President wants to put them in the picture as to what we're planning to do about the situation."

"It's gonna leak," the Press Secretary, Jimmy Desmond, said dolefully. "It always does. Guys are gonna put two and two together . . . "

"We'll have to ride that. But not a word of what we have agreed here today must go out until all possible data have been processed and those groups necessary have been informed by me in person."

"With respect, Mr President," Mark said. "In view of the urgency of the situation, what *have* we agreed here today?"

"We have agreed, Doctor, to seek a national and international consensus for your plan. I hope you're satisfied."

At last something was being done. It might be too late to prevent a great deal of hardship and even, Mark feared, loss of life. It was also an immense leap into the dark. But at least, he felt, it would avert a catastrophe which could well plunge civilisation into another Dark Age.

He had arranged with Obrenski that he would be contacted and given his briefing the moment Mitchell's staff came up with the necessary facts and figures; that had to be within a week at the outside, because the weather was hotting up all the time. Then he'd be on his way to England, which he had chosen as his patch – he felt

160

he knew the British, and could communicate with them better than with anyone else.

Besides, he wanted to call on the Dunnings. Anne had told him that Geoff and Liz Bowman had actually gone ahead and got married. He reckoned that was a sensible decision to make. But he had more than congratulations in mind.

It wasn't a case of asking for Anne's hand of course. But he did want to have a look at the family at first-hand, just to harden the decision which was slowly forming in his mind.

He had never considered marriage in his life before, to anyone. Girls, and then women, had fulfilled a necessary function, great fun to have around when one was in the mood, absolutely necessary from time to time, but unless they happened to be colleagues – and there weren't all that many female vulcanologists – he had not reckoned they were really creatures with whom to share an essentially busy life; they were simply too demanding, of attention, of niceties which a busy man might not always instinctively provide. Never in his life had he even given a girl flowers.

Anne Dunning had changed all of that. She lived her own life, that of an utterly liberated woman, and he knew she would never attempt to interfere with his. But she would always be there, totally organised, interested when he wanted to talk shop, efficient when he wanted efficiency, amusing when he wanted to be amused, and sexy when he wanted sex.

So she was probably an encouragement for him to be even more of a MCP than he already was; but she accepted him for what he was, apparently had no desire to change him in any way, was content to regard him as equal if different.

She was the woman he wanted to marry. If she'd go along with that. He felt that being accepted by her family might be important . . . even if she'd never acknowledge it.

New York, and a dreary wait between trains. Everything was running late, because more people were now using trains. Granted the local airlines weren't affected by the ban, which only applied to aircraft flying at more than 30,000 feet, the ever-present psychological fear of flying had become accentuated by the three disasters in rapid succession.

Mark telephoned Boston. "Should be with you about ten," he said.

"Foddered?"

"I'll grab something on the train."

"How'd it go?"

"We're winning. I'll tell you about it."

"Hurry along," she said.

The train pulled out forty-five minutes late. Mark bought sandwiches and a Coke, settled down with a magazine.

Time drifted, and he was dozing off when the lights went out and the train stopped. People were shouting and swearing, and a guard came down the aisle with a flashlight.

"Sorry, folks. There's been a power outage. They're working on it, but we may be here a little while."

"Can we stretch our legs?" a woman asked out of the gloom.

"Sure thing, ma'am, but I got to tell you . . . it's raining out there."

Mark got up and felt his way through the various pushing bodies to the rear platform. Several people had descended on to the path beside the track. It was impossible to tell if they were near any civilisation; the evening was utterly dark. And the rain was settling everywhere in a steady downpour.

"Christ, what a mess," someone growled. "Every goddam thing is falling apart in this country. No planes, trains running late, electricity outages . . . what the hell is the Government doing?"

"The best it can," Mark suggested.

"Who the hell are you? Some kind of spokesman?"

"Look, buddy, all I said was the Government is doing the best it can," Mark told him.

"Shitting asshole," the man said, and threw a punch.

11

The Party

"You said ten o'clock." Anne Dunning peered at Mark Payton as he came through the door.

"I know. You got any alcohol in this place?"

"Name it."

"Brandy."

"At three o'clock in the morning?" Her shoulders gave a little shudder beneath the dressing-gown as she made her way to the bar and poured. "Let me guess . . . there was a power outage."

"Correct." He took a long draught from the balloon glass, pulling her against him at the same time. "Oh, honey! Does that feel better! And" – his free hand slid over the gown while he buried his face in her hair – "do you feel good."

"You mean I would've done, a couple of hours ago." She looked down at the lace edging of the gown. "For Chrissake, Mark, you're bleeding."

"Not again! I thought they'd fixed me up."

She peered at him. "You're covered in plaster. And blood. And bruises. What in the name of God . . . ?"

"There was this guy . . . "

She guided him to the settee.

"Actually," he explained, "the worst delay was caused by the police . . . "

"Okay," Anne was saying, arranging the pillows. "You're on an assault charge . . . "

"He threw the first punch."

"And then he threw several more, from the look of things. But you're the one on the charge, and $5,000 bail. Right?" The dressing-gown was draped over the back of a chair and she wriggled across the bed to lie against him.

"They just don't understand," Mark grumbled. "None of them do. They were upset by the outage, and the train delays, and the grounding of the planes . . . and the heat. They think no one's doing anything, just letting things slide from bad to worse. And I tried to explain. But it was damned difficult without letting the cat out of the bag. It's all a deadly secret. You do understand, don't you, Annie?"

"You ever call me Annie again and your other eye will be blacked. So the President gave the go-ahead."

"Well, yes and no. He's still hoping."

"Aren't we all! Mark, if he does press the button, do you have any real idea what is going to happen?"

"It has to be better than a fifty-foot rise of tide."

"I hope to God you're right." Her fingers caressed him from head to knee, circling his ears, stroking his neck, playing tantalising games with his nipples. Suddenly she peered at him. "I'm not having much success. Not turning on tonight?"

"Well, I am. But . . . "

"Oh, sure," guessing. "Where'd he kick you?"

"Where it hurts."

She giggled and sat up. "And you're the one on bail. Mark . . . what does *he* look like?"

Mark grinned. "He already had two black eyes when I last saw him. And his mouth was bleeding."

"Now, Mr Appleyard," said the BBC presenter, "there are rumours coming from the United States that the Administration is actually considering the use of nuclear weapons to disperse the ash cloud. May I have your comments on that?"

"I have never heard such nonsense in my life," said Mr Appleyard, a somewhat florid gentleman who was apparently a spokesman for the Government. "And may I point out that the United States Government has absolutely no legal right to explode nuclear weapons in the atmosphere. It is a signatory of the Test Ban Treaty."

"You think the results would be serious, do you?"

"Serious? My dear fellow, it would be disastrous. It would be like loosing a cloud of chlorine gas upon an entire neighbourhood, while the inhabitants are in residence, in order to rid one dwelling of rats."

"Hm. But what of the rise in water levels and the consequent flooding predicted unless something is done?"

"Poppycock, in my opinion. There may well be a rise in water levels. But only in the North Atlantic. My dear fellow, consider the size of the oceans. Any rise will be very rapidly absorbed into that vastness."

"What do you mean by very rapidly? We already have sea level rises of three to four feet in the North Sea, and this is causing problems. If this were to increase dramatically . . . "

"Well, the North Sea is a special situation, of course."

"Why?"

"Simply because it is virtually landlocked. Any rise of sea level coming from the north has to find its way out through the Dover Strait, and that is going to cause a considerable backing up of water and consequent local flooding. But it will all be absorbed in time."

"How much time?"

"I should not put it at longer than a few weeks. Possibly a month."

"From when?"

"Well . . . from when the sea level rise begins."

"It has already begun."

"Well, from when it reaches critical proportions."

"What would you describe as critical proportions?"

Mr Appleyard began to look a little hot under the collar.

"What advice, for instance, would you give a farmer in East Anglia?" the presenter pressed, "during this period between a critical rise in sea level and the dissipation of the flood waters by natural processes?"

"I assure you that the Government is doing all it can. Why, at this moment, levees are being built . . . "

John Dunning turned the set off in disgust.

"Do you reckon that's to keep the water out, or keep it in?" Freddie asked his brother, as they pulled the Land Rover into the side of the road to look at the men building the levee.

Geoffrey glanced from right to left. The dam was being constructed some one hundred yards from the A17, on the seaward side; a huge sluice gate was being constructed over the River Nene. From the beginning there had been a great deal of controversy over it, and over the other levees being built along the seashore and down in Essex, because it meant requisitioning private land, while of course some areas had to be omitted. Of immediate interest to the Dunnings, of course, there was no way that King's Lynn itself could be dammed against a rise in the Great Ouse, while here on the other side of the river, where The Wash threatened Holbeach Marsh and towns like Boston and Wisbech, the area needing protection was so enormous that the cost was becoming astronomical. To add to the furore, questions were being asked in the House about the special measures being taken to secure the safety of the royal residence at Sandringham, south of the Ouse.

As a seaman, Geoffrey could not see that the whole thing was going to be much more than a cosmetic exercise. The sea was too vast, too inexorable an enemy. Right this minute, it was peaceful, lost in the rain mist. But this he found the most frightening thing of all.

It was April, and since last September there had not been a gale. There had hardly been a wind above Force Two. Just a constant drizzle and a steadily increasing heat which had him wiping his neck even now.

In the past there had of course been vast areas of shallow low pressure over the northern hemisphere which had lasted for weeks . . . but never for months. Just as there had never been an entire winter without sunshine before. Equally, there had never been a winter as warm.

Now there was this constant mist, a vast sucking up of water vapour, which had nowhere to go, and would not even rise high enough to condense.

Geoffrey had a terrible feeling that it was all building towards an immense bang. And he was heading south in a week. How he wished he could take Liz with him . . . but *Skyhawk* was fully booked. Too many other people just wanted to get out of England.

He asked Freddie as they drove back to Dunning Farm, "What's your plan?"

"Do I have a plan?" Freddie's shoulders rose and fell. "Borrow, I suppose. And hope that one of these days that cloud goes away."

"Will it be a problem? Borrowing, I mean?"

"Shouldn't be. The Government is virtually underwriting loans for farmers. And a lot of other people besides." He gave a crooked grin. "It'll all have to be paid for, eventually. By us."

"Our first separation," Liz said as she helped Geoffrey put the suitcases into the car. "Since our marriage, I mean."

"I'll be back at the beginning of June. We're going to celebrate Midsummer's Day. That's when the sun is going to come out. According to some pundit."

"What the man said was, if the sun *doesn't* come out on Midsummer's Day, it will be the end of the world. You don't suppose he's right?"

He grinned. "No chance of that. People like your friend Mark Payton are going to make it happen by blowing up the atmosphere." He frowned at her expression. "Sorry, it was a bad joke. They'll never let him do it."

"Geoff . . . " she clung to him. "I'm frightened."

"This time next year it'll all be history," he promised her.

All be history. Was that possible?

Liz watched till Geoffrey's little car was out of sight before she went back into their home and closed the door. She had wondered if she would always feel the Wing was just a corner of the Dunning family home – but strangely enough she didn't. They had definitely made it their own; put their own character stamp on it. While Geoffrey had been at sea last time, she had collected up lots of photos of both their families and had enlarged copies framed. These now hung on the freshly emulsioned walls, together with a set of Australian pictures Aunt Madge had given her as a wedding present. She had bought material for cushion covers that matched the ready-made curtains, and potted ferns provided greenery, occasionally with silk flowers added for colour as fresh blooms were almost impossible to find.

It had been great fun to cook their own meals in the little kitchen, curl up on the velvet-covered Chesterfield in front of the TV in the evenings, and giggle together as the old brass bedstead squawked and groaned its protests under their activities. The family had been so sweet, leaving them strictly alone until Liz and Geoffrey invited themselves over for a meal.

And now? Well, she was going to try hard to control her thinking; not be morbid. There were hundreds of things to do, to make, repair, redecorate. She would keep busy. And if she had time on her hands she would help Mary with one of her projects. And maybe, when she had settled down, she would get the curse again. It had failed to turn up for two months in succession . . . but that was obviously due to a combination of wedding excitement, weather oppression and, finally, the aircrash.

She was grinning to herself as she put her own kettle on the stove and took a cup and saucer, covered in little rosebuds, out of the cupboard. Jennifer had given her the teaset as a present.

"All be history," he had said.

But Geoffrey, as he drove through the rain and mist to Liverpool, admitted he was frightened too. He had this odd feeling that the entire world had been carried back in time; it must've been like this a few million years before. When a lorry loomed out of the mist, for a moment he almost imagined it was a dinosaur.

The thing about a few million years ago was that there had been no people, no elaborate civilisation. Now, slowly, but inexorably, civilisation, at least in the northern hemisphere, was grinding to a halt. As it was happening slowly, people seemed only half aware of it. They could still relate what was happening to events, occurrences, disasters that had happened before. They had not yet grasped the immensity of this crisis, which was all of those past disruptions of society by weather rolled into one. And they were also still hoping that all of a sudden the cloud would disappear and let life get back to normal.

Well . . . it might.

But that was hardly going to alter what was happening, and seemed likely to go on happening this summer. It was not going to restore normal communications in a hurry, nor reverse the apparently catastrophic slide in the stockmarkets; it was not going to restore production levels or ameliorate the swingeing tax increases which would be necessary. Equally it was not immediately going to put an end to all the strikes or all the various failures of electrical equipment resulting from the all-pervading damp.

Most of all, it was not immediately going to dissipate the floodwater which was lying everywhere, and which had turned East Anglia into a vast swamp. And which was driving his family into bankruptcy.

He regarded *Skyhawk* as an island of sanity, but was brought sharply back to reality when Fogarty told him they were first of all going to have to cross the Atlantic to the States to stock up with fuel oil, because there was a shortage in England. It was going to add at least a week to their voyage.

He telephoned Liz. "I'll still be back by Midsummer's Day, I promise," he told her.

"We're booked, Calais-Dover, eleven tomorrow," Charles announced. "Should be south of Paris by nightfall."

"And then, sunny Spain," Jennifer said, hopefully. "Oh, I wish you could all be coming with us."

"Judging by the reports, it isn't all that sunny in Spain right this minute," Freddie warned.

"So it's been raining," Charles said. "But they have had some sunshine as well. The dust cloud doesn't stretch that far south."

"What's the news about Geoff?" Jennifer asked Liz.

He'd been gone six weeks.

"Well, because they apparently had to hunt for fuel, they're going to be late back. But in another three weeks or so he'll be here. Say, Jennie . . . I'd like you to come and tell me what you think about the bedroom curtains. I'll put the kettle on and we can have a natter."

She grabbed an old golf brolly and held it over them both as they dashed round the building to the other front door.

"That's new," Jennifer said, picking up a photograph and examining it.

"My sister sent it ages before the wedding. It's taken months to get here. Her nursing uniform looks more like some kinda space suit, doesn't it?" She put cups and saucers on to a tray.

Jennifer watched. "We usually use mugs at home."

"Oh! I thought I was being ever so English! Your Ma always uses cups."

"All her generation do. Now where are these curtains?"

"What curtains?"

Jennifer laughed. "The ones you asked me to come over and look at." She looked at her sister-in-law suspiciously, "Or was that just an excuse for a private gossip?"

Liz grinned. "Well . . . " She heated the pot before dropping in the teabags " . . . the fact is I haven't had a curse for months." She carried the tray into the sitting-room and curled her feet up in a corner of the Chesterfield.

Jennifer kicked her shoes off and did the same. "So when is junior due?"

"Due! I haven't even worked out how many I've missed. I never was very regular and when the first one didn't turn up I thought it was wedding nerves. Or maybe the weather. Then later, when Mum and Dad died, I thought the emotional stress might have stopped it. But I've been feeling a bit nauseated in the evenings lately."

"Which confirms it!"

"Does it? I thought one got morning sickness . . . not evening."

"Anytime. It was always when I was preparing evening meals that my tummy misbehaved. I was fine in the mornings. Congratulations!" Jennifer added.

"Hold it! You weren't listening properly when I said I thought I missed the first one because of the wedding . . . before the wedding." She watched a big grin spread over Jennifer's face. "It's all very well for you to sit there looking like a Cheshire Cat. What's your Ma going to say when she hears her third grandchild was conceived out of wedlock?"

"Oh, come on! She may have old-fashioned ideas about teacups, but she put me on the pill at sixteen."

"She did! Dammit, she's more mod than I'd thought. And I've been worrying myself spare!" She poured two more cups of tea. "I had the impression from Geoff . . . "

"Good Lord! You don't want to listen to my brother; he's the corniest old stuffed shirt when it comes to family morals. Far worse than our parents. Why, Charlie and I had even speculated on whether you two actually slept together at all before you married."

"We only did once," Liz muttered, not sure if she should be proud or sorry.

"Were you one or two hands?"

Liz raised an eyebrow. "Come again, I'm not with you."

"Did you count your pre-marital lovers on the fingers of one hand or two?" Jennifer explained patiently.

"Oh!" Liz thought she knew Jennifer quite well, and now realised she didn't. "Er . . . two, if I recall rightly."

"I was only one. I got married too young."

Liz thought she detected a note of regret. "Changing the subject ever so slightly, does this mean that if this really is a pregnancy and not one of Freddie's mythical frogs I've got in here, I should produce sometime in November?"

"That's the way it looks." Jennifer got up. "Sorry, but I'll have to go; Charles is anxious about getting back. They were saying at the station in King's Lynn that we might have to be re-routed on the return to London due to water over the tracks. When are you going to tell Mummy your news?"

"When Geoffrey gets home. I think we should wait till then."

"Chicken!"

"You bet I'm chicken!"

"Did you read they're cancelling Wimbledon?" Charles asked. "First time in history."

"And no cricket at all," Freddie commented. "You know what they're going to call this? The year that wasn't."

"For anybody," Charles muttered, pouring himself another whisky.

"What do you think about this American plan? Seems it's official, as they're sending a team of scientists to Europe to explain matters and gain support. I think it's crazy. Maybe it'll work, but . . . what do they say? The operation was a success, but the patient died? All of them? Trouble is, the fellow behind the project is a friend of Geoff's, and Anne's, apparently. Dad's had a letter asking if he can come up here to see us when he's in England. So I suppose we have to be polite to him, even if he is a bloody fool. Did you meet him the last time he was over? Mark Payton?"

"I may have done," Charles said. "Well . . . it may be suicidal, but they have to do something. God, they have to do something."

Freddie frowned at his brother-in-law. "Problems?"

"Well . . . " Charles sighed. "The market's come to a standstill. I've been laid off."

Freddie sat up. "You? But . . . aren't you staff?"

"Yes I am. And it's not redundancy, or anything like that. The fact is, I've been suspended without pay. The MD had us all in. We just aren't doing any business. People have been liquidating in every direction, and there's no sign of anything coming back. Everything's on hold. So, it's a question of whether we quit, or go on hold as well. I've opted to go on hold. The very moment things pick up again, I get my job back."

"Hm. What does Jennie say?"

"Jennie doesn't know."

"Eh?"

"My suspension starts from the day I go on holiday. That is, today. Doesn't seem much point in telling her now and spoiling the holiday, right? I'd be grateful if you wouldn't tell her, either."

"Of course I won't tell her, or anyone," Freddie said.

Charles nodded. "Sorry to lumber you with my problems – you've got more than enough of your own. But I felt I had to tell someone. What I may do is suggest we stay on in Spain for a week or two after our holiday is finished. Anyway, by then things may have started to move. If not . . . we'll have to put the villa on the market."

"Supposing you can find a buyer, the way things are. But Charles . . . Jennie is a big girl now, you know. She can take bad news. And she won't thank you for keeping something like this secret."

"I'll tell her," Charles said. "I just want to choose my time."

He looked up with a bright smile as the women came in.

The north of France, like England, was shrouded in mist and light drizzle, not sufficient to cause a problem, but quite sufficient to make everything wet and soggy.

"Boy, am I looking forward to a hot bath," Jennifer said as they took the A3 towards Paris. They had landed just after lunch, and were following their unvarying routine. "And then, a really big meal. Do you remember that duck we had last year, in apricot sauce? I hope it's on the menu again this year."

Charles stared at the wet road, both hands tight on the wheel. "Actually, we're not staying at the Georges Cinq this year."

"Not . . . why not?"

"Well, I thought we'd give somewhere else a whirl."

"Why didn't you tell me? What have you in mind? The Ritz?" Since marrying Charles Jennifer had become accustomed to five-star hotels.

"Well . . . there's this chain of motels, called Campaniles.. . . "

"Campaniles? Those are bell towers."

"That's their logo, yes."

"But . . . motels? You once told me you wouldn't be caught dead in a motel."

"Did I? Can't imagine why. These places are very nice from all I've heard. The kids'll love it. Won't you?" he asked over his shoulder.

There was a moment's uncertain silence.

"What's a motel?" Jessica asked.

"Ah . . . well . . . we'll be there in a little while. You'll love it. And," he said to Jennifer, "it is one quarter of the price of the Georges Cinq."

"Oh. Is that important?"

"It might be, one of these days. You never can tell."

Jennifer directed him from a map in the little green booklet he produced from his pocket. She was watching unhappily as factory buildings and warehouses flashed by. Rather different from the Champs Elysées. But her attitude softened somewhat when Charles swung the car round and followed the signs into a car park surrounded by neatly cut lawns, hedges and colourful flower borders.

The rooms were tiny, but the convenience of having the carboot of luggage right outside the door was a great improvement on underground parks, lifts and waiting ages for porters to bring up the gear. And the children were thrilled. Their room had a communicating door to their parents', a little bathroom of their own and a TV. The programmes were all in French but that didn't matter; children's cartoons were pretty self-explanatory in any language.

The *pièce de resistance* for the children was being allowed to stay up late and have dinner with their parents in the restaurant, Charles and Jennifer having to apply almost physical restraint when the children saw the colourful buffet waiting for them, plus a special children's menu.

Jackie and Jessica fell asleep at the table before they reached the dessert buffet. Jennifer woke her daughter sufficiently for the child to be led back to their room, while Jackie remained asleep over his mother's shoulder.

Five minutes later Jennifer returned to join Charles at the table for coffee and brandy. "They are both fast asleep," she grinned.

"I won't be far behind them." Charles suppressed a yawn.

"You must be exhausted. I wish you'd let me take a turn driving."

"What, and leave me to entertain the kids!"

*   *   *

As they drove south they left the mist behind, but instead got into some really heavy rain. Charles always followed the same route, the A10 down to Bordeaux, then east along the Route des Deux Mers. Usually they stopped at an hotel just outside Toulouse, but this time he had booked them in at the Campanile south of Perpignan. This met with general approval now.

"Do you think we'll see the sun?" Jennifer asked.

"Has to be there somewhere."

It actually cleared up somewhat as they neared the Mediterranean. Best of all, they left the blackness of the ash cloud behind them. Now they looked at ordinary rain clouds, and there was a good deal of thunder and lightning, which alarmed the children at first.

"What's the matter?" Jennifer said brightly. "Have you forgotten the game of counting how far away it is?" and she soon had them busily marking off incorrect seconds between flash and thunder on their tiny fingers. It distracted the little ones, but as the storm grew fiercer and rain lashed the windscreen she suggested tentatively, "Don't you think we should stop?"

"For lunch, yes. I know just the place, Agen."

They got soaked running from the car to the motorway restaurant, but had a very good meal.

"I do think we should stop until this clears up." Jennifer grimaced at the downpour flooding the car park. "There's bound to be an hotel in Agen. Maybe even a Campanile."

"We're booked in at Perpignan. Anyway, this is bound to stop soon. You are not having very good weather," he remarked to the waitress in atrocious French.

She gaped at him for a moment until comprehension dawned. "Oui, oui. C'est terrible," she agreed. "The worst spring anyone can remember. No one knows where it will end. The Canal du Midi, it is overflowing its banks."

Charles couldn't follow the reply much beyond the word 'terrible'. "I'll bet it's not raining in Spain," he told Jennifer optimistically.

"What odds are you offering?"

"Ten to one."

"Ten pounds. You're on."

"Hey! That's a bit steep!"

"You said it, sweetheart. Want to back off?"

They saw what the girl meant as they drove out of Toulouse; there was water everywhere. But the motorway climbed after the city, and although they couldn't go very fast because of the spray thrown up by other vehicles, the rain began to ease off and the electrical storm faded into the distance.

Leaving Perpignan next day, as they drove round the eastern end of the Pyrenees, the sun began to shine.

"I'd almost forgotten what it's like," Jennifer said. "Oh, this is just marvellous."

Yet Spain too had had a great deal of rain. There was standing water everywhere, and as they drove further south they could see that the fields on both sides of the motorway were waterlogged, while in places the terracing for the orange groves had collapsed beneath the weight of water. It was also very warm, far warmer than they had any right to expect at the end of May.

"So when do you pay up?" Charles demanded.

"What?"

"The bet. I told you it wouldn't be raining in Spain."

"Come off it! It's been pouring!"

"It isn't now."

"But just look at the wet everywhere. It must have been bucketing when we made the bet."

Despite heavy thunderclouds overhead, it didn't actually rain again on the journey, but the playful argument continued spasmodically until they turned off the motorway at Ondara, with Montgo rising some 2,500 feet on their left.

"Home," Charles said cheerfully.

The mountain now loomed enormous. Montgo was one of those curious Spanish features thrown up by some prehistoric earthquake. It rose in comparatively gentle slopes to the north though there were some sheer precipices on the southern side. But Montgo's most interesting feature was its isolation. Several miles from the first mountains to the west, it stood alone, dominating the surrounding valleys, one hunched shoulder reaching due east into the Mediterranean, ending where Cap San Antonio fell hundreds of feet down to the sea.

At its northern foot lay the very old seaport of Denia, founded by the Romans in about 300 BC, and named after their goddess Diana. Although nowadays a considerable resort town, Denia retained its fishing fleet, as well as a large yacht marina, and was very much a business centre. South of Montgo lay the triple township of Javea, Javea Port, and Arenal, known respectively to the locals as El Pueblo, El Puerto, and La Playa.

Javea had begun as a simple fishing village with a small marina, but over the preceding twenty-odd years had grown enormously. It now catered for all nationalities which did not have guaranteed sunshine of their own: Dutch, German, Belgian, French, Swiss, Swedish, Danish, Norwegian and, more numerous than all the rest put together, British. So many British ex-pats had made their homes in this area that one of the in-jokes in Spain during the last days of the quarrel over Gibraltar was that the Spanish Prime Minister once offered his English counterpart a deal: We'll forget about Gibraltar if you'll give us back Javea.

Charles and Jennifer had been coming here for years. On their first visit they had fallen in love with the place, and bought a flat in Arenal overlooking the beach. This had not been a great success, especially when Jessica had come along. The apartment building was noisy, the beach was even more noisy with discos thundering forth until the small hours, and the Spanish habit of letting off firecrackers at the very slightest excuse was noisiest of all. Thus two years ago the flat had been sold, and in its place they had bought a small villa on the slopes of Montgo.

Montgo had rapidly developed into a most popular residential area. Villas, with their attendant access roads, wound their way as high as six hundred feet up the gentle, pine-wooded slopes; the Rowlands' villa was some four hundred feet up. Services were of course limited. The house still did not have a telephone, although the previous owners had applied for and been promised one years ago, and there were no such niceties as rubbish collections or milk and paper deliveries. But the mountain possessed a boon far more important than any of those trappings of civilisation – utter peace and quiet.

Many of the houses belonged to non-residents, people who came down for a few weeks in the winter and let their places during the summer; the beginning of June was a dead period, between one season and another, and therefore there were few lights to be seen as Charles drove in the gathering dusk, through the village of Jesus Pobre – Poor Jesus – and turned on to the Jesus Pobre Road, which led into Javea itself.

He looked at his watch. "We could stop and have a bite to eat at Pedro's before going up. There'll be nothing in the house."

Jennifer nodded. "Good idea."

Jessica and Jackie were becoming quite restless, and for all his potty training Jennifer's alert nostrils suggested that Jackie's pants were at least damp.

Charles pulled off the road and parked outside Pedro's bar/restaurant, where they had often eaten in the past.

"Señor Rowland!" Pedro was large and stout; he drank his own wine. Now he shook Charles' hand before embracing Jennifer and Jackie, and stooping to kiss Jessica. "But it is good to see you." He spoke English very well, although to strangers he pretended to understand only Valenciano Spanish, incomprehensible even to Castilians.

"It's good to see you," Charles told him. "You won't believe how much we've looked forward to this holiday. The weather up north . . . "

"But the weather here has been bad also," Pedro said. "I did not expect you. I do not expect anybody, it has been so bad."

"Nothing could be worse than England," Charles assured him. "Now, we'll have tortillas Espagnole for the kids . . . " he looked at Jennifer.

"Mejillones en vapor for me, con ensalada normal."

"And cordero al horno for me," Charles said. "With una botella de vino tinto, y una botella de agua sin gas, y . . . " he glanced at the children, "dos oranginas."

"Right away," Pedro assured him.

"One really does feel one's come home," Jennifer said. "There's such a welcome."

Charles nodded. "I must just check out his plumbing. It's been a long drive."

"Me too." She vanished into the Ladies with the children.

Charles was back at the table first, poured himself a glass of wine, and found Pedro standing beside him.

"You go up to the villa?" Pedro asked.

"Soon as we've eaten."

"Bien, bien." He nodded, smiling.

Charles looked up and frowned. "Why?"

"There is some crazy man saying that Montgo is not safe. I think he is trying to buy some houses cheap. What do you call them . . . spacu . . . ?"

"Speculators. What is unsafe at the moment? You've had burglaries?"

"No, no. It is the mountain. The rain. He says there will be landslips."

"On Montgo?" There was a good deal of evidence that there had been rockfalls on Montgo in the remote past, huge boulders which had broken away from the escarpment and rolled down the terraced and wooded slopes. But the terraces themselves, now long abandoned as the locals had discovered it was more profitable to sell their land to rich visitors than try to cultivate it, had been there for centuries and were the best guarantee of the stability of the mountain.

Pedro touched his head. "Crazy man. Crazy."

Charles saw Jennifer and the children emerging from the loo. "I agree, crazy. But best not to frighten the women and children, right?"

Pedro nodded, and departed.

"What's the local gossip?" Jennifer asked.

"Just the weather," Charles said.

They were shocked when they let themselves into the villa. Invading damp had left great patches of black mould. Of course the children didn't notice that, but when they rushed through the house for a first glimpse of the pool, the main attraction of the holiday for them, Charles and Jennifer heard Jessica's shouts of dismay. "It's all green and horrid, Mummy. Daddy, come and make it clean!"

"Oh hell! That damned so-called pool cleaner," Charles exploded. The lights in and around the pool revealed the extent of the algae. "And to think I've been sending him a monthly cheque . . . "

"It's too late to swim tonight, anyway, darlings." Jennifer put her arm round each of the children and led them off to bed. "Daddy will buy chlorine in the morning." She was more concerned with checking whether the beds and linen needed airing.

Charles slept heavily for a while, exhausted by his three days' driving, but he woke suddenly about three. For several seconds he lay listening, wondering what could have disturbed him. Beside him, Jennifer breathed slowly and evenly. The only sound was the thunder of heavy rain on the roof. Damned rain. He hoped it wasn't going to spoil their holiday.

He got out of bed, padded down the corridor past the children's bedroom, through the lounge-diner, and on to the naya. Rain was falling in a solid wall obliterating any lights in the valley; water gushed out of the gutters so forcefully that, although there was no wind, spray was sent flying into the air and across the floor of the naya. He stood very still, listening. There was no sound from any of the villas nearby, not that many of them would be occupied. Not even a dog barked. Suddenly he slapped at his arms; the exceptionally warm night had brought out all the mosquitoes from under the pines. How the hell did they manage to fly around in this weather, he wondered?

But maybe it was all to the good. To lie half naked on a beach in glorious sunshine, and have to tell Jennifer that this was the last time . . . it'd be easier in pouring rain.

So what had woken him? There was not a sound above the incessant noise of the rain, except – he took another swipe – for the buzz of mozzies round his head. Must've been all that rubbish Pedro had been telling him.

He went back to bed.

Next morning the rain was still solid. Rivers of water gushed down the driveway carrying stones and debris; filling faster than the drain could cope, the pool overflowed over the surrounding terrace, spreading its·green slime. With windows open, water splashed off the sills into the house, adding to the already unpleasant humidity; closed, and they immediately steamed up.

"Mummy," Jessica wandered through the sitting-room naked. "When can we sunbathe?"

"When the rain stops, darling."

"Beach," Jackie shouted. "Beach."

"Well, we'll have to do something with them ... " Jennifer looked at Charles.

"Might as well go down later and see if it's raining at Arenal," he said.

He spent the first half of the morning in swimming trunks, hair plastered over his ears by the rain, backwashing the pool. Without too much success.

"Thank goodness we didn't bathe in that last night," Jennifer grimaced. "It looks even worse in daylight. Ugh! You know what we need? One of those barracuda things. Then we wouldn't have any problems."

"They only scoop up what's on the bottom," Charles explained. "And someone still has to clean the filters. If the place sits empty for a couple of months, the whole pump will seize up. Anyway, they cost about four hundred quid down here."

"We could employ someone to come in every couple of weeks," Jennifer went on, before his last remark reached her. "Who's suddenly all worried about money then?"

"Who isn't worried about money?" Charles snapped. "Come on, let's go out."

They drove down the narrow mountain road over mud, stones and rubbish, peering through steamed-up car windows, splashing through the deserted pueblo to Arenal. Together under one golf brolly, they made a dash, dodging puddles, to their favourite café and stood under the dripping sun awning, facing out, seawards. The usually popular promenade and beach area was even more depressing than the villa, the view of the sea almost hidden behind the veil of rain.

"It is going to be a bad year," said the waiter who came out to stand mournfully behind them.

The children didn't even suggest going on to the sand.

They drove into the mountains behind Pedreguer to have lunch and occupy Jessica and Jackie, but it wasn't a success. The children had already had enough time in the car as opposed to the beach. Everywhere there was evidence of subsidence and collapsed walls; several roads were closed.

"Charles," Jennifer said, "this is hopeless. I want to go home."

"Let's give it one more day," he said. "If it hasn't improved by then, we'll pack it in."

It was a new experience, this sudden loss of confidence. He had always been so positive, self-assured. Successful. Now his world, if not the whole world, was collapsing around his ears. He, Charles Rowland, a leading light in City finance, head of his own department, owner of two homes and two cars, father of two children whose names were registered at Eton and Roedean from birth . . . had joined the ranks of the Great Unemployed.

And he lacked the courage to admit it to his own wife. He just couldn't face it. It wasn't that he had any doubts as to how she would take it. She would be deeply sympathetic, understanding; she'd be on his side. But subconsciously in her eyes, his stature would be halved immediately. No longer could he play the role of the great, high-income provider who had plucked her from a simple farming background and propelled her into the beautiful social whirl of the Metropolis. It wasn't even as though he was changing jobs. Roles. There was no other role. He was an out-of-work actor. A nothing.

He had brought her down here to tell her . . .

He sat behind the streaming glass in the closed naya, an untouched glass of beer going flat on the tiled table beside him. He was trying to get his act together, while Jennifer put the children to bed. Oh God! If only . . . if . . . if . . . Dammit, it only needed the cloud to lift for all his troubles to be over.

Suddenly he straightened. He'd made a decision . . . to sleep on it.

And awoke to brilliant, baking sunshine.

He wandered out on to the naya, dazed with sleep, and couldn't believe his eyes. There wasn't a cloud in the sky.

He looked up the hill. Now, for the first time, he could see the mountain, watch as the last vestiges of cloud snaked down through clefts in the cliff face where the early sun had not yet penetrated, before melting away into the barancas. There had been some rock falls, that was evident from the fresh red scars on the cliff. But high up. And the rock face, normally a reddish brown, was almost black

179

from the amount of moisture absorbed. But that would dry out with a few days' hot sun.

Jennifer emerged, naked and heading for the pool.

"Who wants to go home now?" he teased.

"This is what it's all about," she said happily.

"Long may it last! And maybe by the time we return the cloud will have gone."

Charles listened to the news on the BBC World Service. There was no sign of the ash cloud dissipating as yet, the reader said, but it might be changing its position and moving slightly north.

That had to be a good thing. At least it was taking the worst of the weather away from Spain, which had had the wettest winter since records had first been kept, with a disastrous effect on crops, some of which were virtually wiped out.

"Shame we can't stay down here until it's all gone," Jennifer remarked.

Charles made no reply, but her remark reminded him of the idea he had aired to Freddie. He could pretend to have telephoned the bank to say he was taking an extra couple of weeks' leave . . . his available cash would just about support that. And then . . . "Come on," he said. "Let's go down to the sea."

They chose a beach near Cap de la Nao, smaller and rockier than at Arenal, but quieter and better for swimming and snorkelling. A few near-naked bodies were sopping up the sun, a young couple were launching a rubber dinghy and offshore two yachts swayed gently at anchor.

Jessica and Jackie stripped their shorts off, stamping impatiently while Charles blew up their armbands and Jennifer threaded them on to little white arms.

"We'll have to smother them in sun cream," Jennifer observed as the children scrambled over rocks and pebbles into the water.

"Perhaps they ought to have T-shirts on, later."

They took turns in swimming out into deep water with snorkel, mask and flippers while the other played with the children, attempting to teach them to swim. The headlands to either side of the bay were more green and lush than Charles could ever remember them, but all the more beautiful for that. He lay back on his towel, eyes closed against the glare, aware of the kids nearby collecting shells, letting the sun dry the damp misery out of his soul, soothe and relax the tension in his body.

Water dripped on his face. "Lunch?" Jennifer asked, towelling her hair.

The high, stone wall behind them was topped by a café terrace.

They ordered cokes and a jug of Sangria, sat waiting for their paella, sipping, watching people enjoying themselves in the way that is peculiarly Spanish, whereby everyone has a great deal to drink, but nobody gets drunk, everyone has a thoroughly good time, but nobody ever gets offensive. It was necessary to move their chairs frequently, to keep in the shade of the sun brolly. The paella was good, washed down by a second jug of Sangria.

All very soporific.

"Please may I get down?" Jessica asked.

Jackie didn't wait for the answer.

"I'll take a turn with them while you have first snooze," Jennifer offered.

Charles blew her a kiss across the table, and called for *la cuenta*.

They drove back home quite late, in the most relaxed mood they had been in for weeks. Even the children were good-humoured despite exhaustion from the day's activities.

Jennifer had bought some lettuce and tomatoes and peppers, as well as ham; Charles had bought some bottles of wine, and the two of them sat out on the naya for supper, looking down the hill at the twinkling lights in the valley as it got dark.

"Kids asleep?" Charles asked.

"They went out like lights."

"Happy?"

"Ever so."

They made love, for the first time since leaving England, and were both fast asleep by 10.30.

And again Charles was awake about three. Must be some kind of new, and damned irritating, sleep pattern, he thought; Jennifer was still out to the world.

But he hadn't woken the previous night.

He turned over to get back to sleep, and cocked his head as a weird noise filtered through to him. For a moment his heart seemed to stop. Burglars? It sounded like a door. A big, heavy door swinging slowly on a rusty hinge. He debated for a second before deciding to wake Jennifer. "Sweetheart," he hissed, shaking her.

"Wha . . . ?" her exclamation was stifled by his hand over her mouth.

"I think we may have company," he breathed into her ear. "Where's the truncheon?" referring to the wooden bauble they'd bought last year in a jolly junk shop.

Jennifer sat up, pulling the sheet round her. "On the dressing-table, I think." Pointing.

He tiptoed across the room in the dark, fumbled, found it and, mouth dry and wondering whether he was a hero or a first-class idiot, carefully opened the bedroom door . . . which gave its usual high-pitched squeak. He held his breath and listened. Through the open bathroom window came the hoot of an owl; nothing else. His bare feet on the tiled floor made no sound as he crept on through the house, eyes becoming sufficiently accustomed to the gloom to enable him to peer into every corner, including under the children's beds. Nothing. What was more, every door, window and *reja* was in place, untouched. He switched on the kitchen light, blinked, and set the kettle on the stove.

They laughed about the nocturnal adventure, next morning, but Charles did make a surreptitious daylight check, nevertheless. He knew he had heard something.

"What's the order of the day, today?" he asked over breakfast.

"Beach!" two young voices pleaded together.

"No, you had enough sea and sun yesterday, darlings. We are going to stay at home and play in and around the pool," Jennifer insisted.

The following day they left early for Guadalest, lunched at El Riu, gave the children donkey rides up to the castle and returned late after supper at Arenal. It was dark . . . and hot. They couldn't see the mountain as they got the children out of the car, but they could feel the intense heat which had been absorbed all day into the rockface.

The noise was a huge groaning, slithering sound, punctuated by sharp crashes. Charles sat bolt upright in bed, trying to orientate, work out the direction it was coming from.

"Whatever is it?" It had woken Jennifer, too.

Dogs began barking frantically, further down the hill.

Charles ran out on to the naya, looking in every direction, eyes narrowed, straining, but the darkness was intense and he could see nothing. Then something landed in the garden with a horrifying thud, and something else bounced all the way down the drive. And the floor of the naya started to shake.

Charles dashed back inside calling, "Jennifer, Jennifer! Quickly. Grab the kids." He switched on the bedroom light and dragged on a pair of pants.

The groaning and crashing got worse.

Jennifer was already in a tracksuit. "What is it?"

"The mountain. Into the car." As he spoke there was an extra violent crash as something hit the back wall of the bedroom and both bedside lights teetered and fell.

Barefoot she raced into the children's room, threw back their sheets and grabbed them in her arms, handing Jessica to Charles. Heads down, they dashed across the car park and Charles didn't even pause to put the child in the back but leapt into the driving seat and dumped her on top of Jackie on Jennifer's knee. The Mercedes' engine shuddered into life at the first try and all four were dry-mouthed with fear as they bumped down the driveway over loose stones, while more chased them down the hill, bouncing off the boot.

"The mountain's coming down," Jessica gasped, and as if to punctuate her statement something heavy struck one side of the gate archway as they shot underneath.

The children, still tangled in their bedclothes and held tightly by Jennifer, started to scream. Now the air was filled with flying debris, mainly mud so far, but Charles had to wrestle with the wheel as the tyres struck chunks of rock. The car careered down the steep road to the accompaniment of an ever-increasing noise, the groaning, tearing sound being accompanied by a steady series of crashes and thumps from close at hand, and now screams too as other sleeping residents woke to realise their houses were about to be engulfed, while from the bottom of the hill there came the whine of a police siren.

Desperately Charles wrenched the wheel round and the car skidded sideways, nearly crashing into the barranca on the far side of the narrow road. Jennifer suppressed a scream, repeatedly trying to reassure the terrified children. Charles got the car back under control and they slid rather than drove down the mud-filled road, taking corners sideways, racing down the lower levels to come to a stop against a four-wheel drive manned by the Guardia Civile.

Freddie was at Gatwick to meet the incoming flight. It had been impossible to drive down, and even his rail journey had been achieved on an oddly roundabout route. He grinned as they came through from Customs in their weird assortment of clothes. Even the ever-immaculate Charles looked like a washed-up beach bum, in filthy pants and an unlikely chequered shirt.

"We had nothing," Jennifer explained, and gave an almost hysterical laugh. "Would you believe I left the house in a muddy tracksuit? The Guardia were wonderful and one of them got a blouse and skirt from his wife for me, until Charles got the bank to let us have some money and bought something for me to wear."

"The British community down there was quite tremendous," Charles said, while Freddie hugged his sister and took charge of Jessica's hand. "They rallied around us with accommodation and endless lifts to and from banks and the insurance office, plus phone calls."

Freddie looked around. "Where's the luggage?"

"There isn't any."

Freddie boggled at them. "What, none at all? Couldn't you get back to the house?"

"I'd like to have seen you try." Charles attempted humour, but his face was grim.

"Where's the car?" Freddie asked, practical as ever.

"Down there, on a dump. It was absolutely wrecked."

"With us in it. God, what an experience," Jennifer said, as she followed the men over to the station for the train to Victoria.

"When you say you couldn't get back to the house, are you saying you lost everything?" Freddie asked.

"Every damned thing," Charles said, staring through the window at the drizzle.

"But you're insured, of course. Might come in handy."

"How do you insure against the collapse of a mountain?"

Freddie shot him a quick glance.

"Fire, theft, storm, we had all of those," Charles muttered morosely. "But a sliding mountain . . . "

"Did it all come down?"

"Oh, good lord, no. There just happened to be a slip right above our place. There were others, but according to the Guardia ours was the worst. I went out with them next day. God, what a mess. The house had been pushed right off its foundations and just collapsed into the pool." He turned his head. "I had hoped to sell it to raise some capital. Now I suppose I'll have to put the Greenwich house on the market."

Freddie felt like saying, join the club, but he gave an encouraging smile. "Sit it out a while longer. Things'll improve. I mean, they can't get any worse."

"Welcome home, darling." Liz hugged her husband, then held him away to look at him. "You brute! You've got a sun tan."

"I had. It's starting to fade." He pulled her against him, feeling the small shape of her, nuzzling her hair and bending to kiss her upturned face. Then it was his turn to hold her away. "And you feel cuddlier than ever. Have you put on weight?"

"Mmmm . . . Possibly."

"What does that mean?"

"There could be a reason." She gave him a coy look.

"You've been letting Mum feed you like she does Freddie, I suppose," he teased.

"Better reason than that! Guess again."

"You've been teaching yourself to cook?"

"No! Come on! What is the best reason in the world for a woman to lose her shape?" Liz prompted impatiently.

"Being preg . . . eh? Are you . . . ?" he watched her face split into a huge grin. "You little doll!" he shouted. "You bloody marvellous little doll!" He scooped her up, cradling her in his arms and marched into their sitting-room to deposit her carefully on the Chesterfield.

"Are you pleased?" She was a trifle anxious.

"Pleased? Isn't it the most wonderful news a man could possibly hear? I bet Dad and Mum are bucked."

"Well . . . I waited till you got home before telling them. You see, junior was conceived out of wedlock."

He cocked his head on one side. "He was? You don't mean that time . . . "

She nodded.

"Wow! Are we well matched! I touch you for the first time and *bingo* you're ignited."

"But what about admitting to your folk . . . "

"They won't give a damn! In fact, if I know Dad he'll pop a bottle of bubbly the minute we tell him." He pulled her to her feet. "Come on. This is the best excuse for a party I've had in years."

When the excitement in the elder Dunnings' sitting-room died down, Geoffrey asked "How're Jenny and Charlie?"

"Still feeling pretty shaken up," his mother replied. "They went home last week. Can you imagine the experience? A whole mountain coming down on top of you?" She looked pretty shaken by the event herself. "And worse than that, from Charlie's point of view: he's lost his job."

"Charlie?"

Liz explained. Charlie had told them all a couple of nights after returning from Spain.

"They must both be feeling shattered!"

"I don't think it's all sunk in yet. So sad for them. But we mustn't dwell on their troubles tonight. John," she held out her glass, "have you got another bottle hidden away somewhere? It's so good to have Geoffrey back and hear their good news."

Geoffrey grinned. "Meaning because I'm the only member of the family still employed. Save for Anne."

"I wish I could meet her," Liz grumbled. "She sounds such a super person."

"She is. But I don't know if you'd go for her. She's too

organised."

"Meaning I'm not?"

"I wouldn't dare mean any such thing," he assured her, pretending to duck from an invisible blow.

12

The Panic

"God, look at it! Ninety-seven. At dawn."

Liz sat on the edge of the bed and thumped the thermometer. She scooped sweat from her neck. "I used to think it could be hot in Oz. Geoff . . . what are we going to do? What's going to happen? It's the end of June, and look at it. The cloud is still there, it's drizzling all the time, acid rain is killing off all the vegetation that has survived the floods so far; the entire country is shrouded in this thick mist; the air is totally polluted . . . do you know people are going down with coughs and colds at the rate of a thousand a day? The hospitals can't cope. They're only admitting emergencies."

"You're coming with me when we go again," Geoffrey said.

"Am I, Geoff? Can I?" She turned on her knees. "Do you think it'll be all right . . . ?" she looked down at her thickening waistline.

"Sure it will. We carry a doctor. And you're not due until the beginning of November. That's a whole four months."

"But your voyages take two months, and most shipping lines won't take women more than six months gone."

He kissed her. "I told you, we carry a doctor. Anyway, it's all been squared. The cabin is booked. One cabin for the round trip. You won't even have to share. And it's the skipper's last voyage before retirement. We're going to have a whale of a time."

"Why didn't you tell me before?"

"Thought I'd wait to see how things were, here. You look as though you need the break. We had been going to Spain, remember?"

"You're darn right I need a break. But it makes me feel a bit guilty when I think of all those people at Stonehenge with their grey, miserable faces."

They had watched the 'ceremony' on TV, when thousands of people had accumulated at the old monument in the hope, and apparently belief, that the cloud would finally lift and the sun be restored. And watched, too, in horror, the angry scenes that had followed their disillusionment.

"It was that that made me decide not to leave you again." His voice was suddenly sharp with anger. "Those people behaved like animals!" He held her tightly in his arms. "Can't think why you should feel guilty towards people like that."

"The hooligan element was only a small portion of the crowd. What about the rest? Everyone needs a change," she said sadly, reaching for the TV remote control and switching on, more in hope than expectation. The electricity situation was so bad that private homes were strictly rationed on a rotated basis, each part of the country getting some for a few hours every other day.

Officially the bulk of the electricity supplies were being reserved for industry, but so much industry had been shut down Geoffrey found it difficult to believe they needed it; apart from the factories producing de-humidifiers. The country was just grinding to a halt. The few remaining train services were in a mess, limited to tracks high enough to avoid floods, and to periods when electricity was available. And from those lines one could see vast areas under water, surrounding many abandoned buildings. Trees and grass were turning black, houses too, covered with mildew. What little fresh food one could find had to be eaten immediately before it turned bad. Everyone prayed that the electric power would not be cut completely, meaning the loss of refrigeration.

He was amazed, and distressed, by how much the mood of the people had changed during the two months he had been away. He had thought, before leaving in April, that people didn't seem to have yet realised what was happening. Now they surely did, and had descended into a general depression, though a few, knowing there was nothing they could do about the situation, merely shrugged, and went on with their own lives as far as that was possible . . . praying for a miracle. But the majority appeared limp, bedraggled, hopeless.

No one had ever known a summer like this before. There had been no sport at all, and holidays were non-existent. This was partly because so many people were short of money due to the huge lay-offs, but it was also caused by the massive cutback in available aircraft. It was a chicken and egg situation for the airlines, forced as they were to fly beneath 30,000 feet by Government regulations, had to put prices up so high they couldn't fill their seats, thus pulling more and more planes out of service until conditions improved. And where there were aircraft, it was a matter of getting them down through the constant mist and fog which had spread down from the Arctic to envelop everywhere north of the Pyrenees and the Alps.

Shipping therefore, was at a premium, and British Ocean Transporters was doing better than ever before, with every cabin booked for the foreseeable future; it had taken a good deal of arm-twisting – and made a big hole in Geoff's savings – to get Liz's berth, at least on the outward leg: most of those who were leaving had no intention of coming back; they were seeking the sunlight of the southern hemisphere until the cloud broke up and disappeared. They were the lucky ones, although many were businessmen or money managers who justified their flight on the grounds that they could no longer conduct their businesses from England.

It was possible, he thought as he shaved, to suppose that what was happening was a decisive shift of power away from the north to the south. Australia and South Africa, India and Pakistan, Brazil and Argentina, Chile and Mexico were the countries where all the business was happening now. With the New York, London and Tokyo stock exchanges virtually shut down, partly from lack of power but also from lack of trading, Sydney and Johannesburg, Calcutta and Karachi, Buenos Aires and Rio de Janeiro were becoming the new financial centres of the world.

Now there was talk of launching a massive aid programme . . . for Europe!

But the sheer physical aspect of the catastrophe hanging over the northern hemisphere was far more terrifying than the economic implications, even if this was not yet apparent, it seemed, to many people. Geoffrey could estimate the situation merely by looking out of his window, at the extent of floodwater on the surrounding farmland. West Walton had become Wet Walton.

Even at low tide the channels were full; so the land didn't get a chance to drain off. When the tide was high in the North Sea, nowadays, it rose some six feet above anything ever recorded before even in storm conditions, and in some areas, the levees were barely able to cope, although the sluices were shut, so that acres of land were polluted with salt, along with those parts of the coast of East Anglia which were already submerged; he was told there had been a number of evacuations, houses and whole villages on the seaward side of the dykes abandoned. Dunning Farm was far enough inland from the coast for that not to have become necessary, yet, because of the buildings being on a slight rise. But the Great Ouse was carrying twice its normal flow; at every high tide the streets of King's Lynn were flooded. It also constantly spilled over in their direction, *behind* the levee. His father reckoned that if the increase in the water level was maintained, the farmhouse would be flooded in less than a month.

The media kept trotting out experts who told the nation that the six-foot rise of sea level was nothing to worry about. Trouble was, too many people were willing to believe them. Tales of massive flooding in Holland, despite the elaborate barriers, merely reminded people that Holland was a very low-lying country. TV pictures of several Bahamian islands virtually under water, as was a good deal of the American coastline, seemed remote. News of the States of Illinois, Missouri, West Tennessee, Arkansas, Mississippi and Louisiana being declared disaster areas because of the flooding of the Mississippi, and of the Carolinas, Georgia and Florida also suffering from massive floods, was too commonplace . . . some disaster or another always seemed to be happening in the States.

No one seemed to understand that it had barely even started yet. Mark Payton had paid the farm a visit a few days previously, immediately after the Midsummer's Day. He had spent a week in England conferring with the Government, and had been due to go on to Paris and Bonn to support the American delegations there, seeking a united front against the catastrophe.

Mark had been unusually serious. "It's getting the message across that's proving so goddamned difficult," he had told Geoffrey and Liz. "I show them photographs I took during my last visit to the Arctic, three weeks ago. Okay, so we're in midsummer and everyone expects the Arctic Ocean to be just a mass of floes. But there isn't any ice at all. Just water. They look at them and say, how remarkable. Some of them, I'm sure, think I faked those photos. Others say, well, yes, this has happened and we have a sea-level rise of six feet. Big deal. Once the cloud goes, the Arctic will freeze up again, and this summer will just seem like a bad dream."

Geoffrey and Liz had looked at the photos in amazement. As Mark said, there was no ice to be seen at all. "Where were these taken?"

"A hundred miles south of the Pole." Geoffrey whistled.

"What people can't understand," Mark said, "and I can't show them, is that the permafrost is now melting, and it is going to gather speed."

"How long?" Geoffrey had asked.

"Two months, I would say. By the end of August that rise is going to be in the order of thirty feet, not six."

Geoffrey had looked out of the window then, too. That would be the end of the farm. It would not merely be a matter of drying out the floors of their home; submerged under that much water over a prolonged period, it would be destroyed completely. The levees could still handle a normal tide – and in fact the Government had gained enormous credit for conceiving and building them, regardless of the expropriation and compulsory purchase rows, the majority of which were still awaiting settlement in the courts, as angry landowners insisted they had not been paid sufficient compensation. It had lulled people in East Anglia, and in Essex and London itself, into a feeling of security, a feeling that all they had to do was sit things out. They had done that before.

But the levees had not been designed to cope with thirty feet of water. It was at that moment that his resolution to get Liz out of England had hardened. He only wished he could take the whole family.

He confided his plan to Mark, who had given one of his twisted grins. "Good idea."

"You don't think I'm acting the rat vis-à-vis the sinking ship?"

"Hell, no. I'd do the same. For God's sake, you *have* to go. Why shouldn't you take your wife with you, if you can?" He had brooded for a few moments. Then he said, "Talking about wives . . . I want to marry your sister."

He had been rather embarrassed, less at the idea of marriage, Geoffrey thought, than the fact that he had obviously visited the farm to vet his prospective in-laws. And Geoffrey had been unable to resist the temptation to tease. "Are you sure the Dunning family comes up to scratch?"

"You're a great family," Mark had said, reddening. "And I just love your mother."

"Nice of you to say so, but . . . have you asked Anne yet?"

"Er . . . no. I was planning to do that next week. And if any of you guys feels like putting in a good word for me . . . "

That had made Geoffrey laugh. "Don't you realise that there is no way any of us could possibly influence Anne's decision about who to marry . . . or anything else? She'd probably do her nut if she knew you'd mentioned it to me at all."

"Oh. Well, don't tell her."

"I won't. But do let us know when you've popped the question. What do *your* parents think of the idea?"

"Ah . . . they don't know anything about it."

"Well, what do they think of Anne?"

"Ah . . . they liked her, when they met at Christmas. But they don't know anything about our er . . . friendship."

Geoffrey scratched his head. "Well, I don't suppose it's much of their business either. But . . . I presume *Anne* knows you're interested?"

"Oh, well, yes, of course. I mean . . . "

"Oh, quite. What happened to Ben?"

"Ben?"

"Forget it. Mark, I couldn't wish for a better brother-in-law. Just be careful you don't blow it."

"Think he'll make it?" Liz had asked, after Mark had left.

"That will depend entirely upon my little sister."

John and Freddie were standing anxiously outside the front door, peering down the slight slope towards the road, which was entirely under water.

"They'll be late," Freddie said gloomily. "This water is a lot deeper than last week."

"Who's going to be late?" Geoffrey asked, joining them.

"The Government truck, with fodder."

"How are the animals, anyway?"

"They don't give milk, if that's what you mean. Poor things haven't seen the sun for nine months."

"Nor have any of you," Geoffrey pointed out. "How serious is the food position?"

"Bloody awful. Haven't you gathered that?"

He had, of course. People were apparently being encouraged to do their own thing, wherever possible, and flour was being issued so that each household, certainly those which were isolated, could make their own bread. Mary had always made the most splendid bread, but the quality of much of this flour was poor, and she was disgusted with the results. And it was almost impossible to keep the flour from going mouldy.

The village store had closed down, so it was now necessary to drive into King's Lynn to shop, quite an expedition with so many roads closed and diversions in every direction. And once there, things were hardly better. Though there was a good deal of meat available, this was in itself a disturbing trend. Thousands of sheep and pigs had been drowned where they hadn't been taken to safe ground soon enough, and others, as well as large numbers of cattle, were being slaughtered simply because there wasn't sufficient fodder. People were saying it was the very end of the home-grown livestock industry.

"We'll be doing the same, soon enough," Freddie said. "Before they starve."

"Or just to feed ourselves," his father pointed out.

The Dunnings had assumed that the food situation was a result of bad distribution with East Anglia suffering most because the flooding was worst there. But ten days before *Skyhawk* was again due to sail, Geoffrey received a telephone call summoning him to London.

192

Here he discovered Fogarty and Turnbull, together with the captains and officers of all the other company ships which happened to be in port. They were assembled in the main hall of the headquarters of British Ocean Transporters off Piccadilly to be addressed by the chairman.

"I have to inform you," Sir James said, "that your ships have been requisitioned by the Government." He paused to let that news sink in. "Let me make it perfectly clear right away that this will make no difference to either your ranks or your pay. It will, however, make a difference to your routes. The fact is, our manufacturers are virtually closed down, and while the demand in Central and South America for manufactured goods is as strong as ever, the food situation in this country is as severe as it was during the two great wars. To alleviate this, the Government has just concluded a deal with Argentina and Brazil, aimed at taking every ounce of their surplus beef and wheat. This agreement goes into effect today. The Government therefore needs every ship it can lay hands on, for this very vital matter. I am sure you will all appreciate the situation.

"Now, the voyages to your destinations and back must be made in the very shortest possible time; it therefore follows that all leave is now cancelled, and each ship will sail just as soon as possible. These are very much emergency measures, and must be seen as such. All passenger traffic has therefore been suspended, for the homeward journeys at any rate. Those booked for outward voyages to the West Indies will still have their accommodation reserved, but we are now in the process of advising them that we will be unable to put them ashore before Rio de Janeiro or Buenos Aires as the case may be. Should they decide to cancel their reservations, then their fares will of course be refunded. Thank you, gentlemen."

Geoffrey remained seated for several moments after Sir James had left the room. Turnbull clapped him on the shoulder. "Why so glum? Pity about the cancelled leave, but it sounds like sense to me, and a pleasant change of scenery."

"What about Liz?"

"Liz? Hell, I'd forgotten, she was coming with us, wasn't she! Well, she'll have to take a raincheck, unless you've got friends in South America."

"Like hell."

He went in search of Fogarty.

"Surely there can be one exception," he argued.

"I'm afraid not, Geoff. One exception would lead to requests for other exceptions. Anyway, there won't be any room."

"You telling me that we are loading our passenger accommodation with food?"

"That's right. Grain."

"Oh, for God's sake . . . we're not a grain carrier. We're not equipped."

"That apparently doesn't matter in this situation. I suppose you could call us the bucket brigade."

"But surely, one cabin . . . "

"Can't be done, Geoff. I'm sorry. Unless of course you would like your wife to stay over there . . . "

Or fly on to Australia to her brothers and sister? She'd be better off there . . .

Geoffrey went home to break the news.

"So why get upset," Liz shrugged. "I felt guilty about going anyway."

"And I feel guilty about leaving you here. Would you like to rejoin your family down under . . . ?"

"No! I've married you. That makes me a Dunning now. So I stay. A break away for a few weeks on board with you was one kinda thing. But no way do I do a runner. I hope to go back to Oz sometime, but only when you agree to come with me. What's more, I married a sailor. You'd have to leave me behind even if this were the best and brightest summer ever," she pointed out. "Look, I'll do a deal with you. I won't have junior until you get back. That's a promise."

He grinned and kissed her. "I'll hold you to that."

But she felt weepy as he drove away into the mist. She supposed she would have done so anyway, but this time . . . she stood outside and looked up at the sky. But she couldn't even see the black cloud, because of the mist.

She telephoned Jennifer. Companions in misery. But Jennifer's misery was much more real than hers; Geoff still had a job, he was coming back . . . and she had never looked catastrophe in the face. Jennifer still shivered a lot of the time, as she remembered, while Charles just sat and stared gloomily into space. To have had so much, and now to have so very little! They had put the Greenwich house on the market, but no one was buying right now.

And there was no end in sight, for them. Oh, indeed, compared with them she had nothing to complain about.

A week later, Mark Payton visited the farm again. "I'm off back to the States tomorrow," he said to Liz, over coffee in the Wing.

"Flying?"

He grinned. "It's regarded as a permissible risk, for scientists."

"And you're going to pop the question?"

"Geoffrey told you!" But he wasn't annoyed. "You bet. First thing. Wish me luck."

"Oh, I do. How has your trip gone?"

"You win some, you lose some. But anyway, we're going to put a stop to all this rubbish, the moment I get back."

"Seriously?"

"Yep."

"You mean the people over here have agreed to your plan?"

"Well, no. But the Russians are with us. So . . . we're going ahead, just as soon as possible."

"You're talking about using atomic power."

He grinned. "That's what the papers say."

"But . . . does the British Government know this?"

"We're going to make an official announcement within the next few days. Then they're just going to have to get their fingers out and prepare. But it has to be done."

"Mark . . . I'm having a baby."

"So it can't be harmed. Not at this stage. Not unless you're harmed yourself, Liz. But if you take proper precautions, if your Government takes proper precautions, you'll be in no danger. Believe me."

Believe you, Liz thought. But to you, even to you, I am just a statistic, and so is my baby. 'It is calculated that X number of people are going to suffer radiation sickness and X percentage of those are going to die, but we have worked it out and that is preferable to the X percentage who will die if the water goes on rising.' Believe you!

Mark settled back into his seat and closed his eyes as the aircraft rose from the Heathrow runway into the mist. This now extended for several thousand feet, but after a few minutes the jet emerged above it, and into the continuous twilight zone between the cloud and the earth, and headed west. The flight had left several hours late, as was usual nowadays, and because of altitude limitations instead of six hours to Boston it was going to take eight, but he'd still be on the ground by dusk. And at Anne's apartment an hour later, at the outside.

And the cabin was air-conditioned, which made sitting in it for eight hours a most comforting experience after the humidity at ground level.

Technically, he supposed he should have flown to Washington first, but that could wait for a couple of days; Dave Obrenski had all the various reactions tabulated, anyway – the President would need to study them before giving the go-ahead.

Mark had actually been surprised by the vehemence of European opposition to the plan. The explanatory trip had thus taken much longer than he had anticipated. It was now the first week of July, and nothing had been done, from Ireland to Poland, to prepare for what might be coming, or for the immediate after effects of the proposed nuclear explosions. Nothing had been done in Russia, either, but the preparation of radiation-resistant clothes, of fallout shelters, and of the immense literature needed to explain what was going to happen and how to survive it in as much safety as possible, had been launched, as it had been launched in Japan.

In Europe, the responses had been wholly negative. The trouble was, he supposed, that the continent which had once virtually ruled the globe had lost all sense of power, of decision-making, of the ability to see anything outside of their own narrow boundaries. Fragmented themselves, unable to agree on the political union which was their only hope for future economic clout, they were subject to the fragmentation of their internal politics, in which splinter groups could command so much media time and subsequent publicity as to paralyse any executive force.

Mark was an environmentalist. He deplored the cutting down of forests and the careless damaging of the ozone, but he was also an historian and a logician, and he understood how much of the public reaction to allegedly environmental destructive trends was hysterical. He agreed entirely with Dr Edwards, whom he had first confronted following Misreal's eruption, that the general tendency of climatic history was away from the last Ice Age, and that the warming process would continue for possibly another five thousand years before an overall reversal would occur, regardless of the amount of carbon dioxide in the atmosphere. But that had nothing to do with the immediate, local, desperate problem that faced mankind.

And mankind was what mattered, to a member of the species. Dogooders might moan about saving this or that species of animal, the lunatic fringe might want to splash paint over expensive fur coats – apparently totally oblivious of the fact that the mink is a highly destructive pest – but when the chips were really down he did not see even the most dedicated vegetarian allowing his wife and children to die simply because the only food available to feed them happened to be a pig.

That was the real issue here. The trouble was, as he had said to the Dunnings, people would not believe the extent of the catastrophe which was about to overwhelm them. Weatherwise, north of the Equator, it had been the worst year in living memory. Economies and industries were suffering disastrous losses – but there had been years like this before, and recovery had invariably been complete.

The rise in the water level had been too slow to be noticed, except for those who had their business on the water, or lived on low-lying ground; he doubted if even the Dunnings, who had become his favourite English people, would have been so wholeheartedly on his side had they lived in the fells of Cumbria and Geoffrey not been a seaman. In England more than anywhere else, the weather was a national joke. It would get better, and no doubt it would, eventually, get worse again. It always did.

Thus the British Government had politely but definitely rejected any idea of dispersing the cloud by using atomic power. "My dear fellow," the Minister for the Environment, with whom he had spent most of his time, had said, "the people simply will not go for it."

He had reminded Mark of the President's Press Secretary.

"You were elected to govern the people, weren't you? That means protecting them, if necessary from their own folly, even if you have to take unpleasant decisions to do it."

"It also means that we are responsible to them, eventually. And scattering lethal amounts of fallout over their heads can hardly be called protecting them," the Minister responded.

"The fallout is going to be less than any danger limit," Mark had repeated wearily.

"You have calculated that to your own satisfaction. But you cannot be sure, Dr Payton. Nobody can. All it needs is for a few freak winds to concentrate the material in one area, and you'd have a major disaster on your hands. Do you realise there are parts of England which are still contaminated by the Chernobyl disaster? And how long ago was that?"

"And do you realise that if the melting of the permafrost is not arrested, and very quickly, the disaster you are going to have to face will equal that of an atomic war?"

The answer was always the same. "That, Dr Payton, is pure speculation. The other we know about."

Well, he supposed as he closed his eyes in utter exhaustion, they were going to know about the other before too long. When it was too late.

If it wasn't too late already.

Mark slept heavily after lunch, and only awoke as the aircraft began its descent into Logan. It was half past nine, and at 20,000 feet was still as broad daylight as it ever was, nowadays, but it grew darker as the plane lost altitude, while below them the lights of Boston twinkled.

One of those lights, Mark knew, was in Anne's apartment. Time to forget the problems of the world, and look forward to the coming night; he'd telephoned just before leaving Heathrow and told her not to wait for dinner, but he knew she'd be waiting for his arrival.

The aircraft landed and he was through Customs and Immigration in half an hour. He hailed a cab, gave the address, and sank into the back seat. Needless to say the car radio was on. " . . . massive flooding around Yellowknife," the newsreader was saying. "The whole area between Great Bear Lake and Great Slave Lake is under water, and reports from further north indicate similar situations. This despite the fact that there has been little heavy rainfall recently."

"They got problems up there," the driver commented.

It's happening, Mark thought; the permafrost is going. That'll surely clinch it. He knew he had to be in Washington tomorrow. But he wanted tonight first.

"In Washington, the President . . . "

"Let's have some music," the driver growled, switching channels. "All that guy does is talk."

A pop group blared into the back of the cab, and Mark winced . . . then the sound died.

"What the hell . . . " the driver remarked, and braked violently as the traffic lights in front of him also disappeared.

There was a screech from behind them, and a thump, accompanied by the sound of shattering glass.

"Holy shit!" the driver snarled aggressively, and got out.

There were screeches of brakes all around them as cars pulled to a halt from every direction. Mark opened his door and also got out, gazed at darkness, apart from the beams of the headlights. All Boston was blacked out.

Another goddam power outage, he thought.

His driver was bawling at the man who had rammed him, who was bawling back. Mark tapped the driver on the shoulder.

"Buddy," he said. "I have someplace to go."

"You mind your own fucking business," the driver shouted, and then looked over his shoulder. "Oh, it's you. You'll have to wait until this asshole gives me the name of his insurance company."

"Look friend," said the other driver. "You stopped without any warning at all. What I want is the name of *your* insurance company."

"What the shit was I supposed to do? The lights went out. You know what, asshole, I oughta punch you right on the nose."

Mark sighed. To turn up with another black eye would be no way to persuade Anne to marry him. He reached into the back of the cab, pulled out his carryall – he always travelled light – and trudged into the gloom.

Around him the city was quiet for perhaps half an hour. Then sounds began, and people, perhaps for that time surprised and shocked by the outage, began to emerge from the darkness. Mark was a big, strong man, and he didn't anticipate any personal trouble, but soon he heard the sound of breaking glass, and then a scream, from down a sidestreet. The outage was proving too great a temptation for the criminal element.

But he was in no mood to play vigilante, and besides, soon enough squad cars were screaming up and down the streets. Yet when he left Commercial Avenue to climb up Binney Street in the direction of Anne's apartment, he found himself in the midst of a surprisingly large crowd of people, of whom a great number seemed to be smashing shop windows, whooping their delight at the sudden windfalls which had come their way. Then there was a shot, followed by several more. People ran in every direction, and Mark ran with them, ducking down a sidestreet and leaning against the wall, gasping for breath.

This is ridiculous, he told himself. I am Dr Mark Payton, an important, even a key, figure in what is going on. I should declare myself to those policemen and obtain an escort to Anne's apartment. But now bullets were flying in both directions along Binney, and to step out on to it was to court death.

Mark was also becoming worried about what might be happening down Anne's usually quiet side street. He felt his way along the street and into an alley. Here there were people clustered but in the darkness they couldn't tell if he was friend or foe, only that the newcomer was large and young. No one attempted to stop him, and a few moments later he emerged into a wider thoroughfare.

All around him now was the howl of sirens, the shattering of doors and windows, the screams of people either being assaulted or terrified by the break-ins, and the sounds of gunshots, some revolvers, most the deeper intonations of shotguns.

Mark ducked along street after street, gradually getting closer to his objective. And at last, there it was. It seemed empty, and as quiet as it always was. He gave a sigh of relief, stepped out of the shadows, and climbed the steps, pressed the bell, and then remembered there was no electricity.

He banged on the door, but this elicited no response; if there were people in the ground floor apartment they weren't coming out.

He chewed his lip, put down his carryall, went down the steps and into the trash area. He opened one of the cans, groped and found an empty tin. He stuffed it with garbage to weight it, wrinkling his nose against the stench, then backed off into the street. At college he'd had a pretty good arm . . .

He threw the can at the third floor. It struck the side of the building several feet below Anne's windows, and fell back to the street with a clatter.

It took Mark several minutes to find it again, all the while listening for the sound of someone opening a window to demand, no doubt from behind the barrel of a shotgun, what the hell he was doing. But the windows remained firmly closed, although he thought he heard a sound on the street. But when he looked left and right he saw nothing. He took up his position once again before Anne's apartment, and hurled the can. This time it struck the edge of her lounge window, before bouncing off again into the blackness. A moment later the window opened.

"Who's there?" Anne asked.

"Me."

"Oh. Mark!" She gave a squeak of pleasure. "I've been so worried. I'll be right down."

He went back up the steps, waited, and heard the noise again. He looked round, and saw several dark figures moving along the pavement, in the deeper shadow of the building next door.

He turned back to the door as he heard the bolts being drawn. "Get back," he said. "Don't open it."

But Anne had already pulled it open and was coming out. "Mark!"

"Back inside," he snapped, but he was too late.

"Get 'em!" someone shouted, and five youths surged up the steps.

"Shit!" Anne complained.

Mark turned back from her and attempted to stem the rush. He thrust out his left arm with closed fist on the end of it, and the first boy ran straight on to it and went tumbling back down the steps, to hit the pavement with a sickening crunch.

The second boy, however, ducked beneath the arm and although Mark then swung his right arm he was too late to save himself from a shoulder charge in the belly which carried him back against the wall.

"Oof," he gasped, as he lost wind.

A third boy was clutching at his jacket. Mark let his legs give way and sank to the floor, out of the embrace of the arms round his waist, heaving forward as he did so, so that his shoulders caught the youth in the groin and upended him against the wall. Mark then reached his feet, looking desperately to his left where he had heard Anne exclaiming a moment previously.

But that fight was also over. Two of the young men had run at Anne. She had stepped back into the hall and slammed the door on the first, as he reached for her dressing gown. Now he was on his hands and knees, screaming and crying that his wrist was broken. Anne had then opened the door again, stepped past the fallen boy, and confronted the last of them. He had attempted to stand his ground, despite the destruction of his comrades, and in turn had reached for the dressing gown, which was now swinging open and revealing, even in the semi-darkness, a good deal of white flesh.

Anne seized his sweater with both hands and brought him against her, raising her knee with all the force she could manage. The boy gave a howl of agony, and fell to his knees. Anne kicked him on the hip, and he rolled down the steps.

"Inside," Mark snapped, and pushed her back into the hallway. He picked up his carryall, heaved the still screaming boy with the broken wrist out of the way, closed and locked the door.

They stared at each other in the darkness.

"You are really something," he said.

She wasn't even panting.

"I was so worried about you," she said.

"About me? Hell."

They listened to shouts and curses from outside, and someone banged on the door.

"Get lost, asshole," Anne said. "Or I'll break your other arm."

The noise died and they went up the stairs together, their arms round each other.

"Remind me never to pick a fight with you," Mark told her.

"Those were just kids." She closed and locked the door, then turned into his arms, her face tilted up for a kiss. "Mmm. Mark . . . do you think we should call an ambulance for that poor boy?"

He shook his head. "The phones are probably out too. Now," tugging off his jacket, "I need a drink."

"What sort of drink? Coffee? Beer? You name it . . . "

"Something to give me courage . . . To strengthen my resolve."

Anne laughed. "For what, bedding with me?"

"No. I've got something to discuss with you."

"What?"

He collapsed wearily on to the settee. "When I've had my drink."

He heard Anne's tongue click behind her teeth as she took the stopper out of the whisky decanter.

"Try that for size," she handed him the glass.

"Come and sit."

She sat on the edge of the chair facing him, examining his expression suspiciously. "Well?"

He drank, took a deep breath and said, "Will you marry me?"

13

The Bombs

"Marry you?" Anne sounded surprised.

"Don't you think it's a good idea?"

"Why spoil a perfect friendship?" She stepped away from him and poured drinks, measuring with some difficulty in the flickering candlelight.

"Because our relationship has gone beyond mere friendship. Or don't you agree?"

Anne cocked her head on one side. "Hadn't thought that deeply about it."

"Don't you ever think about love and permanent relationships?" He took the glass and gulped.

Anne gave a dry laugh. "Oh, I used to . . . in my youth. Those far off days when my anticipation of life was still coloured by the 'happy-ever-after' fairy stories in romantic novels and movies on which kids are reared."

"Do I detect a latent fear of repeated hurt?"

Anne sat down on the settee, leaned back, one shapely leg thrown carelessly across the other. She stared vacantly at the ceiling. "You can say I learned the hard way."

He sat beside her. "You don't have to let one painful incident make you hard."

"I wouldn't, if it was only one." She turned her head to stare at him, and his heart lurched to see the sadness in her face. "I think I have truly loved three blokes. I've been unofficially engaged twice."

"What happened?"

She shrugged. "At the time it seemed like stupid, petty squabbles. In retrospect, I guess we tried to change each other into the kind of partner we wanted. Which was quite different from the way we were."

"Then why did you get engaged in the first place?"

"Sex." Her voice was very matter-of-fact. "We were so sexually compatible we thought every other aspect of our relationship would fall into place. Each time." She sighed.

"So you've settled for sexual compatibility, as and when required, and preserved your independence?"

"Correct."

"And that's all our relationship is to you? Sexual compatibility?"

She shook her head, and turned away so he couldn't see the struggle to control her lower lip.

Mark got up and walked across to the window, stared out at the dark. "Okay, I know you regard yourself as a free agent. You need space to be your own person. But there's one point you've overlooked. We are birds of a feather. I need space, too. I don't want a clinging possessive female who needs to be with me wherever I go, or calling me across continents when we're apart. Nor do I want a little woman patiently waiting at home, warming the nest, with no thought in her head but putting my favourite dinner on the table."

Her head turned, eyes lifted to stare at the curls in the nape of his neck.

He felt in his pocket. "I bought this, before I left London, because" – he swung round to face her – "because I know I have found the right woman for me. We are not only sexually compatible. We are compatible in every possible way. I have never before met a woman I could so totally respect, love and admire. I want a woman with a mind of her own; interests and involvements outside the home. And I'm not talking about raising money for charity – church bazaars and women's clubs for airing complaints about men. I'm talking about someone who can hold a conversation on subjects in which I, too, am interested. I love you, Anne, because you are a business woman. I love the fact that putting on a super meal at the end of a working day is just part of being alive. Not the be-all and end-all of your life." He came back to stand over her, placed the little box in her hands.

Anne opened it, gazed at the ruby set between two diamonds. "Didn't anyone ever tell you this is the end of the twentieth century? People don't go in for this kind of gesture in this day and age." Her voice was tight. She was resisting with difficulty.

"So what's wrong with being romantic? Why don't you try it on?"

Anne slipped it on to her finger. "It's too big."

"Well, we have two choices. We can fatten you up or we can have the ring reduced. Which would you prefer?"

She sat staring down at the ring. Did she dare let it happen again? Lay herself wide open to the same devastating pain as last time . . . and the time before . . . and the time before that?

"I'll go make some coffee," Mark said, and headed for the kitchen. He'd said his piece. Now it was up to her to make up her mind.

He returned with the two mugs on a tray which he put on a small table, cursing the dryness in his throat – the tension in his gut.

She was still wearing the ring on the fourth finger of her left hand, holding the hand out and admiring it. "Looks good, huh?" She got up and stood beside him. "You are absolutely right. We were obviously made for each other."

He held her shoulders and stood back, examining her face. "That was a quick reversal. Are you quite sure?"

"Positive." She leaned against him, relaxed. Trusting. Forcing away the doubts that had held her back.

"Okay. We'll take the ring to a jeweller's in the morning."

She regarded him for several seconds, kissed him firmly on the mouth, then asked, "Are you hungry?"

"Yes. But not for food."

She nodded. "Me too."

He followed her into the bedroom. "You never said if you liked the ring."

"I think it's the most beautiful ring in the world."

He supposed that was as near to an acceptance as he was ever going to get.

"Guess what!" Anne announced. "We have power." The bedside light was already on, and now she found the remote control and switched on the TV.

Sleepily Mark looked at his watch; it was just after six, and actually as daylight as the overcast allowed.

" . . . worst in all the history of the United States," the newsreader was saying. "Reports are still coming in, but it now seems evident that the entire North American grid failed just on dusk last night. The outage lasted for eight hours, or until an hour ago, and plunged the entire continent into chaos. Many people have been trapped in high-rise apartments or their hotel rooms throughout this period, many others have been caught in elevators between floors and are only now being released. But these were the lucky ones. On the streets there have been pitched battles between police and looters who became rioters when attempts were made to control them. It is impossible to estimate at this stage the total casualty figure, but here in Boston alone there are reports of more than twenty people killed, and this does not include those involved in the numerous car accidents which occurred just after the blackout. This morning Boston looks like a battleground, with shop windows smashed, abandoned cars blocking streets, and police patrolling in force; what the tsunami of last autumn failed to accomplish, one night of thuggery has achieved. The Mayor has issued an appeal for calm, but he has also imposed a curfew which will take effect at dusk this evening, and will last until he is satisfied that the city is under control."

Anne went to the window, opened it, and looked out. The street was relatively unscathed – no sign of the five youths who had attacked them.

"In the studio with me I have John Reynolds of the Electricity Company," the newsreader continued. "Mr Reynolds . . . we've had power outages before, and recently they've been quite common. We've been told it is a result of the unending rain and damp, and in many cases the inability of your maintenance engineers to carry out their duties, but there has never been anything on this scale."

"As a matter of fact, the north-eastern seaboard did have a complete outage once before," Reynolds countered. "That was more than twenty years ago, and was regarded as a freak. But it lasted for several hours before additional supplies could be switched from other grids."

"I remember that one," Mark said. "It's claimed the number of births in New England nine months later was double the average."

"You have a one-track mind," Anne told him.

"And last night was another such freak?" the newsreader asked.

"I wish I could say that," Reynolds replied. "Last night was perhaps inevitable, and I'm afraid it may not be an isolated incident. Over the past several months, as you just mentioned, the situation has gradually deteriorated, and this has been happening not only in Boston or New England as a whole, but across the entire northern half of the continent including Canada. We have been doing everything possible in the adverse circumstances, but we have known for some time that a total outage was imminent. It only needed one extra overload. That happened last night. At the peak hour, when everyone was switching on their lights and their ovens, there was a failure in New England. Under normal circumstances additional power would immediately have been requisitioned from a neighbouring grid, either Canada or the midwest. But on this occasion there were simultaneous outages in Montreal and Seattle. These cities naturally also sought additional power from neighbouring grids, and this threw an overload on to the whole system."

"Are you saying that a situation like that of last night could happen again?"

"Very easily, and very soon, unless something is done."

"What do you have in mind?"

"I think we have to introduce some kind of rationing, as they have already in Britain and parts of Europe. At least until this crisis is over."

"Oh, cheer me up," Anne said, switching off. "Running battles in the street! Maybe we got off lightly." She got out of bed, stood in the bathroom doorway to watch him shave. "You're in one of your hurries."

"I have to get down to Washington." He grinned at her in the mirror. "I should've gone last night, but I'm glad I didn't. Although I figure you could've taken on those five on your own."

"If you hadn't turned up, I wouldn't have had to take them on at all," she pointed out. "When do you come back?"

He wiped his face clean of soap, turned, and held her left hand, looking at the ring. "I don't know, for sure."

"You mean the balloon's going up?"

"Just as soon as it can be done. Before civilisation really falls apart. What are you going to do?"

She shrugged. "Get on with living. While it's still practical."

"Yeah. Look, have the ring made smaller, or whatever it is they do. I don't want you losing it the first time you wear it."

"You still think this is a good idea?"

He kissed her. "Don't you?" But after last night he knew she was joking.

"We were all right down here," Obrenski told Mark, as they waited to see the President. "Anyway, we have our emergency generating supplies to fall back on. But it sounds as if it was pretty grim."

"It was. And will be again, if we don't get something done, p.d.q."

The President looked tired; Mark knew that for the past month he had been besieged by lobbyists for every conceivable movement, trying to make him change his mind about setting off the bombs. He was as usual flanked by his advisers, as well as by the men he had appointed to liaise with business and industry.

"Well, gentlemen, I've been through the reports, and I've spent half the morning on the telephone to various heads of state. There is one hell of a lot of opposition ... but as long as Moscow is prepared to work with us I guess we can call the shots. Mr Laverick?"

The industrialist cleared his throat. "We are not quite ready, sir. We are manufacturing protective clothing at the rate of ten thousand suits a day, but we are still short of our target. There is also a distribution problem, of course."

"Give me a date."

"Well . . . five weeks minimum."

"Five weeks?" Mark cried.

The President glanced at him. "It couldn't be sooner than that, anyway, Dr Payton. We may not have obtained the support of the European community, but we have to give them fair warning, and time to prepare."

"The squawk at our unilateral decision to go ahead may well break up the cloud on its own," the Press Secretary opined.

"I have that much in mind. Mr Preston?"

"Well, sir, I can't say any of us is happy about it, but as there seems to be no alternative . . . it will mean a total shut-down of all business activities for a period of three months."

"At least," the Press Secretary muttered.

"Now, sir," Preston went on, "in accordance with your instructions, we have been increasing production as much as possible, and there are considerable stockpiles, both of manufactured goods and raw materials available, but of course there are inevitably going to be the most massive shortages. I'm afraid the strictest rationing is going to have to be imposed. Certainly as severe as anything in World War II."

The President nodded. "I'm asking Congress this afternoon for a state of emergency, nationwide, as from next week, and for a period of three months after the bombs are detonated. I then intend to impose rationing as near immediately as we can make it. Our lobbying indicates that these requests will be granted. My address will also serve to announce our intention to the world, and the Soviet President will make a similar announcement tomorrow."

"Let's all thank God we're not still in the days of the Cold War," Obrenski remarked. "Otherwise we could find ourselves with a war on our hands as well."

"Quite," the President said. "Mr Summers?"

"One hundred million booklets have been printed, and every home in the United States will have received one by now. I can't pretend anyone's happy about the situation, but they're accepting it. It is very important, however, that everything runs smoothly." He looked at the four-star general seated beside him.

"My boys are geared up," General Crowther said. "They know what they have to do. They'll keep order, and they'll deliver the food supplies."

"Ron?" the President asked.

The Federal Reserve Director cleared his throat. "My people have prepared the figures you wanted, Mr President. Funding all of this is going to require the biggest tax increase in the history of this country."

"I think everyone accepts that fact," the President said. "Congress certainly does, save for a few mavericks. Survival is a costly business. But I still want the package presented in the most favourable light." He grinned at the Press Secretary. "Okay, Jimmy, we are probably going to lose the next election, but we may just have saved the nation. Maybe the world." He looked round all of their faces. "Well, gentlemen, I think we'll have to give it six weeks. But not a moment longer. I will therefore tell you now the date on which the bombs will be fired . . . 5 September. Thank you."

"Six weeks!" Mark protested to Obrenski. "Another six weeks."

"People have to be given time to prepare," Dave pointed out. "We can't just fire off bombs while everybody is outside looking on."

"Six weeks is going to be three weeks too late. At the very least," Mark groaned. "I'm going back to Boston."

Liz was in Greenwich with Jennifer and Charles when the news broke. The three of them were watching the President's speech to the Joint Houses of Congress on television.

"Are they *mad*!" Jennifer squeaked, bouncing up and down. "My God, the children . . . "

"Ssssh!" Charles recommended, as the newsreader went on to say that the British Government, although deeply deploring the Russo-American plan, recognising that the decision was irrevocable, would within forty-eight hours publish guidelines for the public to follow during the period after the bombs had been fired.

"Asked about protective clothing," the newsreader went on, "the Government spokesman informed us that there were only sufficient supplies for the essential services, which in this context includes those responsible for food deliveries; it is assumed this will be the province of the Army. It therefore seems probable that for most of us, the three months following 5 September will have to be spent indoors."

"Three months, indoors?" Jennifer demanded, her small frame quivering with rage. "Jessica and Jackie, locked up for three months? That has to be the most ridiculous idea yet! What on earth will we do with them? I mean, what will any family do?"

"Grin and bear it," Charles suggested, chin jutting.

"Oh, you . . . you just sit there," Jennifer stormed.

"Look, darling, *something* has to be done. Our people don't seem able to make up their minds, so thank God for Washington and Moscow."

"All our lives are going to be at risk."

"Aren't they already at risk? Quite apart from the flood water, what about all the new, previously unknown bacteria that are filling the hospitals. Old and young are dropping like flies. Anyway, even if the kids do go outside at present, in their wellies and macs, the air is so disgustingly polluted they risk far worse than if they stay indoors."

"They have to go to playschool," Jennifer pointed out.

"No, they do not. It is quite unnecessary, besides being an additional risk to their health. I think you should telephone Miss Whatshername and tell her they are not attending till further notice." He'd really got the bit between his teeth now. "I'm at home all day, now; I'll take them over for three hours every morning. Teach them to read and count."

"You don't know what you're saying!" Jennifer tried not to laugh, wondering how long he'd last. She caught Liz's eye and both girls quickly looked away.

Liz was going back to Dunning Farm the next morning, for which she was very grateful. She thought this time she was going to stay put, until after the baby was born. Well, she would have to, once the bombs were fired. She loved being here with Jennifer, but she loved her home, too. In it she could potter about, do things. Staying with friends was all very well, but it was lovely to be in a place of one's own. She would stay in the Wing and wait for Geoffrey to come back. And what about Geoffrey? By the end of August he'd be on his return voyage. There wouldn't be any protective clothing at sea! She turned to Charles in alarm.

"Don't let it faze you! They're not all dummies in the Merchant Navy. They'll pick up the gear in the States or wherever before starting the crossing."

She prayed he was right. And after calling Freddie to let him know what train she was hoping to arrive on – British Rail was maintaining a mainline service but it was very uncertain – she hugged and kissed everyone, trying not to think about how long it might be before she saw them again, and took a taxi from Greenwich right across London to King's Cross.

Every time she did this trip it became more alarming. At Greenwich itself the river was wide, and if it was always higher than usual – and when the tide in the Channel was high and the Barrier needed to be open for the passage of ships the water was lapping at the embankment and some of the landing stages were submerged – somehow it lacked any menace. It was as she drove into London, along the embankment, that the extent of the flooding became apparent. This wasn't tide so much as a sheer swelling of the river above the locks, which could no longer cope. At high water, when the Barrier was normally closed, the embankment itself was under water, several inches deep, and although on each low tide this was taken off when the Barrier was opened, she knew that all the houses near to the river had been evacuated.

Government spokesmen kept reassuring the public that the levees and the Barrier would prevent any risk of catastrophe, but reassurances could hardly compensate the people who had now been out of their homes for months, and who had to know that those homes, after all that time under water, would hardly be habitable again without the spending of a great deal of money.

And now, on top of all of this, the highly dubious decision – in her opinion, anyway – to fire off atomic bombs into the atmosphere . . .

Traffic on the bridge at Westminster was bumper to bumper.

"It's the tubes, see," her driver said. "Most of them ain't running, and most of the mainline trains are out as well. Too much water, and too much damp for the circuits. You know something, our civilisation ain't geared up to cope with nothing like this. It's just too . . . well, civilised. Everything's too dependent on everything else working well and to full capacity. I mean, even fifty years ago, when we still had steam trains, all this weather wouldn't have meant a damn. Now the country is just solidifying because there isn't enough electricity. Can you beat that? Anyway, the Government has lifted parking restrictions, while making it a traffic offence to drive into town with less than three people in the car. Mind you, they're saying our fuel supplies are so short even that's going to stop in the near future. Add that to the fact that half the traffic lights are out all the time . . . "

"At least we haven't had a total blackout like they had in the States the other night," she pointed out.

"Only because the Yanks are even more civilised than us. Rationing," he said. "The Americans don't go for that. Big spenders."

The taxi came to a halt in a seemingly unending stream of traffic. "Lights out up ahead," he explained. "This whole street has been knocked out. Water in the underground electric conduits. Dangerous, you know. Water and electricity don't mix."

He wasn't too unhappy, as his meter was ticking away, but Liz began to chafe; she had allowed herself what she thought was plenty of time, but now her train was to leave in only half an hour.

They moved a few feet, and stopped again. Liz looked out of her window as she heard a vague commotion, and watched several men running along the pavement, carrying an assortment of bags and valises, and also a couple of shotguns, while from round the corner there came shouts.

"What on earth . . . ?"

"It's a robbery," the driver explained. "Happens all the time, nowadays."

"But . . . shouldn't we *do* something?"

"You don't want to get involved. You could miss your train. And those fellows are armed."

Liz stared at the men as they drew abreast of the taxi, and then began to cross the road. Cars coming in the opposite direction screeched to a stop, and the policeman on point duty came running along the pavement.

"Oh, lord," remarked the driver. "Here's trouble."

The policeman held up his hand, and one of the robbers levelled his shotgun and fired.

"Oh, my God!" Liz screamed, as the policeman fell backwards and blood scattered across the pavement.

In the distance they heard the wail of a siren, but it wasn't getting any closer.

"They have it all figured out," the taxi driver said. "They go for areas where they know the electricity has been cut off, so all the alarms are out as well. That gives them an extra half an hour at least in their getaway. Hey, lady, you don't want to get involved . . . "

Liz had opened the door and was dodging cars as she ran across the street to kneel beside the stricken policeman. He was alive, but very badly hurt, and bleeding profusely.

"Hey, lady, the traffic's moving," called her driver, at the same time blowing his horn.

"Fuck the traffic," Liz muttered, using her handkerchief to attempt to staunch the blood. By now several other people had gathered round. The taxi driver pulled into the kerb and joined them. No doubt, Liz supposed, his meter was still running.

Freddie was waiting at King's Lynn Station.

"I'm sorry I'm late," Liz said. "Did you get my message?"

Freddie nodded. "You're in no condition to take on armed bandits, you know."

"I didn't take them on," she protested. "They ran off. I just couldn't leave that cop lying there. Hell, Freddie, that ride was terrifying. The way those thugs rampaged, and then shot the poor guy straight in the gut . . . "

"It's happening all over," Freddie said gloomily, as they drove through the lake that spread across the station yard. "I suppose the point of view is, if the world is going to come to an end, one way or the other, the best thing to do is grab what you can while you can."

He gave a twisted grin. "The thing is, you needn't have come home at all."

"Eh?"

"We've just had what amounts to an order from the County Council, this morning. Dunning Farm, and all of West Walton, has to be evacuated."

"Why?"

"There is a spring tide in a week, and water levels are already ten feet above normal; there's been a massive increase over the past week or so. The levee may not keep it out. In any event, the drains can no longer cope as they are never above water level. So it's just going to get higher. I've got a small boat in the barn, but we can't depend on that to get us all we need."

"Oh, hell. When do we have to go?"

"By the end of the week. The animals leave tomorrow."

"But . . . " she thought of the beautiful home she and Geoffrey had made out of the Granny Wing, the furniture that they had lovingly restored, the plans she had made for the baby . . .

The baby!

"How long will we have to stay away?"

"Search me. Until water levels return to normal."

"But that may not be until next winter."

"That's what they're saying. No matter what the Yanks and Russians do in the atmosphere."

She wanted to weep, and the more so as they came in sight of the farm buildings. She had never seen this place in sunshine, with everything going well, yet she had come to regard it as home. Especially since the death of her parents had made such a break in her ties with Australia; she didn't know when she would ever return.

The Land Rover splashed to a halt in the yard, and Liz hurried inside to find her mother-in-law. "Mary, I am so terribly sorry."

"I don't think I properly understand what's happening," Mary said. "The letter only arrived late this morning. Now . . . " she looked around herself. "There's so much to be done."

"What are we going to do? I mean, where will we go?"

"The Government has various hostels available, of course, and it's started opening camps. But they sound pretty grim, and apparently we are welcome to make our own arrangements if we can. In fact they'd prefer that, as accommodation is really short. I thought we might ask Jennifer and Charles if we could move in with them. We'd pay them rent, of course . . . it might be a help."

The thought of them all cooped up in the Greenwich house was dismaying, but Liz couldn't very well say that to Mary. "I'm sure they'd love to have you. Us. Have you spoken to them yet?"

"No, I was waiting for you to get home. You look bothered."

"I can't help wondering if it's a good thing to go to them. They are quite near the river. Would we really be gaining anything?"

"Oh yes. The house is well up the hill . . . "

"But . . . "

" . . . and besides, I'd much rather keep all the family together. Once we are separated, and if things get worse, one never knows when . . . " Mary's voice trailed off.

"Well . . . " Liz endeavoured to give a bright smile. "I'm here now. Let's see if we can get through."

Mary stood in the middle of the sitting-room and stared – first in one direction then, swivelling slowly on the heel of her shoe, into the next, and the next. What to take? What to abandon? She closed her eyes, and a weird noise, part gasp, part sob, part moan, welled up from her very soul. In this room her whole life was encapsulated. Family portraits, both painted and photographed in sepia; of grandparents and great-grandparents. Framed photographic reminders of all the important events in their lives: with her parents at Buckingham Palace when Dad received the OBE, John in dress uniform, bemedalled; the children's christenings and confirmations, the lovely silver-framed picture of Jennifer's wedding standing alongside a similar one of herself and John. Jackie and Jessica . . . Her eyes moved to the glass cabinet and the collection of porcelain figurines. She heard a noise in the kitchen. "Have you got any boxes in the barn, Freddie?"

"Some. What sort? Wood, cardboard?" He came to the doorway, drinking tea from a mug.

"Preferably wood."

"How many?"

"As many as you can lay hands on. I'm going to start packing stuff away, upstairs." She opened the cabinet and began removing the precious contents.

Freddie stood watching her for a moment, open-mouthed. He had to admire her, dear old Mum whom he had teased and derided over the years; Mum, who seemed so old-fashioned, fussy, feeble in her attitudes to contemporary life and technology. Here she was, her whole existence tumbling around her ears, not sitting weeping over endless cups of tea and complaining of headaches, but demanding materials to get weaving on the job of salvaging everything possible.

Now she was taking pictures out of the frames. "We can't take all these heavy mounts with us, they'll have to stay, but the pictures themselves need to be kept dry," she explained.

"Of course," Freddie agreed, and dragged on his wellies again, to wade across to the barn. At least, when this was all over, there would be years in which to rebuild his own future, but how much time would Dad and Mum have? Well, if Mum was prepared to expend that much energy and effort . . . In the barn he gave the tractor's engine casing an affectionate smack. "Can't get you into the attic, old girl. Somehow or other we're just going to have to replace you."

"How's it going?" Liz stood in Mary's bedroom doorway studying the stacked crates and boxes amidst the remains of screwed up newspapers and kitchen roll.

Mary straightened her back with an effort. Her face was red and perspiration matted her hair into punk points. "I could go on for another fortnight. Unfortunately there isn't another fortnight available so I'll just have to stop when the lorry comes."

"Have you packed up everything you're taking?"

"I've done that three times. Then emptied the cases and started again. Keep changing my mind." She laughed. "Good thing you've come over. Stop me doing it a fourth time. Let's put on the kettle." Tea was, after all, the best placebo in the world.

Liz sat on a kitchen chair and the dog came and rested his chin on her knee. "Jason looks miserable. Anyone would think he knows what's happening."

"It's the suitcases. He always goes into a decline when they come out. But don't under-estimate him. He senses our moods, so he's known that something was wrong for months."

The entire parish was being evacuated, including the village church. Roy Chubb had of course been invited for a drink back in April, after the wedding party had returned, and had offered a suitable blend of condolence and congratulation. Now he was coming round to say goodbye. Clearly his own ebullient, optimistic, confident personality could not retreat into biblical prophecies based on the vengeance of the Lord for mankind's relentless pursuit of Mammon, as some were doing. But equally clearly, he could not accept that such a catastrophe should be allowed to hover above the earth. He shook hands with each member of the family, and then took his leave. At a loss for words.

Liz had done all she could, packed their clothes and most precious small items into two large suitcases, praying there might be storage room in Greenwich for them. Larger things like crockery and cutlery she carried up into Mary's attic.

When her packing was complete and Mary had assured her there was nothing more she could do to help in the main house, Liz wandered out to the barn. "Any chance we could drive out to the levees to see just how the water level is looking?" she asked Freddie's back as he hauled another load of farm gear up to one of the barn beams. "If you have enough petrol."

"May as well use the last ration. But it would be a pretty round-about route, trying to pick the roads that are built up high enough." He criss-crossed the coil of rope round a cleat on an upright, finishing it off with a reverse turn. "I went out there just over a week ago and it was tricky then. But there's no harm in trying. When had you in mind?"

"Whenever it suits."

"I've just about finished here. And I was meaning to go into King's Lynn, anyway. Let's have a coffee and then we'll take the Land Rover."

Freddie manoeuvred the vehicle on to the grid of narrow roads, most of which still cleared the water and mud, though it was necessary to do some awkward shunting to avoid those that positively did not. The tide was out and the town was dry if damp, but the waters of the Great Ouse were swirling up to the bridge as they drove across it.

"Lines are out," Freddie explained, as he parked in front of what was Doreen's parents' house. Liz didn't offer to go in, especially when Freddie said, "Shan't be long." In fact he was back in five minutes, looking thunderstruck.

"They've gone."

"Just like that? Oh, Freddie . . . "

"There's a note. Says she tried to get in touch, without success. There's a letter in the mail." He brooded for a few minutes. "Sensible thing to do, really." He grinned at her. "Come on, you wanted to look at the levee."

Liz bit her lip. There was nothing she could say. She only knew that she could never have walked away from this big, friendly bear, no matter how frightened she was, without making a real attempt to see him and make future plans.

Perhaps the plans were in the letter.

Although the mist limited visibility, it was possible to see across the surrounding water. "Ever been to Spain?" Freddie asked.

"No. Why?"

"This all looks a bit like the rice fields just south of Valencia."

"If the weather stays warm as this you can head the market into a new crop."

"And if the water level didn't rise any further. Which it will. You can't grow rice on the seabed."

Liz glanced at his face. It was grim.

Freddie was able to get the Land Rover right up to the embankment . . . and hoped he wouldn't live to regret it: he was no Canute. For as they watched, less than four hundred yards away the rising tide was coming inexorably towards them.

"Will you just look at the speed it's coming across that beach," Liz gasped. "That is quite awesome."

"And that beach was once green fields."

"In the olden days . . . " she mused.

Freddie snorted. "Like a month ago?"

"You can't be serious! Will they ever be usable as agricultural land again?" Liz asked.

"After being inundated with salt water? Not for one hell of a long time."

The dam was patrolled by soldiers, and also by engineers, for it had been hastily put together and there had been no time to pour the amount of concrete necessary for a true sea wall.

Two soldiers were passing when Freddie said he thought they should get back, rapidly.

"Oh, it'll hold," one of the engineers told them. "As long as we don't have any storms to push the water too hard. In that respect, we've been jolly lucky."

Lucky, Liz thought miserably, as they returned to the Land Rover, and then had to form part of a long queue taking the road back towards Wisbech; an enormous number of people had come out for a last look before leaving – most of the town was also being evacuated. . . .

"What about Geoff?" Liz asked.

"What about Geoff?"

"Well . . . shouldn't he be told that the ancestral home is being abandoned?"

"I reckon we'll wait until he's nearer to home," Freddie decided. "Heck, he won't even have reached South America yet. There's damn all he can do, except worry."

She supposed he was right.

They dined on a miscellaneous collection of leftovers on the last night. "Amazing what one finds stuck at the back of the fridge," Mary said to no one in particular. "I found all sorts of things I didn't know I had. And as for the freezer . . . "

"Is it all cleaned out and switched off?" John asked.

"Of course. And the lid propped open. Now," she opened a

plastic container, "would you like some of this ham?"

"How green is it, Mum? Are you sure it doesn't bite?"

"Do like Jason. Bite back," Mary suggested.

"I hope the sewerage system is working well in Greenwich," John feigned a growl. "We're all going to have the runs by the time we finish this lot."

"Well, Jason doesn't agree. He's having a ball," Freddie noted, slipping the unknown contents of another anonymous package on to the floor.

Liz thought the three Dunnings were fantastic, the way they laughed and leg-pulled. The magnificent silver and crystal with which their lovely dining table was normally laid, had been replaced with plastic boxes and freezer bags. Their instant coffee was creamed with powdered milk, and they drank it from ancient, chipped mugs. Yet listening to them, you'd never believe the misery they were suffering. Freddie had said not a word about Doreen, even if, with the mail in chaos, he must know there was very little chance of his ever receiving her letter. And of course their spirit helped. No point in going into a decline at this stage; negative thinking was only destructive. Follow their lead, she told herself. Be positive.

"So that's where the smell was coming from!" she exclaimed as she opened an elderly box of Gorgonzola. "And all this time I thought the drains were blocked." She could play their game, too.

But she didn't sleep that night, at all. Nor did the others.

Liz dozed just before dawn, then sat up with a start. She couldn't imagine what had disturbed her.

She heard voices, got out of bed, pulled on her dressing-gown, and joined the family downstairs.

"It was a funny sound," John explained.

Freddie was on the telephone, trying to get through to the police station, but the lines were still dead.

"Listen," Mary said.

Through the night they had heard the screech of a siren, assuming it was a distant police patrol.

Freddie put the phone down and opened the front door, as the police motor cyclist emerged from the mist.

"Emergency, sir," the policeman said. "You must leave the farm immediately."

"The van is coming for our things at eight o'clock," Freddie protested.

"Can't wait for that, sir. You must take only what you can carry. The water's coming over the top of the dam, and the tide's still rising. It'll be here in half an hour."

Mary's eyes closed, momentarily. Then she swallowed hard and said, "Let's get these other things upstairs, boys. Freddie, that will have to stay, and that. Anything else you want to put in the attic, Liz, before we lock up?"

14

A Lot of Water

"Wowie," Hudson commented. "There's a green and pleasant land."

The mist had to a large extent cleared over the Arctic as temperatures had equalised, and visibility was quite good. Flying at 8,000 feet, Mark could look down on Greenland, and on a sight he had never hoped to see in his lifetime. Below him, this high central plateau might not yet be a green and pleasant land as it was round the southern coast, but it was just about devoid of snow. Water was running everywhere, gushing down hillsides and foaming through valleys, heading for the sea. He had known the permafrost was going to melt, with all that that implied . . . but once it began he had not expected it to accelerate at such a pace.

"That's happening all over Canada as well," Hudson remarked as he turned the aircraft for Thule. "When are you guys letting off your bombs, Doctor?"

"It doesn't matter now," Mark said gloomily. "We're too late."

"Tom Kinnear has been trying to get you," Anne said, when Mark telephoned.

"Oh, yeah?"

"He said it was very urgent."

"I'm sure he did. If only he hadn't killed my interview last February . . . "

"Anyway, I told him you'd call when you got back. When's that going to be?"

"Day after tomorrow."

"14 August," Anne said. "Three weeks and counting. We have things to talk about."

"I'm all in favour of that," Mark said.

*　　　*　　　*

So that no matter what happened, it would be the two of them, if necessary against the world. What was left of it.

The sudden collapse of the permafrost had taken everyone except Mark by surprise. Only a fortnight previously governments and experts had been dealing in a matter of ten feet at the top of each tide, and expressing considerable confidence. Now the water level was twenty feet above normal, and catastrophe had arrived. Every seaside town and port was in a state of emergency; most docks were under water, and as life had to go on as best it could, shipping was unloading into lighters offshore, their cargoes then being ferried ashore, across esplanades and down streets where shops and office blocks rose out of the water like relics of a bygone age, until at the first rise of ground improvised ramps would be put into use for the stevedores.

In countries like Holland, there was no rising ground for miles inland from the sea. Holland had been reduced to a series of islets, and a massive evacuation of the population had taken place into West Germany. But the evacuations themselves were another source of disruption and chaos; there were simply not enough places for the evacuees to go, and the hills of Picardy were covered in huge, tented refugee camps. This was no serious hardship for the moment, apart from the agonising misery of having abandoned one's home to the water, because of the extremely high temperatures . . . but the temperatures themselves were becoming a problem. Even in the absence of direct sunshine they regularly climbed past a hundred degrees Fahrenheit every day – at least there was no shortage of bathing or swimming facilities.

In England, East Anglia had been turned into a gigantic sea lake, almost the whole of Norfolk and Suffolk having had to be evacuated; only the roofs of houses and church spires marked where there had once been thriving communities; electricity pylons poked up from the gentle waves like surrealistic mooring buoys. Further south conditions were a little better, as the Essex dyke had been made higher, and the countryside itself was an extra few feet above sea level; the dam included massive sluices to take off the top of the tide, while the Thames Tidal Barrier also seemed to be coping, although below it there was massive flooding in Chatham and the Isle of Sheppey. In London, the Underground system had had to be abandoned.

Islands like Jersey and Guernsey had lost a third of their areas, and more than a third of their houses and businesses. Again, most people had been evacuated; only a handful were clinging to the higher ground, supplied by daily airlifts from the mainland.

But conditions were no better on the other side of the Atlantic.

In Boston itself the Neck, so laboriously reclaimed from the sea over the past hundred years, was once again submerged, and people had been forced to leave their homes. Lower Manhattan was inundated on every tide, the water flowing over the Battery and along Wall Street; the financial centres had been moved out of New York altogether, and reassembled on the mainland in White Plains.

Further south, Atlantic City, Norfolk, Charleston, and Savannah, were virtually flooded ghost towns, their residents moved inland into improvised camps. The offshore islands had all but disappeared. The rising water level was equally devastating in Florida. Miami Beach had been evacuated as had all the coastal strip east of the Intra-Coastal Waterway which was now all but part of the sea itself in most places. Sea water flowed inland through gardens and houses, shops and restaurants, crossing the Interstate 95 and the South Dixie Highway and, most disastrously, contaminating the State water supply as it swept into Lake Okeechobee. Low-lying island groups such as Bermuda and the Bahamas had been reduced in area to minute islets, their airports under water. In Nassau itself, Bay Street had vanished and Government House stood at the top of Shirley Street with water swirling through the houses immediately below. Most Bahamians had been evacuated to restricted camps in the States; although they were being constantly assured they could go home when the water receded, no one was convinced it would ever happen and many of them sat out in the wet, refusing to eat, weeping and wailing to the Lord for deliverance.

The death toll was mounting, too. Apart from the inevitable accidents, the ever-thickening atmosphere had caused a sharp upsurge in bronchial complaints. Most northern governments had by now just about banned any factories emitting smoke – and indeed many had simply closed down for lack of fuel or labour – but it was rather like closing one's front door after the water has come in, and expecting the carpet to dry.

And there were still twenty-one days to the explosion of the bombs. They could have no effect now, Mark knew, save to add a radiation hazard to those already existing; sure, if they dispersed the cloud the next winter should see a return to normal atmospheric conditions – but could civilisation ever return to normal? If only they could have been fired three months ago, while there was still some chill in the air.

And yet, they still *had* to be fired, now, if there was to be any hope of civilisation even surviving.

*   *   *

A Lot of Water

DON'T PANIC. The words bombarded one from every angle. Posters on hoardings, full-page spreads in newspapers; TV, radio . . . They made one want to close one's eyes, put one's hands over one's ears and run. Liz sat on the lid of the loo, hands over the bulge in her lap, feeling the tiny limbs in there kicking and punching . . . wondering if he or she would ever see this hellish world before it disintegrated. There was nothing worth seeing in it, that was for sure.

The loo was the only place in the house where one could be alone – sit thinking without the feeling that someone was watching your face, analysing your thoughts. The fact that everyone else was far too busy with equally miserable thoughts of their own to bother analysing yours, didn't overcome the desperate need for occasional privacy. Living tight-packed with so many people, even folks as super as this family, tended to fray relationships. From the privacy of the Wing, she had never noticed Freddie's fluctuating moods. John's pipe never stank so offensively, and Mary's calm, jovial personality had only been a source of admiration. When she had stayed with the Rowlands previously, Jenny's inability to discipline the children had been laughable and she'd not been aware how fiercely Charles over-compensated.

Everyone was suffering, trying in one way or another to cope with their private miseries; it was when, accidentally, and publicly, those private miseries got temporarily out of hand that sparks flew and people readily snapped each other's heads off. Of course there were tears and apologies afterwards, but each spate tended to worsen the overall atmosphere, with everyone speaking to each other over-cautiously, tense for the fear of causing offence. So the loo became the most relaxing corner of the house.

Unfortunately one couldn't stay in the loo for long, there were only two, both much in demand. Liz pulled the flush after she heard someone try the doorhandle . . . she hadn't used it but she had to pretend and, in the circumstances, she couldn't be accused of wasting water. There wasn't exactly a shortage.

"Oh, it's you." Charles stood aside, unsmiling, to let her pass.

"Hope I didn't keep you waiting." She smiled, ignoring his curt manner.

"No. I'm only just back."

"Where have you been?" she asked, surprised he could go anywhere; then she wished she hadn't spoken, afraid he'd be annoyed at her for prying.

But he wasn't. "Just down the hill as far as I could."

"How's the water level?"

"Up another couple of inches."

His voiced sounded odd and when she looked closely in the gloom of the hallway she realised with horror that he was on the verge of breaking down. Charles! Big, strong Charles, the financial whizzkid. You poor beggar, she thought, you've lost so much more than most of us: you had so much more to lose. She squeezed his arm. "Well at least this family's better off than a lot of folks. We've none of us gone down with anything more serious than the odd cough and cold. So many families have been decimated by viral diseases."

Charles gave a watery grin. "Trust our little Oz to make one imagine one is bloody lucky!" He feinted a cuff on her chin, stepped past her into the small room and locked the door. It was his turn for privacy.

TV and radio had been given over to Government announcements – mainly a list of street corners where the next food deliveries were to be made by the army – *Pink Panther, Fred Flintstone* and weather reports . . . none of which ever varied, all interspersed with jolly music. And of course the news, which didn't vary much, either. Every lunchtime during their limited electricity ration, they sat round the dining table shushing the kids, hoping for one good item in the news report. But the news only deteriorated steadily, and today was the worst yet: the bombs were due for detonation in a fortnight. That was bad enough, but if the water kept on rising . . . and after the bombs had gone off, how could they possibly be evacuated, even supposing there was some place to go?

The adults looked at each other in turn, shrugging, shaking their heads, unable to think of anything to say.

Raucous music invaded the miserable scene and Jackie and Jessica whooped with joy as yet another cartoon burst into life.

Jason started barking at the sudden excitement and Charles demanded the remote control to turn it off.

"No Daddy, please. We want it." The children screamed, but before he could press the button the electricity failed, the picture dwindled to a blue spot and disappeared and the light over the table went out.

Both the children started to cry.

Afraid of Charles's reaction, Jennifer shouted at them to shut up; it was so unusual for her to raise her voice to them that they were stunned into temporary obedience.

"Oh hell! I'm getting out of here." Charles shoved his chair back from the table. "Come on, Jason. Come outside and have a leak. Add your contribution to the flood."

The rest of the family sat in embarrassed silence as he stamped up the hallway, wrestled his brolly from the congestion in the umbrella stand, and slammed out of the front door. And just as they started to move and collect up dirty plates they heard the door flung open again.

Charles came back into the room looking as though he'd seen a ghost. "Will someone come outside with me a minute and tell me if I've gone round the bend?"

"What is it?"

"Why?"

"What's up?"

"What have you done?"

They scrambled to follow him, wide-eyed. Mystified.

In the front garden he stopped and stared up at the mist. "Well?"

Everyone followed suit, including the children.

"It's gone lighter," Jessica announced.

Mary's mouth fell open. "She's right! It has!"

"There," Freddie shouted, pointing, "look up there."

"I daren't believe it," Liz whispered in awe.

Other people, strangers, were spilling into the road, shouting, calling to their friends and relations still indoors. "Come on out! The sun! It's the sun! The cloud's breaking up. It's all over!"

Which was a slight exaggeration. The sun was not visible, but there was a definite lighter patch in that part of the sky where the sun should be at 2.15 on an August afternoon.

But it was enough. Charles and Jennifer openly wept in each other's arms. John embraced Mary, and in the absence of Geoffrey and Doreen, Liz hugged Freddie who hugged her back enthusiastically. The children rushed about excitedly, hugging everyone in turn, while Jason barked.

Traditionally, Trafalgar Square was the place where events of national importance were celebrated, and inevitably people began to congregate. Youngsters waded through the water where the fountain no longer played, to climb up round the foot of Nelson's Column. Others scrambled up on to the somnolent lions. Every few minutes cheers would go up from one group or another, setting everyone off again. Clergy appeared on the steps of St Martin-in-the-Fields and began prayers. People nearby began to sing the Crimond version of the twenty-third psalm, taken up by others until it reverberated round and round the square. Many were moved to tears, while others rushed from one group to another kissing everyone they could reach.

The Rowlands and Dunnings held open house to their neighbours. With all the élan of the once wealthy, Charles brought up the last remaining bottles of champagne from his cellar, followed by claret, burgundy and the Spanish wines which over the years he had smuggled back from Javea in his car. Latecomers were sent back home to fetch glasses . . . or plastic mugs. Ladies produced biscuits and nibbles on which all the children descended like locusts, and although the weather was still decidedly damp, everyone spilled out into the road, taking chairs with them for the older celebrants.

In East Anglia the faintly brighter day dimmed into night, beautifying the scene, obliterating the unpleasant sight of animal carcasses moving gently with the rise of tide, bouncing against the roof of the Dunnings' farmhouse. They were mostly wild animals and strays, but unlike the Dunnings, not everyone had been able to move or slaughter their livestock in time, so occasionally a hugely bloated cow carcass appeared, or a pig. Dusk can make the most obnoxious picture appear mystical or romantic. But it cannot annihilate the stench.

That evening, when the children were finally persuaded to go to sleep, the Dunnings and Rowlands settled down in the sitting-room to enjoy the luxury of an extended electricity ration and watch the celebrations on television. Scenes from numerous places accessible to local TV stations were relayed. Some were sombre, some joyful, many drunken and hysterical. The religious aspect was well represented, packed churches holding impromptu thanksgiving services. Cameo interviews were shown: a man told the story of the rescue of his cat, two elderly sisters laughed as they recalled the two days and nights they had sat perched on their roof waiting for the army to arrive in a rubber dinghy. A child sat in a cot while the audience was told why he was the sole survivor of his whole family . . . The producer had even obtained footage from abroad.

"The northern hemisphere seems to be in a solid state of conviviality," Charles remarked to the room in general, as the newsreader pointed out that now the bombs would no longer be needed.

"Oh, thank God for that," Mary said. "I was so afraid. Now . . . even if it takes weeks for the floods to subside, it is a joy to sit with the windows open and smell fresh air." Her face was tired, grey and drawn, and she was trying to count their blessings – not think about their beloved home, submerged. If necessary, the whole house could be rebuilt, but the contents, family linen edged with handmade lace, furniture generations old, her ruined tapestries, those things could never be replaced. But her family was safe and well. Now they could all start to re-structure their lives, even though things would never quite be the same, ever again.

"Without that beastly mist swirling in and soaking the furniture," Jennifer added.

"It'll be your first view of England in sunshine, won't it?" Freddie asked Liz.

"Yes. Something I've been looking forward to ever since I arrived." She knew that it would be a much longer time before England became a green and pleasant land again, but she didn't think Freddie needed reminding of that.

The programme ended with a warning of more power cuts. "I wonder how many weeks it'll take to get the electricity supply back to normal?" Charles liked his creature comforts.

"I don't give a damn," Freddie said, "as long as the bloody sun comes out and stays out."

"Most people on that programme seemed to be very happy, I thought," Liz remarked.

"Except the weather forecaster." John was frowning. "Did you notice? That Met man is usually quite a bright, humorous character but he certainly wasn't tonight."

"It's probably the prospect of having to start work again with satellite pictures and complicated weather maps that's depressing him," Jennifer suggested. "He's had no work to do for months."

Her father smiled and nodded. He wouldn't spoil the family's evening by sharing his private worries, even if he could find words to express them. He knew as much about weather as any farmer worth his salt. Years of observation tended to develop in one a kind of instinct about it; what a woman would call intuition. And he couldn't completely suppress the unreasoned fears which had gnawed away in his chest ever since Charles had called them all out into the road. He kept the fears to himself, but they wouldn't go away.

Mark picked up a paper when he landed at Keene. A local airport in Vermont some eighty miles north-west of Boston, Keene had been hastily converted into an international airport, because Logan was now under water on every high tide.

THE SUN! screamed the banner headlines. SIGHTED IN BRITAIN AND ON THE NORMANDY COAST. TRUE OR HOAX?

But there was a photograph, of a watery looking sun peering through the mist.

Mark looked up. The sky was still dark over New England, at any rate. But if the sun was coming out . . .

There was a bus service into the city, and he was there by mid-afternoon. He had telephoned his parents from the airport to let them know he was back, then went to the apartment; he had his own key now.

Anne wanted to talk to him. And he wanted to talk to her.

Everyone on the bus had been speculating about the sudden re-appearance of the sun over southern Britain and northern France. When Mark switched on the TV, there was a chat show going on about the implications.

"Oh, definitely," one pundit was saying, "the cloud is breaking up, and now that it has started, it will probably do so quite quickly. Mind you, we always knew this was going to happen. It was just a matter of when."

"What does that mean, in real terms, Professor?"

"Why, a return to normalcy."

"You mean the flood waters should now start to recede?"

"Oh, well, not overnight, you understand. But yes, they will certainly commence to go down in the near future, especially as we get into autumn and temperatures begin to drop in the Arctic."

"Then in your opinion, Professor, the crisis is over?"

"Oh, well, obviously there remains a great deal to be done. Land inundated by salt water is going to require massive irrigation and soil hygiene to restore it to its former fertility. There are still millions of homeless people, whose houses may have been wrecked beyond repair. Oh, yes, indeed, there is a lot to be done. But . . . " the Professor's plump red face broke into a smile, "you could say that we have turned the corner, and without the use of those hydrogen bombs."

Mark switched off the set in disgust, and tried calling Washington, but the lines were all busy. He sighed. He would have to get down there and find out what was going on, and whether those people understood the real impact of what was happening.

But first . . . he listened to the feet outside the door, and a moment later it swung in.

"Mark, lover!" Anne kicked the door shut and was in his arms. "Isn't the news marvellous?"

"You reckon?"

She stuck out her tongue at him. "You're just mad because now you won't get to fire off your bombs."

"Believe me, I'm happy enough about that, if it happens to be true. But if this cloud breaks up real quick . . . there could be problems."

"Oh, boo. Listen . . . " she sat beside him on the settee. "Last week, when there seemed no alternative to the bombs, I thought I should go home."

"Eh?"

"Well, I haven't seen my parents for years, and if we were

moving into some kind of Doomsday situation, I felt I wanted to see them again. Be with them, at least for a while."

"You never told me about this."

"You weren't around long enough. Anyway . . . " she looked him in the eye, "I thought we were remaining free agents?"

"Well, sure we are. But going off to England . . . "

"Well, up yours. You go off to England every couple of weeks."

"That's business."

"So how about trying it for pleasure? If you're not firing off those bombs, you don't have to hang about Washington. So why not come with me. Meet your prospective parents-in-law."

"I've done that," Mark said absently.

"Oh yes, I remember. Someone told you that if you wanted to know what a girl would be like in twenty years' time, look at her mother."

"Exactly. And I liked what I saw and came back and proposed."

He kissed her, and she suddenly laughed, got up, and mixed them both a drink. "I was looking forward to telling them about us. You know they've had to evacuate the farm?"

"No. Is that a fact? Damn. What about the levee?"

"Didn't do much good when high tides started going over ten feet, much less twenty."

"Then where are they?"

"Staying with my sister Jennifer, in Greenwich. By the Thames. You haven't met Jennifer."

"She the one who nearly got buried in that Spanish avalanche?"

"That's the one. Apparently she's been in a pretty upset state ever since. I should've gone over long ago. So . . . will you come with me?"

"I'd like to. How're you flying?"

"I'm not. I'm booked on a steamer. I wanted to go by Geoff's ship, but he's not doing the North American run right now; all freight carriers have been diverted to South America and South Africa for food supplies."

"Steamer? That's going to take a week."

"At least. I'm due in England 3 September. I worked it out. That was to be two days before the bombs went off."

"And then what?" He frowned, realising for the first time what she was actually telling him. "You'd have been stuck there, for three months."

"Yes."

"While I was stuck here?"

"You'd have been working, in your little protective suit. I'd have been stuck in the apartment. Mark, if the world was going to come

229

to an end, I felt I should be with my folks."

He knew she had a point, even if he felt resentful.

"The world wasn't going to come to an end."

"Nobody, not even you, could be sure of that. Mark, say you understand."

"Oh ... hell, I understand, sure. I just wish you'd told me sooner."

"Like when? Last time you were here, the idea was just kind of taking shape. Anyway ... " she gave a bright smile, "now it doesn't matter, does it?"

"You're cancelling?"

"No, of course not. I really want to go and see them. But now it'll be a proper vacation. I'm taking just over a month's leave. A week there, a fortnight in England, and a week back. Mark, it'd be great if you'd come with me."

"A month's vacation may be okay for those who are virtually head of the company. I'm not, remember."

"Surely you can take a vacation? You've been working like a dog these last six months."

"And it's not over yet. Listen, I can't spare that much time, but I'll see if I can fly over and join you in the UK for a week. How about that?"

"You reckon they'll have the planes flying again by then?"

"If all the news is right, one hell of a lot may have happened by then. Now, doll, you going to bed me or not?"

"Don't tell me," she fixed a pained expression on her face. "You're off to Washington in the morning."

"You got it. But I'll be back. Say, when are you leaving?"

"Monday night."

"I'll be back Saturday."

"You better."

Mark had not before seen so many smiling faces in the Oval Office.

"If you knew what a weight has been lifted from my shoulders," the President said. "What's your latest report, General Mitchell?"

"Our observation planes have been as close as they dare to that ash, and we've also been using satellite coverage, and there can be no doubt that it's starting to break up quite fast. Seems that the jet stream has at last got to the right spot and up to the right altitude. It's tearing the cloud apart."

"Fine. But how long a breaking-up period are we talking about?"

"For it to disperse completely? Well, the process seems to be accelerating, it could all be gone as soon as two weeks."

"That's what I wanted to hear. I'm going on nationwide television just as soon as you can confirm that, General, to let the country, the whole world, know, that the crisis, in terms of catastrophe, is over. Now we have to pick up the pieces. It's going to be one hell of a job. But we'll do it."

"You going to cancel the emergency powers?" the Press Secretary asked.

"I guess we're going to have to retain some, until we get things sorted out. This whole nation, hell, the whole hemisphere, is a disaster area. I have to retain the power to assign priorities. But obviously that power will be relaxed as much as possible, in things like permitting movement of people. We also have to get the airline networks back to some semblance of normalcy as soon as is practical." He looked from face to face. "Gentlemen, I want to thank you for all you've done, the immense amount of work you've put in these last six months. I know you're just as happy as I am that it's all going into the trash can. Dr Payton, my especial thanks to you. Sure, maybe we should have acted on your advice sooner, but . . . all's well that ends well, eh?"

"With respect, sir . . . it isn't over yet."

"I understand that, Doctor. I just said so."

"I'm not talking about cleaning up, sir, about getting back to normal. We can't do that until the weather gets back to normal. I wanted to talk about this last month, but I kind of got sidetracked."

"So the weather gets back to normal," said the Press Secretary. "Ain't that all good news?"

"You ever read any H. G. Wells, Mr Desmond?"

"I don't go much for science fiction, Doctor."

"Wells once wrote a short story about a guy who was given three wishes. He tried out the first wish on something unimportant, and it worked. So he reckoned he'd go to town on the second. He didn't much like the state of the world, so his second wish was that it would stand still while he sorted things out. His wish was granted immediately. But he hadn't realised it would be granted literally, without regard to anything else."

"Say, I remember that story," the President said. "The world just stopped, but as it had been spinning at whatever it is miles per second, everything else kept on going at that speed. There were houses flying through the air, whole cities collapsing, oceans pouring across the land . . . "

"So how'd he get out of it?" Desmond inquired.

"Well, he still had another wish, remember. He was being blown along with everyone else, but he managed to make his wish, which was to restore everything to exactly how it had been the moment before he had made his second wish. That happened, and the status quo was restored, with nobody except our hero remembering what had happened. Like all of Wells's stories, of course, there was a moral: think before you act."

"Sure. That's a great story, sir," Desmond said in total boredom. "And that's what we did, about those bombs, with the result that we won't have to use them. Nice story, Doctor. Now, if we can get on to serious business . . . "

"This is serious business, Mr Desmond," Mark said. "I wasn't thinking of the moral. I was thinking of this: we have a situation just like that tale, now, in reverse. For the past ten months, world weather has been on hold, as it were. There have been only minimal barometric fluctuations, nothing but light winds . . . the ash cloud has been blotting out all pressure gradients. When it goes, the weather is going to return to normal, just like that chap making his wish."

They stared at him.

"What are you?" Desmond asked at last. "Some kind of Cassandra?"

"I'm trying to be realistic about the situation. I'll be as happy as anyone to see the back of that cloud, but when it goes, if it happens too suddenly, I reckon we could have bigger problems than we do now. I raised this point before, you may remember, and then we were talking in terms of a ten-foot rise in sea level. That rise is now twenty feet and with every day it's getting higher. Right now we have calm oceans. Should that water start to move anywhere in a hurry . . . "

The President stroked his chin, and looked at General Mitchell.

"So we could have some big storms," the General said. "Nothing we can't handle. Certainly there'll be no problems compared with those we would have had if we'd had to send up those bombs."

The President looked at Mark, not unsympathetically. "I guess you've been working real hard, Doctor," he said. "But the crisis really is over. You leave it to us, now."

Pompous ass. Mark supposed he had nearly said, 'the experts', instead of 'us'. He wanted to stand up and grab each one of this bunch by their shirtfronts and shake them till their teeth rattled.

Dave Obrenski took him out to lunch. "I guess the boss is right," he remarked. "We've all been under one hell of a lot of pressure, and of course he's still under it. People might have been willing to accept almost anything while their lives were in danger, but now, first thing you know there'll be complaints, strikes, God alone knows what else."

"Dave," Mark said. "Mitchell was talking kibosh, and you know it.

We carry on about the awesome power we have at our fingertips in those little bombs. You know as well as I do that the power we command isn't one millionth part of the power nature has at *her* fingertips. That's all going to be let loose sometime in the next month. People's lives are still in danger. More than ever. That's the message I want to get across."

"You don't reckon the President's right, and they've had all the bad news they can take?"

"There's no bad news quite comparable to dying."

Sun! Amazing how much it affected everyone psychologically. Liz lay out on a sunbed on the Rowlands' back patio, eyes closed, thinking and basking. Not that the sun was visible all the time; high stretches of dark cloud and low swirls of mist still drew veils across her patch of sky every few minutes, but that didn't matter. They couldn't obscure the fact that the ash cloud was vanishing – fast. And with it went the nation's despair, depression, its pessimistic view of the future. People were smiling, breathing sighs of relief as they flung open all their windows to let in clean, fresh air, and hung damp clothes and bedding out to dry . . . those people who were more fortunate than the Dunnings, whose home was still completely submerged. In fact, the water level was still rising, but that didn't stem the tide of optimism which flowed through every conversation and was projected through every TV programme. Problems remained monumental and would almost certainly get worse. The telephone service was at best unreliable. As there were no such things as drains any more, sewage was ever present; the very air was thick with the stench of rotting vegetation and human excreta. Because all the water reservoirs were contaminated, all supplies had to be boiled . . . but this could only be done when the electricity was on – gas supplies were non-existent – which meant that there was never enough. It seemed the height of absurdity to be surrounded by water and yet have to be sparing with it.

Food was delivered by army personnel who charged round hap-pily in inflatables with powerful outboards, causing even more damage with their huge wakes driving the flood waters further than ever. Although here in Greenwich they had been lucky enough, so far, to get a ration of electricity each day, many areas were without any power at all, and thus boiling water or preserving food for more than a day was a nightmare. And the food itself was dreadful. Thank goodness for Mary; at least she was born in an era before people became so dependent on fast foods from giant freezers in supermarkets. Somehow, with the assistance of Jennifer and herself, her mother-in-law created reasonably palatable meals out of tins and packets, stuff imported from the southern hemi-sphere . . . stuff one wouldn't dream of buying normally. Some of the TV programmes were a hoot. Cooking tips on the use of powdered eggs; how to make biscuits to replace non-existent bread, dreadful squares of cardboard that tasted of shoe polish . . . for reasons one wouldn't dare to investigate. Some programmes offered suggestions on getting rid of mould marks on clothes and crazy ideas on making do and mend. At least they provided a reliable source of entertainment.

The British Government was apparently very proud of itself for the way it had handled the disaster. Ministers appeared on the box offering each other oral pats on the back and announcing the printing of ever more leaflets to be distributed with the food rations, instructing the public how to get their lives back to normal: how to get to work; how to make best use of the electrical power available; and how to be self-sufficient and put as little strain as possible on public services. "All we need now is a little patience," the Home Secretary assured viewers in a news interview at lunch-time. "The sun is shining, and soon we will see our countryside drying out and the waters receding, and we can start to build a new future with joy and optimism."

A cold, wet nose nudged her neck and a heavy paw descended on her chest. Jason had come out to enjoy the sun, even if the heat did make him pant.

"Poor old Jason," she rolled over and hugged his big golden head. "Are you longing to get home?" She wondered for the millionth time whether the farm would ever be habitable again. The house and wing might possibly be okay when the sea had ebbed away, back within its original bounds. But not the land. It would be years before anything would grow there . . . So what was the point of going back? Better, surely, to start again in an area high above sea level where the soil was merely contaminated with the ash dust. Aunt Madge had left London quite early on, to go and stay with friends in Wales, and she had told Liz on the phone only a few days ago that she had no intention of returning for a long time, adding the suggestion that Liz and Geoffrey could do worse than join her in Denbigh where they might rent a house until they finally decided where to settle.

She stretched sensuously as the sun reappeared. Geoff would soon be home. She'd see what he thought of the idea.

The phone was ringing; amazingly, in some parts of London these were still functioning, and Greenwich was again being lucky. But no one seemed to be answering. Geoff? She swung her legs to the ground and rushed inside to answer. "Hello?"

"Rowland residence?" a female voice demanded.

"Yes."

"Who is that speaking?"

"Liz Dunning. Who are you?"

"Oh hi! I'm Anne Dunning. Say, I'm coming over to meet you, real soon. I wanted to tell Mum my schedule: is she around?"

"She can't be very far; probably out in the street talking to neighbours. Hold on, I'll go and see."

Liz ran down the hall and out into the front garden. "Mary? Anyone seen . . . "

Mary came in through the gate. "Want me?"

"Oh, there you are. Anne wants a word with you."

"Anne! Oh how lovely." She grabbed the receiver. "Hallo!"

They talked for some minutes before Mary put the phone down and turned to hug Liz with excitement. "She's going to be here next week. And . . . can you believe it, she is bringing her fiancé to meet us. Guess who?"

Liz feigned ignorance.

"Why, that nice American scientist who came up to see Geoffrey. You know, Dr Mark Payton."

A big lump formed in Liz's throat. Mary's excitement reminded her so much of the way her own mother used to get so involved with her children: so happy with their successes, so sad with their disappointments. "Wonderful!" She squeezed Mary's hands. "Where are the others? Let's go tell them the news."

Mark caught the train up from Washington next day. In New York he had to change from Grand Central to Penn and, as there was an hour between connections, he wandered out on to the streets.

Manhattan was packed. No one seemed to be doing any work; they were all just rubber-necking at the sky. Even the fact that it was high tide and water was lapping at the long evacuated United Nations building, or that thousands of people had lost their homes and businesses, couldn't dampen the spirit of euphoria.

"Ain't that just the greatest sight you ever saw?" asked the taxi driver he hailed.

Mark was inclined to ask, what? The sky was still dark and impenetrable; there was no sign of the sun here. It was merely that it was lighter than it had been for some time – the cloud was definitely thinning.

"Yeah," Mark agreed.

He reached Boston that evening. As usual, Anne was already home.

"That was a quick turnaround. I didn't expect you back until the weekend."

"Did you hear the President's speech?"

"You bet. You know something? The whole office stood up and cheered. I reckon people were more scared than they'd let on, about those bombs. And have you looked outside, recently?" She held his hand and pulled him to the window. "Those are stars. You remember what stars look like? It's just a shame there's no moon."

"Well, I see one star."

"There's another over there, dummy. That thing is dissolving."

"Say . . . when are you leaving?"

"I told you . . . Monday night."

"You wouldn't like to cancel?"

"To go where instead?"

"To stay here. Just for a couple of weeks, until we see what the weather is going to do."

"The weather is just beautiful."

"Right now, yes. But I'm serious, Anne."

"Well, you can forget it. My folks are expecting me. Everyone is expecting me. Geoff's going to be there by then, too. Look, you are coming over, right?"

"Yeah, sure I am, just as soon as I can make it."

"Right. Because I kind of thought we might get married over there."

He gazed at her. "You serious?"

"I've been thinking about it, and if it's what you want to do . . . "

"Oh, sweetheart." He hugged and kissed her for several minutes, then pulled his head back. "Listen, doll, why not cancel your passage and fly?"

"Because that would mean a delay of several weeks. I've checked that out. The airlines haven't got their act back together yet, and they have a backlog of bookings as long as your arm. Besides . . . I want to go by ship. I think it's going to be fun. I could be going to meet the great romance of my life." She blew him a kiss as she watched his expression change. "Or at least have a last fling." She put her arms round his neck. "I'm only teasing, silly. What's gotten into you, anyway?"

"Thesis. Anti-thesis. We've had unnaturally calm weather for damn near a year. I just have a hunch there's going to be some unnaturally nasty weather coming to make up for it. And it has one hell of a lot of material to play with."

"A lot of water. But that's why ships were invented, to be on top of the water, right? They float much better than planes. And I don't get seasick, you know. Come on to bed. You're over-tired.

You'll feel a whole lot different in the morning."

She wasn't an easy woman to argue with. And she was going to be his wife.

Mark was up early, looking at the weather channel. It was concentrating mainly on satellite pictures of the break-up of the ash cloud, which was quite dramatic from outer space, as it was happening moment by moment.

"Now," the forecaster said, "I guess we can get back to normal weather patterns. Well, maybe not yet. That cloud is going to take a day or two to disappear altogether. For today, therefore, the readings and prospects are much as we've had the past year: there will remain almost total cloud cover – note the word 'almost', folks, with probably some light rain or drizzle. Visibility moderate to good, winds light or variable. So what's new? This will take us over the weekend. But next week we're expecting some quite dramatic changes.

"The first result of the lifting of the ash cloud is liable to be a sharp rise in pressure, and, you may be surprised at this, an equally sharp drop in temperatures. Right now the barometer is steady at 1,002 millibars, that's just over 29½ inches, and that's what it's been showing, give or take a millibar or two, throughout the year. Over the next couple of weeks it could shoot up to 1,030, before equalisation sets in and we have our normal run of lows and highs. This equalisation could bring with it some strong winds, especially as the temperatures will also be equalising. Right now the temperature on the Atlantic seaboard is 73 degrees Fahrenheit, and by noon today we expect it to reach a new high of 112 in the shade. That is hot, folks! But again, over the next couple of weeks that is going to return to normal. Now remember, hot air rises, and is replaced by cold. Our trouble the past year has been that the rising air hasn't really had anywhere to go, and there hasn't been any cold air to replace it. Well, we can expect that to change, and quite dramatically, over the next month. So . . . "

Mark switched off, went back into the bedroom and stood looking down at the sleeping Anne. She looked so . . . so young, and vulnerable, when she was asleep. A thick coil of black hair had fallen across her face, a few strands tangling in her long lashes, the soft curl at the end moving gently on her lips as she exhaled. He attempted to remove it without disturbing her but her eyelids fluttered and opened. Immediately she saw him her arms reached up round his neck, to pull him down on to her. He did not resist.

"Mmm," she purred. "My darling Mark, I do love you. Ours is going to be the most wonderful, happy marriage that ever was."

When the kissing stopped for air he drew back, very, very slightly, frowning.

"What's up. Want a divorce already?" She pecked his nose.

"Never! No, I was just wondering what your reaction would be if you accidentally got pregnant."

She pushed him away and sat up. " Pregnant! Why I'd . . . I'd . . . have to go out and buy some books on the subject. I know nothing about babies."

His head tilted to one side. "Are you telling me you wouldn't be livid? You wouldn't want to terminate . . . "

"Well, I guess I'd have to give it a lot of thought. It would all depend on what it was likely to be, wouldn't it?"

He frowned. "I'm not with you."

"Well, if it was going to be a miniature Anne, why, that would be wonderful. But a little Mark . . . I don't know if I could handle two of you."

"Are you saying you'd give up business . . . "

"Hey! Hang in there. I'm saying no such thing. Haven't you ever heard of nannies? I might cut down my business involvements to spend more time at home, but I wouldn't . . . "

He'd had all the reassurance he needed. The rest of her answer was smothered in kisses.

When he was finished, she rolled out of bed and went into the kitchen to make coffee, returned a moment later with two cups.

"Hey," she said. "Guess what. The barometer's rising."

15

The Wind

"Isn't that something?" Lloyd Turnbull asked, as he stood beside Geoffrey on the bridge and gazed at the brilliant sunshine ahead of them.

"Had to happen," Geoffrey said buoyantly.

He was only a week away from home. A home which was presently under water, and which was going to cost a fortune to restore. Yet the mere fact that it was over, that the cloud was gone, had lifted his spirits and those of everyone on board.

The voyage had taken a fortnight longer than had been expected. They had encountered Argentinian and Brazilian bureaucracy and procrastination. Fogarty had at times nearly exploded with angry frustration. Yet the meat and grain had finally been loaded, the meat in refrigerated containers, the grain in special sacks for stowage in every available nook and cranny, including the passenger cabins and the saloons. *Skyhawk* was indeed overloaded; her Plimsoll line was eighteen inches beneath the surface, but no maritime inspector was going to worry about that in an emergency like this; the important thing was to get the food home, and now they were steaming as fast as their ancient engines would permit.

Geoffrey went inside to write up the log. Even this was a pleasure. There had been plenty of weather activity south of the Equator. They had had their share of gales and the barometer had bobbed about like a yoyo. Now they were returning north to high pressure and a brisk north-easterly breeze, just sufficient to whip the tops off the waves and send the occasional rattle of spray over the bows. This was the North Atlantic on which he had been brought up.

He sat at the desk in the chartroom, made the necessary entries, called out. "Give me the barometric reading, will you, Walsh?"

239

"Ten twenty-six, sir," Walsh replied.

Geoffrey entered the figure, then frowned at the page. Turnbull's last entry, four hours previously, had been ten thirty-two, to which level the glass had risen slowly but steadily since crossing the Equator. "Repeat that reading, will you, Walsh."

"Ten twenty-six . . . no, ten twenty-five, sir."

Geoffrey picked up the phone and called Fogarty's cabin. "Just thought you'd like to know, sir, that the glass has started to fall again. Fast."

The water was flat calm, a sheet of polished steel reaching into infinity. Only an occasional capricious movement of air, drawing horizontal lines across the surface, indicated where sea and sky met. The scene was almost tropical in its shimmering heat, except that there were no exotic coral atolls crowned with seagrapes; the idyll of waving palms standing in line along the shore replaced with skeletal rows of electric pylons and a few tops of telegraph poles, grotesque flotsam entangled in their trailing wires. A scene not of beauty but of utter desolation.

The noise of the powerful Volvo Penta cut across the stillness disturbing clubs of seagulls into irritable flight above putrefying carcasses, its propeller leaving a syrupy, widening vee.

"Where are we, Tony?" Charles Rowland asked.

The man in khaki checked the map on his lap then pointed. "That church spire over the port bow must be in March, so Downham Market must be on the starboard beam, beyond the railway."

"So we've reached the Fens."

"Yes." Tony Melville wished he could be somewhere else, right now. But when his old schoolfriend Charles had phoned to ask this favour, he couldn't refuse. He was indebted to Charlie for kind, free financial advice last year. Very indebted. But bringing Charlie Rowland's family out here, cruising over the destruction of their entire lives, was not his idea of fun. It was bad enough having this army assignment, charting the flood levels here in East Anglia. The regular tour out from Newmarket, steering through the stench of bloated carcasses and rotted vegetation was not funny. Fortunately most of the bodies were of rats, mice and chickens; one didn't get too rattled by those. He hadn't been too nauseated even when he saw the swollen remains of sheep and cattle. But that poor little Cairn terrier . . . that was worst of all, much worse than the two humans, tramps by the look of them, they had fished out last week.

"That must be our roof, then. Up ahead," Freddie pointed.

His father looked left and right, frowning. Bewildered. "Is it? I cannot get orientated. I don't recognise anything."

"Yes, surely that's your weathercock," Charlie shouted, turning the knobs on his binoculars.

"I suppose it is. Yes. You're right." John leaned forward over the bow, then quickly withdrew as the sunscorched rubber gunwale burned his hand. "Any chance of getting us alongside? I want to get to that gable window."

Captain Melville raised a questioning eyebrow at the young private who was enjoying himself on the tiller. "Can you make it?"

"No problem, sir."

Freddie moved forward, painter in hand, as the engine idled, allowing the inflatable to coast gently up to the sloping roof. Tony Melville used a wooden paddle to fend off and nudge along to the end tiles where Freddie could grab the facia.

"Can you find anywhere to make her fast?" Charles asked.

"I'll try." Freddie lifted a tile and slipped the end of the painter under a slat, leaving enough slack to allow him to manoeuvre the boat up to the window. "There you go."

Father and son stood together, clutching the window frame. It wasn't easy to see anything. The attic was dark and the window grimy on the inside. But as their eyes strained against the reflections and penetrated the gloom, shapes formed.

"There should be water in there, seeing the water is above the eaves," Freddie said.

"True, but we packed the attic so tight there wasn't a square inch of floor left. Ah! That's your mother's box of china, on the left. And her chairs with the tapestry seats are well clear. That'll please her." It was little enough. Thank God she wasn't here to see this mess. It would break her heart. Bad enough when time came to start the clear-up. But by then at least she could do something about it. Not just sit in Jennifer's sitting-room, brooding.

Freddie turned his back on the window to peer down through the water into the yard. The reflected sky made it impossible to see through the surface, but he could picture the barn down there, with the tractor and the Rototiller, the electric milking machines and all the other equipment he had persuaded his father to buy last year, rusting away. But what did it matter? Nothing would grow here for years. So much for his degree in horticulture. He tried to fix a smile on his face before turning back to his father, but it wasn't easy. All these smiling faces round one, people rejoicing that the cloud was finally breaking up; didn't they realise that their lives would never be the same again, that all they had worked and studied for was wasted? He dared not think what he could do with the rest of his life. He was qualified for nothing that could be of the faintest use. So how could he possibly expect Doreen to marry him? Thank God he'd not got round to asking her.

A sudden gust of wind swung the inflatable round and he nearly overbalanced into the water. He fell rather than sat, his father beside him.

Melville saw the old man grasp Freddie's wrist, attempting an encouraging smile. Poor old beggar; he looked awful, grey and drawn, yet he was obviously more concerned about his son than himself.

Charles saw the gesture, too, and wished he hadn't let the two men persuade him to ask this favour of Tony. But they had insisted they must come out and see for themselves.

The breeze was more persistent, now. Foot-high wavelets were slopping against the wall and rolling up the cant of the roof.

John looked at the sky and frowned. "Weather."

Tony Melville nodded at the young private, who turned the engine key.

"Better be getting back to base, don't you think?"

Even the wind was hot as the boat bounced over the disturbed water.

Sitting together in the bow, John and Freddie watched the roof of their home dwindling over the engine cowling, neither daring to speak.

"Glad to have you back, Mark," said Peter Grosvenor, President of the Ballard Foundation. "But I guess you're glad it's over."

"I wish to God it were," Mark said.

Grosvenor followed him into his office. "You mean the possibility of some more odd weather? Well, that's outside our province, I'm happy to say. But there's some volcanic activity in the East Indies you may care to have a look at. Now we're talking about real volcanoes."

"Misreal was real all right," Mark said. "Okay, Chief, I'll check into them." He waited for the door to close, then called his secretary. "I want every weather map you have for the northern hemisphere," he told her. "As of this morning."

She raised her eyebrows, but was used to her boss's idiosyncrasies. Half an hour later the maps were on his desk, and she was studying them with him.

"Pressure has been rising pretty steadily over the whole hemisphere as the cloud has broken up," she remarked. "But it seems to have peaked."

"Yeah," Mark muttered. The rise, as the girl had said, had been universal and meteoric. The falls were being less general, and as was to be expected, the sharpest were coming in over the Atlantic. "What do the Met boys say?"

"Strong winds expected, with possibility of increased flooding. Some more evacuations have been ordered."

"I mean at sea."

"Gales. Maybe even storms. But we all expected that, didn't we?"

"Yes," Mark said savagely.

Harper had been on to the Met Office in London.

"Seems the pressure variations are pretty extreme, holding high in some places, collapsing in others," he told Fogarty and Geoffrey. "And quite honestly, in view of the unique weather over the last year, nobody seems quite sure what is going to happen next. But the Met boys do recommend we prepare for some weather."

"It'll be almost like old times," Fogarty said. "You'll check ship, Mr Dunning."

"Yes, sir."

"At least we've no passengers to worry about," Turnbull commented.

"Just an overloaded ship," Fogarty growled. The Captain had found the frustrations of Latin-American bureaucracy more irritating than any of them, and he was looking positively ill.

Geoffrey prowled from hold to hold, Allen at his shoulder. The containers were as tightly packed as was humanly possible, and they were so heavy he didn't see them shifting unless the ship turned upside down.

"They're not going anywhere, Mr Dunning," the carpenter asserted reassuringly. "They're bedded."

"I still wish we weren't drawing two feet too many."

They also checked out the passenger cabins, which had been stripped of their usual fittings and all filled with sacks of grain.

"These are the things to worry about," Allen said. "But, with that extra weight in the hold, she should stay upright."

"Should?"

Allen grinned. "No use in worrying about the other, Mr Dunning. Not now."

Geoffrey had a cup of coffee with Evans.

"All well?"

"Whenever you ask me that, Geoff, boyo, your next question is, can I do something special?"

"We've weather coming."

"Big deal."

"This could be exceptional."

"Well, it's the hurricane season."

"Trouble is, I don't think it's going to be an ordinary hurricane. You know, because they're so concentrated, you can take evasion action when there's one of those ahead of you, and even if you get side-swiped, you know it can't last more than a day or so if you keep steaming away. In these circumstances, I wouldn't like to say what's going to happen."

Evans grinned. "How far are we from Liverpool?"

"Six days."

"Then it can't last longer than that, can it, boyo?"

Geoffrey wished he could be certain of that.

Fogarty was studying the latest print-out from the Weatherfax machine; because of the ash cloud, for most of the year they hadn't been able to use their satellite-linked instruments when north of the Equator. "That trough is dead ahead of us," he said. "And it is deep."

Geoffrey looked at the figure indicated, and gave a low whistle: 960 millibars. He looked at their own barometer: 1015 and still falling. But it had another 50 millibars to fall! And the trough stretched right across the North Atlantic, in a north-west/south-east direction, from just west of Greenland to Cape Verde; it was the biggest he had ever seen. There would be no going round it.

The sky was still bright to port, but darkening to starboard and ahead; the wind was north-west, just over fifteen knots according to the anemometer, but dropping all the time.

"It's not a hurricane," Turnbull pointed out. "Just a real deep trough. Moving north, quite quickly."

They both looked at Fogarty.

The Captain stroked his chin. "Our orders are to get this food back to the UK just as fast as we can, gentlemen. We'll alter course two points to starboard."

The officers exchanged glances, as Fogarty saw.

"Straight for the centre, eh? But I'm not quite round the twist. As Lloyd says, that bugger is moving north, and high pressure is holding to the south and east of it. I reckon we can cut through his back end."

"And if he stalls?"

Fogarty sighed. "Then we'll think again."

Throughout the next twenty-four hours the wind dropped, until there was none at all, although a huge swell came out of the east, some forty feet from trough to crest; the horizon disappeared as *Skyhawk* dipped into each one.

By now, too, the entire sky was darkening. "You'd think that damned ash cloud had come back," Harry Trent remarked.

"We may well wish it had, before too long," Turnbull told him.

But the Fax print-outs which came in every hour showed that the trough was steadily moving north, and that on their present course they would pass some hundred miles south-east of the deepest barometric reading. That was reassuring, even if the Fax picture itself was amazing, and frightening. Pressure was high over Newfoundland and the western Atlantic, and high over Western Europe; in between it slid downwards in some of the deepest barometric slopes any of *Skyhawk*'s officers had ever seen.

"Makes you think of relief maps of East Africa," Fogarty remarked. "With the Great Rift Valley dead ahead."

"If it's such a huge area, the winds can't be that strong," Turnbull argued.

"I don't think they'll be strong at all in the centre," Geoffrey said. "But going in and coming out . . . !"

That night they began the slide into the trough. Looking from the ship's position on the chart to the Weatherfax really gave the impression of careering down a precipice; the pressure was dropping at the rate of a millibar every fifteen minutes. Geoffrey was reminded of a cartoon painting he had once seen in a West Indian bar, of Columbus's three ships reaching the edge of the world and falling off, while one of the crew remarked, "I told you so!"

The wind had now backed to the south-west, and was steadily increasing in speed. At thirty-five knots, it was tearing the tops off the swell, and creating great, rolling, six-foot-high waves of white foam. But the movement was as yet regular, because of the length of each wave. *Skyhawk* climbed slowly up the slope in front of her, burst into a flail of flying water, and then gathered speed as she slid down the far side. Her speed was controlled by the officer of the watch, but the adjustments required were small, and with the wind astern the motion was not at all uncomfortable. Only the size of the wave still waiting for them, and all the others beyond that, gave an impression of lurking danger.

But nothing they had not encountered before.

"What's the word from England?" Geoffrey asked Harper at dinner, as the plates slid gently to and fro, restrained by the fiddles.

"Strong westerly gales. That's actually the best weather they could be having, if they have to have weather at all. It's pushing all that flood water in East Anglia back."

"Into Holland," Fogarty suggested.

"Well, yes," Harper conceded. "But the winds are dropping all the time as the trough spreads across the area and in fact the weather over the North Sea isn't at all bad, at the moment. The centre of the trough stretches all the way up there. Actually, the weather boys aren't calling it a trough – they're calling it a deep."

"And it's still slipping away north-west. What happens when it clears the UK? Won't the wind veer easterly, and probably strongly?"

"That would be the normal pattern. I don't think anyone's very happy about it." Geoffrey thought of the farm; although he knew it had been evacuated, it was still there for when the flood waters receded. But would it be there if it got chewed up in an easterly gale?

"Well, we could have troubles of our own before then." Turnbull put the latest Weatherfax on the table beside Fogarty's plate, and they all craned their heads to look at it. The trough, or deep, had now moved further north, and stretched from the Azores to the Arctic, but it had taken on a most peculiar shape, rather like a gigantic question-mark. The southern end was the narrow tail, in the centre of which was *Skyhawk*'s position, while the bulk of the curve lay, as Harper had suggested, right over the British Isles and the North Sea, clutching the islands in a kind of soggy embrace.

"Wind's shifting too," Turnbull said. "It's veered back to the north-west, and is still going."

As usual, they looked at the Captain.

"We have a choice," Fogarty agreed. "We can alter course and try to keep in the middle of this trough . . . but it's moving north-west probably faster than we can. Alternatively we can hold our course, take the weather that's ahead, and then hope to be in reasonable conditions for the run up the Irish Sea. I'm in favour of the latter, gentlemen. If we're going to have weather, let's have it where we have lots of sea room."

The wind continued to veer, and freshen again, and by the next morning they were ploughing their way into a north-easterly gale. Now the swell was shorter, and the breaking crests higher. *Skyhawk* plunged into them, with spray flying high over the bridge, engines racing as she slid down the troughs beyond, water pouring along the decks to spew out of the scuppers like rivers.

"There's fifty knots of this up ahead," Harper told them. "Storm force."

Well, they could see that from looking at the Fax print-outs.

Geoffrey went below with Allen to make sure everything was

shipshape in the holds. The noise was tremendous, with the slapping of the waves against the hull competing with the thudding of the water falling on the deck above, and the bullet-like rattle of spray, while over all there was the constant howl of the wind. But the holds were dry and the containers motionless.

He was less happy with the situation on the cabin deck, where several of the sacks had become dislodged, one or two had even split open with the violence of the motion, and there was grain everywhere.

"I told them we weren't a grain carrier," he grumbled.

"There's going to be a hell of a mess to clean up, in Liverpool," Allen agreed.

Geoffrey was even less happy when he returned to the bridge, and watched the swing of the clinometer. In conditions like this *Skyhawk* would be expected to roll through some forty degrees, from twenty to twenty ... but today she was rolling twenty-five/twenty-five. In normal circumstances it was generally accepted that a well-found ship could roll up to thirty-five degrees – through seventy – and recover ... but these conditions were far from normal.

"How's she handling?" he asked Walsh, who was monitoring the yaw control on the autopilot.

"Recovery is sometimes a little sluggish," the coxswain replied. "But we're carrying a lot of weight."

"Maybe too much." Geoffrey went along to Fogarty's cabin, where the Captain was lying down; he was looking very tired. "I'd like permission to alter course two points to starboard, sir."

"Eh?" Fogarty raised his head. "We're bound for Liverpool, not Dover."

"She's top-heavy," Geoffrey reminded him. "And there's too much on the beam. We need to take the seas bows on until they die a bit."

"I'll come up," Fogarty said, and got out of his bunk.

Geoffrey left the cabin and stood for a moment on the bridge wing, gazing at the afternoon. It was a wild and yet beautiful scene, one he had looked at often before, but which had never failed to fascinate him. They were leaving the 'deep' and climbing back up the pressure gradient, thus the heavy clouds of yesterday were dispersing, and there were large patches of blue ahead. The sun, just beginning its droop to the west, kept darting in and out of the patches – now mostly white – illuminating the flying spray, the heaving blue water, and then plunging it into shadow again.

The seas themselves were dramatic in the extreme, for if the swell was now travelling with them, it was as big as ever, and the wind coming the other way was pushing up huge walls of water, while to either side the blue was smothered in streaks of white spindrift, which formed little broken egg-whites as they surged astern.

To a novice the prospect would have been terrifying. The water-mountains rearing up on the starboard bow appeared far taller than the ship, and the curling crests always seemed about to break exactly on the deck and perhaps smash open a hatch-cover, to send thousands of tons of water crashing into the bowels of the ship. But *Skyhawk* always wriggled out of the end of each swell, leaving it to break harmlessly astern, while she braced herself for the next.

She was rolling, however, and with each roll the needle of the clinometer edged a fraction further, especially to port, the leeward side. Geoffrey snapped his fingers impatiently, and gave a sigh of relief as Fogarty appeared.

The Captain peered through the bridge windows, then turned to the chart to study their position.

"Big one," Walsh muttered.

Geoffrey looked up and caught his breath. He had been at sea long enough to know that the tradition that every seventh wave was bigger than average was often true. And every seventieth was bigger yet, while one could reasonably expect every seven hundredth to be a monster. He reckoned this had to be a seven thousandth. Not only was it higher than any of the previous ones, it was also longer. There was no chance of *Skyhawk* slipping out the end of this one.

He glanced at Fogarty as the Captain also straightened, but Fogarty was temporarily speechless, his face suffused, his mouth sagging open as he gasped for air. Geoffrey hadn't the time to work out whether he was ill or just horrified. He leapt forward to stand beside Walsh.

"We're going to have to come up," he said. "Use manual."

Walsh nodded, face grim as he disengaged the autopilot and wrapped his hands round the spokes.

"Stand-by engine-room," Geoffrey said into the intercom. "We have a big one."

He stared at the water wall surging up beside him. It was a matter of timing the manoeuvre to the last second, but time seemed to be standing still, while the wave moved closer, and rose higher.

"Three points starboard," he said, no longer able to wait for the Captain's decision . . .

Walsh responded immediately, bringing the helm hard down to his right. *Skyhawk* started to turn, but too slowly because of her enormous overweight. "Oh, shit," Walsh commented.

The bows were rising to the water wall, but still obliquely, and the overhanging crest was now immediately above them.

"Everyone hold on," Geoffrey said into the tannoy.

The wave broke.

Skyhawk disappeared almost entirely beneath white water; even the bridge was for a moment submerged. Holding on with all his strength Geoffrey kept his feet, but Walsh was hurled from the helm and thudded into the leeward bridge door, and Fogarty hit the deck without a sound.

Geoffrey hadn't time to worry about them. *Skyhawk* was on her beam ends, and not recovering. Voices spluttered up the telephones, but he ignored them as well as he grasped the helm and dragged on it.

"Power!" he shouted down to the engine-room. "I need power."

Skyhawk responded, and came up, a little way. It was possible to see forward. The huge wave had gone on its way, but the next one was already taking shape, and the freighter was lying to port at an angle of twelve degrees, held there by the enormous weight on the upper deck.

"You all right, Walsh?" Geoffrey snapped, still leaning on the helm, but knowing he wasn't going to get a response.

"Yes, sir. But the Captain . . . "

Geoffrey looked down at Fogarty, who must have hit his head as he fell; he had rolled against the port bulkhead, and was now lying absolutely still.

"Dr Bennett to the bridge!" Geoffrey snapped into the intercom. "Two helmsmen to the bridge. All hands to the upper deck. Take her, Walsh."

The next wave struck. Once again *Skyhawk* was obliterated by surging water, and once again she thudded on to her beam ends.

Walsh clung to the spokes. "Course."

"Just bring her up, if you can." Geoffrey was clawing his way up the steeply sloping deck to the door.

"She ain't responding, Mr Dunning." A note of panic had entered Walsh's voice. "She's going to go over."

"Keep trying." Geoffrey went down the ladder, clinging to the rail so as not to overbalance, jacket whipping in the breeze, and realised he was hatless. As if that mattered. From the passenger deck he could look down on a terrifying sight, the port welldeck bulwark almost beneath water, while there was another wave building on the starboard bow.

Trent and Turnbull were waiting for him, as well as Allen and the watch below.

"That grain," Geoffrey told them. "It has to go. Quickly."

They followed him into the corridor between the passenger cabins, formed a human chain. Turnbull and Geoffrey took the lead, dragging on the heavy bags and heaving them through the doors, to where the sailors waited. The next wave struck and *Skyhawk* went over again, throwing men about like toys, and again she lay sluggishly, listing some fifteen degrees.

But the crew kept at work. The sacks of grain were passed out of the cabins, along the corridor, and heaved over the side. Again and again the ship was struck down, and again and again the men fell to their hands and knees or were thrown into bulkheads. Blood flew as hands and faces were cut, but no one stopped work. Gradually the weight was being reduced.

"When you're clear here, work on the saloons," Geoffrey told Turnbull, and made his way aft to the promenade deck. This was the most dangerous situation, as the men here were exposed to both wind and water, but Allen, in charge, had made sure everyone was equipped with a safety harness, and although they were skidding about as they lost their footing and from time to time sliding down to the lee rail in a swelter of water and grain, they too never stopped working. While downwind of the stricken ship a huge grey porridge was spreading over the surface of the sea, limiting the whitecaps.

Geoffrey thought it was a pity they hadn't been able to throw the stuff to windward, like oil. But he could feel the ship becoming more responsive. As long as they weren't struck by another monster . . . "We're winning, Chips," he told Allen, and returned to the bridge, where Walsh was coping very well, although *Skyhawk* was still seriously listing, and being buffeted by every wave.

Bennett's face was grim. "The old man's dead," he told Geoffrey.

"Good God! You mean he hit his head that hard?" Geoffrey knelt beside the still figure of the Captain.

"No. He was dead before he ever hit the floor. I suspect he had a heart attack."

Geoffrey thought of the stricken expression on the Captain's face as he had looked up at the giant wave. It must have been happening at that moment. He sighed. Fogarty had been a good friend for the past three years, ever since Geoffrey had joined *Skyhawk.*

And now he was in command. He pushed himself to his feet, stood by Walsh.

"She's responding," Walsh said. "Better and better."

Geoffrey picked up the telephone. "Mr Harper," he said. "Call Liverpool and tell them the emergency is over, but Captain Fogarty is dead, we think of a heart attack. Inform them that I am taking command."

There was a moment's silence as Harper digested what he had been told. Then he said, "We've lost our aerials."

"Oh, bugger it. Have you any range at all?"

"I'm afraid not. Even the VHF has gone."

"Well . . . we'll just have to plug on, then. As soon as this eases off, see if you can rig a jury aerial."

"Will do. There's a message came in, just before we went over."

"Yes?"

"In view of exceptional weather and possibility of damage, when situation is under control proceed Southampton instead of Liverpool. Acknowledge."

"Now, that is the best news I've heard this voyage," Geoffrey said. "The *only* good news I've had this voyage." He relaid the course, then gave it to Walsh. "Let's go home."

"Will we make it?" Harper asked.

Geoffrey's smile was savage. "We're sure as hell going to try."

16

The Sea

"Geoff and I could move into a hotel," Liz suggested.

"No, no. We'll cope, somehow." Jennifer stood in the middle of the sitting-room, a pile of sheets clutched in her arms.

"Come on, Jenny, why not? There are more than enough of us crammed in here as it is."

"For heaven's sake don't argue, Liz," Charles snapped. "Most of the hotels in London are closed, anyway. With no staff and no lifts there is no way they can possibly operate. The few that are open are already bursting their seams with evacuees. You'll have to stay here whether you like it or not."

Liz didn't take offence at his tone; everyone was feeling wretchedly short-tempered and edgy, not least herself. "I like it fine here. It's you lot, having us all dumped on you. I'm just trying to ease the/ situation. It won't be much fun for Anne's big family reunion if she's got to kip in a sleeping-bag on the floor."

"For Chrissake get your thinking straight. You've just lost your new home; the in-laws have just about lost everything they ever possessed, and you're worrying that Anne, who has lost nothing, and Jennifer and I are being inconvenienced. Try not to be boneheaded."

Liz threw back her head and laughed. "You lovely, stuffy old Pom, you. And you look so frigging serious, too."

Jennifer collapsed on the settee with the sheets in a heap on her lap. "That's telling you, sweetheart!" Not even she had ever dared rib Charles when he was in one of his determinedly gloomy moods. Only Liz could get away with it.

Charles glared at the tiny Australian girl with the now grotesquely swollen stomach, trying unsuccessfully to keep his face straight. Through teeth clenched against the insistent desire to grin, he said, "Can't really expect an overblown Aussie balloon to have any brain!" and attempted a dignified exit.

After the men had returned from the trip out on the flood water over the farm, the four younger adults in the house had taken the first opportunity for a conference. They were worried about John and Mary, wanting to discuss the future of the old folk. There would be no home for them to go back to, nowhere to live, even when the floods had subsided. The farm was gone for ever, finished, and although this was a grim enough fact for Freddie to face, at least he was young enough to start again, with the prospect of making something of his life. But there was no such prospect for his parents.

All four were willing to do anything to help. Freddie said he would take them wherever he went. Charles and Jennifer said they could stay in Greenwich, though Liz thought it would not be a good idea for them to live in an urban environment, they were country folk. Much better, she had said, if she and Geoffrey moved to Wales, for the old folk to come and live with them. "After all, with Geoff away so much, it will be great for me to have their company." But she felt sad, remembering all the possessions they'd so recently acquired, lying under all that water, ruined. Perhaps the lovely tea-service Jennifer and Charles had given them might survive.

Charles had remained worried. He worried now. He shared John's feeling that this catastrophe wasn't over yet. Maybe it was only the oppressive weather, hot, humid, as though they were about to be hit by a massive storm, but he could raise little optimism, despite daily Government assurances in the pamphlets distributed with the food, and on what media were available. But in truth it was that hideous boat ride with Tony Melville that had shattered him; the death and destruction was beyond belief. And worst of all had been the awful finality of it. How could there possibly be a future for anyone in that area within the next fifty years?

Jennifer's parents were holding desperately to the meagre consolation that some of their precious possessions, stored in the attic, had remained above flood level; but hell! What good were a few bits of china and eight tapestry-seated chairs going to be? Their property was worthless. There was no way insurance companies could meet a fraction of the claims ensuing from a disaster of this magnitude. Nor could the Government. Any money available for relief would have to go into industry and cleaning up ash- and salt-polluted land. Hotels would be requisitioned to house the homeless, food sources would be commandeered . . . and the thousands of elderly people, like John and Mary, would stand no chance of returning to the comfortable retirement for which they had worked all their lives. They were committed to living out their natural span as dependants, on their children or the community, without more than a handful of their accumulated memorabilia.

He mooched out on to the back patio to try and mend Jackie's big, plastic truck, and left the girls to sort out the housing problem alone.

"We will have to put Freddie up in the boxroom in the attic," Jennifer decided. "And Mummy and Daddy will go into the little attic bedroom. Jessica and Jackie will have put-u-ups on our bedroom floor and you and Geoffrey will have the spare bedroom."

"What about Anne?"

Jennifer patted the settee beside her. "She'll be on here. It's a long three-seater; perfectly adequate even for my big sister." She smiled. "And she is big, you know. Five foot eight, at least."

"Wow! Six inches taller than me."

"That's not difficult."

"Hark who's talking!"

"Don't worry. She won't be nearly as wide as you."

Liz threw a cushion at her sister-in-law's head. Spot on target.

"When I've put these sheets away we'll have a cup of tea and you can tell me all you remember about my prospective American brother-in-law."

"You Dunnings really are dead chuffed about Anne and Mark, aren't you?" Liz shook her head. "I just love the way you care so much about each other. We Bowmans do too, of course," she added hastily, "but we don't seem to show it like you do. I like it. It's nice." She hauled herself to her feet. "I'll go put the kettle on, if that's what you want. Personally I'd prefer something cool. It's so darned hot."

"You're right. Pity we haven't any ice. We could have iced tea."

Mary straightened her back, not without effort. "What shall we do with all this rubbish?"

John looked at the heap of dead growth they had hacked away from the front wall of the house. "Carry it down the road and dump it in the water, I imagine."

"John!"

"Well, why not? It's not as though it's any different from all the other vegetation floating about out there."

They both felt better having something to do, and Jennifer seemed grateful that they were doing a job usually left to her. Charles was no gardener. John mopped his face on his shirt sleeve, glanced at Mary. She was bearing up very well, all things considered. Only very occasionally did he see her in an unguarded moment, face grey and sad, eyes watery with tears she wouldn't allow to fall.

"There, if you really think it'll be all right." She looked down at the heap. "Can you carry it like that, or do you want it in a dustbin sack?"

"I'll take it as it is. We've run out of bin sacks, anyway." He hefted a bundle into his arms and Mary held the gate, watching him down the hill. When he returned he said, "You should come down. There's quite a brisk westerly, blowing off the water."

"Not pushing up waves, I hope?"

"A bit. But from the right direction. It's an easterly we've got to watch out for." He frowned up at the sky. The weather pattern was building up to something. And there was another big tide due. The North Sea and the Channel were now some twenty feet above their normal level. Greenwich was forty miles up the Thames from the sea, but even so the tidal rise was dramatic, flooding the country-side on both banks. The London Water Authorities continued to issue assurances that the Tidal Barrier would hold no matter what, although on the top of each tide water was now lapping and sometimes spurting over the top, but they were the only people who thought so. The Rowlands and their neighbours felt it was a Government ploy to stop people trying to evacuate the area . . . Simply because there was nowhere to put them. Canvas cities were already springing up in the Surrey Hills, the Cotswolds, on any piece of high ground, regardless of ownership. A situation fraught with problems.

"Prefer to go back?" Freddie asked. He and Liz were taking Jason for a walk up to the Observatory, hoping to be cooled by the freshening wind. But the term 'freshening' didn't apply. The wind was hot and humid, and he was suddenly aware it was backing. He squinted up at the sky, but the steel grey glare obscured any cloud formation. Not a sky farmers liked.

Liz paused, panting. "No, let's keep going. Sorry to be taking so long."

"I'm not in a hurry! Why don't you hang on to my arm?" He crooked his elbow and she slid her hand through.

"Ta. I need extra horsepower with this load." She was very fond of Freddie, the cuddly teddybear type of man, but it would be wonderful if this could be Geoff's arm she was holding. Only thoughts of Geoff, of how soon he would be home again, kept her going without completely losing her marbles. She was so short, the bulge had little place to go but outwards. Even at five months she swore she had been bigger than girl friends back home were when they were due to drop. Now, at just seven months, she wasn't walking at all, just waddling, swaying. She felt like a frigging duck. And a hot, sweaty, irritable duck, at that. Dammit! What a time and situation to be expecting an infant. And what awful food to be feeding it on, all tinned or dried stuff. Not one fresh green vegetable or piece of fruit for weeks. One presumed the baby was healthy, but she hadn't seen a doctor for months. Just happened there wasn't one marooned with them on this bit of Greenwich which was now an isthmus, and she'd no intention of being carted off by a bunch of soldiers in one of those army lorries or a rubber dinghy, just to be told junior was still in there. She knew that only too well. At least she had quite a decent layette, dug out of a suitcase in Jenny's attic . . . nice having the things that had been used by Jessica and Jackie. Family.

Arriving at the Observatory, they sat down on some flagstone steps while Jason conversed with an Alsatian, and Liz tried to get her breath back.

"Did you ever come up here before the floods?" Freddie asked.

"Oh yes. Jenny and I used to bring the children up here for walks. I'm trying to identify the buildings she'd pointed out to me. They all look so different now. Down there, slightly right," she pointed. "Isn't that the roof of the Royal Naval College with the flags still flying?"

"Yes. And look at the mast tops; all that's left of the Cutty Sark. Isn't that sad . . . So much history submerged . . . " He was silent for a few moments. "As for further north, just look. The Canary Wharf tower's still visible but the Isle of Dogs is totally submerged. The river is flowing straight through the Royal Albert and Victoria Docks from the West India Docks. At high tide I'll bet the floods go right up the river Lee to the Warwick Reservoir."

"Charles and Jennifer are very lucky their house is above flood level."

"So far."

Liz shot him a quick glance. "What are you saying? It could still happen?"

Freddie shrugged. "Take no notice of me. Afraid I'm not in the most optimistic of moods at the moment." He stood up. "Better get back. I promised Jessica I'd mend her doll's pram before she goes to bed. Anyway, the weather seems to be on the blink." He held out the palm of his hand. "Look. Huge raindrops." Just a few.

Sudden violent gusts came at them from varying directions, tearing at their clothes and hair. Freddie gave Liz a hand, hoisting her to her feet, whistled Jason, and the three hurried, as best Liz could, back down the footpaths across the park.

But they didn't make it before the heavens opened and they were thoroughly drenched by the time they reached the front door, rain driven by a southerly wind lashing their backs. They slammed the door behind them, dripping on to the mat.

"Dammit!" Liz exploded. "I left the pillowslips outside on the line," and she rushed down the hallway past a soldier standing talking to John and Charles, through the kitchen into the utility . . . and screamed.

Lemons. A strong smell of lemons. Why? Not unpleasant – just strangely disturbing. Better perhaps to breathe under the sheet . . . The sheet felt stiff and hard like brown wrapping paper. Or cardboard. Cardboard boxes . . . packed with food and clothes . . . Hurry! The storm!

Liz sat up, heart pounding with panic – and fell back against the stack of pillows as the pain stabbed through her side. Her eyes were wide with fear, rolling as she looked at the curtains drawn all round the bed, and up at the square of pale blue ceiling. In the middle of the square was a light, steel or aluminium holding a plain white inverted bowl . . . Hospital! It was all coming back. The wet utility floor. The flip-flops she was wearing skating under her – sending her hurtling through the open door and down the steps on to the patio.

Her frown deepened as pain punched again, but this time in her back as well as her side. Slowly, moving one limb at a time, she managed to roll on to her right hip . . . but it didn't help. There were voices in the background, and a cough from the other side of the curtain. Footsteps grew louder, squeaking along the polished floor and part of the curtain was flung back, rattling the hooks.

"Hello, Mrs Dunning. You're awake again." A woman in a green smock and trousers, hair pushed out of sight under a shapeless green cap, bent over to peer into her face. "I'll tell Doctor and he'll come and look at you."

"Was I awake before? I don't remember."

"Half. You were trying to tell us about packing food or something."

"The storm! Jenny and Charles's house! Oh Lord! Ahh!" She doubled up in the bed as a vicious wave of pain swamped through her entire body.

"Hold on there, dear. I'll get Doctor." The nurse bolted.

The pain subsided leaving her nauseated and shaken, and worried about the baby. It was far too early yet . . .

"Mrs Dunning, here's Doctor to see you."

Liz opened her eyes.

"I'm Tom Shields. Obstetrics." A short, fat, round-faced young man was smiling at her.

"Hi," she whispered, "I'm Liz Dunning."

"You're Australian! Floated all the way here on the flood?"

"My accent still that thick?" She attempted a smile before asking, "What's happening? Something wrong with baby?"

"We did a scan while you were still unconscious. One of the babies is fine but I'm worried about the other one. You did some damage I'm afraid when you made that unscheduled exit into the garden."

"Other one? Are you telling me there are two in there?"

The doctor and nurse looked at each other then back at Liz.

"You mean you didn't know? Your doctor didn't tell you?" The doctor looked amazed.

"I'd no idea. Possibly because I don't have a doctor. We've been cut off by the floods . . . ahh!" She doubled up again. "Quick," she whispered, " I think I need to go to the loo."

Then everything became a blur. Noise. Feet. Herself being lifted. The IV needle in the back of her hand.

Mark Payton lunched with an old friend, Tom Dyce, UBC's chief weather forecaster. Dyce had provided much of the statistical background for Mark's book, and this morning, at Mark's request, had brought along the latest weather map.

"It's an odd one," he agreed.

"I want to know what's happening out there, Tom."

"Well . . . what's happening is even odder than the look of the thing. You can see that this really huge depression is centred mainly over the British Isles, stretching north up to Iceland. Now the centre of that contains very low pressure, but is so wide that it really is quite weak as regards winds, although there is a lot of thundery activity. You could say it's the residue of the weather we had while the cloud was up there.

"Now, as you can see, over the European continent, just as here in the States, pressure has risen very sharply, and is continuing to do so. Our situation is fairly straightforward. On the other side, you have a reversal of normal patterns, with the anti-cyclone trying to push that low away. Well, you could say it's winning, because the low is moving. But it's moving in its own good time. Where the two meet, of course, there are very deep pressure gradients indeed, and a lot of wind."

"I want to know what's happening on this side of the low."

"Well, there is high pressure over the western North Atlantic, an extension of our ridge here. Again, where the two systems meet, there are some steep gradients and strong winds. Nothing out of the ordinary, although they extend over a larger area than is normal. It's where that low is over the sea, just to the west of the British Isles, that we have the real freaks. That water is so warm, you see, that in places it is forcing the air to rise, which is of course perfectly normal, but the pressures and the temperatures are so unusual that when the air starts to do that it's doing it very suddenly and very rapidly. You could almost describe what is happening as a series of tornados over the sea, whereas you know, because of the heat required, tornados almost always occur over the land. Where they occur over the sea as waterspouts, they can of course be quite dangerous to shipping. These are very local occurrences, so we're getting these little patches of fierce weather, quite unexpectedly. It's a forecaster's nightmare, I can tell you."

"What kind of winds are we talking about in these mini-hurricanes?"

"Oh, a hundred miles an hour plus, then pfft. Nothing."

"And you say they're dangerous to shipping?"

"Well, obviously a hundred-mile-an-hour wind just springing up from nowhere can be dangerous for shipping. The normal pattern, of course, is for the locality and incidence of these disturbances to be charted and shipping advised, so that they can take evasive action in good time. But in these conditions, where they are just appearing from nowhere, that isn't proving practical. So we've been having reports of ships in trouble from all over. Only yesterday a British freighter went down. Can you imagine, a ten-thousand tonner being thrown on her beam ends like some racing yacht? That's what the last radio report from her said was happening. I believe she was overloaded and topheavy, but even so . . . "

"And you say she sank?"

"Seems so. All contact with her has been lost."

"And she was ten thousand tons," Mark brooded. "I was on a ten-thousand tonner in that tsunami. She didn't seem to have any problems handling it."

"Well, normally, a well-found ship can handle almost any weather. Short of real freaks, of course."

"Like they're having in the North Atlantic right this moment," Mark growled. "Thanks a million. You have quite spoiled my lunch."

He went back to the Institute, called in Penny. "I'd like to place a shore-to-ship telephone call, SS *Roberta*."

"Has to be person to person."

"I know. Ms Anne Dunning."

Penny wrote the name down very carefully, refraining from comment. She'd rather guessed that her boss, most unusually, had something on his mind apart from his work during the past couple of months. But this was the first time she'd had a name.

"ASAP," Mark told her.

"Right away."

But it took well over an hour to get through, and then a further ten minutes to locate Anne and get her up to the radio cabin.

"Mark? What's happened?"

"Not a thing. How're things with you?"

"Couldn't be better."

"No bad weather?"

"Hot and muggy."

"No wind?"

"Not a ripple. Mind you, they say it could change. That'll be a relief. Say, did you call me just to ask about the weather?"

"I just wanted to hear your voice."

"Silly man," she commented. "When are you coming over?"

Mark had just made a decision. "I'll be there to meet you," he said. "When do you dock?"

"Three days' time. At Southampton."

"I'll be there. Take care."

He blew a kiss into the phone and hung up. "I need a flight to Heathrow the day after tomorrow," he told Penny.

"May not be easy. All the airlines are jampacked now that people can fly again."

"Just get me a seat."

Anne was grinning all the way back to her cabin. What was it he'd said about the girl friend who'd telephoned him all over the world, nursing her 'togetherness'? Dope. But it gave one good vibes. He was lovely; strange she had ever thought otherwise. A peculiar mixture of strengths and weaknesses more noticeable in him than in most people because of his very positive public face. Deceptively so. Made one think he'd be like that in his private life . . . Nice he would be at Southampton. She hugged herself, looked at the date on her watch, and noticed the time. Wedding bells or not, she was still enjoying the attentions of the ship's officers, and one of them was waiting in the bar to have lunch with her.

Second Officer James Parker could only match Anne's height when they were sitting down, so he was perched on a barstool deliberately not springing to attention when she eventually arrived.

"Sorry I'm late. Had a phone call."

"You did? Let me guess. Your boss trying to pile the workload?"

"Wrong. I'm my own boss, and this isn't a business trip."

"Have a drink while I try again."

"The bar steward does a gorgeous Pimm's. May I have one?" She pulled up another stool and perched beside him.

"Your car rental is confirmed?"

"Eh? Oh, you mean the call. No. You'll never guess. It was my fiancé; he just wanted to hear my voice."

He poked his tongue into his cheek, trying not to laugh. "Keeping tabs on you. Don't blame him. You are far too attractive to be allowed out alone."

"Only in areas where the wolves are extra ferocious."

Lunch was fun. They shared a table with a middle-aged English businessman and his wife, both of whom were treating the voyage as a holiday before getting down to importing all the food they'd bought in the previous month. They were full of humorous anecdotes, drank liberal amounts of wine and the meal turned into a mini-riot before James had to go back on watch.

Siesta was vital, Anne decided, if she was to face another lively meal that evening. But by then not only had the weather become yet more muggy, accompanied by a large, uneasy swell out of the east, but those officers who were using the ship's dining-room appeared to have lost all their available humour. They were quiet, not to say morose.

"They're having some terrible weather, up ahead," a steward explained. "Some old cargo boat turned over."

"Jees! Nobody lost, was there?" another diner asked.

"Could be the lot. All radio contact with her has been lost. Couldn't happen to a modern ship like this," he added reassuringly.

Anne wasn't sorry when the evening broke up early and most passengers retired.

Her bedtime routine followed its usual pattern. She sat up in bed to write her five-year diary; smiled at the photo of Mark which advanced through the book one page per day, then swapped the diary for her current novel. Reading at night invariably had a deliciously soporific effect, a point which would doubtless not be appreciated by the author.

She thought about Mark's call, again. Happy thoughts. She had almost despaired of ever trusting a relationship again sufficiently to allow herself to feel quite this elated. But this was for real; something very, very special. It was impossible to imagine their feelings for each other ever breaking down. They were going to be married and live happily ever after . . . For ever and ever.

*   *   *

Anne awoke to a shuddering jar which had her sliding down her bunk, and then up again as the ship moved the other way.

She looked at her watch. 2.15 a.m.

Now she was aware of noise. The wind was howling, and there were waves battering at the ship. She got out of bed and stood at the porthole, but it was too dark to see anything, especially as spray was scattering across the outside of the glass. Then there was a vivid flash of lightning, striking right down to the sea with a sound like a whiplash, and for a dazzling moment lighting up the entire ocean.

Anne gasped. The ship was in the midst of a maze of gigantic whitecaps, which seemed to be coming from every direction at once.

After the flash the darkness was even more intense. She felt for the switch of the cabin light, found it – and was thrown on to the bed, catching her funnybone on the edge of the bedside table. "Damn!" she swore aloud, more to relieve the tension than the pain. It was all rather scary. She didn't know why; she was not a woman who was easily frightened, and this was just a storm at sea. Surely. They had been expecting it, but it had happened so suddenly.

She knew she wasn't going to sleep any more, so she pulled on slacks and a sweater, and opened her cabin door. Lights glowed reassuringly in the corridor, but standing was not easy as the ship was rolling heavily, as well as plunging. The stairs to the saloon deck were particularly difficult and she had to sit down on a step for a few moments, clinging for dear life to the handrail. Reaching the rather grand lobby with its gilt-framed pictures and essential potted palm, she encountered a steward.

"Get you something, miss?"

"Where did all this weather come from?"

"Search me, miss. Skipper didn't mention it. Fierce out there."

"Um."

The steward could see she was uneasy. "You go and sit down in the saloon, miss, and I'll get you a nice cup of coffee."

"Oh, that would be great." Clutching at various grab rails and door handles, Anne made her way into the saloon and collapsed into one of the leather armchairs. She tried to envisage what might be happening on the bridge, where presumably the officers were gathered, staring into the darkness . . . but they had all those instruments . . . the ship gave another quite startling lurch, and seemed to drop about a thousand feet. Anne's stomach stayed put, and as a result felt as if it was in her throat. She swallowed saliva, clutched the arms of the chair, listened to an enormous flowing sound as water poured along the decks, and watched in stark horror as one of the bulkhead doors burst open.

Water rushed in, and she screamed and drew herself up on the chair, watched the steward come lurching back from his pantry.

"The door . . . !"

He hurled himself at it, and was driven back by another surge of water which flowed across the carpet and swirled around the chairs. These were chained to the floor, of course, but Anne, kneeling on hers, felt as if she was clinging to some half-tide rock . . . with the tide rising. The bulkhead door had been virtually torn from its hinges.

The noise from outside was tremendous as the wind shrieked and the waves roared, but it was louder than it should have been, and Anne suddenly realised why: there was no reassuring growl of engines from beneath her feet.

She stared at the steward, who had been knocked over by the last inrush of water, and washed right across the carpet between the legs of chairs and tables. Now he was picking himself up as the ship rolled the other way, and the water flowed back out through the door. Some of it. A great deal had poured along the corridor and down the stairs to the cabin deck.

"What's happening?" she shouted, more annoyed than frightened at this moment.

The steward looked at her, a stricken expression on his face. Then the alarm bells jangled.

For some reason Anne looked at her watch. It was 2.20. Only ten minutes ago she had been snugly asleep in her bunk. But in those minutes . . . the ship rolled again, and another wave smashed at the open doorway, pouring across the saloon and into the bowels of the vessel.

Second Officer Parker appeared with the purser, both capless, soaking and panting. "Lifejackets!" James snapped. "Get everyone up, Conroy. For God's sake, can't they hear the bell?"

Anne wanted to hug him; she so desperately needed the reassurance of someone who knew what he was doing.

He gazed at her, apparently noticing her for the first time. "Anne!" he shouted, and moved towards her, clutching furniture to keep his balance.

"What's happening?" she gasped.

"This just blew up, ten minutes ago. It's as if the whole surface of the sea has been caught up in some kind of explosion. Not a sign on radar or the weathermap. We thought we'd drive through it, but that engine failure . . . "

The ship gave another of those terrifying, uncontrollable

263

lurches, and he was hurled sideways. Anne screamed as his head struck a table and he fell heavily to the floor. Then she was out of her chair, slithering across the deck, half submerged in water, to reach him. But he lay absolutely still. He was breathing, but had knocked himself out.

She shook him and splashed water on his face, and was surrounded by wailing, shouting people as passengers hurried up from below.

"James!" she shouted. "For God's sake, James!"

But he wouldn't wake up. She heaved him up into a sitting position to keep his face above the water.

"Aaaagh!" someone screamed as another wave broke into the doorway. "We're sinking. She's going down!"

Anne realised the woman could be right. There were several stewards in the saloon now, carrying armfuls of lifejackets, slipping and sliding about the place, falling over people who were also unable to keep their footing.

And not only had this last wave not flowed back out through the door, but more and more water was coming in.

"The lifeboats," one of the stewards was shouting. "Get to the lifeboats."

But the lifeboats could only be reached by going on deck, and the deck was now constantly awash. One of the stewards edged out of the door, and the next huge wave swept him away, his voice a fading scream of terror.

The noise in the saloon was unbearable, as people yelled or prayed or begged. The disaster had developed too suddenly for the passengers or the crew to take control of themselves, or the situation. Anne looked at her watch again; it was not yet 2.30.

Parker stirred, and she slapped his face. "James, for God's sake wake up."

He blinked at her, then looked past her, and his eyes seemed to go dead.

"The lifeboats," she said.

He shook his head. "Anne, sweetheart . . . " he held her tightly as they were enveloped in an immense gurgling sound, and the deck seemed to drop away beneath them.

I am going to be married, Anne thought, in two weeks' time. She felt herself floating, away from Parker, and then her head bumped, and the water rose around her nostrils.

Oh, dammit! she thought.

The alteration in course took *Skyhawk* to the east, and into steadily improving conditions. Geoffrey was able to set both watches to cleaning up the mess caused by the knockdowns, and to adjusting what was left of the grain; most of the deck cargo had also gone overboard, and there was substantial damage apart from the radio aerials. Several lengths of rail had been smashed, and three lifeboats carried away. Most serious of all, there were no electronics, as all the other aerials had also been carried away.

But the ship was dry and seaworthy, and had it not been for Fogarty's body lying on his bunk, Geoffrey could have been almost happy; there is no sensation that quite equals the exhilaration of having fought one's way through really heavy weather.

"Sextants, gentlemen," he told Turnbull and Trent. "And dead reckoning. We still have the auto-pilot and the log. I want you each to work out the exact moment we will sight the Needles."

"You realise we won't be able to call for a pilot," Harper grumbled. "I can't do anything with the VHF aerial."

"So we'll do without a pilot, and answer questions later. Wait a mo, though, don't we have a lamp? We must have a lamp."

"Well, I suppose we do," Turnbull said. "But I'm not sure any of us can work it well enough to be understood."

"I did my stint in the Navy, Mr Turnbull," Walsh said. "I can handle a signalling lamp."

"Good man," Geoffrey said. "We'll signal the lighthouse and explain the situation."

Everyone was feeling fairly euphoric, and a great deal of textbook navigation was practised. Geoffrey intended to keep them busy, because it was an eerie, and unique situation for them. They had all been brought up on electronics. Of course to gain their mate's tickets they had had to pass examinations in real navigation, and good skippers like John Fogarty had insisted that their officers shoot the sun every day and work out longitude as well . . . but always there had been the comforting feeling that it didn't really matter, when the satellite navigator, and the Loran, and the radar were all humming away, and the Weatherfax was showing them exactly what lay ahead, and Harper was in constant touch with both sides of the Atlantic . . . now they were suddenly absolutely blind, in every way. The only instruments remaining were those like the barometer and chronometer, which lived on their own, as it were.

And that afternoon the barometer started to rise, quite steeply, while the wind freshened up again . . . once more from the east.

"That 'deep' is shifting," Geoffrey told Turnbull. "It could be another wild night. I think you'd better check everything all over again."

Turnbull nodded lugubriously, and went about his duties. But that evening he was happy he'd done so, when the wind was screaming and the seas were growing very big all over again.

Skyhawk was well under control, however. Geoffrey never left the bridge, although he elevated Trent to full watch-keeping duties. With her top-heavy cargo jettisoned, the freighter pushed her way into the seas which curled green over her bows and sent spray rattling aft, but presented no immediate danger; Chief Evans, who was far senior to Geoffrey and had every right to take command, was happy to hand over to the younger man and keep control of his engines.

Towards dawn Geoffrey dozed in his chair, but was awakened by Trent after an hour.

"The Needles light, sir, one point on the port bow."

Geoffrey levelled his binoculars, counted the flashes. It was the Needles all right. "What time do you estimate, Harry?"

"Well, actually, 0600."

"Hm. What about Lloyd?"

"He made it 0500."

"And it's 0333. You fellows are going to have to practise."

"What time did you enter, sir?"

"0400. It's in my notebook."

"Um," Trent said enviously.

It was now distinctly wild, but as the wind was coming out of the north-east it was offshore as they closed the Isle of Wight, and the seas were actually beginning to go down. The tide was falling, which meant that it was flowing with the wind, and that helped as well. Ocean-going vessels were normally required to anchor or heave-to under power, and wait for the pilot, while equally, for economic reasons, it was normal to wait for the tide to turn, but Geoffrey had no intention of doing that: he wanted to get home. He had navigated the Solent before, and as the tides were running some twenty feet higher than usual there was very little chance of his hitting anything, while apart from Fogarty, he didn't like to think of what a strong north-easterly might be doing to all the flood water in East Anglia . . . and the south-east. When he had telephoned from Buenos Aires and been told that Dunning Farm had had to be evacuated, they told him the family had all moved down to Greenwich. Now he was none too sure how safe Greenwich was.

Skyhawk steamed on, into the shallowing waters south-west of the Isle of Wight, while Geoffrey studied both the Needles Lighthouse and Hurst Castle on the north shore through his binoculars. He had no doubt they were both calling him, and swearing as he did not reply, but stood on for the narrow channel between Hurst and the rocks on which the lighthouse stood, and which would take him into the shelter of the Solent. When lights began to flash he had Walsh reply with the signalling lamp, and as a result a pilot cutter was waiting for him as *Skyhawk* fought her way up the channel against both wind and tide.

"When contact was lost, we thought you'd gone down," the pilot told Geoffrey as he took command.

"We were knocked down," Geoffrey confessed. "I think that's when the skipper died."

The pilot nodded. "You were lucky."

"Well . . . " Geoffrey decided against arguing the point, although he would have said they owed their survival to skill and prompt action.

"There have been some alarming casualties," the pilot told him. "A thirteen-thousand ton liner, *Roberta*, has just disappeared."

Geoffrey frowned at him. "Come again?"

"Fact."

"Thirteen-thousand ton ships do not just disappear," Geoffrey remarked.

"This one did. There was not even a mayday. But a ship which was seventeen miles away from *Roberta*'s last calculated position has reported being on the edge of a sudden disturbance which topped hurricane force."

"And you think she could have been overwhelmed? Thirteen thousand tons?"

"That's what we think happened, yes. The crew must've been taken completely unawares."

Geoffrey gave a low whistle. "Maybe we were lucky, after all."

Southampton Docks being under water, *Skyhawk* joined an armada of other ships and anchored, just before noon; British Ocean Transporter officials came out by launch, the pilot cutter having used its radio to call ahead and bring them up to date.

"Mr Dunning? Well done. Sorry about the old man."

"Yes," Geoffrey said. "So am I."

"The important thing is that you brought the ship home. I have an idea you may be confirmed in command."

"Hell," Geoffrey commented. It went against the grain to be elated about anything, with Fogarty lying dead only a few feet away . . . but it was difficult to resist.

"Now you'll want to get ashore," the dock captain told him.

"There's a hell of a lot to be done here."

"Let your people do it. You have an emergency. A personal message has been forwarded to us from Liverpool, saying your wife has been taken to hospital. Something to do with her pregnancy."

"Oh my God! When? Did they say when?"

"No. But that doesn't matter. You want to hurry. And listen, take care. The whole of south-east England has been placed under a state of emergency, because of the high tide expected tonight and these very strong winds. You may not be able even to get to her."

"I'll get to her," Geoffrey told him. "Lloyd, you're in command." He ran for the gangway.

17

The Flood

Geoffrey tried to telephone Greenwich, but the lines were out. He didn't want to hang about, so he hired a car, with some difficulty. Not only was it a Sunday, but there had been precious little demand for hire cars over the past few months and most firms were closed down; there weren't all that many places to drive to . . . or much fuel available. But at last he secured a Ford Fiesta.

"You'll be bringing it back here?" the girl asked anxiously.

"I'll let you know. What the devil is that item?"

"Insurance."

"Fifty pounds?"

"The rates are very high now, sir. We never know when one of our cars is simply going to be abandoned and left where the water can get at it."

"This car is going to London," Geoffrey said firmly.

"That's where we lose most of them, sir."

He took the M3 motorway intending to approach Greenwich via Lewisham on the South Circular. It was still stormy, with clouds scudding across the sky, driven by the strong easterly breeze. Yet there was no rain, and every so often the sun shone quite brilliantly.

But Geoffrey was in no mood to admire nature, or even to feel any satisfaction at having brought his ship safely home. Only reaching London mattered, and Liz.

And then, he supposed, at some stage Jane Fogarty. She wouldn't even know of her husband's death, as yet.

There was not a great deal of traffic, but it built up as he neared London, most cars heading west. Nearing the Orbital, notices appeared: beyond the Orbital the M3 was closed due to flooding. So he followed the signs on to the M25 without difficulty, scarcely noticing the water-logged low-lying ground he passed on the way. It was good going, fast, so he elected to stay on it to Junction 7 and turn north past Croydon on the A23; but then he joined an enormous tailback, which filled the road as far as he could see.

He wound down his window. "What the hell is going on?" he asked the driver of the car beside him.

"Search me. Probably a police roadblock. They have them all over the place nowadays, telling you where you can and cannot go."

The traffic had come to a complete halt, the minutes were ticking by – and Geoffrey became increasingly aware that he hadn't had any breakfast or made provision for lunch: he had expected to be in Greenwich by now.

It took an hour to reach Purley, and even then there was no end in sight to the jam. Geoffrey decided to abandon it, and with much hooting and arm signalling, got on to a side road and parked in the first available spot. He just had to eat, and he wanted to try telephoning Greenwich again to find out which hospital Liz was in.

He wrestled with coins in the box, standing in the entrance lobby of a pub, but every time he punched out the numbers he got a continuous buzz. The confounded lines were still out.

"Making for London?" asked the publican as he served steak and kidney pie.

"Greenwich."

"Shouldn't think you'll get there."

"Sugar! Why not?"

"Police have the approaches to the river sealed off. This easterly wind is causing breeches in the Essex levee, and there are doubts even about the Barrier. Seems there's a very big tide tonight, and if this wind strengthens, there could be some serious problems."

"If the situation is that serious, then presumably the whole area has been evacuated."

"Well, no, it hasn't. The Government has been appealing for people who live in areas thirty feet or more above sea level to stay put. There's been so much evacuation that they've run out of places to put them."

"My family live in Greenwich. Including my pregnant wife!"

"That's bad news," the publican sympathised. "You mean they're still there?"

"I don't know," Geoffrey groaned. "I just don't know. I've driven up from Southampton this morning and I can't get in touch." He paid for the meal. "Thanks anyway."

He didn't know where Liz was, nor the rest of the family. And he had no idea how to find out . . . except by getting to them.

*   *   *

At Waddon he turned off into Croydon; here the only delay was caused by the stream of traffic which, another driver explained, consisted of evacuees heading for the army tents on Addington Hills. There was comparatively little on the A212, all the way to Catford, but having crossed the South Circular there was another complete hold-up. He found out why when he reached Lewisham and ran into a police roadblock.

"I'm sorry, sir, but no traffic is permitted beyond this point," the Sergeant said.

"I have to get to Greenwich."

"To look at the Barrier, eh? I'm sorry, sir, but sight-seeing is quite definitely out."

"I have no desire to look at the bloody Barrier!" Geoffrey exploded. "My family live in Greenwich, and my wife is having a premature delivery, or a miscarriage, I don't know what. I have to get there."

The Sergeant stroked his chin. "On the level?"

"Yes. On the level."

He looked at Geoffrey's uniform. "Then you'd better go through." He signalled his men. "You know tonight's the biggest tide of this cycle?"

Geoffrey nodded.

"You may not be able to get back out until after midnight."

"I just want to get *there*."

The barrier had been opened.

"Best of luck," the Sergeant said.

Jason could almost have been a descendant of Nana Darling, straight out of Peter Pan: he had infinite patience with children. Which was just as well; it was more than could be said of anyone else in the house. He sat in the middle of the living-room carpet looking utterly ridiculous in one of Jessica's cardigans, a scarf tied round his head, unable to move if he'd wanted to as he was hobbled by one of Jennifer's old skirts. What was more, you could tell by the expression on his face that he felt ridiculous. At least the children were happily occupied for a few minutes ... Long may it last, Jennifer thought as she ferreted about in one of the cardboard boxes in the hallway, looking for the margarine and some biscuits.

John edged past her, accidentally treading on her skirt, causing her to cry out, "Oh, look where you're going!"

She frowned at her own short temper.

"Silly place to keep the groceries, isn't it?" her father riposted as he opened the front door. Which created a draught and the back door slammed with a crash.

271

"Oh good heavens!" Mary rushed to the head of the stairs. "What was that?"

"Daddy going out, *again*, to see if the army have come to fetch us," Jennifer snapped. "The back door slammed."

"Poor Daddy. He is so anxious." Mary came down, slowly. She was feeling desperately tired, though she couldn't imagine why. There was absolutely nothing to do, except wait.

"Aren't we all?" Jenny stood up with the margarine and oatmeal biscuits, cursing under her breath at the person, or persons, un- known who had put them away in the wrong box, and headed for the kitchen.

"I was going to offer to help with the children's tea, but if that's the mood you're in I won't bother." There was a cool edge in Mary's voice. A tone Jennifer had never heard before.

"Oh Mummy, I am a perfect bitch, aren't I?" Her arms circled her mother, food still clutched in each hand.

"No worse than I am." Mary hugged her daughter and the two women sobbed, clinging together in despair.

The tears turned to almost hysterical laughter when they heard a shout from the other side of the front door. And men's voices.

"It's Geoffrey!" Mary cried, and rushed to the door. "How mar- vellous."

It opened as her hand reached for the latch. "Hello, Mum." Geoffrey pulled her into his arms for a quick hug. "Any news of Liz?"

"Not a thing. But the phone is no longer working . . . "

"I found that out! Phew!" He stood back to peel off his jacket, hitched it over the newel post with his cap over the top. "Hell, it's hot. How do you stick this humidity?"

"We did have de-humidifiers but there isn't any electricity at all, now," his father explained.

"None at all? What about fridges, etcetera?"

"We have been without since Liz's accident, yesterday," Mary told him. "Luckily we still had the phone then and were able to get help."

"What happened?"

The three went into the sitting-room, to the end farthest from the children's game with Jason.

"Liz and Freddie took Jason up to the Observatory for a walk. We didn't know the weather was deteriorating . . . "

"Well," John interrupted. "We knew, but we had no idea of the speed . . . "

"Quite. Well, while they were out a lorryload of soldiers arrived, visiting all the houses and warning us to be ready for immediate evacuation should it become necessary. While they were here the wind picked up and it started raining in buckets, didn't it, dear?"

"Yes," John agreed. "First really heavy stuff we've seen for months."

"Freddie and Liz dashed home and she went straight through to the back to bring in the washing. She was wearing those Australian flip-flops of hers. The soles were wet and she skidded out of the utility door and down the stone steps to the patio."

"How badly hurt was she?"

"We don't know. We could see the grazes on her hands and legs, but it was the awkwardness of the fall which seems to have caused the problem . . . "

"And the baby?"

John leaned forward, empty pipe in hand. "We have no idea. They said they would try to get her into St David's, but couldn't guarantee it. In fact she could be in any of a number of hospitals. The trouble is the phone went dead soon after they left."

"Oh Lord!" Geoffrey ran his fingers through his hair. "Then how the hell do I find her? I must get to her."

"Best to wait . . . " his father looked at his watch " . . . another half-hour. The next supply boat is due then. Those are the boys who are most likely to know."

Geoffrey got up and started to pace around. "How long did it take for the ambulance to get here?"

"It wasn't an ambulance, dear," Mary corrected. "They carried the stretcher down the road to a rubber dinghy . . . and transferred her to a river launch. The soldiers said it would be better and quicker than trying to get round by road, south of the river."

Geoffrey shook his head. He was tired, worried sick. Dazed. "How was she?"

His parents looked at each other. John shrugged and nodded.

"Concussed," Mary admitted. "But there was a doctor with them who examined her. He said she would be all right. But . . . he couldn't say anything about the baby."

Geoffrey knew it would be senseless to head straight for St David's. If she wasn't there it was unlikely they'd know where she'd been taken. But he was waiting, along with Charles and Freddie, down the hill, where a stiff wind was throwing waves up the tarmacked road, when an army Avon finally nosed up as far as possible. The soldiers, all in fishermen's thigh boots, began heaving sacks and boxes over the side.

Geoffrey stepped up to the corporal in charge. "Hello. The name's Dunning. I believe one of your lot collected my wife and took her to hospital after a fall . . . "

"You mean the little auburn-haired girl. Pregnant?" He was a freckle-faced young man of no more than twenty.

"Yes. That fits. You remember her?"

"Sure thing. We got her to an ambulance launch which shot straight up river with her. They'd radioed an ambulance to meet them by Vauxhall Bridge. They arranged for her admittance to St David's while we were still alongside."

Geoffrey breathed a sigh of relief. At least he'd established where she was. He looked at the inflatable. "Any hope of a lift up river?"

"Sorry, mate. Not a chance. We've several more deliveries down river yet." The corporal seemed genuinely apologetic. "Got a car?"

Geoffrey nodded.

"Keep south of the river. Slow, but it's your best bet."

"Are you sure it's the wise thing to do?" Charles asked. "They did announce that no one was to go out unless it was absolutely essential, until after ten o'clock tonight. That's half-tide down," he added helpfully.

"You don't suppose it is essential I am with Liz at this moment?"

"Well . . . " Charles scratched his head. "I mean, your being there can't affect what is going to happen. It can't help in any way."

"Supposing you get there," Freddie added, "the weather is deteriorating all the time. There must be a full gale out there, veering to the east. It'll push up much more water."

"I'll get there," Geoffrey told them. "As for helping . . . of course it's going to help. Liz will want me there."

The time was 5.30, an hour and a half before the big high tide. They were all looking anxious, John repeatedly going out to Croom's Hill, hidden under a heavy, yellow plastic mac with a hood, and in green wellies, to gauge the water level.

"I think it would be better to wait till morning . . . " he said when Geoffrey gave his arm an affectionate farewell squeeze.

Mary and Jennifer were checking the boxes, adding things, taking things out.

Geoffrey shook his head. "I'll make it. Don't worry. You just look after this lot." He kissed the children, said goodbye, and ran out to the car. Heading for Deptford and Camberwell, he meant to cross the river at either Lambeth or Vauxhall, but he hadn't got very far when he was stopped by a police patrol.

"May I ask where you are going, sir?"

"St David's hospital."

"Are you ill?"

"No, I'm not ill," Geoffrey tried to keep his cool. "But my wife is. I'm trying to reach her."

"I'll have to call ahead and get permission for you to cross the bridge, sir," the Sergeant said. "Shouldn't be long."

He had some kind of command vehicle waiting at the side of the road.

"Well, for God's sake hurry up," Geoffrey snapped.

A radio sputtered from the squad car, and the other policemen were listening, clearly very interested, fiddling with knobs to improve reception.

"I am standing on the observation platform looking down the river," a news reporter was saying, "and it is really a terrifying sight. We are told the tide in the Channel is now some twenty feet above normal. Well, as it has spread right across Essex – we are hearing reports that the levee has given way in several places – it is not quite so high here, but it is coming up the river like a series of ocean waves, pushed by this gale-force easterly wind. The tops of the gates are nearly fourteen feet above normal tide height, and I can tell you that the water is spilling over the top at several thousand gallons a minute. But at least the Barrier is restraining the main force of the flood tide, as it is intended to do, although the area to either side of the river bed is flooded to a distance of perhaps a mile on the south, and much more extensively on the north. In view of what is happening in Essex, it is certainly possible that the whole East End will shortly be under water. There are air-sea rescue helicopters out there as well as rubber boats, but they are having a hard time of it.

"Immediately beneath me, as I have said, the Barrier stands firm, creaking a bit as it withstands this immense volume of water being thrust against it. We are within an hour of high water, and therefore it would appear we are at the critical moment. Soon . . . "

The Sergeant came hurrying back. "That's all right, sir. You have permission to cross Vauxhall Bridge." He handed Geoffrey a slip of paper. "This will take you through any other roadblocks. But having got to St David's you will have to remain there until half tide down."

"Don't worry," Geoffrey told him. "I won't be going anywhere for some time."

He put the car into drive, and listened to shouts from the radio.

"My God!" the reporter was yelling. "It's going, it's cracking beneath the strain. The Barrier's going! My . . . "

"Why do you keep going out, Daddy?" Jennifer demanded. "You trail mud and water in with you every time you come back."

Geoffrey had left half an hour ago in filthy weather, but not nearly as bad as it was now. Wind and rain lashed the back of the house, rattling the old sash windows, driving trickles of water up and on to the inner sills, and under the back door. It was so dark they needed candles to see at all, making the blue lightning seem much more intense.

"Everyone in the area is feeling very nervous, not to say panicky. If we do need to get out we don't want to be on the end of the queue."

Mary looked at John as he spoke. He had aged ten years in the past few months. The once firm flesh of his face now sagged in grey folds, his eyes sunk deep in dark-ringed sockets. He no longer walked straight and upright. He was like a bent, old man.

"If you reckon it's important to keep an eye out there, why don't you let me go?" Freddie said. "I thought you were only going out as a matter of interest."

"It would be better if we both went together. Then one of us can keep seats in the lorry while the other comes back for the girls and the children."

"And the luggage," Jennifer added.

"You won't stand a hope of taking all the stuff you've stacked in the hall," Charles warned.

"But we must! We've got to have clothes and food," she protested.

Freddie disappeared, returning a few minutes later in oilskins and boots like his father's, and the two men set off again.

"I suppose we should get our waterproofs ready, and the children's. If the lorryride is a long one we don't want to be sitting in wet clothes for hours." Mary went out to the utility.

The children were tired, whining and squabbling.

"Do shut up, you two," Jennifer pleaded.

"I want to dress Jason up again," Jessica demanded.

"Jason has had enough. He doesn't enjoy it."

"He does!" both the children yelled together.

Mary came back into the room with an armful of macs and dropped them over a chair. "Come and sit by me and I'll tell you a story."

The children threw themselves at her and a story commenced, while Jennifer started collecting ornaments from the mantelpiece to take upstairs.

Suddenly there was a huge noise, an enormous, rolling rumble.

"Oh, my God!" Charles burst into the room. "The Barrier!"

"Freddie!" Mary screamed. "John!"

"I'll see if I can call them." Jennifer kicked off her sandals, it wasn't worth bothering with boots. "Oh damn. The rain is coming in under the door." She opened it . . . and gasped as water, several inches deep, flooded into the hall. Through the rain she could see filthy waves surge round the gate and up the flagstone path. "Charles!" she screamed, and staggered to the gate shouting "Daddy! Freddie!"

Other people were shouting and screaming, neighbours who lived above and below. Wind whined between the houses and the headlights of a vehicle shone from further up the hill. Above and behind it all the great roaring rumble continued.

"Daddy! Freddie!"

"Come back, for God's sake, Jenny," Charles called from the door. "Come and get the children. We've got to get out of here."

Mary had her mac on, helped Jenny into hers, though it seemed a waste of time as she was already soaked to the skin, her brolly having blown inside out. The three grown-ups wrestled with the children's clothes and boots.

"That'll do. Out," Charles commanded. "Hang on to Jackie, both of you. I'll bring Jessica."

"The food!" Jennifer yelled across the cardboard boxes now standing in inches of water. "Our clothes!"

"Forget it. Just come. And you, Jason." He led them out into the storm.

Faces averted from the stinging rain, they joined the throng of neighbours trudging up Croom's Hill. Ahead of them they saw the headlights swing as the vehicle turned.

"What's happening?" Charles asked the man in front of him.

"Lorry's full."

"Aren't there others?"

"They say they're needed in other districts." The man's voice was dull, toneless.

"What about us?"

"They say they'll be back as soon as they can."

If they can. And that could be hours! "We're not staying out here," he told the women. "Let's see if we can get across the park to the museum."

"You go," Mary said. "I'll stay and wait for John and Freddie."

"You won't find them in this crush. Come on, Mary. You must come with us. We'll find them later."

She didn't argue.

The great dome of the world-famous observatory was invisible through the rain. Some thoughtful person had opened the doors of the Flamstead Museum and already miserable throngs of sodden people were dripping pools of water on to the floors.

The Rowlands sat with Mary on the stairs. A woman next to Mary was weeping and a young boy beyond her said, "She's upset, seeing your dog. She's just remembered we've left the budgerigar behind."

"Budgerigar! What about the poor people who were washed away?" snapped a skinny little woman in a sodden trilby hat.

"How many?"

"Didn't count. More than necessary, though. It was obvious that nobody could get back out of it, not all dressed up in boots and that; yet some silly youngster jumps in after an old man. Never saw either of them again. Must have been six or seven of them, all told."

For a moment Geoffrey was in a quandary. He didn't know what might be happening back in Greenwich. He did know that Jennifer's house was only just over thirty feet above water level, and if more than thirty feet of water had just burst through the dam . . . but Freddie and Charles, and Dad, were all capable men, and his instincts still drew him to the hospital.

"I think you had better wait while I call again, sir," the Sergeant suggested.

Geoffrey shook his head, and gunned the engine. The policemen stepped back, and he drove for the bridge. Progress was slow, because there were so many people about, shouting at each other, running into the street as if expecting a torrent of water to come down it at any moment . . . well, he supposed it could happen.

At the foot of the bridge there was another police barrier. Geoffrey braked, and waved his piece of paper.

"Sorry, sir," the Inspector said. "But all passes have been cancelled. Too dangerous."

Geoffrey looked at him, then at the bridge; the barrier was only a thin piece of wood. Again he gunned the engine, and drove at it. The policemen shouted, and ran behind him. The car struck the wood, but it was thicker than he had supposed. It broke all right, but for a moment he lost control, and skidded sideways on to the bridge itself.

As he fought the wheel, he looked along the river, which bent away from him about a quarter of a mile away. And gasped. Round the bend was coming a huge wave of water still at least twenty feet high, like the biggest tidal bore in history, making him remember what he had read of the fearsome Seine *mascaret*, travelling at immense speed and carrying on its crest a mind-boggling assortment of debris, tree branches, park benches, shattered boats and miscellaneous pieces of timber . . . and human bodies. How incred-

ible if he were to survive a tsunami at sea only to be drowned by one
on land!

The policemen were nearly up to him, shouting and bawling
instructions. Geoffrey twisted the wheel and drove at the north
bank, where there was another barrier, and more shouting, arm-
waving men. But their attention was also caught by the coming
liquid juggernaut. Geoffrey drove at the barrier, smashed into it,
and this time lost control completely. The car again slewed round
and smashed backwards into a lamp post, the engine dying. When
he twisted the starter key, there was no response.

He opened the door and got out, and a police Sergeant ran
towards him.

"You," the Sergeant shouted, "are under arrest. You . . . "

Geoffrey started to run too, as the water smashed into the
bridge. The wave flew high into the air, with a deafening roar, and
then descended to either side. The almost solid roof of water
knocked both Geoffrey and the policemen right over. For a moment he was scattered breathless on the street, then the water
receded and he got back to his knees and struggled to his feet. All
around him were screams and shrieks, overlaid by the roar of the
wave, which was continuing on its way up the river.

The Sergeant was sitting up, shaking water from his hair.

"See you around," Geoffrey said, and waded into the dusk.

London was a crescendo of noise, of screaming people, wailing
sirens, crashes and bangs. Geoffrey was ploughing through knee-
deep water most of the time, as the river had now quite burst its
banks even within the city and was spreading out in a huge gush to
either side, joining the tidal wave which had now swept right across
Essex. It flowed down into the tube stations, and the drains, and
came bubbling up again, a thick stinking soup. All current had long
been cut off, and there did not appear to be many casualties,
although he came across groups of firemen evacuating people
from basement flats which had been thought safe this far up-river.

People shouted at him for help, but he ignored them as he
struggled forward, following the rising ground now, until he was
clear of the water. Here there were crowds, peering down streets,
asking silly questions, plaintively inquiring after relatives, held back
by policemen and troops, out in force. Reluctantly they allowed the
capless man wearing the torn and mudstained remnants of a uniform into their ranks, and he pressed through them, asking directions to the hospital.

Liz looked drained and weary, her face white, auburn curls damp

279

and matted with sweat.

Geoffrey stood at the opening in the floral curtains round her bed, his heart aching with love and pity. As he moved towards her she opened her eyes, her whole face lighting up with joy, for an instant, before twisting with sadness. But both arms reached out for him and he paused only to throw his soaking jacket over a chair before slipping his hands under her back against the pillows.

They clung together in silence for a few moments until Geoffrey could no longer resist asking, "Well, what have we – a boy or a girl?"

"Oh, Geoff . . . You mean they didn't tell you?"

"Who tell me . . . what?"

"The nurses."

"I haven't spoken with any nurses. This place is in total chaos, with all the casualties. I just walked in."

"Oh!"

"Well. You tell me," he demanded, and watched the tears dribbling from her eyes. "Oh, no," he muttered.

"You have a son," she whispered.

"A son?" he shouted. "But that's marvellous. Oh, my darling!" He held her close, felt her stiffness, slowly laid her back on the pillow. "He's not . . . all right?"

"He's fine, Geoff. Just fine. So they say. But . . . he had a sister."

"Twins?" His mouth hung open. "Liz, my darling. When did you know . . . "

"About an hour before they were born."

"Where are they? I want to see them."

Her face twisted again. "Him."

Geoffrey stared at her, and felt her fingers tighten on his.

"Oh, my darling."

"It was that fall I had," she said. "Geoff . . . I'm so terribly sorry."

She was in his arms again. "What have you to be sorry about, my dearest girl? I should've been here. Oh, hell . . . "

The door behind him opened. "Mrs Dunning?" a nurse asked anxiously.

"It's all right," Liz explained. "This is my husband."

The nurse did a double-take as she gazed at the tatterdemalion creature in front of her, and then at the mud on Liz's sheets and nightgown.

"Everyone seemed sort of busy, so I thought I'd find my own way," Geoffrey explained.

"Hm," the nurse commented, and then her face softened. "Would you like to see your baby?"

He glanced at Liz, who gave a quick nod. So he followed the

nurse out of the ward and down a crowded corridor, people rushing in all directions. "I thought new babies were kept with their mothers, nowadays."

"Yes, in normal circumstances. But with so many viral infections about at the moment, we have to be extra careful."

He gazed at his son. There was precious little flesh on his skull, so huge in proportion to his little body, and there was a bandage round his middle. The nappy was enormous, causing his skinny legs to stick out like matchsticks. But it was wonderful to see his big, dark blue eyes, his tiny flailing hands.

"Has your wife told you?" the nurse asked.

"Yes."

"I'm sorry. We're all sorry." She half turned as a stretcher was wheeled past in the corridor outside. "About everything. There is so much . . . "

"Yes," Geoffrey said.

She seemed to pull herself together. "I don't wish to be rude, Mr Dunning, but not only are your clothes dripping all over the floor, you ah . . . smell, absolutely dreadful."

"There's an awful lot of stinking water out there. Sorry. Perhaps if I could shower you might lend me a hospital gown? I'd like to stay awhile with my wife."

"You were a long time," Liz murmured sleepily when he eventually returned. Then she opened her eyes, and smiled. "New patient? I'm glad you changed. You smelt terrible!"

He sniffed his hands. "Can't say carbolic soap makes the greatest improvement. Liz, I'm so proud of our son. Of you. I'm so sorry I wasn't back in time for the birth. When was he born?"

"Last night. Or rather, this morning at about two o'clock." She took his hand and kissed it. "I'm the one who should be apologising to you. I'd promised I'd wait till you were home."

"You did. I was. Well, back in the Solent, anyway. It's been a little difficult getting to you."

She listened to the storm lashing the window at the end of the ward. "Sounds terrible out there. How are the family coping?"

He was wondering that, too. He didn't want to alarm her so his reply was noncommittal, but he knew that wall of water he'd seen on his way here must have caused havoc in Greenwich.

"You know the farm is finished?" She watched his face as she spoke.

"Dad told me. Want to go to Aunt Madge in Wales?"

"I want to be where you are. When you are ashore, that is," she added quickly.

281

He squeezed her hands. "Fogarty is dead."

"Oh, Geoff . . . "

He nodded. "I liked him. Very much indeed. And I think he liked me. I'm terribly sorry. But Liz . . . I think I'm going to get *Skyhawk*."

"Oh, Geoff!"

"I know we don't really have a lot to celebrate, apart from our son's arrival. But . . . we'll be able to afford somewhere decent as soon as such a thing becomes available again."

"It will," she said." "We've survived, Geoff. You, me . . . and our son. And the family."

He prayed she was right.

The tide started to recede soon after seven, and by ten that night the crisis was over; soon afterwards the storm blew itself out. But for those driven from their homes and refuges by this last excess of the flood water it was still a wet and dismal night, as they worried about their loved ones.

Next morning, walking, hitching rides on army vehicles, and finally on an amphibious landing craft, Geoffrey got back to Greenwich. Another high tide had come and gone, and he stared in horror at the shambles which had been the Rowlands' house.

"Some mess," Freddie commented.

Geoffrey turned, seized his brother's hand. "God, am I glad to see you. The others . . . "

"More or less okay . . . Except for Dad. They're up at the Observatory. There's quite a crowd up there." His face was grey.

"What about Dad . . . ?"

Freddie shook his head. "He and I were at the water's edge when the dam broke."

"Oh, Lord. What happened?"

"We were both swept away. I tried to get to him, but . . . Geoff, he was dead already. I could only just hold him up. Then we got stuck in a tree and I managed to hold on."

"With Dad?"

Freddie gave a miserable nod. "The army inflatable came by after a couple of hours and rescued us. Me. It was their medic told me Dad had almost certainly died of a massive heart attack when he went in. We tried to persuade him not to go out . . . "

Geoffrey didn't have the heart to tell him of his own tragedy. "You held on to Dad in the middle of the river in that weather for a couple of hours!" He hugged his brother. "You bloody hero. You must be fitter than you look."

*   *   *

They climbed the slope together to the museum, and soon Geoffrey was holding his mother in his arms. Then he could tell them about Liz, and the babies.

All the tears had already been shed. And at least one of the twins had survived. Young life, new life, had to mean hope.

Geoffrey sat beside Charles.

"What happens now?"

"The army was here this morning, handing out food. We're all to be moved to a camp as soon as transport is available. Some time today."

"I was talking about, well . . . next, I suppose."

Charles pulled Jason's ears. "I reckon it's a long hard haul. Shoulders to the wheel and all that." He forced a grin. "We'll make it. We have to. At least we'll all be together. Even Anne. She's due in today. I wonder what she'll say to living in a camp."

"Today? Do you know the name of the ship? I must try to get in touch with her."

"Ah . . . " he looked across at the others. "Jennifer, can you remember the name of the ship Anne was travelling on?"

"A girl's name. The *Roberta*," she said.

An icy hand gripped Geoffrey's stomach. "Are you sure?"

Charles's eyebrows drew together as he saw Geoffrey's expression change. "Why, do you know it?"

"Yes," Geoffrey said. "I know it."

He couldn't bring himself to tell them. He went back to St David's to see Liz, then reported to British Ocean Transporters Headquarters.

"Congratulations," the Marine Superintendent said when he heard about the baby. "Now I think you'd better rejoin your ship, Captain Dunning. Your rank is confirmed."

"Thank you, sir. I was wondering about Jane Fogarty . . . "

"Leave that one with us. We've had the body brought ashore, and someone is with Mrs Fogarty now. But there's a lot of work to be done on *Skyhawk*."

"Yes, sir. May I ask . . . have you any information on what happened to *Roberta*? News of survivors?"

"I'm afraid not, Captain. Good luck."

No trains were running, so Geoffrey had to hitch rides on various army vehicles down to Southampton. From there he could make inquiries, as well as regain his ship.

But there was no good news to be had.

"I'm sorry, Mr Dunning," said the shipping agent. "There were no survivors from the *Roberta*."

"How can you be sure?"

"Simply that the area has been scoured time and again. Only a very limited amount of flotsam has been found: a few lifebelts, a shattered lifeboat. She seems to have gone straight down."

Geoffrey wandered across to the window, watched the tide coming up Southampton Water; in another couple of hours the ground floor of this building would be several feet deep in water. But he could look at the ships, anchored off, and pick out *Skyhawk*. His command. Due for a massive repair job, which would keep her in dry dock for several weeks. If a dry dock could be found. Weeks in which he and hopefully Liz – as soon as she was strong enough – would look for somewhere to live, on the top of a hill, he hoped. They had all to live for. Everyone who had survived had all to live for, their values perhaps restored from the greedy crawl after wealth to something more intrinsic, the sheer glory of being able to see the sun, and feel the breeze . . . all except Anne, who perhaps had had more than any of them to anticipate. And perhaps more to offer as well.

Anne! So vital, so much in command of herself, and every situation.

"Geoff? Geoff Dunning?"

He turned, and gazed at Mark Payton, standing at the counter. A Mark who had suddenly aged a dozen years.

"Where the devil . . . "

"Got in this morning. Anne and I were to meet here."

"Oh! You've heard . . . ?"

Mark nodded, walked to the window, gripped the sill as he stared down the Water. "Old *Skyhawk*." He swallowed hard. "I heard there was trouble in London, last night."

"A slight understatement, possibly."

"Family okay?"

Geoffrey could tell the scientist was close to breaking down. So he said, "Yes."

"Do they know . . . ?"

"Not yet."

Mark turned, and Geoffrey saw with consternation that tears were streaming down his face.

"I loved her," Mark said. "God, I loved her."

"We all loved her," Geoffrey told him. "She was that kind of woman. You'd better come and have a drink."

Mark drank Scotch, slowly and remorselessly. Geoffrey realised he might be going to have a problem. But then, he felt like doing the same.

Instead he telephoned the hire car company. "Remember me?" he asked. "Geoffrey Dunning. I hired a car from you yesterday morning."

"Yes, Mr Dunning." The girl's voice was watchful.

"Well, you were absolutely right. I had to leave the car in London."

"Is it . . . ?"

"Wrecked and swamped," he said. "I'm afraid so. You may find it at the north end of Vauxhall Bridge. But the operative word is may. I really am most terribly sorry, but I'm afraid I was overtaken by a flood."

"That's what they all say," the girl said wearily. "All right, Mr Dunning. We'll see if we can find it."

"A son," Mark said, drinking his third whisky; Geoffrey had told him nothing more than that. "That's terrific. Anne and I . . . " he changed his mind about what he was going to say.

"You're going to come up with me to see him. Liz would like that."

"Yeah. Sure. Next time I'm over, I will. Right now . . . they want me Stateside. I only came across to get married." They left the pub, and looked up at the sky. The storm had gone, and only occasional white clouds drifted across the sun. "You think Anne saw the sun?"

"Yes," Geoffrey said. "We saw the sun out there," tilting his head towards the south-west. "Before the worst of the weather."

"I sure hope she did," Mark said. "She'd wanted to for so long." His shoulders humped. "It's all so pointless."

"Anne?"

"The whole thing. Do you realise that what we've experienced over the past year is what's soon going to happen, permanently?"

"Not tomorrow, I hope," Geoffrey said, trying to lighten his mood.

Mark shrugged. "Not too many tomorrows, that's for sure. Maybe Misreal was nature's way of warning us, we don't have all that much time to play with."

Geoffrey stared at him. "Seriously?"

"Seriously." He ran his fingers through his unruly hair.

"Maybe, just maybe, if we can convince world governments how vital it is to protect our environment . . . immediately . . . Then there may just be a chance."

He clutched Geoffrey's arm.

"You be happy, with your wife, and your kid, Geoff. And pray."

"And you?" Geoffrey asked in some alarm.

"I'll get back to work. Who knows, perhaps the fact that I was right about the ash cloud will mean they'll listen to me this time . . .

before it's too late."

He wandered out into the muddy street to thumb a lift from one of the army trucks, in the direction of the airport.